PRAISE FOR 7

DAUGHTER SERIES

"Swift and sure, compelling as any conspiracy theory, persuasive as any spasm of paranoia, *The Dark Monk* grips you at the base of your skull and doesn't let go."

—Gregory Maguire, author of *Wicked* and *Out of Oz*

"Oliver Pötzsch has brought to life the heady smells and tastes, the true reality of an era we've never seen quite like this before. The hangman Jakob and his feisty daughter Magdalena are characters we will want to root for in many books to come."

—Katherine Neville, bestselling author of *The Eight* and *The Magic Circle*

"I loved every page, character, and plot twist of *The Hangman's Daughter*, an inventive historical novel about a seventeenth-century hangman's quest to save a witch – from himself."

—Scott Turow

"Oliver Pötzsch takes readers on a darkly atmospheric visit to seventeenth-century Bavaria in his latest adventure. With enough mystery and intrigue to satisfy those who like gritty historical fiction, *The Dark Monk* has convincing characters, rip-roaring action, and finely drawn settings."

—Deborah Harkness, author of *A Discovery of Witches* and the forthcoming *Shadow of Night*

"In this subtle, meticulously crafted story, every word is a possible clue, and the characters are so engaging that it's impossible not to get involved in trying to help them figure the riddle out."

—Oprah.com

The Play of Death

Also by Oliver Pötzsch

IN THE HANGMAN'S DAUGHTER SERIES

The Hangman's Daughter

The Dark Monk

The Beggar King

The Poisoned Pilgrim

The Werewolf of Bamberg

Castle of Kings

The Ludwig Conspiracy

FOR YOUNG READERS

Book of the Night (The Black Musketeers)

Knight Kyle and the Magic Silver Lance (Adventures Beyond Dragon Mountain)

OLIVER PÖTZSCH

The Play of Death

A Hangman's Daughter Tale

**TRANSLATED BY
LEE CHADEAYNE**

amazon crossing

Previously published as *Die Henkerstochter und das Spiel des Todes* by Ullstein Buchverlag in Germany in 2016. Translated from German by Lee Chadeayne. First published in English by AmazonCrossing in 2017.

Published by AmazonCrossing, Seattle

www.apub.com

Amazon, the Amazon logo, and AmazonCrossing are trademarks of Amazon.com, Inc., or its affiliates.

ISBN-13: 9781477848319
ISBN-10: 1477848312

Cover design by Houghton Mifflin Harcourt

*In memory of my grandmother Hermelinde Werner,
who told me for the first time about our ancestors, the
Kuisls, and now rests with them.
Her long life was more exciting than any novel.*

The bi-ba-bogeyman, the bogeyman is back . . .
He picks up little boys and girls and throws them in
his sack.

—An old German nursery rhyme originally
describing a demon or dwarf-like monster

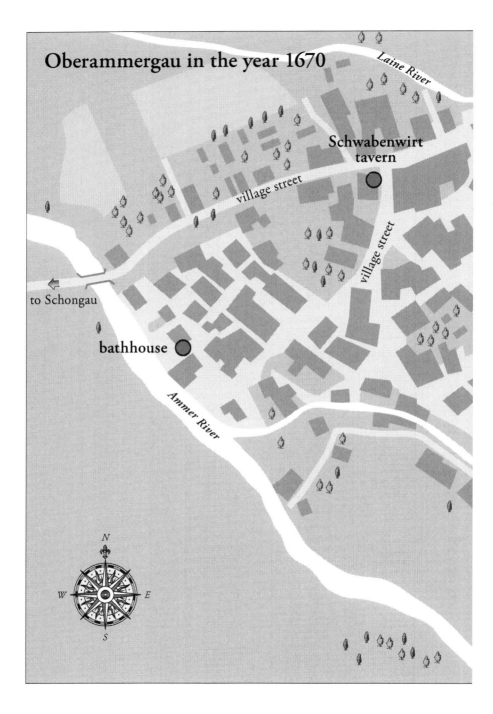

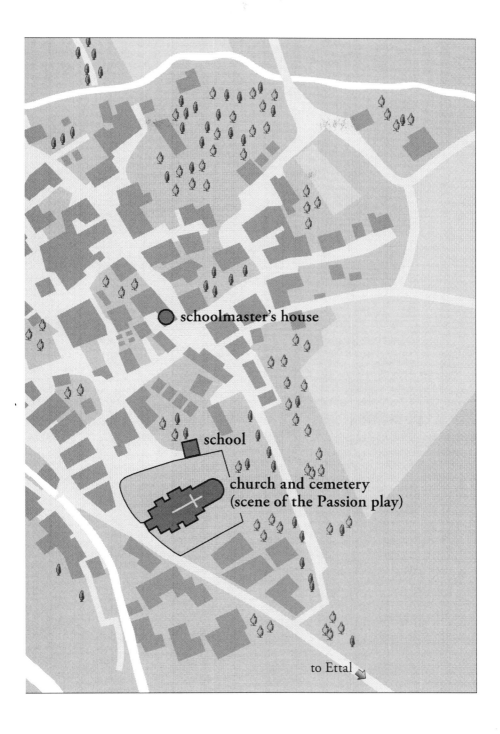

schoolmaster's house

school

church and cemetery
(scene of the Passion play)

to Ettal

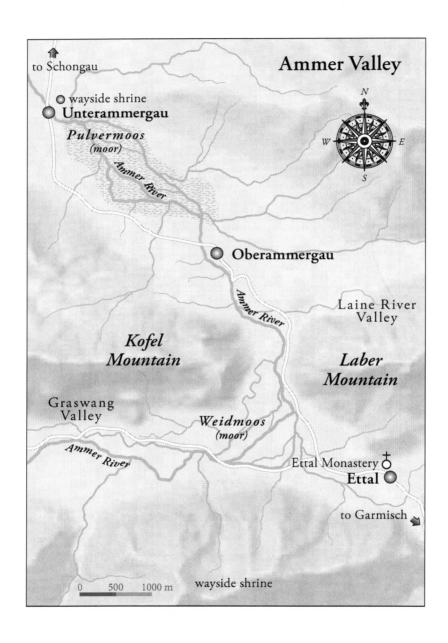

to Schongau

Ammer Valley

wayside shrine
Unterammergau

Pulvermoos
(moor)

Ammer River

N
W   E
S

Oberammergau

Laine River
Valley

Kofel
Mountain

Laber
Mountain

Graswang
Valley

Weidmoos
(moor)

Ammer River

Ammer River

Ettal Monastery
Ettal

to Garmisch

0   500   1000 m

wayside shrine

DRAMATIS PERSONAE

THE KUISL FAMILY, SCHONGAU

JAKOB KUISL, Schongau hangman and executioner
MAGDALENA FRONWIESER (NÉE KUISL), Jakob's elder daughter
BARBARA KUISL, Jakob's younger daughter
SIMON FRONWIESER, Schongau bathhouse keeper, Magdalena's husband
PETER AND PAUL Fronwieser, sons of Magdalena and Simon
GEORG KUISL, Jakob's son, currently in Bamberg

OTHER SCHONGAUERS

JOHANN LECHNER, secretary
MELCHIOR RANSMAYER, town physician
MATTHÄUS BUCHNER, first burgomaster
JAKOB SCHREEVOGL, member of town council and second burgomaster
MARTHA STECHLIN, midwife
LUKAS BAUMGARTNER, wagon driver

OBERAMMERGAUERS

KONRAD FAISTENMANTEL, merchant and chairman of Oberammergau
  Town Council
DOMINIK, KASPAR, and Sebastian Faistenmantel, his sons
JOHANNES RIEGER, Ammergau judge
TOBIAS HERELE, priest
GEORG KAISER, schoolmaster and scriptwriter of the Passion play
ADAM GÖBL, painter of religious figurines and member of the Council of Six

HANS, PETER, AND JAKOBUS GÖBL, his sons

URBAN GABLER, WAGON DRIVER and member of the Council of Six

FRANZ WÜRMSEER, leader of the Oberammergau wagon drivers, member of the Council of Six, and vice-chairman of the town council

SEBASTIAN SAILER, manager of the Ballenhaus (town office building and storage facility) and member of the Council of Six

AUGUSTIN SPRENGER, miller and member of the Council of Six

XAVER EYRL, also called Red Xaver, carver of religious figurines

BENEDIKT ECKART, abbot of Ettal Monastery

ALOIS MAYER, forester in the Laine Valley

KASPAR LANDES, recently deceased bathhouse keeper

HANNES, CALLED POXHANNES, teacher's assistant

NEPOMUK, MARTL, AND WASTL, Oberammergau schoolchildren

JOSSI AND MAXL, children of immigrant workers, friends of Peter Fronwieser

PROLOGUE

Jesus was nailed to a cross and died, but this time there would be no resurrection.

Though it was pitch-black, Dominik Faistenmantel could see the rough outlines of the gravestones in front of the Oberammergau village church. Now and then he could hear the fluttering of wings and assumed the sound came from ravens sitting on the gravestones, watching him curiously. The huge, intelligent birds were no rarity in the Ammergau Valley. Their nests were high up in the mountains, but they often came down into the valley to hunt and forage for rotting carcasses. Faistenmantel shuddered.

If help didn't come soon, he, too, would be a corpse for them to feed on.

The young woodcarver groaned, and when he tried to raise his head, a searing, almost unearthly pain shot through the tense sinews in his neck. His cry was muffled by the filthy rag filling his mouth. He slumped down again, coughed, and gasped for air, but the only sound that came through the gag was a rattling gurgle.

This is the way our Saviour died, he thought. *What agony! With the burden of the world on his shoulders. Lord, come and help me!*

But the Lord did not come, no one came, and once again, despite the gag, Dominik tried to shout for help. It was not yet dawn, and most people in the village were sleeping. Wouldn't the sacristan for early mass be awake? His house stood right next to the cemetery wall, just a few yards away, but no matter how hard Dominik tried, all he could do was groan and whimper. It was so cold, so damned cold. Here, in this Alpine valley, even a night in May felt like the middle of winter. It was a dark and starless night, and he was nailed to a cross dressed only in a loincloth, freezing and trembling from the cold as the ravens stared at him.

If I fall asleep, they'll fly over here. Your eyes are the tenderest place, they say. That's where they'll start. I . . . mustn't . . . fall . . . asleep . . .

While Dominik Faistenmantel struggled to stay awake, little scraps of memory passed through his addled brain, memories of the rehearsal that afternoon. As he'd spoken the final words of the Saviour on the cross, a few rotted boards on the stage had caught his eye. He'd asked Hans Göbl, who was about his age and playing the part of the apostle John, to have the boards replaced immediately, before there was an accident. But Göbl had just rolled his eyes and whispered something to the other actors, whereupon they all broke out laughing. Dominik knew that the hot-tempered Göbl couldn't stand him. Hans wanted more than anything to play the role of Jesus in the Passion play, and he had been generally viewed as the favourite for the part. But the council had given it to Dominik. Should he have turned it down? His father, a powerful merchant in town, had made the final decision, and no one dared to contradict him – not the priest, not the elders on the town council, not even his own son.

Dominik was just about to emerge from under the shadow of his father, and he had dreamed of going to Venice or perhaps even farther, over the great ocean to the New World, where gold and silver flowed from the mountains like water. If his plan had worked, he could have brushed off his father, whom he hated – and also loved very much – and said farewell forever.

But his plan had failed horribly.

Once again, Dominik tried to pull himself up on the cross, and once again he began coughing violently and collapsed. The little wooden step that always had supported his feet in the rehearsals had been removed, and his cramped posture made it harder and harder for him to breathe. He tugged on the heavy ropes binding his arms and legs tightly to the wooden beams, but they held him as firmly as if they were metal wires. In any case, he was too weak to pull himself away.

His head still hurt from the blow he'd received. He had heard a *whoosh* of air behind his head, felt a sudden, searing pain, and when he came to, he was tied to the cross, freezing and naked – a living stage prop staring down at the graves still partially covered with snow.

"Help!" he cried through the gag. "Help . . . me!"

The muffled sounds were carried away by the cold wind sweeping down from the Ammergau Alps into the valley. The houses remained dark; a few cows mooed, but otherwise there was not a sound. Behind Ederle's house a small light suddenly appeared. Probably old man Ederle going to the latrine out back, holding a burning pinewood shaving. The house was only a stone's throw away from the cemetery, but it could just as well have been a hundred miles.

"Help!" Dominik gasped again.

Actually, he'd known for a while he was going to die, either by freezing to death or suffocating first. Even now, hanging there, he could barely breathe, and it became harder and harder for him to think. The only thing that kept him going was his certainty about the perpetrator's identity. He'd underestimated him. Never would he have thought the man capable of such a deed. This was madness, the work of a demon. Someone had to warn the villagers of the devil who was loose in their midst. Dominik had seen the madness flashing in the man's eyes. He should have known.

Now it was too late.

Once again there was a fluttering of wings coming from the direction of the gravestones and, opening his eyes briefly, he saw a few dark shadows flying towards the cross, settling on both sides of the crossbeam.

There was a cawing that sounded almost like a human voice, and a patter and scratching of feet as the birds moved closer.

Father, Father, why hast Thou forsaken me? he thought.

Then the ravens were there.

1

WITH GLASSY EYES, THE SCHONGAU LINEN WEAVER Thomas Zeilinger stared at the rusty tongs ominously coming closer and closer to his lips. A thin stream of saliva ran from the corner of his mouth, and his hands trembled as he clung to the arms of the chair. He opened his mouth, closed it again, and finally shook his head dejectedly.

"I think . . . I think I need another swallow, Frau Fronwieser," he stammered. "Can I . . . have another little swallow?"

With a sigh, Magdalena put down the tongs and reached for the little glass vial standing on the table in the barber-surgeon's workroom. Carefully she poured a precisely measured dose on to a wooden spoon.

"Now this really is enough," she scolded. "Ordinarily I don't give even a horse this much theriaca."

Zeilinger grinned, and the blackened stump of a tooth that was giving him so much trouble became clearly visible. Magdalena breathed in the stench of cheap liquor that mixed with smoke from the poorly vented fireplace in the barber-surgeon's room. A worn, wobbly stool served as the treatment chair, and alongside it was a cracked bowl used as a spittoon for the blood. On the scratched table were all sorts of crucibles and glasses, including the one with the home-brewed theriaca, by far the most precious of the medicines. The afternoon sun fell through the small open window, causing dust particles to dance in the light.

"I'll pay more than a horse, I promise," the linen weaver babbled. It was clear he'd tossed down a good dose of courage on his way to the Tanners' Quarter.

"It won't do me any good if you die on me now," Magdalena replied, putting the spoon in his mouth. "There's so much mandrake and opium in my potion that before long you'll hear the angels singing. What shall I tell Secretary Lechner, eh? That the biggest coward in Schongau would rather die in my office than have a bad tooth pulled? They'll charge me with murder and drown me in the town moat."

"But it hurts so much," Zeilinger wailed.

"I'll go and get my father, the hangman. He'll show you something that really hurts," Magdalena shot back. "Now just hold still. Martha, are you ready?"

The last words were directed at the midwife Martha Stechlin, standing behind the whimpering Zeilinger, holding his head firmly as Magdalena grabbed the bad molar with her tongs. Cursing softly, she pulled on the black stump. Did this jackass Zeilinger have any idea how much theriaca cost? This miracle drug often used as an anaesthetic contained more than three dozen ingredients. Well, the bill would be high enough that the linen weaver would no doubt pull the next tooth himself.

Once again, Thomas Zeilinger flinched and shook his head so hard that Magdalena had to take the tongs out of his mouth. Standing behind him, Martha rolled her eyes.

"Maybe we should wait for your husband, the bathhouse keeper, to come home?" Zeilinger suggested anxiously.

"Simon won't be back for a couple of days," Magdalena replied, growing impatient. "I told you that before. Do you really want to wait that long?"

"I could, uh, go to the doctor in town," said Zeilinger, trying again.

"You want to go to that quack?" Martha retorted, butting in. Her hair had turned grey and her face more and more wrinkled in recent years, looking somewhat like an apple that had been in storage too long. "This so-called *doctor* Ransmayer has studied medicine but can't tell the difference between *Liebtreu* and forget-me-not," she hissed. She glared angrily at the trembling linen weaver. "But go right ahead, do whatever you want. I've also heard that the venerable councilman Stangassinger went to him to have a tooth pulled and two weeks later he was found in his bed, cold and dead."

These words struck home, and Zeilinger finally resigned himself to his fate. He opened his mouth and Magdalena once again grabbed hold of the tooth, which was already loose. There was a loud crack and she held the rotten, stinking stump up in the air triumphantly.

"A wonderful specimen," she exulted, turning to her ashen-faced patient. "If you like, you can now rinse out with some brandy."

This was a suggestion that Zeilinger was only too glad to follow, and he took another deep swallow from the jug he'd brought along. Suddenly his eyes turned up towards the ceiling, his head fell to one side, and he began to snore blissfully, as the jug, almost empty, rolled across the floor.

"At least now he'll keep his mouth shut," Martha said with a grin.

"I couldn't have put up with his moaning and complaining much longer. I'm feeling dizzy again." With an ashen face and a sigh, Magdalena sank into a chair and wiped the sweat from her brow. Martha was the only one so far to know that Magdalena was expecting another child. She hadn't even told her younger sister, Barbara, yet.

"If Zeilinger had waited any longer, I would probably have thrown up in front of him," Magdalena said weakly. Gratefully she stepped to the open window and took a breath of the cool fresh air.

"You really should tell Simon that you're pregnant," Martha scolded her. "In any case, it's a complete mystery to me why he hasn't noticed anything yet. His own wife! Your belly is getting larger every day, and your appetite for sour pickles . . ."

"I'll tell him when he gets back from Oberammergau, I promise. I just don't want to get his hopes up too soon." She hesitated. "Not a second time. It . . . it would break his heart."

Magdalena had known Martha for many years. Magdalena's father, the Schongau executioner, had once saved the midwife from being put to the stake when she was accused of witchcraft and infanticide. Ever since then, Stechlin had felt a close bond of loyalty and friendship with the Kuisls – even if her constant chattering sometimes tested Magdalena's patience.

"It was important for Simon to take Peter to his new school in Oberammergau," Magdalena continued. "It's only a day's journey from here, but we won't see much of the boy in the next few years. I wanted very much to go along," she said, her voice catching, "but someone has to stay here and keep the bathhouse open so that everything doesn't go to the dogs. Barbara is much too young to take charge, and besides, she doesn't know anything about the healing arts."

With a heavy heart, Magdalena thought back on the parting early that morning. Even though Peter was just seven years old, he'd been very brave and hadn't cried, in contrast to his mother, who couldn't hold back her tears. Even Peter's younger brother, Paul, who would ordinarily not let any opportunity pass to tease his older sibling, had remained subdued.

Alongside her, Thomas Zeilinger started grunting softly, tearing her from her melancholy thoughts. The linen weaver burped and wiped his mouth, which still showed some traces of blood. With disgust, Magdalena roused herself.

"Hey, the procedure is over," she said loudly. "You can go home. And remember: nothing but warm small beer and barley porridge for a week, until the wound has healed."

Zeilinger started to get up, wavering slightly, but Magdalena put her hand on his shoulder and held him back. "You owe me half a guilder."

Suddenly the linen weaver became stone-cold sober. "Half a guilder?" he grumbled, then let out a scornful laugh. "Was that pair of tooth tongs made of pure gold?"

"No, but you guzzled down almost all my supply of theriaca, and that's expensive stuff, so hand over the money." She stretched her hand out insistently.

Without responding, Zeilinger tried to walk around her, but the two women blocked his way, their arms crossed.

"And suppose I don't pay? What then, eh?" the linen weaver asked.

"Then I'll send you to see my father, the hangman," Magdalena replied. "He'll pull all your other teeth out. For free."

Grumbling, Zeilinger fumbled around and took a few coins from the purse on his belt. "Very well," he grumbled, placing the coins on the table. "But take care, bathhouse keeper's wife." He gave Magdalena a sly look. "Who knows what you two have put in this drink. Perhaps they're forbidden witches' herbs that the town council should hear about? Not everyone on the council is your friend. Just recently the head of the town council said—"

"Get the hell out before I cast a spell and give you warts," Martha Stechlin snapped. "Look what we get for helping you. But I can tell you one thing. The next time you need a potion so you can get it up in bed, don't come to us."

"Ugh! Your watered-down love potion never worked, anyway. And since we're talking about sex now . . ." – Zeilinger gave Magdalena a dirty look – "your sister, Barbara, better watch out. She's wagging her arse around a little too much over in the taverns. Some people think she's there to cast a spell on the young men."

"Now get out!" Magdalena shouted. She handed Zeilinger his crumpled hat. "Sober up first before you go around talking nonsense like that."

Zeilinger headed for the door, muttering under his breath, while making signs with his hands to ward off evil magic. After the door finally slammed shut behind him, Magdalena turned to Martha.

"You shouldn't have said that about the warts," she warned her. "You know yourself how quickly women healers are branded as witches."

The midwife shrugged. "It's always been that way," Martha replied sharply. "They've been talking behind our backs for years, and it doesn't take much to make the pot boil over. Zeilinger's right when he says the town council tolerates us, at best." She hesitated before continuing. "And as far as Barbara is concerned . . ."

Magdalena stared at her, waiting for what would come next. "Just say it, before it gets stuck in your throat."

"Well, your sister should really try to control herself a bit. Recently I saw her up in the Stern flirting with three fellows in that tavern all at the same time. She knows she's attractive, and she likes to turn them on. People talk."

"My God, Martha, she's only seventeen. You used to be young, too."

"Yes, but I knew my place." Martha stared at her wrinkled hands with their cracked fingernails. "My father was a simple charcoal burner. We lived out in the forest. Naturally we went to church fairs, but I never would have dared to dance with the son of a wealthy farm owner."

"Is that all you want to tell me? If Barbara had come from a respectable family, it would be all right for her to swing her hips around, but as a hangman's daughter she immediately gets branded a whore?" Magdalena could feel the anger boiling up inside her. Actually, she had to agree with Martha that sometimes Barbara overdid it. She combed her hair like a princess and sometimes even used belladonna juice to enlarge her pupils. She wouldn't let anyone push her around, and her laugh was often a bit too loud, her speech a bit too disrespectful for a dishonourable girl from the Tanners' Quarter.

At least in this respect, she takes after her father, Magdalena thought.

"Sometimes I wish Barbara would find a gentle, loyal husband to bring her under control," she mumbled, more to herself. But Martha Stechlin had heard it.

"Not everyone can be as lucky as you, Magdalena," the midwife replied softly. "Not everyone has someone to care for them and look after them. I wish I did." With a grim look, she continued. "That's another reason, by the way, why your husband should come home again as soon as possible. A dishonourable bathhouse keeper is always viewed with suspicion, and a woman running a bathhouse on her own while her husband is away on a trip can quickly be viewed as a woman in league with the devil. We can only pray that no one in town tries to exploit this situation."

Magdalena shuddered and, despite the warm fire on the hearth, she suddenly felt a chill.

A frosty wind swept down from the Ammergau Alps directly into Simon's face.

Though it was already the beginning of May, there were still patches of snow in the meadows and moors, and snow began to fall as they approached Oberammergau. Frost was not uncommon at night even into June here in the Bavarian foothills, and there were occasionally even snowstorms. Together with his son Peter, Simon was crouched down in a horse-drawn wagon whose driver had picked them up in the little town of Soyen. He apparently had taken pity on the serious-looking, slender lad who didn't seem up to the long walk.

Simon glanced lovingly at his elder son, who was absorbed in one of the anatomical drawings he'd traced from his grandfather's books on to tattered scraps of paper and was now carrying with him in a large folder. The sketches were Peter's pride and joy. In rapt attention, the seven-year-old ran his fingers over the filigree of muscles belonging to a bloodied man.

"Do you see, Father?" he said, without taking his eyes off the drawing. "Here is the *pectoralis major*, and that's the *rectus abdominis*. Is that right?"

"Indeed," Simon replied with a smile. "But in Oberammergau I'd refrain from using Latin words, for the most part. It's much more important there for you to learn to speak Bavarian fluently and be faithful in attending mass."

Only now did Peter look up from the sketches. His face was still a bit pale, as if he were unaccustomed to fresh air, and his straggly dark hair hung down over his eyes. He sniffled loudly, as he had caught another one of his frequent colds.

"I don't want to go to Oberammergau," he whispered. "Why couldn't I stay in my school in Schongau?"

"Do you really want to spend the rest of your life just counting apples and pears, and memorizing the catechism?" his father asked gruffly. "Your teacher there is an old drunk who's quicker with his paddle than with his head, and as the son of a dishonourable bathhouse keeper you aren't allowed to learn Latin. Once the authorities have made up their minds, there's no point complaining about it."

For a while they fell silent, as Simon once again pondered the decision he and Magdalena had made a few months ago. It had become quite evident that Peter was not being sufficiently challenged in the Schongau school, in contrast to his brother, Paul, who was a year younger, cut classes often, and regarded school as torture. But Peter was different. While other children had trouble memorizing the confession of faith, Peter knew the alphabet, the basics of arithmetic, and even spoke some Latin. But for the grandson of the local executioner, further schooling in Schongau was out of the question. Simon knew a talented schoolmaster in Oberammergau who didn't care about Peter's background and lower class and was willing to accept him.

Peter crossed his arms defiantly and turned to his father again. "I want to stay with you, Father. You're the best teacher I could ever ask for."

"Oh, don't say that," Simon said in a deliberately cheerful tone. "Schoolmaster Georg Kaiser is a very intelligent man, and moreover very pleasant. Back when I was at the university in Ingolstadt, he was my favourite teacher and even instructed the children of a baron. Oberammergau can consider itself lucky that he returned to his home town a few years ago, and so should you. I don't think I've ever heard of any child from a hangman's family—"

"Who's allowed to study with such a learned gentleman," Peter added, finishing his father's sentence. "Yes, I know, but still—"

"Just take a look at these huge mountains," Simon interrupted, trying to change the topic. "If you were a bird, you could fly all the way to Venice, but people like us need to take the steep mountain passes." He smiled as he pointed to the chain of low mountains stretching from east to west, with tall peaks and entire ranges towering up in the distance. A wide valley opened up before them, interspersed with snow-covered moors and heaths, and in the middle the Ammer, the river that gave this region its name, a raging flood in late spring. Before them they saw a chapel with a small village behind it, and in the background gently rolling grassy hills rising to the forested and craggy mountains.

"In front of us is Unterammergau," Simon continued. "Now we're almost there." He winked at Peter. "It was this route that the Romans presumably took on their trip over the Alps. It leads down to Garmisch and, beyond that, the pass over the mountains to Lombardy. Many foreigners and other interesting people take this route through the region. And then there's the Passion play taking place next month in Oberammergau. You'll like it here, I'm sure, and I promise we'll come to visit you a few times a year."

Peter nodded silently and went back to staring at the sketch in front of him.

With squeaking wheels the wagon moved along through the slushy snow, and now and then they'd have to climb down and help pull when it got stuck in one of the many ruts. Now the mountains rose up on both sides of the road. The sun, which had until then shone down brightly and cheerfully on the moss-covered ground and forests, disappeared behind dark grey clouds, and the shadows seemed to be reaching out with long fingers to grasp the travellers.

At a crossroads near the river, the wagon driver suddenly stopped and got down from his box. He approached the wayside shrine that was covered with moss and lichen; it was standing a bit lopsided. Snowdrops were sprouting all around from the leaf-covered ground. The wagon driver removed his hat and began to pray quietly. After some hesitation, Simon followed him and joined him in prayer. He wasn't an especially religious person, but the sudden darkness in the valley and the prospect of having to leave his son here for such a long time saddened him.

As Simon stood there with folded hands, his eyes wandered over the cracked and weathered stone that had probably been there since ancient times. Strange runes were scratched into it, and Simon even thought he recognized a devil's face. The man alongside him was murmuring the Lord's Prayer again when suddenly a long, drawn-out rumbling could be heard in the distance, as if a giant were dragging a heavy sack of stones behind him.

"What was that?" Simon asked, startled.

The driver turned around to spit, then crossed his fingers. "The accursed Kofel," he answered finally. "Somewhere on its rock face there's probably been an avalanche." He pointed towards a cone-shaped mountain on his right that was barren of vegetation and cast a shadow across the valley. "The Kofel is an evil thing. It's no wonder that people here think it's really a devil. There are many stories about it."

"What kind of stories?" asked Peter, who had run to his father on hearing the terrifying crash.

"Well, evil spirits are said to live up there, and the Kofel witch has a cave there, where he takes children and bakes them in his oven. It's said that, in ancient times, sacrifices were made up on the summit. And then there are the little men from Venice that live deep in the mountain and—"

"Now just stop this superstitious nonsense," Simon scolded. "You're scaring the boy."

"But suppose it's true," the driver persisted. "I've never been able to stand this accursed valley. I'm always happy when I'm headed down the Kienberg into the Loisach Valley."

"What are those strange stones?" Peter suddenly asked, pointing at a circle of white pebbles aligned around the foot of the cross. Until then, Simon hadn't noticed them. Four branches pointed away from the circle, like the points of a compass, making it look like a drawing of the sun.

"That?" The wagon driver shrugged. "No idea. Some children must have done that. It's time we got moving. There's still a long way to go."

He turned away gruffly, and Simon thought he noticed a nervous twitch in the man's face. He seemed to be hiding something from them.

Sullenly, he climbed back into the driver's box and whipped his horses on. He was in such a hurry that Simon and Peter barely had time to get back in.

Strange people here, Simon thought. *Tight-lipped and superstitious to the core. Perhaps it wasn't such a good idea after all to bring Peter to Oberammergau.*

As the wagon moved forwards, Simon's gaze rested for a long time on the moss-covered, crooked stone cross, until it finally disappeared behind a hill.

"The fish live in the water, the doe live in the wood, and so they stay together, as young and old they should . . ."

Barbara sang the old tune her mother had taught her long ago to the rhythm of a country folk dance as she swept the last of the soiled reeds out the door. In her mind she was already at the dance that would take place that evening at the Stern Tavern up in town. A few itinerant minstrels were scheduled to be there, and the innkeeper would open the large ballroom for the occasion. Karl Sailer, who lived in the Tanners' Quarter, had promised to take Barbara with him. Such an invitation couldn't be taken for granted, since as a dishonourable person she was actually forbidden to attend dance parties unless she could find an honourable young man willing to overlook established prejudices and invite her. With his fractured nose, Karl, the tanner's journeyman, was not the handsomest lad in town – nor the brightest – but at least Barbara could attend the dance. Her father had given her permission only because she'd agreed to give his room a thorough cleaning beforehand. The sun was already setting behind the roofs, so she had to hurry. After all, she still had to clean out the stable, feed the chickens under the bench in the main room, and prepare the evening meal. Then she wanted to change her dress and wash off the dirt and ashes with some cheap bone soap she'd bought from the butcher.

Well, at least it gave you healthy-looking red cheeks.

With a sigh, Barbara put the broom aside and began cleaning the dirty dishes. Dry bits of oat porridge clung to a bowl, a dead fly floated in a cup of small beer, and crumbs of tobacco lay all over the table. Ever since Mother died several years ago, Father was neglecting himself more and more, and it was Barbara who had to clean up after him and do the cooking. That was the arrangement she had with her big sister.

Only last year, the hangman had moved to the little house down by the river and left the large executioner's house to Magdalena, Simon, and their children. Barbara still had her own room there, but during the day she cared for her father. At the moment he'd gone shopping in town, but he'd be back soon and no doubt have some complaint about what she'd done.

"So they stay together, as young and old they should," she sang again, a little softer. Suddenly the song sounded like a mockery. Was that her fate? To care for her father until he died while her older sister made money and gained recognition as the wife of the bathhouse keeper? It was a lucky stroke for Magdalena that the secretary Johann Lechner had a few years ago approved her marriage to Simon, the son of the former city doctor. Barbara's future looked far less rosy. Basically, she was allowed to marry only someone of her own social caste, and that meant knackers, hangmen's journeymen, or the crippled Schongau gravedigger who had proposed to her twice already.

But before that could happen, she'd kill herself.

Barbara polished one of the copper plates, casting a furtive glance at her reflection in the shiny surface. She was a black-haired tomboy with sparkling eyes and bushy eyebrows, just like her older sister. Further, she had about her something untamed, saucy, that magically attracted men. Her bust had grown considerably in recent years, and she enjoyed it when young men in the tavern secretly glanced at her. Often they told her she was pretty – beautiful as a starless night, some said, a bride of Satan. When they got drunk, they'd make salacious remarks and break out in dirty laughs. Sometimes Barbara would sit down with them and a few other girls at a table in the tavern and let them buy her a tankard of beer, but the others always made her feel that she didn't belong. She was, after all, the daughter of the Schongau executioner, a dishonourable hangman's girl.

The plates clattered as Barbara cleaned up and put the dishes back in the cupboard over the table. *Those are the rules. Either I marry the hunchbacked gravedigger or I clean up after my father until I'm an old maid . . .*

Barbara spent many sleepless nights thinking about leaving this stinking town forever, and once, about two years ago, at the wedding of her uncle in Bamberg, she almost did. But she knew it would break her father's heart. Jakob Kuisl's only son, Georg, her beloved twin brother, was serving as a hangman's journeyman in that distant city. It was doubtful he'd ever return, and thus she kept putting off her decision.

Until I'm so old I'm no longer able. And until then, I'll clean and cook and . . .

With a grim face she wiped the cobwebs from the shelves that held the books on healing herbs and poisons that her father had taken with him to his small quarters down by the river. The books had always been his favourite possessions, along with the large chest that stood next to them. He had forbidden her from ever looking inside, but of course she'd disregarded this order. Most of what it held was just old junk, anyway – stuff from the war like a rusty handgun, a shortsword that was equally rusty, and a soldier's uniform with so many moth-holes that you could see through it in places. They were her father's memorabilia from the time he'd served as a sergeant in the army.

Much more interesting were the contents of a smaller trunk with ornamental fittings standing alongside it. This is where Father kept what he referred to as magic and hocus-pocus – a length of gallows rope, vials of the congealed blood of executed men, scraps of tanned human skin, and tiny bones fashioned into amulets. From time to time Jakob sold such objects to superstitious townspeople and got a good price for them. There had been a time when Barbara also thought of these things as magic, but all that changed suddenly when she happened to find some objects Father must never know she had.

Ever since then, Barbara could not get enough of magic.

Now the trunk gave off a somewhat musty odour, and she wrinkled her nose. Curious, she raised the lid and at first saw just the usual pans, tins, and boxes, but now another object was lying inside. It wasn't much larger than a burl on a tree branch and it was wrapped in a soiled rag. She couldn't resist. She reached carefully into the trunk and unwrapped it, then with a scream she dropped it on the floor.

Before her lay a severed thumb.

After the initial shock wore off, she examined it more closely. It had been cut off cleanly just below the ball of the hand, and here and there dried muscle fibres still clung to it. It had already turned black, the nail had fallen off, and it had a god-awful stench. The odour was spreading throughout the room, as if someone had shaken out a burial shroud.

"If you're finished screaming, you can put the piece back in the chest. You're scaring the whole Tanners' Quarter."

The familiar deep voice made Barbara jump. With a flush of guilt she spun around and saw her father bent over in the doorway. In one hand he held a sack with dark wet spots all over it, and with the other he was waving a jug of foaming beer.

Grimly, Jakob Kuisl glared at his younger daughter. With his height of over six feet, broad shoulders, and prominent hooked nose, he was still a frightening figure, but now the once black hair and bushy beard had turned grey and his face was deeply furrowed. As he so often did, he clenched a pipe stem between his lips. The hangman had acquired a habit of leaving the pipe in his mouth when he spoke, making his few words sound even more like the growls of a beast.

"I said put the piece back in the chest before I tan your hide, you nosy wench," Jakob snarled. "Haven't I forbidden you from opening the trunk?"

"What *is* it, for heaven's sake?" Barbara replied with disgust, without answering her father's question. Gingerly she wrapped the rotten piece of flesh in the cloth again and put it back in the chest.

"Well, what do you think it is? A thumb," he said. "To be exact, a left thumb, and to be more exact, that of Hartl the shepherd."

"You . . . you mean the thief and drifter you hanged more than two weeks ago?" Barbara asked. She felt like she was going to throw up.

Jakob nodded. "Simon Rössle, the owner of the big farm in Altenstadt, is going to pay me a lot for it – he thinks the thumb of a thief in his cattle trough makes his cows' pelts shiny and soft." He grinned and held up the dripping sack. "Now he's heard from somebody that a thief's heart buried under the oak tree in front of his house will ward off burglars. Well, that naturally costs more."

Barbara was about to let out another loud scream, but quickly clapped her hand over her mouth. "You're not telling me you went back to Gallows Hill . . ." But her father waved her off, grinning.

"Nonsense, it's a pig's heart. I got it from the butcher, who promised not to tell anyone," he added with a wink. Evidently he'd already forgiven her for poking around in the trunk. "People are so dumb, they can't tell a pig from a person. Aside from the doctors, the only ones who can tell the difference between this and a human heart are executioners. So keep your mouth shut, will you? Recently there haven't been so many hangings, and we can use a little extra money."

"If you charged a decent price for your healing herbs and treatments, like Magdalena and Simon, perhaps you could afford a new shirt now and then," Barbara shot back. "It's almost impossible to get the stains out any more."

Jakob snorted. "Everyone pays what they can. How can I squeeze the last few coins from poor people? They'll be healthy, but they'll die of hunger."

"Promise me at least you won't keep that heart here in the house but out in the shed," Barbara replied with a sigh. She didn't mention they needed the money because Father had been drinking more and more recently. Even now the sickly-sweet odour of alcohol hung over the room, though at least it masked the stench of the rotting thumb.

Her father took the sack over to the shed and soon returned, and in the meantime Barbara had tidied up the room and taken a seat on one of the stools.

"Do you believe all that about the thief's heart?" she wanted to know. "I mean, that there's really something magic about it?"

Jakob took a seat alongside her and silently poured himself another mug of beer. "If that were the case, soon I wouldn't have any more work," he said after a while, "because then everyone would bury a heart in front of his house, and there wouldn't be any more burglaries." He took a deep swig and wiped his mouth. "Let people believe what they want – I'm not telling anyone what to do."

"But what if there really are such things as magicians and witches?" Barbara persisted. "Your grandfather Jörg Abriel accused some women of being witches, then he tortured and burned them. Didn't he ever tell your father anything? Maybe there were some real witches among them."

Jakob set his cup down and eyed his daughter suspiciously. More than eighty years ago, during the great Schongau witch trials, their ancestor had executed several dozen women. Barbara was afraid she'd probed too far with her questions.

A sudden thought flashed through her mind. *He suspects something!*

"Why do you ask that?" Jakob asked.

Barbara tried to look innocent. "Well, wouldn't it be good if there really were sorcerers and magicians? I mean, those who could do good things? I thought maybe you could tell me more about them."

Abruptly, her father slammed his fist down on the table. "How often have I told you I don't want to hear such nonsense! It's enough that half the town council believes in it. It's already caused so much bloodshed."

"This blood is also on the hands of our family," Barbara mumbled in a flat voice, but it seemed her father hadn't heard her.

"That's enough," he grumbled. "Is the stew ready? I'm hungry."

Barbara shrugged. Secretly she was glad her father hadn't asked any more questions. "It's simmering on the hearth, but the meat is still pretty tough. I'm afraid it will be a while."

Jakob stroked his beard. "In the meantime you can bring your tired old father some fresh beer from town." He held up the old jug. "This one here is almost empty."

Barbara glared at him. "Don't you think you've had enough? And by the way, you'd let Karl take me to the dance tonight."

"Once you've finished your chores. In the meantime, I've been thinking, and perhaps it's not such a good idea for you to go to the dance. People in the taverns are gossiping about you, especially the young lads."

Barbara jumped to her feet, furious. "You promised me! All afternoon I've been slaving away for you. You could do a little cleaning up yourself. I'm not your maid, as Mother used to be."

She stopped short, realizing she'd gone too far, and for a moment it seemed her father was about to go into one of his famous fits of rage, but then he just nodded and got to his feet.

"Very well, I'll go myself. The air in here is too poisonous for me, anyway."

Barbara watched sadly as her father left, a defiant, lonesome giant, stomping down the garden path past the apple orchard to the road leading to the Lech Gate. She was sorry about her last remark but couldn't take the words back now.

He's so alone now that Mother is gone and Georg has left, too, she thought.

But then she brushed aside the gloomy thoughts and walked over to the stable. Yes, she'd go to the dance that evening, she'd laugh and joke around, and there was nothing her grumbling, stubborn, sour-faced father could do about that.

And perhaps after that she'd have a look at the books . . .

Those books whose reappearance Jakob Kuisl must never know about.

Creaking and groaning, the wagon moved along over the Ammergau moor as Simon pondered the strange roadside cross. Their trip now took them along the Ammer River, past hedges and low bushes where some blackbirds were chirping. They passed other wayside shrines and crosses, but the wagon driver just kept on moving. Simon didn't see any other stone circles, and Peter had turned back to his pictures, engrossed in them as if in a trance. Simon admired his son's ability to block out the rest of the world, while he himself couldn't help brooding and worrying constantly. His mind never actually seemed to rest.

I hope it was the right decision to bring Peter here, he thought. *But at least in this valley he's no longer just the grandson of a hangman.*

After a while, another village right on the riverbank appeared before them. Not far away, a brook poured down from the mountains into a swirling pool while a few scrawny-looking cows grazed in the Alpine meadows above.

"Oberammergau," the wagon driver grumbled. "If you ask me, I'd never spend a night in this place. All you find here are barren fields, moorland, rocky cliffs, and a lot of weird stories. The people in Oberammergau can be glad the old trade route goes by this miserable place, or nobody would ever venture out here. I'm telling you, not even an old billy goat, well, maybe a crazy one—"

"Thanks. I think we've got the idea," Simon interrupted as he watched Peter put on a long face and start to turn pale on hearing the man's words. This superstitious fool would make his son start believing in ghosts and demons again.

In fact, Oberammergau was not an especially hospitable place. A row of dingy farmhouses huddled along the river and behind them were a few larger buildings with a stone church in the middle. To the right was the strange Kofel Mountain, and to the left other high mountains, making the valley especially narrow at this point. Simon felt like he was locked up in a musty cage. They were passing some isolated farms and dilapidated stables when suddenly a man on horseback came towards them at full gallop, his horse foaming at the mouth. The man, dressed in black, bent far down over his horse and raced by so close that the wagon driver's two horses shied away.

"Hey, you idiot!" the driver called after the rider. "Watch what you're doing!" He shook his head angrily. "May God see to it that he breaks his neck."

"Evidently someone else who can't stand it in Oberammergau," said Simon with a grin.

The driver gave him a sullen look, then turned to the two horses and tried to calm them down. Then the wagon moved forwards again, shortly thereafter arriving in Oberammergau.

A wooden bridge spanned the rushing Ammer River, and the road on the other side led straight through the centre of town. Simon could now see, scattered among the simple farm houses, a few fine-looking taverns and multistorey buildings, some with shops on the ground floor. He knew from previous visits that Oberammergau certainly had a better side. The once busy trade route had brought a degree of prosperity to some villagers.

The wagon stopped at a crossing where a few especially handsome buildings stood, among them the house of the village judge and the Ballenhaus, an office and warehouse where the wagon drivers stored their merchandise. The wagon driver planned to spend the night in the adjacent Schwabenwirt tavern, the best place in town, and put up his horses in its stables. Simon thanked him, then continued on his way with Peter. Night was already falling, and it was deathly quiet in the manure-spattered street. The only sound was the occasional whinnying of horses in their stalls. Simon sensed a mood of depression in the town. The few people they saw were stooped over and passed by without saying a word. An old farmer seemed to hiss an evil oath at them as he passed, but his voice was so low it was impossible to say.

Simon suddenly noticed the many bouquets of St John's wort hanging on the closed doors everywhere, said to drive away the devil and evil spirits. The bouquets, sprinkled with holy water, were usually put out on Walpurgis Night, when witches were said to gather for their secret meetings. But Walpurgis Night was already a week ago, and the bouquets looked very fresh.

Almost as if they'd been hung on the doors just this morning, Simon mused. *What in God's name has happened here?*

The schoolmaster's house was just a stone's throw from the church. It was an attractive little building with a vegetable garden and some green already appearing amid the last remnants of the winter's snow. Muffled sounds of men's voices could be heard coming from the open window.

"You'll soon get to meet your teacher," Simon said in a deliberately cheerful voice, turning to Peter as he opened the squeaking garden gate. "It's really extremely kind of Georg Kaiser to take you into his house," he said with a smile. "Do you know I also lived with him for a few months when I was a young student? That was in Ingolstadt. I had my own room in his house, and it cost just a few kreuzer a week. And his wife—"

At that moment the front door opened, and two men emerged. The elder one wore a priest's cassock, and the other was a tall young man dressed as a simple labourer and carrying a rolled-up bundle of papers. Both men seemed very serious, though Simon noticed a certain gleam in the eyes of the younger one that didn't seem in keeping with his sad face.

"I'll see you in two days at the rehearsal," the older man said to the other. "And make sure you've learned the text by then, Hans, or we may have to change our minds about doing this."

With a brief nod the priest walked past Simon and Peter, as if he hadn't noticed them. His face looked like it had turned to stone. The young man walked behind him in silence, completely ignoring the two visitors.

"A good day to you as well," Simon mumbled and shrugged. Then he knocked on the front door that had just closed. Quick steps approached, the door was torn open, and Simon found himself face to face with a withered, slightly stooped man about sixty years old. On his nose he was wearing pince-nez, and he looked at the new visitors with annoyance.

"Good Lord in Heaven, what in the world—" he started to say, then his face suddenly brightened.

"Oh my God, it's Simon!" he cried. "How could I forget? You said you would be coming today." He embraced his friend warmly then stooped down to Peter, who was hiding bashfully behind his father.

"And you must be the child prodigy I've heard so much about," he continued with a smile, and held out his hand. "It's good that you've come. I'm Georg Kaiser, the Oberammergau schoolmaster."

When Peter bashfully reached out his hand, a few of his sketches slipped from it, landing on the floor, wet from the melting snow. When Kaiser leaned down to pick them up, he uttered a cry of astonishment.

"Did you do these yourself?" he asked, handing the drawings back to Peter.

The boy nodded silently, and Simon answered for him.

"He insisted on bringing them along," he said with paternal pride. "Sometimes he works on a page like that for several days. Peter is fascinated by everything that has to do with anatomy – he's always prodding me with questions about medicine."

Kaiser smiled. "Just the way you pestered me back in those days, Simon. Do you remember? What you always were asking me, though, was about which taverns had the best music and where to find the cheapest wine in Ingolstadt."

"Thank God Peter hasn't got to that stage yet," Simon answered with a laugh. But then his face darkened. For Simon, his university days in Ingolstadt were an embarrassment. He'd studied medicine there for only a few semesters before his money ran out, partly because he'd spent it less on furthering his education than on fine clothing, wine, and gambling, but also because his stingy father never gave him more than the bare essentials. Georg Kaiser had been Simon's salvation back then. Kaiser was teaching theology and music in Ingolstadt and adopted the young playboy, treating him like a son.

Actually, I really was a son to him, Simon thought, grimly. He'd never had a warm relationship with his own father, who was now dead.

"But come on in and warm yourself up," Kaiser said finally, in order to break the embarrassing silence. "You must be hungry."

Together they entered the narrow, dark hallway with a sooty little kitchen. An old, almost toothless maid was stirring a pot and looking at the guests expectantly.

"Go ahead and make a bit more, Anni," Kaiser told the maid. "This boy looks like he still has a bit of growing to do. And be generous with the honey in the porridge."

"Porridge?" Peter's eyes sparkled for the first time that day. Just like Simon, he'd had only a little bread and hard cheese since the morning.

Georg Kaiser winked at Peter. "And first, a tasty fish stew left over from Sunday. Doesn't that sound all right? But before the food comes I have a surprise for you. I think you'll like this." With a cheerful nod he opened the door to a candle-lit room where dozens of books stood on several rough-hewn boards. Peter stood there in astonishment, his mouth agape.

"But . . . there are more books here than all the ones Grandfather and Father have put together," he stammered.

"My private library," Kaiser explained. "I brought them with me from Ingolstadt. In one or the other of those books you'll surely find anatomical sketches." He pointed into the room. "On the table over there you'll find paper, ink, and a quill. Just help yourself."

Visibly elated, Peter hurried over to the shelves and started leafing through the books. Georg Kaiser closed the door and waved Simon over to the room across the hall. In that room, a jumble of printed sheets and pages covered with handwriting were piled on another table. The cheerful expression on Kaiser's face suddenly vanished, and he looked tired and upset.

"Unfortunately, you've chosen the worst possible time to arrive here with your highly gifted son," he said, collapsing on a stool. He coughed, removed his pince-nez, and rubbed his reddened eyes. "And that's not just because I'm suffering from a cold."

"I was getting that impression, too," Simon replied. "The whole town seems anxious about something. On our way to town we had a few strange experiences. If you believed in ghosts, this valley would be a good place to find them." He laughed softly, but Kaiser looked earnest and remained silent.

Simon looked with curiosity at the many crumpled sheets of paper on the table. Most of them were text passages assigned to individuals in a play. Many words were crossed out and replaced with new passages. Simon read the names: Jesus, Peter, Pontius Pilate.

"The Passion play?" Simon asked.

The schoolmaster nodded. "It's an old text that I'm trying to rewrite. The villagers asked me to do that the last time the play was performed, but there's a lot that still seems stiff and old-fashioned, and I'm having a lot of trouble with the verse form. And as soon as I finish a few pages, the priest comes and changes it all. The venerable Tobias Herele is very devout and conservative. Any change for him is almost blasphemous." Kaiser rolled his eyes. "Almost five thousand verses! Good Lord, I should never have got involved in this play. The whole thing is becoming more and more my own personal passion."

Simon smiled. Georg Kaiser had written to tell him he'd accepted the assignment of rewriting the text of the Oberammergau Passion play and was directing it together with the priest. Just half a century earlier, the last of the plagues had passed through Oberammergau, and there were deaths in almost every family. In that dark hour, the citizens had sworn to perform a Passion play once every ten years if they were spared further deaths. In fact, the Plague had passed them by, and since then there had been performances that were well received by residents of surrounding towns and even talked about in Schongau.

"I don't understand why you will be performing the play this year at Pentecost and not four years from now, as custom dictates," said Simon with a frown as he studied the sheets of paper on the table. "That could cause a lot of hard feelings."

"You're telling me," Kaiser sighed. "But Konrad Faistenmantel has got it into his head to move up the schedule. He's the most powerful man here in town, and in addition he's the head of the town council. Whatever he says is the law." He shrugged. "Faistenmantel is no spring chicken and wants to make the play a sort of monument to himself. Right now it looks like he'll go down in the town's history as a tragic figure," the schoolmaster added gloomily.

"For heaven's sake, what happened?" Simon asked. "I saw the bouquets of St John's wort on the doors everywhere. People seem to be so gloomy, as if struggling under a heavy burden. Even the priest I saw just a few minutes ago looked like a corpse."

"How can you blame him?" Kaiser sighed again. "A lot of people say the devil has been loose in Oberammergau since last night." He leaned forwards and lowered his voice. "In the early morning hours, the priest found the actor playing Jesus dead in the cemetery."

"A murder?" Simon asked.

"We assume so. The poor man couldn't have hung himself on the cross, in any case."

"My God!" Simon exclaimed. "Someone actually . . . crucified him?"

"As terrible as that sounds, yes." Kaiser looked distressed. "And not just on any cross, but the one being constructed for the play. The perpetrator bound him to the cross with ropes, then set it in the ground upright. Well, at least Dominik Faistenmantel was given the chance to die just like our Saviour."

"Dominik Faistenmantel?" Simon asked with surprise. "Is he . . ."

"Yes, the youngest son of the powerful town council chairman, Konrad Faistenmantel," said Kaiser. "There are plenty of people who believe we are being punished by God because Faistenmantel wants to stage the play four years early. The old man, by the way, remains stubborn and insists on sticking to that schedule. He had recently quarrelled a lot with his son, and their relationship was not the best, to put it mildly. Faistenmantel has already ordered me and the priest to find a new Jesus, and the job will no doubt fall to Hans Göbl, our Saint John the Apostle." He pointed towards the door. "You saw him briefly as you arrived, I think. Our conversation had just ended. We'll start the rehearsals in three days."

"Hold on," Simon said. "Someone dies on the cross, and on the same day his own father tells you to find his successor in the play and orders new rehearsals? How heartless can he be?"

Kaiser shrugged. "That's just the way Konrad Faistenmantel is, but he's amassed a considerable fortune." He pointed through the grimy bull's-eye glass windows towards the cemetery, where night was falling. "By the way, the poor lad's still out there in St Ann's Chapel because the judge in Ammergau wanted to examine the body again – even though he doesn't understand a thing about medicine." Georg Kaiser coughed and spat into a bowl under the table.

"Excuse me," he gasped. "I just can't get rid of this accursed cold that's been hanging on since February, and our old medicus and bathhouse keeper, God bless his soul, died just two weeks ago of smallpox. It would have been better if he'd been here to have a look at the corpse." Kaiser caught his breath and looked at Simon, thinking.

"Do you have any plans for the evening?" he finally asked.

Simon sighed. "Probably I do. I assume I'll have to take a closer look at your crucified Jesus."

"You'd be doing the town a great favour." Georg Kaiser smiled sadly. "If it's true what people have been saying about you in recent years, you're a bright, reasonable man, Simon." The schoolmaster got to his feet and put on his pince-nez. "That's what we need now: the sober gaze of an expert. Otherwise, I'm afraid it won't stop with just a few pretty bouquets of St John's wort to ward off the devil."

2

Hunched down in the shadows of the houses, Barbara hurried through the narrow lanes of Schongau towards the Tanners' Quarter, beyond the city walls. The so-called beer bell announcing the closing of the city gates at nine o'clock had rung some time ago, so, as she'd done before, she'd have to slip through the door at the old entrance. The drunken watchman, Johannes, had bent the rules a bit in the past and let her through, and she could only hope he'd do the same this time. In return, she'd probably have to flatter him a bit.

She broke out in a cold sweat and, despite the late hour, she felt wide awake. She'd danced so wildly that towards the end of the night she even knocked over a table. The tavern keeper was going to throw her out, but her friend Karl intervened. What followed was a wild brawl in which chairs were broken and beer mugs smashed. In the end, everyone blamed her, the dissolute hangman's daughter. She had fled at the last moment, before the night watchmen arrived. Barbara grinned.

Well, at least she'd had a good time.

She heard someone whistling at her from behind and drew her shawl more tightly around her head in hopes of not being recognized in the darkness, though her wild curls were visible just the same. The last thing she needed was to meet her father. Karl, the tanner's journeyman, had seen him that evening in the tavern Zur Sonne, frequented by the simple labourers and farmers. It was quite possible that her father was also on his way back after the curfew. Jakob Kuisl knew most of the guards at the city gates, caring for many of them when they were sick or injured. Among the lower classes, the hangman was popular as a healer, and therefore Jakob often had a last glass of brandy with the guards before setting out for home.

Lost in her thoughts, Barbara hurried along towards the old entrance. She was still sorry she had flared up at her father earlier. Perhaps it was mostly because of her fear he'd discover her secret. She loved him despite his gruff manner and grumpy disposition; they concealed a sensitivity so atypical of a hangman. Her father was not only strong, he was extremely perceptive and well read, more so than most of the dim-witted Schongauers, in any case. Only Secretary Lechner was any match for him with regard to intelligence, and it made Barbara all the sadder that her father was a drinker. Alcohol changed his character and, what was worse, when he was drunk, she could no longer be proud of him.

She was ashamed of him.

Her sister, Magdalena, once told her that their grandfather had died a drunkard. Barbara could only pray this was not the predestined fate of everyone in the family.

Perhaps our fate will be different, she thought, *and I can figure out what it is going to be. These books . . .*

She paused on hearing a hissing sound. At first she thought it was just another admirer trying to get her attention, but then she began to wonder. The sounds clearly came from the old cemetery behind the church, which hadn't been used for a long time. A wall with a rusty iron gate separated it from the narrow lane, and inside she caught sight of some rough-hewn rocks, sacks of mortar, and a few tilted gravestones. She watched with curiosity as two figures stood behind the gate talking quietly, then she heard the jingling of coins and sounds of laughter.

She pressed her forehead against the iron gate, trying to learn more. The men were hard to see in the darkness, but at least one seemed very well dressed, with a large dark cloak and a wide-brimmed hat. The other was wearing a Stopselhut – a tall, bell-shaped hat, traditional in the high Alps and Bavaria, but almost unknown in the Schongau area. Barbara was certain they weren't drifters or beggars that one might expect to find in such a place, nor were they drunken journeymen.

So what were they doing here?

The man wearing the Stopselhut nodded a farewell and headed towards the gate. Barbara ducked down but kept watching through a crack in the wall. The stranger was strongly built and moved with the swaggering motion of a tough brawler. The brim of his hat was pulled so far down that she couldn't see his face, but there was something menacing about him. He turned again to the other man with a whispered farewell.

"Be prepared," he said. "You'll hear from us soon."

His voice had a strange, hard tone. It took a moment for Barbara to realize he was speaking a Tyrolean dialect, with an accent not often heard in the Priest's Corner, in southwest Bavaria.

A cold shiver went through her body as she hurried away down the lane so the second man wouldn't see her. When she'd gone a good distance, she heard steps behind her quickly approaching. Was the man following her? Had she seen something she shouldn't have?

Barbara turned around and uttered a faint cry. Someone was standing in the lane. She couldn't tell for sure if it was one of the men from the cemetery, but he was wearing a dark coat. He took off his hat and smiled broadly.

"Barbara, my dear," the man cried as if he'd just recognized her in the half-light. "What a pleasure it is to see you," he continued, opening his arms. "The sight of you brings a delightful end to this hard day of work."

Barbara gave a sigh of relief. "Ah, it's you, Doctor Ransmayer. You gave me a real scare. I thought—"

"What did you think?" the stylishly dressed gentlemen asked, drawing closer.

"Let's forget it," Barbara said with a wave of her hand. "I thought you were someone else." Then she added with a chuckle, "Or do you hang around in dark streets with shady characters?"

"Shady characters? Oh God, no!" the doctor laughed, but it sounded a bit forced. "Very well, I'll admit I saw you a while ago with the lads up in the Stern and hoped I'd see you here later." He raised his arms in an expression of surrender. "Touché."

"Well, if you were so interested in meeting me, Herr Doktor, the bathhouse would have been a more suitable place," Barbara replied.

"I'm afraid your elder sister and especially her husband wouldn't be so happy to see me there." Ransmayer politely held out his arm to her. "May I?"

"Thanks, I can manage by myself."

Ransmayer sighed. "Then at least let me take you to the one-man door. The watchman is one of my patients. All it will take is a word from me and he'll let you through without any questions."

Reluctantly, Barbara accepted his offer, as she didn't want any trouble at the gate. In return, she'd put up with the company of the arrogant doctor for a while. Melchior Ransmayer was in his mid-forties but took great pains to appear younger. He wore a felt hat adorned with colourful flowers and a pitch-black full-bottomed wig – a French fashion now rapidly spreading in Bavaria as well. His pointed beard was twirled and rubbed with beeswax, and a white lace collar circled his neck.

Barbara had never been quite able to figure out this doctor who'd been living a full three years in Schongau and was such strong competition for her brother-in-law, Simon.

Ransmayer seemed to have taken a real liking to her and had been courting her occasionally. Until now Barbara had refrained from telling

Magdalena and Simon about these rendezvous, as she knew Simon couldn't stand Ransmayer and thought he was a quack. But perhaps her brother-in-law's dislike for him was due to the extremely expensive and exquisite clothing the doctor wore and that Simon only wished he could afford. Even now Ransmayer was dressed in petticoat breeches and a doublet of red silk underneath his coat.

"Did I hear that your esteemed brother-in-law is out of town for a few days?" Ransmayer asked as they walked together through the dark street. "Oberammergau, so I hear."

Barbara nodded hesitantly. "Simon is taking Peter there for his schooling, as he is not permitted to attend the Latin school here."

"You don't say." Ransmayer assumed a troubled look. "What a pity that such a talented child is not permitted to attend the grammar school. People say wonderful things about your little nephew," he said, patting Barbara's hand. Barbara could smell his breath and knew that the good doctor had had a bit too much to drink. "Believe me, my dear, if I had any influence in the town council, I would try to change that."

"But you do have influence," Barbara retorted. "You are, after all, a learned doctor."

"Do you think so?" Ransmayer rocked his head thoughtfully from side to side as if he'd just come to that realization too. "Perhaps you are right. I could at least speak with Burgomaster Buchner . . ."

"You would really do that?" Barbara looked at him, elated.

"I would." Ransmayer smiled, but suddenly there was a cold glitter in his eyes. "But one hand washes the other, as the saying goes." Suddenly he stopped. "How about this . . . I'll take care of your little Peter, and you . . ." He ran his fingers through her hair. "You'll look after me a bit. Of course, it will be just between the two of us."

"What . . . do you mean by that?" Barbara asked, though she already suspected what Ransmayer had in mind.

"Let's start with your showing me what's underneath that pretty bodice." Suddenly the doctor pushed Barbara into a side lane and his hands moved from her hair to her breasts. The man was clearly drunk, and the strong smell of brandy on his breath made her feel sick.

"Hey, stop that," Barbara cried, trying to push his hand away. "Who do you think I am? A prostitute?" But the doctor's grip on her breasts was so tight that she winced in pain. Instinctively she rammed her attacker between the legs. Ransmayer cried out, gasped, and let her go.

"You cheap little hussy," he hissed. His gallant tone of voice had suddenly disappeared and he sounded like any ordinary tavern brawler. "Here I go offering my help, and this is what I get. You just wait, you little tramp!"

He grabbed her by the hair and she screamed, scratched, and fought like a cat, but Ransmayer was stronger. He pressed her against a wall and lifted up her skirt. "Ah," he whispered, fumbling with his flies. "And now you're going to behave and do what—"

"Damnitalltohellandback! Take your filthy hands off my daughter before I chop them off, you bastard!"

Shocked, Ransmayer stopped and looked down towards the end of the lane, where the colossal shadow of a man was visible. The body that went with it was only slightly smaller. The man held a beer stein in one hand, which he smacked into his other hand in a threatening gesture. Next to him stood a young boy, Barbara's nephew Paul.

"Father!" Barbara cried out with relief, suddenly very happy to see him after all. "Thank God! You're a gift from heaven."

"The heavens are about to come down on someone's head."

The Schongau hangman tottered slightly, but the earthen mug in his hand and his determined gait left no doubt about his intention to clean all the muck out of this little alley.

The moment he heard the first cry, Jakob had known his younger daughter was in danger.

The Schongau executioner had just left the Zur Sonne tavern, where he'd spent the last few hours. Actually he'd gone up into town only to get away from his little spat with Barbara and find himself a fresh jug of beer, but then he'd decided to stay in town and finish his beer there. Very well, it wasn't just one, but probably six or seven – he couldn't really remember any more. In any case, at over six feet tall and well over two hundred pounds he could handle it better than those dubious young workers and skinny riffraff that spent the time after work in the tavern and tonight had glanced anxiously at the hangman, even if at the age of almost sixty he no longer looked quite as fit as he used to.

In the tavern, he had been sitting silently, lost in his thoughts, until Paul arrived. As often happened, Magdalena had sent her youngest out to fetch Grandpa and bring him back home. The youngster's whining regularly managed to spoil even the smallest sip of beer, but with enough sweets or a freshly polished pocketknife, Jakob had always managed to postpone the trip back home a bit.

When the hangman heard the screaming, he immediately ran off, and right on his heels came little Paul, for whom this night-time outing was a splendid adventure. Though he was one year younger than his brother, Paul loved roughhousing of any sort. He watched with fascination as his grandfather, snorting and raising his beer stein in the air, stomped towards Barbara and her attacker.

"Grampy, what's the man there doing with Aunt Barbara?" asked little Paul, running along beside him. Fascinated, the boy stared at Melchior Ransmayer, still standing there with his trousers halfway down, clinging to the struggling Barbara.

"Wait and see what Grampy's going to do with the man now," Jakob growled as he charged at the doctor.

"Don't you dare lay a hand on me, hangman!" Ransmayer warned as he quickly pulled up his trousers. His voice sounded shrill, and it was clear he was terrified. "I'm an honourable citizen of this city, and—"

"To me you're nothing but scum," Jakob interrupted. "I'll break every finger, one by one, of anyone who dares to lay a hand on my daughter, and then I'll break them again. I'm the executioner here and I know how to do that."

"Hooray, Grandpa!" Paul cried. "You show him!"

"It's not what it looks like," said Ransmayer, trying to weasel his way out of his dilemma. He pointed at Barbara. "She was making eyes at me and wiggling her behind. You know how young girls are. I only wanted to give her a kiss."

"With your trousers pulled down?" Barbara said sarcastically. In the meantime she had pulled herself together. Her eyes flashing, she looked Ransmayer up and down as she straightened out her bodice. "Don't make an ass of yourself, Herr Doktor. The only thing going for you is that you're clearly drunk and not in control of yourself."

"Apparently not drunk enough, or I never would have been so crazy as to get involved with a dishonourable woman like you," Ransmayer said, his face turning crimson. Evidently his pride had won out over his fear. "That's what happens when one treats people like you as equals," he continued in an arrogant tone before turning to Jakob. "Hangman, you really should keep a better eye on your daughter. She's a crafty little hussy with devilish charms."

The beer mug struck Ransmayer on the side of his head. He stumbled and stared at Jakob with horror in his eyes. "You'll pay for that," he croaked. "Just wait until I speak to the council . . ." Then his voice suddenly failed him and he fell face-first into the muddy lane, where he remained motionless, his fur-trimmed coat covering him like a shroud.

"Ha! Grampy really gave it to him," Paul rejoiced, hopping up and down. "Grandpa is the strongest."

"Are you crazy?" Barbara hissed at her father as she bent down and listened for Ransmayer's breath. "Thank God he's alive," she said with relief, straightening the wig that had slipped from his head. A trickle of blood flowed across his forehead. "We can count ourselves lucky you didn't break his skull."

"Ha! I wish I had," Jakob grumbled, "but an educated fathead like him can stand a lot. Besides, what should I have done, eh? Shake his hand after he almost raped you and then insulted you?"

"A slap in the face would have sufficed," Barbara replied. "Nothing really happened."

"Nothing happened?" Jakob stared at his daughter through bloodshot eyes, then his anger exploded like lava from a volcano. *"Nothing happened?"* he roared. "This fellow called you a crafty little hussy with devilish charms, and you say nothing happened? No one drags our family name through the mud – no one!"

"Nobody has to do that now – he's muddy enough," Barbara replied angrily. "I'm nothing but the youngest daughter of the Schongau executioner, who by the way is as drunk as an entire regiment of Swedish soldiers and has just got our whole family into a lot of trouble." Evidently the fright at the attempted rape was just now catching up with her, and she started to tremble.

"Just look at you." With disgust she pointed at her father, whose beard was dripping sticky beer foam. "It's been going on like this for more than a year. Either you're pouting or drinking, and mostly both at the same time. People have never spoken well of us, but they used to at least respect us, and now they just gossip about what a drunk you are."

"How dare you speak to your father like that," Kuisl bellowed. He raised his hand threateningly and only at the last moment realized he was still holding the beer stein.

"Oh, do you want to beat me senseless just like the doctor?" Barbara sneered. "Is that the way you take care of problems? With a mug of beer? You either drink from it or hit people over the head with it." Her eyes filled with tears. "I'm . . . so sick of it," she whispered. "You don't have any idea how much all you men disgust me." Sobbing, she turned away and ran towards the city gate.

"Barbara!" Jakob shouted as she disappeared down the lane. "Barbara! Wait! I didn't mean it that way."

But his daughter had already disappeared in the darkness.

"Barbara!" he called again.

"Quiet down there," a voice shouted. A shutter opened and an old, almost toothless woman stared down at him. "Is it you again, hangman?" she scolded. "Go sleep it off somewhere else – honourable people live here."

The shutter slammed shut and silence fell over the street, broken only by the regular rattling breaths of the unconscious doctor.

"Grandpa, why is Auntie Barbara so angry at you?" little Paul finally asked in a soft voice.

"Because . . . Because . . ." Jakob struggled for words.

Because she's right, he thought to himself.

His quarrel with Barbara had sobered him up a bit. He'd got so angry because his daughter was speaking the truth.

Either you're pouting or drinking . . .

He had become an old drunk. It had all started four years ago, insidiously, gradually, with the death of his beloved wife, Anna-Maria. It had worsened three years afterwards, when he learned that his beloved son, Georg, would remain as a journeyman with his uncle, the hangman in Bamberg. Some years ago, Georg had had a fight with a Schongau citizen, leaving the man crippled, and for that reason he had been banished from town. Actually, he'd been banished for just two years, but Georg enjoyed his new position in the larger and more cosmopolitan city of Bamberg, far from his father. Georg's decision to stay there almost broke his father's heart, and since then the hangman had been drowning his sorrows in alcohol.

And with the alcohol, all the dark memories returned.

All the corpses . . . hanging on the branches of trees like giant rotten apples. The screaming, whimpering, begging for mercy . . . With the sword I shall separate the wheat from the chaff . . .

But above all, there was one memory that woke him up at night and each time caused him to break out in a sweat.

My father, staggering towards the scaffold, drunk . . . the raging mob . . . a bloody, severed ear lying in the white snow . . . I'm becoming like my father . . . my father, the drunkard . . .

"Grandfather, what's wrong?" Paul asked.

Jakob was jolted out of his reveries. "Nothing," he said, shaking his head as if trying to drive away a bad dream. "I was just thinking of something that happened when I was a child."

Paul smiled. "I want to become an executioner like you someday." Reverentially he stared up into his grandfather's face, as if he were a knight, or the kaiser himself. "I want everyone to be afraid of me."

Jakob nodded. "I know, Paul," he replied hesitantly. "I know. But sometimes you become afraid of yourself. That's the worst fear."

Then he took his grandson by the hand and slowly began walking with him towards the Lech Gate.

It was just a short walk from Georg Kaiser's house over to the Oberammergau village church. Kaiser walked in front with a lantern to light their way. A chest-high wall surrounded the church and the cemetery, but as they approached, Simon saw tall individual gravestones and a larger wooden structure, whose purpose seemed a mystery to him. A slightly sweet odour was in the air, and Simon knew all too well what that was. It was the odour of decay that often emanated from cemeteries, especially when the graves were close together, as they were here.

The autopsy that the schoolteacher had asked him to attend was at nine o'clock in the evening at St Ann's Chapel. The witnesses were Georg Kaiser as well as the priest and Konrad Faistenmantel, who evidently wanted to say one last goodbye to his son. Before they left, Simon had put Peter to bed. Georg Kaiser had given the boy his own room under the rafters, which even had its own fireplace, and Peter finally fell asleep with an illustrated book by the anatomist Andreas Vesalius in his hands. Simon gradually began to feel comfortable with the idea of Peter spending the next few years here in Oberammergau, due in no small part to Kaiser's well-stocked library, but also because of the kind schoolmaster himself.

The schoolmaster opened a rusty, squeaking side gate, and he and Simon entered the dark cemetery. Now the Schongau medicus had a closer look at not only the many gravestones, but also the strange wooden structure he'd noticed earlier. It was around twenty feet long and three feet high. Rough-hewn wood beams formed another framework above the platform. On the left and right sides there were two entrances. A wheelbarrow and a pile of old ropes indicated that the structure was not completely finished.

"The stage for the Passion play!" Simon cried in astonishment. "It's actually here in the cemetery."

Kaiser nodded. "We're still in the middle of rehearsals, but by Pentecost at the latest everything has to be ready for opening day — costumes, backdrops, Pilate's house, hell . . ." His sweeping gesture included the stage and all the props lying around. "The whole town is helping. At present, we're still rehearsing in the Schwabenwirt tavern, but yesterday afternoon we also rehearsed here for the first time. Dominik Faistenmantel insisted on being hung on the cross in order to know how it felt."

"He succeeded," Simon replied darkly. "It was Friday, so he even picked the right day for his crucifixion." He pointed at the wooden platform, where a large dark object could be seen. "Is that the cross?"

"Indeed." Kaiser climbed a small wooden stairway alongside the platform and beckoned for Simon to follow. There was a depression in the ground, presumably representing Jesus's grave, and next to it a trapdoor. In the centre of the platform lay a cross well over six feet long, made of spruce wood and still smelling of resin.

The schoolmaster pointed to a small hole bored through the lower part of the vertical beam. "Normally there's a footrest here, which was apparently removed," he explained. "The actor portraying Jesus is tied with rope and then hoisted up by the Roman soldiers. With the footrest in place, it's possible to tolerate it up there for a while. For nails we use dummies that the blacksmith makes for us." Georg now pointed at a square cut-out in the stage floor. "And this is where the cross is inserted so it stands upright. Faistenmantel was in this position when the priest found him in the morning."

Simon tried to pick up the head of the crossbeam, but it felt like it weighed a ton.

"It's impossible to stand it up like this," he groaned, letting the cross back down on the stage floor. "How could anyone do that with a grown man tied to it?"

Kaiser thought for a moment. "That's just what some of us were thinking. The perpetrator must have been pretty strong, or else there were a number of them. Or—"

"Or it was the devil himself," Simon said. "I see what you're saying – it's no wonder people in town are hanging out bouquets of St John's wort."

Simon was freezing; he rubbed his arms. Only now did he realize he was much too lightly dressed for the late-night outing. He was wearing a shirt with a tight-fitting jacket over it that Magdalena had already mended in places. In his haste, he'd left his beloved wide-brimmed red hat in the schoolmaster's house.

Simon's gaze fell on the muddy ground in front of the staging. It was ripped up, as if a herd of wild pigs had been rooting around in it.

"There's clearly no point in looking for footprints," he mumbled. "It looks like half of Oberammergau visited the scene of the crime today."

Simon looked around the small cemetery then turned his gaze back to the stage and the cross lying on it. Something was bothering him.

There's something wrong here, he thought, *but what?*

After turning it over in his mind for a long time, he gave up. Perhaps it would come to him later.

"Where will the audience be standing?" he asked instead. "There's hardly any room in front of the stage."

Kaiser smiled. "Some will watch from up on the cemetery wall, but most of them will stand on the gravestones."

"*On* the gravestones?" Simon was perplexed.

"The gravestones will be turned down for the performance and later set upright again. That's what they did the last few times." Georg shrugged. "There are constant discussions about whether to move the play to another location, especially now that more and more people are attending, but until now people have adhered to tradition, even if Konrad Faistenmantel has been demanding a larger venue, perhaps one farther from town."

"Who is this Faistenmantel, anyway, and why is he so powerful?" Simon asked. "Is he a large landholder?"

"No, he's . . ." Kaiser suddenly fell silent and nodded towards two figures approaching them from the cemetery's front gate.

"Speak of the devil," he continued in an undertone. "Here comes Faistenmantel in person, and the other man is no doubt the Ammergau judge, Johannes Rieger."

The two men carried lanterns that cast a dim light over their path. One was around fifty years old and wearing the official uniform of a rural official, with a beret and cloak. He was slightly stooped and leaned on a walking stick. His weasel-like appearance was accentuated by his long face and thinning brown hair. The man at his side was about the same age but was a giant of a man – muscular, at least six feet tall, and with a potbelly and a broad back. A bushy beard fell down over his tight-fitting waistcoat. The large man raised his lantern, and Simon could now see his imposing bald head. Tiny porcine eyes glared distrustfully at the two men on the stage.

"Good day, Master Kaiser," the large man – presumably Konrad Faistenmantel – wheezed. "Do you really intend to perform the autopsy at this late hour? I'd like to know the role of the fellow standing at your side. He's clearly too short and skinny to be the Roman soldier Longinus we've been seeking for such a long time."

"My name is not Longinus, but Simon Fronwieser," Simon retorted, jutting his jaw forwards. He hated it when people teased him because of his size. "I'm the medicus from Schongau, visiting here in Oberammergau. It seems you'll have to look around for another Roman," he said. "But remember that Saint Longinus is remembered less for his size and strength than his wisdom and mercy."

Faistenmantel gave a loud, raucous laugh that seemed strangely out of place in the dark cemetery. Simon couldn't help remembering that this was the man whose son had met a horrible end in this very place less than a day ago.

"Excuse me, Herr Medicus," Faistenmantel said. "It was not my intent to offend you. Everyone's nerves are stretched to the breaking point at present."

"But I'd still like to know what business you have in the cemetery at this hour," snarled the wiry man at his side, the Ammergau judge, Johannes Rieger, "so speak up before I have you arrested."

"Gentlemen, please." Georg Kaiser raised his arms, trying to calm them down. "I myself asked Herr Fronwieser to come along. He is a highly experienced medicus, and since our barber-surgeon, old Kaspar Landes, God rest his soul, is no longer among us, I thought it couldn't hurt to bring along a professional observer."

"I have explicit directions from the abbot at Ettal Monastery to make sure that as few outsiders as possible find out about this embarrassing matter," said Rieger. "If His Excellency knew that a visitor from Schongau—"

"Oh, come now, Rieger, don't make such a fuss," Faistenmantel interrupted. "Herr Kaiser is right. The faster we can get this matter behind us, and the more professional and matter-of-fact we are, the quicker we can resume the rehearsals. We need a reasonable explanation for the death of my youngest son, and if the medicus can help us, we should be glad for that."

The judge was about to respond, but Faistenmantel was already stomping towards the south side of the church, where a shed with a low doorway was located. Simon thought he detected a flash of raw anger in Rieger's eyes. Evidently, the judge was very annoyed at how Faistenmantel brushed him off in front of the others.

Konrad Faistenmantel pounded the door with his fist, and the grey-faced priest opened it at once. His name was Tobias Herele, as Simon had learned from Georg Kaiser on his arrival. Father Herele also didn't seem especially pleased to see Simon there. He looked Simon up and down distrustfully, almost with disgust, as if he were an annoying parasite.

What delightful people, these Oberammergauers, Simon thought. *Anyone who doesn't live here but comes from somewhere else can just go to hell. What in the world have I got myself into now?*

His eyes wandered around the interior of the small, simple chapel that was connected by another door to the church. Before the altar, a makeshift wooden bier had been erected, and on top of it lay the corpse of a long-haired fellow about twenty years old. Simon eyed him thoughtfully. Despite its slightly bluish tint, the young man's face was pleasant to look at, except for the two black, blood-encrusted holes where his eyes used to be. His lips were full and nicely contoured, and his fine facial features gave him an almost feminine appearance. In his burial shroud he looked like a blinded angel that had fallen to earth.

Candles burned in candelabra positioned around the corpse, and there was a strong odour of incense, as if someone was trying to drive off the evil spirits that had surely inspired this heinous deed – but Simon thought he could already detect behind it the stench of decay.

From the corner of his eye he observed the corpulent Konrad Faistenmantel staring fixedly at his dead son. Everyone was silent; the only sound was the priest murmuring a short Latin prayer for the dead.

"That with the eyes – that must have been the ravens," Judge Rieger said, breaking the silence. "Damn smart creatures, and they all should be poisoned, but it was something else that killed him."

"Could it simply have been suicide?" Faistenmantel asked. "My youngest boy always had such a delicate, theatrical nature, and recently he often talked rubbish – about a new life, and things like that. Maybe he really thought of himself as the Saviour and was trying to emulate him."

"Nonsense. Suicide is out of the question," Rieger snapped. "How could he have hung himself on the cross, eh?" He turned to the priest. "Did Dominik Faistenmantel perhaps have an argument with any of the other actors, Father?"

"Argument?" The question clearly made Herele uncomfortable. "Well, what do you mean, argument? There were a few angry words – not everyone agreed that Dominik should play the role of Jesus."

"I gave the church a heap of money so that my son would get the role," Faistenmantel growled. "Don't forget that, Father. He was just the right person for the part. Look for yourself." He pointed at the pale corpse in front of them. "The blond hair, the narrow face, the full lips . . . God knows, the boy didn't take after me." He paused to get his composure before continuing. "But he would have made a wonderful Jesus. He truly would have been better suited to that role than to that of my son."

A bitter twitch played around his mouth, and for the first time Simon thought he noticed something resembling grief in his face.

"Who else wanted the part of Jesus?" asked Rieger.

"Well, most of all Hans Göbl," Georg Kaiser replied. "He asked me for the part months ago, but I had to tell him the role was already taken." The schoolmaster coughed nervously and put his hand to his mouth before continuing. "After Dominik's death we assigned him the role after all. Göbl has an astonishing resemblance to the Saviour in the votive pictures in the church, and in addition he has a loud and pleasant voice and can read a bit. Given the quantity of text there is, that's important."

"You say there was an argument between him and Dominik Faistenmantel?" Johannes Rieger persisted. "Are there any witnesses?"

Kaiser shrugged. "Two days ago Göbl came to me and complained bitterly because he hadn't got the part of Jesus, though he was better suited for it. I told him the selection was not up to me but was determined by the town council. And . . ." He hesitated.

"And what happened then?" the judge demanded. "Are you keeping something from us?"

"Well, later Dominik stopped by and said Göbl had come to his house and threatened him. And after he left, a few important pages of Dominik's text were missing, specifically, the scene on the cross in which Jesus laments, 'My Father, My Father, why—'"

"'Why hast Thou forsaken me?'" Simon mumbled under his breath as he looked at Konrad Faistenmantel, who stood there without a flicker of emotion.

"Do you think Hans Göbl stole the pages from Dominik in order to harm him?" Johannes Rieger asked.

"Ha! The Göbls could never stand us Faistenmantels," the fat town council chairman said. "Those miserable, jealous whiners. You see how logic flies out the window when your feelings take over." He turned to the judge. "It looks like Göbl might actually be the murderer, so do your duty."

"I'll deal with Hans Göbl tomorrow," responded Johannes Rieger with a shrug. "The abbot wants this matter to go away as quickly as possible, and at present we don't have any other suspects."

"Arrest Göbl, and better now than tomorrow," Faistenmantel insisted. "Squeeze him, torture him, whatever, but hurry up, Rieger.

We have just a few weeks left, and the rehearsal must not be put off unnecessarily."

"I'm not going to let you tell me how to do my work," Rieger snapped. "Calm down, Faistenmantel. I'm still the judge in this valley and I report directly to the abbot."

"Don't worry, I only want this matter cleared up as soon as possible." Faistenmantel grimaced, and his bald head shimmered in the light of the lantern like a polished apple. "Otherwise, I may need to tell the abbot about your little business."

"How dare you . . ." Rieger turned crimson and gasped for air as he raised his walking stick menacingly and appeared about to attack Faistenmantel.

"Calm down!" the priest demanded. "Let there be peace in my church. There's already too much misery in this village." He made the sign of the cross, and the two combatants backed off.

"I'm praying fervently that this incident will be explained rationally," Herele pleaded, "because if it isn't . . ." He didn't complete his sentence but looked over at the altar, where a picture hung of the Archangel Gabriel driving Satan back to hell with his sword. Simon was alarmed to see that even on the altar there was a bouquet of St John's wort alongside a bowl of smoking incense. Evidently not even the priest was immune to superstition.

"Well, perhaps I could finally inspect the corpse?" Simon asked, breaking the silence. "Just so my visit won't be entirely in vain."

Rieger took a deep breath and turned around. "Please . . . please do what you must, Herr Medicus, even though it's quite obvious what happened. The man died on the cross – isn't that really all there is to it?"

"Let him have a look at the deceased anyway," said Georg Kaiser, turning to the judge. "Master Fronwieser is well known as an enlightened individual and perhaps he'll see something that has escaped even your discerning eyes."

Silently the judge stepped aside, and Simon began the examination. There was clotted blood and bruises on the wrists and ankles of the corpse, no doubt inflicted by the ropes. His face had turned blue, and there were clumps of clotted blood in his eye sockets. On examining the back of the dead man's head, Simon found further traces of blood and an indentation the size of an egg that had been concealed up to then beneath the long blond hair. He contemplated the sticky blood between his fingers.

"Before he was put on the cross, the fellow was subjected to a hard blow on the back of the head," said Simon, turning to the others, who were observing him intently. "Perhaps with an axe, or something of similar size. He was probably unconscious when he was hung on the cross, which explains the rather superficial injuries left by the ropes. If he were awake, he would have resisted much more." Simon pointed at the bluish tinge on the face. "It probably took him several hours to die, due to suffocation. When the arms lose their strength, the body assumes a position that makes breathing almost impossible. If the boy was lucky, he froze to death first."

"That's quite possible," the judge said. "When he was found, he was wearing only a loincloth, just like our Saviour, though our cross is situated in the frosty town of Oberammergau, not in a warm region like Palestine."

"What happened to his clothing?" Simon wondered out loud.

Rieger shrugged. "Who knows? The attacker evidently disposed of it, probably after he'd struck down the poor lad, wanting to make sure he was dead before the priest found him in the morning."

There was a barely audible grinding sound, and it took Simon a while to realize it was Konrad Faistenmantel gnashing his teeth. The huge man was clenching his fists as he looked down at his dead son. Despite the cold, little beads of sweat formed on his bald head.

"But why didn't he cry for help?" Father Herele asked Simon. He had crossed his arms over his chest and was shifting nervously from one foot to the other. "Isn't it possible he awoke from his unconscious state at some point in time?"

"I've been wondering about that, too. I assume we'll find the solution in there," Simon said, tapping the mouth of the corpse. "Unfortunately rigor mortis has set in, but . . ." He bent over for a closer look, his head now only a few inches above the lips. Now he could clearly smell the faint odour of decomposition.

But he also saw something that had escaped him during the first superficial examination.

"Eureka!" Simon cried. He tugged gently on a grey fibre hanging from the lips – and there was a second one next to it.

"What is it?" Rieger asked. "Bits of food?"

"Bits of a gag, I assume," said Simon, holding up the thread. "The one in his mouth used to silence him – and that's why poor Dominik couldn't call for help." He turned to the priest. "Was a gag found at the scene of the crime?"

Tobias Herele shook his head defiantly. "Not to my knowledge. In any case, the poor man didn't have one in his mouth when I discovered him in the morning. That can only lead to the conclusion that your theory—"

"That actually leads to only one conclusion," said Simon, cutting him off. "Namely that the murderer returned in order to cover his tracks. He wanted the deed to look like a curse, a sign from God. A man on a cross . . ." He hesitated.

"What's the matter?" Georg Kaiser asked. "Are you all right? I hope you didn't catch my cold."

"No, no." Simon shook his head. "I just have the feeling I overlooked something out there in the cemetery. Something . . ."

"Well, I think up to now you've done quite a thorough job," said Faistenmantel, patting Simon on the shoulder. "For a simple medicus you're pretty smart, I must say. Better than old Kaspar Landes, God rest his soul. He'd have dragged it out all day just to get in his hours, the old money-grubber."

Simon smiled. "I don't like to drag things out. A sick man, like the one who killed your son, needs all the help he can get."

"I'll make you an offer," Faistenmantel said. "Stay a bit longer in Oberammergau, let's say four weeks, until the Passion play." He pointed at Georg Kaiser, who had just been seized by a fit of coughing. "Just like the schoolteacher, many here in town have caught this illness going around. We urgently need a medicus here, and furthermore, I want to see a solution to the murder of my son as soon as possible. You could be a great help to us."

"I'm afraid that's not as easy as you think," Simon replied, raising his hands defensively. "I have a bathhouse in Schongau and my patients will be waiting for me, and furthermore—"

"Nonsense, I'll pay you ten guilders a week."

"Ten . . . ?"

Simon almost choked. Ten guilders was almost twice what he usually earned in Schongau in a week. Some of his patients had switched over to that quack doctor, Ransmayer, and ever since then his earnings had been falling. A little additional income would in fact be more than welcome, but could he leave his wife and little Paul alone for such a long time?

"Let's say twelve guilders, my final offer." Konrad Faistenmantel reached out his huge hand. "You could live in the bathhouse here, which is empty, as old Landes had no family, and I'll provide a horse so you can ride back to Schongau on Sundays. Shake."

Simon was still hesitant, but then he thought of Peter and his fear of the strange new place, the unaccustomed environment. Peter had always been his favourite, even if he would never admit it to Magdalena. The decision to send him to Oberammergau weighed more heavily on him than on his wife. Staying a few weeks with him would make parting easier for both of them, and they really could use the money.

In the meantime, Magdalena and the midwife Martha Stechlin could handle the simpler cases.

"Very well," he said finally, shaking hands with Faistenmantel, "but only until the Passion play starts, and not one day longer."

"Not one day longer, I promise."

While the large man's hand wrapped around Simon's like a vice, Simon glanced over at Johannes Rieger and the priest, Tobias Herele. Both glared at him with eyes that seemed full of hate.

Welcome to Oberammergau, Simon thought. *The place where strangers are still strangers.*

He smiled back bravely, and couldn't help but wonder whether a bouquet of St John's wort also hung on the deceased bathhouse keeper's door to ward off evil.

He had the feeling he might need it.

3

WHEN SHE AWOKE, A SUDDEN FEELING OF NAUSEA hit Magdalena in the pit of her stomach. She jumped out of bed and ran to the washbowl standing in a corner of the room, but all that came out was bitter green bile. She'd been feeling sick for several days, and Martha Stechlin had told her it was certainly related to her pregnancy, a sign that the child was growing and thriving. To judge from that, the child would be a real bundle of joy.

As so often, Magdalena wondered why women had to assume the full burden of bringing children into the world. First they were as sick as a dog, then for several months they looked like a pouch full of wine, and finally they suffered all the pain of childbirth – and then, all too often, died like cattle. Men's part in this was extremely simple and satisfying – and every time another child came into the world, the men puffed out their chests like the cock of the walk.

And if the baby dies, it starts all over again, Magdalena thought.

Bent over the basin, she vomited again. At least it helped her forget the painful memories that kept coming back. It was four years ago that she and Simon had lost little Anna-Maria just a few weeks after she was born, and since then, Magdalena had had three miscarriages, one of them not until the second trimester. The child had looked like a tiny doll – her fingers, toes, and everything were already formed. By then, people had started whispering behind her back, and for this reason Magdalena had refrained from telling Simon and the rest of the family about it, not wanting to awaken any false hopes.

"Madam!" came the sudden sound of a man's voice outside the bathhouse. Magdalena cringed. There was a knock on the door, first softly, then more and more urgently.

"Frau Fronwieser, are you home?" the person called again. "Please open the door."

"My husband isn't here," she replied, gasping, as she leaned over the basin again. "If . . . it's an emergency, I think you'll have to . . ."

"I'm not looking for your husband, but your father," replied the voice outside. "It's me, the constable, Andreas."

"The constable?" Magdalena whispered, wiping the corners of her mouth with a linen rag before carefully getting to her feet. "Damn. Just as I thought."

The night before, little Paul didn't get home until well after the town gates were closed. Excitedly, he told his mother that Grandpa had had a fight with another man, who had been playing some strange game with Barbara. Magdalena hadn't spoken with either her father or her sister that morning, but she didn't have to be clairvoyant to figure out that the man, the fight, and what Paul called a game were somehow all related. She was afraid her father had got himself into trouble again.

She quickly washed her face with cold water to freshen up, then she opened the door. The city constable, Andreas, stood before her, halberd in hand, staring nervously at her low-cut neckline.

"How many times do I have to tell you town guards that my father now lives in the little house at the back by the pond?" she asked the guard, pointing down the little path. She still felt a bit sick.

"Uh, that I know, Frau Fronwieser," Andreas replied, "but if he won't open the door . . ."

"Then he's just not there," Magdalena said. "Perhaps he's working down at the jail or cleaning up the muck in the streets. Just open your eyes and look around."

"But I can hear loud snoring in the house."

Magdalena sighed, threw a shawl over her shoulders, and went down the narrow, muddy path through the garden to the pond, where the so-called retirement house was located. For hundreds of years each older generation had moved in here to make room for the younger folks. It was a sunny morning and, though it was still cool, the first hint of summer was in the air. Leeks and onions were sprouting in the little garden, spreading their sharp fragrance.

Her father himself had suggested he move into the little house by the water, making room for Magdalena and her family in the large hangman's house with its stable. Jakob Kuisl, now almost sixty years old, was still in better shape than many people in their forties, and he was still the official hangman of Schongau, but he realized that he didn't need all that room after the death of his wife. Simon and Magdalena moved into the hangman's house, which was far larger and roomier than the bathhouse keeper's quarters up in town.

Magdalena pounded on the door energetically. "Father?" she called. "Open up. The constable is here." But the only sound they heard was loud snoring. Andreas grinned and picked his teeth.

"Seems the executioner had a bit too much to drink again," he said.

"What business is that of yours?" Magdalena snapped. Then, in a softer voice, she continued. "What sort of trouble did he get into this time?"

"Dunno . . . I'm just supposed to bring him to see Lechner."

Magdalena shook her head. It was probably just as she feared. Johann Lechner was secretary of the Schongau Court, and thus the representative of the elector in town. Evidently he'd already got wind of the fight the day before. If Jakob's luck ran out, he could find himself in the dungeon, and they'd probably send for the executioner in Steingaden to come and put his Schongau colleague in the pillory. Magdalena knew her father would survive this, but it would be a great humiliation for the family. She could only be glad that little Paul was somewhere down on the Lech River and wouldn't see his grandfather, whom he adored so much, being led away. It was a disgrace.

"For God's sake, Father, wake up before they burn the house down around you." She pounded on the door again, and this time something could be heard moving inside. Something large and heavy fell to the floor, then came the sound of a breaking dish, and then someone shuffled to the door and pushed the bolt aside.

The door opened, and the stale smell of alcohol came wafting towards them. Jakob Kuisl seemed in a very bad mood, and he glared down at Magdalena and the constable with narrow, tired eyes. If Magdalena hadn't been his daughter, she would have been terrified of this angry-looking giant.

"I've got no time now, so beat it," he said through clenched teeth.

"My God, Father," Magdalena hissed. "If you could see yourself . . ."

"Don't have to," he responded curtly. "What the hell do you want from me? Can't a decent man sleep a little late on Sunday?"

"The bells have already rung nine o'clock, and Lechner wants to see you," Magdalena said. She pointed at Andreas, standing next to her and grinning. "The constable is going to take you with him now, and—"

The door slammed shut.

"Hey!" Andreas shouted as he pounded on the door with his halberd. "This is an order from the judge, Kuisl. Come out right now or—"

"Or what, you fool?" came the voice of Jakob Kuisl from inside. "Are you going to get the hangman? You'll have to be patient if that's who you're looking for."

Grumbling, Andreas took a seat on the bench outside the house and stared morosely at the town atop a bluff over the Lech River. The look on the constable's face suggested he would have much preferred sitting down with his colleagues for a pint of beer to escorting a grumpy, hung-over hangman to the Schongau city hall.

"You know how he is," Magdalena said, trying to calm him down. "I'm sure he'll come out soon."

"I'll wait until the bell sounds the next hour," Andreas said in a firm voice. "Until the next bell, and no longer. Then . . . then I'll go to Lechner, and your father will really be in trouble."

Magdalena remained silent – she knew only too well that if her father had his mind set on something, he couldn't be swayed, not by the constable, by Lechner, nor even by the dear Lord Himself.

Barbara was coming towards them across the wetland, holding a basket. Today, Sunday, was her day off, and she'd spent the early morning down on the Lech with other young women, collecting sweet woodruff. When she saw Magdalena and the constable standing in front of the house, she quickened her pace.

"What's going on?" she asked breathlessly and set the basket down between two flower beds.

"You probably know better than anyone," Magdalena responded, pulling her aside where the constable wouldn't hear them. "What was that fight about last night?" she whispered.

Barbara rolled her eyes, then she told her older sister what had happened. Every drop of blood drained out of Magdalena's face as she heard what Barbara had to say.

"Father whacked Ransmayer over the head?" She groaned. "My God, that's a lot worse than I expected. The doctor is an esteemed citizen, and Lechner is a patient of his, and so are half the members of the town council and the burgomaster himself. If Ransmayer wants, he can have Father whipped and dragged through the streets."

"A whoremonger! That's what he is," Barbara hissed. "The esteemed doctor met me again down by the river and threatened that he was going to make a lot of trouble for Father. He'll have him beaten and driven out of town." She smiled darkly. "But perhaps we can make some trouble for the doctor, as well."

"Just what do you mean by that?" Magdalena whispered.

Barbara turned around cautiously and looked at Andreas, who was sitting on the bench, dozing in the morning sun.

"Last night I saw Ransmayer in the old cemetery behind the church. He met someone there, a strange, foreign-looking fellow, and some money changed hands. Later, when I asked Ransmayer about it, he said it wasn't him, but I'm sure it was." Barbara lowered her voice. "Perhaps he's involved in some shady deals, and if we can catch him at it, we've got him where we want him."

Magdalena smiled despairingly. Sometimes her younger sister sounded just like the little girl she had sung to sleep not all that long ago. "I'm afraid, Barbara, you've been reading too many of these bloody fliers with all their sensational news. Isn't it possible the doctor was simply selling medicine to someone?"

"In the cemetery?" Barbara shook her head. "Hardly. You'll see . . . I'll find out what's going on. He'll be sorry he crossed swords with the Kuisls."

"If you hadn't been flirting with the doctor, this fight would never have happened," Magdalena admonished her sister. "Didn't you realize that the whole time he was just trying to pump you for information about Simon and his methods? Ransmayer's a quack. Remember last year? Treating syphilis with mercury was Simon's idea, and Ransmayer simply stole it."

"I didn't flirt with him," Barbara shot back, stamping the ground angrily. "You're just like everyone else, thinking I'm trying to fling myself at men."

Magdalena sighed. "That's not at all what I'm saying, but if you'd just restrain yourself a bit, we'd not always—"

At that moment, the door to the little house behind them swung open and their father appeared, looking grim. Jakob Kuisl had cut his hair, trimmed his beard, and put on a fresh shirt. He wore a leather jerkin over his shoulders, and his boots were freshly waxed, but his face was still pale, his cheeks sunken, and his hooked nose jutted out like an eagle's beak. Magdalena stared at her father, thinking once again how old he looked.

But then she looked into his eyes, alert and intelligent, sparkling between the wrinkles in his face; she saw his upper arms, as big around as tree trunks, and his hands, as large as beer steins, which he clenched into fists until his knuckles cracked.

Magdalena would have to revise her opinion. Even at the age of almost sixty and fighting a hangover, her father still looked like he could put up a good fight.

A scornful expression played around his mouth as he turned to the constable, who was fumbling nervously with his halberd.

"Well, then, let's go," the hangman grumbled. "The most important thing is that I'm well dressed for my own execution."

Around twenty miles away, Simon stared at the soot-stained ceiling of the Oberammergau bathhouse. He'd decided to avoid the bedroom of the deceased Kaspar Landes and spend the night instead on a hard bench next to the stove. In view of everything that had happened recently, Simon felt uneasy about using Kaspar's bed, and in any case wanted first to fumigate the house. Who knew what really killed the old bathhouse owner?

The bathhouse was on the outskirts of the village, not far from the Ammer River, and had a pretty little garden where the first medicinal plants of spring were beginning to sprout. Looking out a window darkened by dust and cobwebs, Simon could see the yarrow, ribwort, and lavender growing there, and the wild garlic was in full bloom, its fragrance wafting through the house.

Judging by the cups, bottles, and pans on the shelves alongside the tile stove, Simon knew that Kaspar Landes was a typical bathhouse keeper. The whole place was teeming with the kinds of ingredients one would find in the so-called dirt pharmacies, among them snakes and toads preserved in alcohol, fat taken from the corpses of executed criminals, and the usual mumia, brown powder from the crushed remains of ancient Egyptian mummies, viewed as a universal remedy. Simon, too, had such things in Schongau, not because he believed in their effectiveness, but because his patients expressly asked for these medicines. Sometimes he even used crushed skull fragments in his pills and had considerable success treating epilepsy with that.

All night, Simon had been agonizing about whether it had been a wise decision to remain in Oberammergau as the interim bathhouse keeper. His family really needed the money, and in this way at least he got the chance to stay longer with Peter. On the other hand, it probably meant he'd lose more clients in Schongau to the quack doctor, Ransmayer, not to mention that Magdalena would really give him hell. Early that morning he'd written her a letter and handed it to a messenger. He'd asked for understanding, but at the same time realized how much trouble it would cause her.

There was of course another reason Simon was determined to stay here, which became clear to him over the course of the night.

It was that crucified man.

As so often in his life, Simon was gripped by an almost childlike curiosity, and once again found himself confronted by a riddle. This was a trait he shared with his grumpy father-in-law, Jakob Kuisl. What exactly was going on here in Oberammergau? A cloak of fear and hate had settled over the village, something he had sensed so clearly on the street the day before, but especially at the strange postmortem in St Ann's Chapel – everyone seemed so hostile towards everyone else.

Simon stretched, stood up from the hard bench, and went over to the stove to stir the coals. Before he could think of what the new day would bring, he needed his coffee. He loved the little black beans he always carried with him whenever he was travelling. Recently he'd even bought himself a little hand grinder. Carefully he ground the beans, put them in a pot, and poured boiling water over them, and at once an aroma arose that sharpened his mind. With a steaming cup of the hot brew in his hands, he sat back down at the table, closed his eyes, and sipped the hot brew. The first sip was always the best. After his coffee, he'd look in on Peter, and then . . .

The front door squeaked, and he could hear footsteps in the hallway. Simon was startled and put down the cup he was holding. Who could it be? Perhaps Georg Kaiser, stopping by with Peter? But he would probably have knocked. Simon couldn't help thinking how people were said to scurry through the house for weeks after their demise. He shook his head.

This village is making me crazy . . .

Suddenly the footsteps stopped, as if the visitor had just noticed there was someone in the house. Simon held his breath, but now it was deadly quiet out in the hall as well. Carefully, he got to his feet and reached for the candlestick standing on the table. Thus armed, he crept towards the door and depressed the latch.

At that moment, a plank beneath his feet creaked, and he heard someone running down the hallway and out of the house. When Simon reached the hallway, he got a quick glimpse of a figure at the front door, who turned right on to the narrow lane leading down to the Ammer. It was a large man with several tufts of fire-red hair protruding from beneath a wide-brimmed hat.

"Hey, you!" Simon called after him as he ran down the hallway. "Stop! What the hell are you doing here?"

He stepped on a pot of fat left by the doorway for people to shine their shoes with and he slipped, landing flat in the mud outside the door. By the time he had scrambled to his feet, the stranger had disappeared.

Disgustedly, he brushed off his clothing, which was now soiled with horse droppings. This was the only suit of clothes he had with him. If he really intended to stay a while in Oberammergau, he'd have to pay a bit more attention to his appearance. He didn't even want to think of being forced to wear the clothing of the deceased bathhouse keeper. He looked cautiously right and left down the muddy lane at some children dressed in rags playing amid the cowpats. They just looked at him curiously.

"Did you happen to see the man who just went storming out of the house?" he asked. But the children didn't answer. They just glared at him suspiciously and went back to playing with their marbles and hoops.

"Thanks so much for the information," he mumbled. "You children here in Oberammergau are really good kids."

He returned to the house and was just about to enter the main room when he noticed something strange alongside the fireplace.

It was a small carved wooden figurine.

It caught his eye because, in contrast to the dirty pots and pans, it appeared spotless and new. He stopped to think – he couldn't remember having seen the finger-sized figurine earlier.

He picked it up and looked at it more closely. It represented a sort of priest with a shroud-like headdress, and when he turned it over he noticed two short Latin words scratched on the bottom.

ET TU . . .

"And you?" Simon murmured. "What in the world . . ."

Again the front door squeaked. Simon was startled, put the figurine aside, and turned around. Had the stranger returned? He was relieved to see that this time it really was Georg Kaiser. The schoolteacher was carrying a large basket filled to the top with food, with a fat hock of ham sticking out.

"Old Faistenmantel told me to bring you this," Kaiser said. "A sort of housewarming gift. The town council chairman was clearly impressed with your remarks yesterday in the chapel. Since it's Sunday and there's no school today, I thought I'd pay you a visit."

He paused upon seeing how upset Simon looked and noticed his mud-spattered clothing.

"Did you fall down outside?" he asked.

Simon nodded. "I was trying to catch a man who broke into the house, but unfortunately I didn't get a very good look at him. Do you have any idea who that might be? He was wearing a soft floppy hat and had bright red hair."

"A floppy hat?" Kaiser shrugged. "Perhaps an itinerant pedlar — there are some now in the village. Maybe the rascal heard the bathhouse keeper was dead and thought he could fill up his knapsack." He laughed. "Well, no doubt he was more afraid of you than you were of him."

Simon waved dismissively and led Kaiser into the main room, where they sat down at the table. "You're right," he said. "How foolish of me." He stared with growing appetite at the basket full of ham, cheese, bread, and wine.

"Help yourself," said Kaiser. "Faistenmantel wants to have a strong, healthy bathhouse keeper and medicus in town."

Simon dug in eagerly. For a moment he considered telling Kaiser about the carved figurine, but then the entire matter felt almost as silly to him as the supposed attempted burglary. With a full mouth, he turned to his old friend.

"How is my son?" he asked.

Kaiser laughed. "He sits in my library and has lost all sense of time. You don't have to worry about Peter. I know that I'll have to go and get more books every so often; he will have read all my books very soon."

Simon nodded contentedly. It was good to hear that Peter felt comfortable with Kaiser. Evidently he needed his father less than Simon had expected.

"Now exactly what does this Faistenmantel do?" he asked after a while, as he continued eating. "Chairman of the city council is not a job, after all."

"He's a merchant in Oberammergau," Kaiser replied. Simon gave him a quizzical look, and the schoolteacher continued. "As you have perhaps already noticed, there's much about this village that's different from what you'd find in other Bavarian towns. First of all, many of the residents make their living not as farmers, but as woodcarvers."

"And you can make a living at that?" Simon asked with surprise.

Kaiser nodded. "Yes, and a rather good one, too. It all started with Oberammergauers making carved crucifixes and figurines of saints that they sold to pilgrims on their way to the nearby Ettal Monastery. The soil is poor here, and that was often all they were able to do to make money, but over time the Oberammergauers turned it into a good business. They carve crucifixes, puppets, jumping jacks, animals, and all sorts of things. The little figurines are sold as far away as Venice and Amsterdam. Konrad Faistenmantel organizes the sales and in return buys tools, wood, and food for the woodcarvers. They work for him, and he makes a good profit."

"At least enough, it appears, that he can play God here," Simon replied as he sipped on his coffee, which in the meantime had cooled down. He pointed at the pot on the hearth. "Would you like a cup, too?"

Kaiser smiled and shook his head. "You offered me that stuff a few months ago when you came for a visit. It's too bitter for me – I really don't know what you see in it."

"It helps me think, but I suspect by now I've become as addicted to it as some people are to brandy." Simon took another long sip and fell silent. His friend's remark reminded him how seldom they saw each other, even though they lived no more than a day's journey apart.

After a slight pause, Simon continued. "I couldn't help noticing yesterday how Faistenmantel treated the Ammergau judge, this Johannes Rieger. Evidently he knows something about Rieger that has to be kept quiet, something that might have sent anyone else off to prison."

"Anyone but Konrad Faistenmantel, who for that reason was able to advance the schedule for the Passion play. Faistenmantel is assigning the roles, providing the costumes, and even paying a lot for the services of a new medicus." Kaiser winked at him. "He wants to make sure no other shadow falls over the play."

"The death of his own son is surely more than enough," Simon said bitterly.

Kaiser shrugged. "Actually, the two of them never got along – they were too different. Dominik was Konrad Faistenmantel's youngest son, and the father always looked on him as a failure, though he was in fact a real artist. There were not many people as skilled as Dominik in the use of gouges and woodcarving knives." The schoolmaster smiled sadly. "His father must have loved him in some fashion, or he wouldn't have got this role for him in the play."

"What did Faistenmantel mean when he said his son was just spouting nonsense?" Simon asked.

"Oh, Dominik was always saying he wanted to leave this place and go to Venice or the New World, but his father never gave him even a kreuzer, so he couldn't do that." Kaiser stood up and started putting the food on the shelves alongside the pickled snakes and toads. With his back to Simon, he continued. "In the meantime, Faistenmantel has persuaded the judge that young Hans Göbl is behind it all, and this morning Rieger took the lad back with him to the monastery in Ettal." Kaiser sighed deeply. "I'm slowly running out of actors to play the part of Christ."

"And you?" asked Simon. "Do you also believe it was this Göbl?"

Georg Kaiser had such a fit of coughing that he had to hold on to the shelves. When he'd got himself together and could speak again, he shook his head. "That's not like him. Besides, Göbl couldn't have tied Dominik to the cross all by himself and then set the cross upright. There had to be accomplices. You said that yourself last night." He appeared lost in thought. "On the other hand, the Faistenmantel and the Göbl families have been feuding for a long time. The Göbls are painters – they see to it that the carvings are painted artistically, and in this way have risen to become the second most powerful family in town. Just like the Faistenmantels, they're members of the so-called Council of Six that decides the town's destiny."

"Let me guess," Simon replied. "In this Council of Six, are they all feuding with one another?"

"Let's just say they're all headstrong – and that's why the Passion play is so important. It binds together the residents of the town, at least once every ten years." Kaiser's mien turned grim, and he sat back down at the table.

"I'll never understand why you came back to your birthplace," Simon mused, shaking his head. "I mean, you had it all in Ingolstadt – a position at the university, a large apartment, a loving wife . . ."

"Back then, ten years ago, when my Grete died," Kaiser said softly, "I was suddenly alone. I couldn't stand living in that large, beautiful professor's house in Ingolstadt all by myself, and that's no doubt the reason I came back eight years ago. This is where I was born. It's my home."

"I'm sorry," Simon replied. "That was really stupid of me."

"Forget it." Georg waved his hand dismissively. "But you're right, it's hard to understand. Let's just say, at least I know the people here, and I have a job." He smiled. "The children love me, and a few of them will probably continue with their education later. I'll definitely be able to make a scholar out of your son, perhaps a priest or—"

Simon laughed. "Anything but a priest. Your gloomy Oberammergau grouch is more than I can take. What's his name? Herele? Sounds like a sour-faced Swabian." He frowned. "The venerable Father seems to have something against me, just like this judge Johannes Rieger. Just the fact that I'm from Schongau made me a thorn in his flesh."

"People here don't like it when strangers stick their noses in our business – even if they come from just a few miles away." Kaiser winked. "But don't worry – as long as Konrad Faistenmantel is watching after you, you have nothing to fear in Oberammergau."

"Oh, isn't that just fine," Simon groaned. "Now I feel a lot safer."

Suddenly he had a hunch that the stranger who had entered the house earlier was perhaps not a harmless pedlar or a tramp. In addition, Simon couldn't imagine that Hans Göbl would crucify anyone just because he was intent on taking away his part in the Passion play. There had to be more to it than that.

Georg Kaiser cleared his throat loudly, interrupting Simon's thoughts. "It's time I told you something about your patients and what you're in for," he began sardonically. "Over on that corner lives old Frau Reiser, presently suffering from a bad cough, just like most people here. Adam Zwink, the blacksmith, has been suffering from rheumatism for a long time, and his wife has a green, slimy discharge that you should take a careful look at, and . . ."

Stoically, Simon listened to all the individual case histories, many of which resembled the symptoms he heard so often from his Schongau patients, though many of the Oberammergauers seemed to be suffering from a fever. Sympathetically, the Schongau medicus watched as Kaiser, pale and unshaven, kept coughing during his report. It seemed he had a bad case himself.

The longer Simon listened, the more he became convinced that the weekly salary of twelve guilders wasn't overly generous after all.

In the high mountains above Ammergau, fog lay over the peaks like a huge funeral shroud. Ravens cawed loudly as they circled the rocky, snow-covered cone of Kofel Mountain, which had been standing watch over this region for hundreds of thousands of years.

The Kofel had witnessed the coming of the little men dressed in furs and leather who performed bloody sacrifices at the foot of the mountain they revered as their god. Soon after that, it had looked down stoically on the Roman armies that had hewn a road through its gorges and over its passes on their way to war. It took no sides in the battle between the men in armour and the men in furs and leather, and no avalanche had come down to wreak destruction upon the warriors. The mountain had simply watched as they bashed each other's skulls in. New blood, new sacrificial offerings followed. The screams of the tortured and executed men could be heard up on the rocky, ice-cold summits where eagles had built their eyries.

The mountain was indifferent – as it had always been.

Then came the knights, and with them the castle whose building blocks had been ripped from the mountain's body. The castle had crumbled long ago, and only scattered, moss-covered blocks of stone gave evidence of its builders' childish desire for power.

A monastery had been built, and pilgrims and merchants had made their way through the mountain's passes, bringing with them war and the Plague. Like tiny ants the two-legged creatures had poured into the valley in a steady stream, always enthusiastic, eager not to offend the mountain – and when they died, others came to replace them.

They played a strange, senseless game.

The Kofel had seen so many of them it wasn't surprised at the strange new creatures now coming through the passes. They were small, even smaller than the other creatures, wearing pointed hats and using ice axes and shovels to dig their way through the snow, which even now, in May, lay as heavy as lead over the rock.

The little creatures hummed a song, no doubt to make the work easier, but it was a sad song and their hoods trembled slightly, as if they were crying.

Their ice axes made tiny holes in the mountain's side.

Chop . . . chop . . . chop.

The hacking and humming were carried away by the wind. *Chop . . . chop . . . chop.*

Sometimes, at intervals that were just moments for the mountain but centuries for the creatures, the Kofel stirred. Then the earth rumbled and shook, and the little buildings inhabited by men collapsed.

The mountain was listening to its own inner voice.

Soon it would stir again.

But until then it would observe the strange little creatures with their pointed hats, their ice axes, and their sad song.

Chop . . . chop . . . chop.

Chop . . . chop.

Chop.

The mountain was indifferent to them and their plans.

4

Grumbling, and with his head pounding, Jakob Kuisl stomped along behind the diminutive Constable Andreas, who kept turning around anxiously to eye the hangman. It had just occurred to Jakob that he'd left his beloved tobacco back at the house. A few puffs would perhaps have helped his mood a bit, but then he remembered that the secretary, Johann Lechner, despised tobacco. If Schongau had not been a Catholic town through and through, the secretary could have been viewed as a crotchety, pleasure-hating Protestant.

The constable and the hangman walked together through the stinking Tanners' Quarter down by the river. The odd pair was observed from the windows above by the tanners as they hung out their leather hides to dry. A few called down some taunting remarks, but most were silent or simply made the sign of the cross when the hulking giant walked past.

The executioner was a feared man in Schongau, avoided by everyone. In addition to executions and torture, Kuisl was also responsible for cleaning up dirt and rubbish in town and making sure that dead animals were not left lying too long in the streets. He was also considered a skilful healer. Despite all these useful occupations, the good citizens of Schongau shunned Jakob Kuisl as much as possible. The very sight of an executioner supposedly brought misfortune; accidental contact with the hangman had cost many respectable workers their membership in the guild.

As he climbed the hill towards the Lech Gate with the constable, the hangman was fighting his hangover and racking his brain, trying to figure out the last time he'd spent an evening without getting sloshed. That must have been before the time he learned his son, Georg, would not return to Schongau. Jakob's younger grandson, Paul, seemed interested in his family's trade, but as he was just six years old, he was of course much too young. It was unlikely that Jakob would live long enough to take him on as his successor.

His family legacy would die out, and there was nothing he could do about it.

They passed through the Lech Gate, entering Schongau from the south, where the small, shabby taverns that in recent years had been Jakob's second home were located. Usually the hangman would sit at a table alone, away from other guests, silently drinking his beer. People didn't dare to criticize him publicly, but he could feel their stares like daggers in his back.

Jakob looked up at the plaster falling from the taverns, the junk shops, and the homes of the workers. Then his eyes passed over piles of rubbish, the crumbling city wall, and all the beggars and injured war veterans huddling in the entryways to the houses. The hangman couldn't help thinking back to his childhood, when Schongau was a rich, powerful city. Merchants from far away came through town via the Lech River and the major commercial routes, bringing amber, spices, pickled herring, cloth, silk, and precious salt from Reichenhall and Hall in Tyrol. But since then, the major commercial routes had been relocated, and Schongau wagon drivers had complained for a long time that their business was declining more and more. Many of them had taken second jobs as labourers down on the river or in the pottery shops sprouting up in town. Money, which had once flowed so abundantly in Schongau, had gone elsewhere.

The second Sunday mass, attended primarily by noble families, had just come to an end, and amid the sounds of many church bells, people streamed from the parish church towards the market square, which was pleasant and warm in the morning sun. People chatted, gossiped, and laughed, but when the hangman passed by, they suddenly fell silent or looked away in embarrassment. Jakob Kuisl held his head high and regarded them with disdain. He had done so much for this town – he'd driven away and executed the robbers, and ten years ago it was only his sharp thinking that led to the apprehension and execution of an insane child murderer. Kuisl's cures had saved many lives, yet the noblemen always treated him like dirt. The poor people, however, respected and sometimes revered him.

But all that was about to change.

"Ah, Herr Kuisl," came a voice from the crowd. It was Melchior Ransmayer, just exiting the church. The doctor was wearing a bandage under his wig, and his smile was thin and extremely hostile. "So they finally got you out of the house, you old drunkard and ruffian. I see the constable is already leading you to the dungeon, where you'll pay for your vile attack."

"I'm not taking him to the dungeon, but to Lechner," Andreas responded wearily. "The secretary wanted to see him and—"

Ransmayer seemed not even to have heard the constable and stepped right up to the hangman. "I'll make sure they whip you and drive you out of town, Kuisl," he snarled. "You can go and join the robbers that you are accustomed to hanging. And who knows, perhaps in a few years a new hangman will put the old one on the wheel and break his bones."

"Better watch your tongue, Herr Doktor," Kuisl said, looking down at Ransmayer, who was at least two heads shorter. His voice was loud enough that bystanders could hear him. "I once hanged a quack doctor just like you. He hadn't been able to keep his flies closed either and was jumping like a goat on women in town until finally a decent man caught him in the act out in the street. He confessed on the gallows, but it didn't save him."

Melchior Ransmayer turned white as a sheet. "How dare you threaten me, hangman!" he snapped. He turned to the churchgoers who had been following the argument silently and with their heads lowered up to that point.

Ransmayer pointed at Kuisl. "This man maliciously struck me down yesterday," he announced. "It's a miracle I didn't die."

"Indeed, that's a miracle," Kuisl said. "Anyone who gropes my daughter usually doesn't see the light of day again. Barbara may only be a hangman's daughter, but we Kuisls also have our pride."

Some of the more poorly dressed churchgoers nodded approvingly, but the noblemen all had angry faces.

"All the things one has to put up with nowadays from dishonourable people," said an old lady with a stiff ruff collar as she fumbled with her prayer book. "Stick the old hangman in a wine barrel, throw it in the Lech, and let's find another one."

Another lady in a black dress agreed. "It's time the town council put the lower class in their place, just as Burgomaster Buchner demanded long ago. This city needs a stronger hand." She pointed at the hangman in disgust. "You see what it leads to."

"Indeed," her husband chimed in. He was the elderly Wilhelm Hardenberg, a trustee of the Holy Ghost Hospital, who in recent decades had acquired much money and an impressive paunch. He gave Kuisl a withering glance. "I remember his father well – he was just the same," he informed the bystanders. "At that time I was still a child, but I remember very well how we threw stones at the old drunk."

That was too much for Jakob. He lunged like a bull at Hardenberg, who froze with fear. Only at the last moment did Andreas grab the hangman by the shirt collar, which ripped with an ugly sound.

"Eh, it's probably better for us to hurry over to the palace," Andreas whispered, "before another unfortunate incident occurs here that we'll all regret."

Jakob nodded slowly. He took a deep breath, then followed the constable through the broad Münzgasse, the main street of the town, while Ransmayer continued shouting behind them.

"Your father was a drunkard, and so are you, hangman!" he cried. "You have dishonour in your blood to the seventh generation. Remember my words when they start breaking your bones."

Jakob Kuisl tried not to listen and continued stomping along behind Andreas.

"Don't pay any attention to him," the constable said quietly. "I know enough people who hope the doctor and also old Hardenberg die of the Plague and go to hell. This town may be ruled by the rich but it's we simple Schongau people who keep them alive . . . and the dishonourable ones too," he said with a faint smile. "By the way, my wife needs some more of the ointment you prepared at the last full moon."

"She can just stop by at my house," Kuisl said. "I won't bite anyone's head off, even if she's the wife of the town constable."

Soon Ransmayer's shouts faded in the distance and the street became emptier. The city dungeon now appeared in front of them, and alongside it the Schongau Palace on the northern edge of the town.

In recent years, the inhabitants of Schongau had been trying to gradually repair the damage from the Great War, but the building in front of them hardly deserved the name "palace". At one time, the great electors had stopped here, but now the massive structure with its war-damaged tower, dilapidated sheds, and threshing floor served only for minor administrative purposes. As he had so often done, Kuisl crossed the ivy-covered inner courtyard, where a few soldiers on duty were lounging around the rusty cannons. When they saw their colleague with the hangman, they grinned.

"Well, you really screwed up trying to arrest the hangman, eh?" a fat old guard called. "But the hangman didn't eat you up, even if you're such a sweet little fruitcake."

"Aw, shut up," Andreas replied. "Just tell me where Lechner is."

The other man shrugged. "Well, where do you think? Doing paperwork up in the office, unless maybe you've seen the boring old scribbler somewhere else."

The other guards broke out laughing but abruptly fell silent on seeing a haggard figure in the doorway at the top of the stairs. He had a black cloak and an equally black beard with two piercing eyes in his almost unnaturally pale face.

"The old scribbler is working on the weekly pay for the watchmen at the castle," the man said in a voice that was soft and slightly nasal. "But I can also put off this work for a few months. On further thought, I'll do that in at least one case."

The heavyset watchman cleared his throat and his face turned bright red. "Your Excellency, I'm sorry if I—"

Lechner silenced him with a slight wave of his hand, then nodded to Jakob. "Delighted, hangman, that you've stopped by, even if it took longer than I expected. Did you two get lost?"

"Eh, there were some disturbances by the church," Andreas replied. "But thank God all of us here have a calm disposition."

Lechner smirked. "I know. Especially our esteemed hangman." He motioned to Jakob. "Come on in, without the guards. We have some things to talk about."

Under the suspicious eyes of the watchmen, Jakob Kuisl climbed the worn steps as Lechner disappeared again inside his dark office. The executioner stooped in order to get through the low portal and found himself in an almost bare, windowless room illuminated only by the light of a few candles in the niches of the wall. Books and parchment rolls were piled on a table in the middle of the room. Lechner took a seat behind the desk and motioned for Kuisl to sit down on a low wooden stool.

The hangman tried to remember how many times he'd sat there before. Johann Lechner worked in Schongau especially in major criminal cases as court secretary on behalf of the elector, one of the German princes entitled to elect the Emperor, the ruler of the Holy Roman Empire. Many times in the past Lechner had summoned the Schongau hangman to this room to dictate the type of execution and the harshness of the torture.

I do the dirty work, and he records it all in the files, Kuisl thought. *To be fair, he should at least sign in blood.*

"Very unfortunate, what happened between you and the doctor," said the secretary, getting right to the point.

"Do you know what Ransmayer did?" But Lechner waved him off.

"Don't tell me about Melchior Ransmayer, hangman," he said. "He's a whoremonger, I know that myself, but at the same time he's our only doctor and otherwise an honourable man. In contrast to you," Lechner added with a shrug. He folded his hands, as if in prayer. "A dishonourable hangman strikes down a doctor. You tell me what you'd do if you were in my place, hangman."

"I'd at least call for an investigation."

"With no witnesses? The testimony of a hangman and his daughter against a highly educated doctor?" Lechner shook his head. "The Inner Council would never allow that."

Jakob Kuisl ground his teeth silently. Perhaps, as usual, Lechner was right. The Inner Council, which determined the destiny of the town, was composed of six councillors, among them three deputy burgomasters and the first burgomaster, Matthäus Buchner, considered a very vain man. They were all from old, well-established patrician families and attached great weight to their positions.

And most of them are Ransmayer's patients, Kuisl thought. *One crow never pecks out the eye of another one.*

"On the other hand, I need you, hangman," Lechner continued in a gentler vein. "You're experienced, clever, and, above all, I have no one else to take the job. But your drunkenness, arrogance, and bad temper are always a problem."

"If the sermon is over, I have a lot to do," Kuisl grumbled.

Lechner raised his hand. "Don't be so impatient. I've already found a solution that will be good for us all." He leaned down over his documents and began leafing through them. "To placate everyone here and spare you from Ransmayer's anger, we'll have to send you away for a while."

Kuisl didn't bat an eye, but inwardly he was seething. "You want to banish me from town?" he finally asked in a soft voice.

"I wouldn't put it that way," Lechner replied. Finally, he raised his eyes from the papers and looked directly at Jakob. "You're just going to take a little trip with me to Oberammergau."

"Eh? Oberammergau?" Kuisl looked at the secretary, perplexed. "To see the Passion play?"

Lechner chuckled, something that coming from him sounded very peculiar, Jakob thought.

"Unfortunately not. I don't have the time," he answered finally. "But a little bird told me there was a very ugly murder in Oberammergau – a crucifixion in the cemetery. They already have a suspect, and after one or two trips to the torture chamber, he'll no doubt confess."

"I'm going to Oberammergau as an executioner?" Jakob asked, puzzled. "But isn't that under the jurisdiction of Murnau?"

"The Murnau judge, Franz Stanislaus Gespeck, died last year," Lechner said, "and the position has not yet been filled. It's possible they'll merge into one district with Schongau. Very distressing, the whole thing." He made a sad face as he played with his quill. "In any case, Schongau is responsible for the Ammergau district for now, even if the abbot at Ettal Monastery disapproves. I have already sent a messenger to Munich requesting the approval. A mere formality.

The messenger should arrive in Oberammergau about the same time we do."

"Hold on." Jakob grinned and scratched his beard, as he gradually began to understand. "You think if you can solve the case, you will be given jurisdiction over Murnau? You are interested in becoming administrator of the Murnau district, aren't you?"

The secretary had already gone back to his work and was signing papers. "As I already said, hangman, you're smart, and that's the reason I need you with me in Oberammergau, not just to torture people. It's not a bad move for you." The quill made scratching sounds as he continued writing. "I can't stand Ransmayer either," Lechner continued, but now in a low, almost inaudible voice. "It's quite possible we'll find something that will bring him to his senses. One hand washes the other. On the other hand, if you fail . . ." He looked up again. "How is your son, Georg, doing in Bamberg?" he asked suddenly.

Kuisl felt anxiety rising inside him. "He's an apprentice right now, and will surely be a good hangman someday. I'm still hoping he'll return to Schongau and take over my job."

"For that to happen, the council would naturally have to agree. Why did he have to go and make a cripple out of Berchtholdt's boy?" Lechner made a mournful face. "The Berchtholdts still have a lot of influence, and I really don't know if there's anything I can do. But we should never give up hope, should we?"

For a long while, the only sound in the room was the scratching of the quill. Finally, the secretary put the quill away, folded his hands, and stared at Kuisl.

"It's so quiet here – did you say something, hangman? Or did I?"

Kuisl shook his head as if he didn't know what to say. "I heard nothing, Your Excellency. When are we leaving?"

"Tomorrow at the crack of dawn – before the Ettal abbot beats us to it and comes up with some random suspect." The quill rasped noisily over the paper. "And now leave me alone again, hangman. I still have some things to do."

Jakob Kuisl nodded, got up, and stepped out of the dark room into the bright light of day. There weren't many people he feared.

But Johann Lechner was one of them.

Hidden behind a stone column, Barbara watched the good Schongau churchgoers on their way home. Tears of anger filled her eyes while Paul tugged impatiently on her hand.

Actually, she'd been sent out by Magdalena only to look for Paul and bring him home. She finally found him in an overgrown garden close to the city wall, sitting under a linden tree and carving a wooden sword. He could be absorbed for hours in such handiwork, but he never went to school. He also wasn't especially interested in playing with other children; if he did, he fought with them, and he didn't shrink from picking a fight with older boys.

On her way back to the Tanners' Quarter Barbara had heard the commotion in the market square. She ran there with Paul and saw how her father was insulted and jeered at by the rich Schongau citizens. Because she feared being spotted by Ransmayer, Barbara had hidden behind a column near the entrance portal – much to Paul's displeasure; he was intent on defending his grandfather's honour with his little wooden sword.

"Why are the people saying such mean things about Grandpa?" he asked. "And why do we have to hide? We haven't done anything wrong."

"Because . . . because . . ." Barbara stuttered then just fell silent. "I'm afraid you're not old enough to understand that yet, but be quiet now before someone sees us here and takes out his anger on us."

Some of the churchgoers were whispering among themselves about the dispute between the doctor and the hangman, with most of them siding with Ransmayer. For a long time, the patricians in particular had been in favour of dealing more harshly with the lower classes, as many of them felt that the old traditional values were being threatened.

"His younger daughter, this Barbara, is a slut. Everyone knows that," said the wife of Josef Seiler, the richest cloth merchant in town. "She gets involved with any fellow who comes along, and when she gets pregnant, well, the wife of the bathhouse keeper, her sister, gets rid of it. Blood is thicker than water." She giggled, and Barbara had trouble restraining herself – she wanted to jump out from behind the column and scratch the old witch's eyes out. Frau Seiler had visited the bathhouse just a few days earlier because of a festering abscess, and Magdalena prepared a healing ointment for her that the old woman had been all too happy to get.

"Watch out, the next time we'll mix some buckthorn in the crucible to give you the shits," Barbara whispered. "Or some moonflower, you old witch."

"Who is a witch?" Paul asked, clutching his sword. "If she's a witch, I'm going to run her through, and—"

"Sh!" Barbara placed her hand over the boy's mouth, and he started to kick. Now the other women started shouting about the Kuisls.

"It really was the best thing for them to do to send little Peter to school in Oberammergau," said an elderly lady who was wearing a bonnet and had almost no teeth left. "He's the only one of this brood that will amount to anything. His brother, this Paul, is already a monster. Some time ago I saw myself how he pulled out little Ludwig Hallhuber's hair in bloody clumps, and one time he got hold of our neighbour's cat, and . . ."

That was more than Barbara could take. With clenched teeth, she turned around and pulled Paul away with her. She was quite aware that her little nephew could be a real devil. But did he have a choice? The other children teased him and his older brother as often as they could, just because they were the grandsons of the town executioner.

Paul had as much courage and determination as all the other Schongau boys put together.

Just as Barbara rounded the corner into the little lane leading to the Lech Gate, she caught sight of Melchior Ransmayer, evidently on his way home. Strangely, he didn't cross the market square but headed towards the back of the church where the old cemetery was located, the same place where she thought she'd seen the doctor the night before. What was Ransmayer up to?

After hesitating briefly, Barbara decided to act.

"Listen, Paul," she said, turning with a smile to her nephew. "We're going to play a little game. We're going to follow the silly doctor as closely as we can without getting caught. If he sees us, we lose; if not, you'll get a piece of liquorice later on, all right?"

Paul nodded excitedly and together they followed Melchior Ransmayer. At this hour a lot of wagons stood in the lane behind the church, providing a good hiding place. Ransmayer opened the squeaking gate to the cemetery and crossed the old graveyard with its sacks of mortar, piles of earth, and carved headstones. From there, he continued on through a door in the rear of the church. Barbara waited a moment and then came scurrying out from behind a wagon with Paul; they entered the building almost on the doctor's heels.

Now, just after the conclusion of the mass, the church seemed deadly quiet, but clouds of incense still hovered in the air, obscuring the view of the unfinished north side of the nave. Two years ago, the clock tower had collapsed, almost completely destroying the choir loft and the vestry at a time when more than a hundred people were in the church. An elderly widow, Regina Reichart, was crushed in the rubble, and it took three days and three nights of digging to find the buried monstrance.

The construction work on the new steeple and choir loft was still in progress, and the old cemetery was being used to store the debris and the new building materials. Bricks and sacks of mortar were piled up in the chancel, and the only way up to the bell tower was an open staircase. Through the haze of incense, Barbara could see the doctor hurrying up the stairs then stopping briefly to look around. At the last moment, she was able to pull Paul behind a pew, and then they heard the creaking stairs as Ransmayer continued upwards.

Well, it's unlikely that Herr Doktor left anything behind up there during the mass . . .

Her heart beat faster. It looked as if Ransmayer really did have something to hide. She had been right.

"This is a good game," Paul whispered. "Lots better than that boring service."

Barbara smiled. Shortly after daybreak that morning, she and her nephew had attended the early mass for the workers and simple people. Paul was right – this was a lot more exciting, but not without danger. If Ransmayer caught them, there would be some embarrassing questions.

As quietly as possible, Barbara and Paul approached the bottom of the staircase and looked up. In the oblique light falling through a church window they could see two pairs of boots standing on a landing about twelve feet above. One pair clearly belonged to Ransmayer, but Barbara had no idea who the person in the second pair might be, though the boots were of the finest leather and certainly didn't belong to a poor man.

"You want more?" said a voice up above that seemed strangely familiar to her. "Are you crazy, Ransmayer?"

"Well, I also had expenses," the doctor replied, "and the matter turns out to be more complicated than I thought at first. If my modest demands seem unreasonable to you, you can ask someone else . . ."

"Hold your tongue," the other man snapped. "You're already getting more than you deserve."

In the meantime, Barbara and Paul had tiptoed a few steps higher. They just had to see who Ransmayer was talking to. He was not speaking in a Tyrolean dialect, so it had to be someone different from the man last night. They advanced very slowly, step by step, so that none of the fresh pine boards would squeak. Now they could see not just the stranger's feet, but his clothes as well. Fine clothing, dyed wool . . . Clearly, the person standing next to the doctor was a Schongau patrician. One more step, and now Barbara could finally see his face. She held her breath.

It was not just some patrician, but none less than the first burgomaster, Matthäus Buchner.

At just that moment, Paul lost his grip on the little wooden sword, and it clattered down the stairs. To Barbara it sounded louder than all the church bells ringing at the same time. She started running back down with Paul, but it was too late. Buchner bent over, peered down the steps, and saw them both. The astonishment on his face changed to a horrible grimace. The burgomaster was a stocky man around fifty years old, with small, piercing eyes that shone like polished buttons in his puffy face. He was regarded as a strict Catholic and staunch defender of the Old Order, which he sought to impose at all costs.

"What are you two doing here?" he shouted at Barbara. "Have you been eavesdropping, you dishonourable woman?"

"Uh, no, Herr Burgomaster . . . abso-absolutely not," Barbara stuttered. "I just wanted to see how far along the building of the steeple—"

"Naturally she was eavesdropping," Ransmayer interrupted. "She's a lying slut. I rebuffed her yesterday, and now she's stalking me and trying to embarrass me. It's outrageous."

"*I* stalked *you*?" For a moment, Barbara was so stunned by Ransmayer's nerve that she forgot her fear. "What are you saying? You attacked me like a rutting pig."

"Ha! Listen to her!" said Ransmayer, turning to the burgomaster. "This brat is lying through her teeth. The pig was her father."

"Grandfather is no pig," shouted little Paul, who up to then had been hiding anxiously behind Barbara. He was about to charge at Ransmayer, but at the last moment his aunt seized him by his dirty shirt collar.

"Just look at them, this riffraff," Ransmayer said. "They're like wild animals. They should all be rounded up and thrown in the dungeon."

"Be quiet!" With an angry wave of his hand, Matthäus Buchner silenced the doctor and suspiciously eyed Barbara.

"What have you heard?" he asked finally.

"Uh, actually nothing," Barbara replied. "We just got here."

Buchner's piercing eyes seemed to bore straight through her. After what seemed like an eternity, he shrugged.

"Oh, why should I care what you heard, you dishonourable brat? You can go, both of you."

"But . . ." Ransmayer started to say.

"I said, you may go." Buchner's lips twisted into an evil sneer. "For the time being, in any case."

Barbara didn't have to be told twice. Nodding, she silently spun on her heels and ran down the stairs with Paul to the side entrance of the church. Once outside in the marketplace, she shook herself, as if just awakening from a bad dream.

The words of the first burgomaster were still resonating inside her. *You may go . . . For the time being . . .*

"I think the burgomaster is a bad man," Paul said. "He has such evil eyes. They say something different from what comes from his mouth."

"I fear so, too, Paul," Barbara replied, trembling. "Now let's run home as fast as we can. We lost this game, but you'll get the liquorice just the same."

She took her nephew firmly by the hand and ran through the muddy lanes, her skirt blowing in the breeze, down to the Tanners' Quarter. She suspected she'd made a very bad mistake.

"You did *what?*"

Magdalena, who was crushing fresh linden leaves in a mortar for a potion to cure colds, stopped and stared at her younger sister. That

Sunday she had finally been able to take a break and had just taken a seat next to her father at the table when Barbara and Paul came bursting excitedly through the door. What her headstrong little sister told her was really unbelievable. Couldn't there be just one single day of peace and quiet in this family?

"Just so I get this straight," Magdalena said again, struggling to lower her voice. "First, Father has another fight with Ransmayer in front of all the nobles, and nearly sets off a riot. Then you and Paul stalk the doctor and the first burgomaster, listen to their conversation, and get caught doing it?"

"Those two are up to something," Barbara replied, still out of breath from running. "Listen, if we can figure out what Ransmayer is doing, then—"

"Did you even stop to think that perhaps Ransmayer was just trying to sell some expensive medicine to the burgomaster?" Magdalena interrupted angrily. "After all, the burgomaster is his patient. Everything you tell me about this conversation suggests that's the case. Ransmayer had expenses and wanted more money. Well? Where is the crime?"

"Barbara is right," Paul said. "The doctor is an evil man – he says very bad things about Grandpa."

"Oh, Grandpa can take care of himself," Magdalena replied. "If need be with a good slap in the face that gets his family in a lot of trouble, right?" she added, with an angry side glance at her father. Then she turned back to Barbara. "We have enough to worry about already, and we don't need your foolishness on top of it."

"But why are those two meeting secretly in the church?" Barbara objected, now visibly unsure of herself. "Why doesn't Buchner simply go to the doctor's house, if it's just about getting some medicine, as you believe?"

"What do I know? Because Buchner happened to be in the church, that's all." Magdalena shook her head. "Don't you realize that with your clumsy snooping you're just making more trouble for us?"

"You can't talk to me like that," Barbara said furiously. "You're always treating me like a child, and I'm not going to put up with it any longer. It's enough that I have to clean up after Father, like a maid."

"Everyone in this family has to pull their weight, even if you don't like it," Magdalena replied coolly. "And until you have a husband to look after you—"

"I guess that means *you're* off the hook, sister," Barbara said. "Back then, Lechner gave you permission to marry out of your class, but how about me? Do I have to marry the gravedigger or end up an old maid? You can forget about that."

"Quiet, for God's sake!" shouted Jakob, pounding the table so hard that the plates rattled in the cupboard and little Paul crept under the bench by the stove, whining. "If you don't stop at once, I'm going to lock you two harpies in the stocks. We're a family. Have you forgotten that?"

Magdalena and Barbara fell silent, and Jakob continued in a calmer voice. "Matthäus Buchner is in charge of construction work at the parish church, and he personally owns the three lime kilns in this area." The hangman watched as the smoke from his pipe rose towards the ceiling. Suddenly he looked as gentle as a lamb. "The construction work in the church is the biggest deal since the Tower of Babel for Buchner, and he's making a killing on it. Almost every day I see him harassing his workers there, so it's not unusual that he meets the accursed quack doctor in the bell tower."

"But how about the meeting last night in the old cemetery?" Barbara quickly replied. She had calmed down a bit, but she still cast a defiant glance at Magdalena. "Did I just imagine that, too?"

Magdalena sighed. She took her younger sister by both hands, and Barbara reluctantly let herself be led to the table. "I do understand your desire to help Father," Magdalena said, "but believe me, young lady, you're in way over your head. Don't you understand what you've done? Now not only is the doctor mad at us, but the first burgomaster is, too.

Matthäus Buchner has never liked us Kuisls. He's been trying for years to cut back even more on the rights of the dishonourable class. Basically, he's just waiting to strike back, and you're giving him the excuse."

Barbara sat on the bench, looking grim, while Paul had wandered off to a corner of the room and was trying to shoo away a lost chicken. From time to time there was a furious cackling.

"I'm sure those two are up to some mischief," Barbara mumbled after a while. "I just wanted to help."

Magdalena nodded as if she understood, but her thoughts were racing. Three years ago, after the death of the old burgomaster, Karl Semer, Matthäus Buchner took over as chairman of the town council. Magdalena knew that Buchner, along with a few other members of the council, had been trying for some time to get rid of her father as the hangman because he was so stubborn and wouldn't follow orders. A couple of times already Jakob had terminated a torture on his own because he thought it didn't make much sense. Only the younger third burgomaster, Jakob Schreevogl, was on their side. Years ago, Kuisl had saved the life of Schreevogl's daughter, Clara, and ever since then, the patrician was indebted to him. But in this case, there probably wasn't much he could do.

Suddenly Magdalena felt sick. She bent over and held her hand in front of her mouth.

"What's the matter?" her father asked. "Didn't the mutton stew we had for breakfast agree with you? I'll admit it was a bit rancid, but still quite edible."

Magdalena shook her head. "I'm . . . all right now." She sat up and tried to smile confidently. "In any case, we need to keep quiet now." With raised eyebrows she turned to her father. "That applies especially to you – no boorish behaviour, no late-night drinking binges—"

"Hey, that's no way to talk to your father," Jakob interrupted. "In any case I'll be out of your way here for a while. Tomorrow at the crack of dawn, Lechner is taking me to Oberammergau."

Magdalena looked at him with surprise. "What did you just say?" she asked. "And you're just telling us now?"

"Until just now you two women have been arguing," Jakob grumbled.

In a few words he told them about his conversation with the secretary about the murder in Oberammergau.

"A crucifixion in the cemetery?" Barbara gasped. The gruesome news seemed to make her completely forget her argument with Magdalena. "That's awful! And it would be a shame if the Passion play were cancelled this year because of it. I've also been thinking of going there . . ."

"To look around for a man?" Jakob asked. "Forget it. Not without my permission. The reputation you have here is already more than I can take."

"That's mean!" wailed Paul, who had been listening closely to what his grandfather had to say. "You'll let Peter help you torture and execute people in Oberammergau – why not me?"

"You're not going anywhere," Magdalena scolded. "Your brother is going to school there and won't be hanging around the dungeon." She rubbed her tired eyes and turned to her father. "Well, perhaps it's not a bad idea for you to get out of the line of fire for a while. I just hope that before long Simon will—"

There was a knock on the door, and Magdalena cringed. "Maybe that's the constable again, only this time he's coming to pick up Barbara," she said gloomily. "What a fine family we have." She went and opened the door, and outside stood a messenger in a mud-splattered coat. His horse was grazing nearby in the noontime sun. The young man anxiously eyed Jakob, who was still sitting on the bench smoking his pipe. Everywhere in the area around Schongau, the executioner was well known and feared.

"Calm down, he's not going to chop your head off," Magdalena said impatiently as she pointed to the leather mail pouch the messenger was holding in his hand, "unless you bring us bad news. So what is it?"

"Eh, I have a letter from your husband, the bathhouse keeper," the man answered uncertainly. "He gave it to me this morning in Oberammergau. It's already paid for." He pulled out the letter and handed it to her, then lowered his head. After she'd given him an additional kreuzer, he jumped on to his horse with a sigh of relief and rode off.

Magdalena unfolded the wrinkled paper and started to read.

"And just what does my honourable Herr Son-in-Law desire?" Jakob Kuisl inquired. "Has my grandson forgotten to take his schoolbooks?"

Magdalena shook her head silently as all the blood started draining from her face. For a moment she was so angry she didn't know how to answer.

"Well, it looks like Martha and I will have to manage the bathhouse by ourselves for a while," she said finally, digging her fingers into the little sheet of paper. "Simon will be staying longer in Oberammergau. I can only hope no major problems come up here in Schongau while he's away, and by that I mean no more than we already have."

Another wave of nausea came over her.

5

SIMON LEANED AGAINST A GRAVESTONE AND watched as the simple wooden coffin was slowly lowered into the grave in front of the priest. At the head and foot of the long pinewood box stood the two stocky Faistenmantel brothers as they entrusted the soul of their younger brother to the Lord. They lowered the coffin on ropes, their faces rigid as masks, their lips pressed tightly together. A bell in the tower of the Oberammergau village church announced the burial.

"Ashes to ashes, dust to dust," intoned Father Herele as he scattered a handful of earth over the grave.

Almost the entire village had assembled at the cemetery, standing silently between the stone crosses marking the graves or squeezed against the wall. The gnarled fingers of woodcarvers clutched their old, battered hats as most of them looked heavenward, as if some explanation would come from up there for the calamity that had been visited on their town. The large cross on which Dominik Faistenmantel had been crucified had wisely been removed from the stage, but the platform that had been nailed together was there still, reminding the mourners of what had happened three nights ago.

Judge Johannes Rieger had just that day released the body for burial, allegedly because the postmortem examinations were only now concluded, though there were rumours in the village that in this way Rieger wanted to show Konrad Faistenmantel who was in charge in Oberammergau. In the first row in front of the grave, leaning on his cane, stood the father of the dead man, the head of the town council. His face was flushed with anger and his nostrils flared out like those of a wild bull. It looked to Simon as if Faistenmantel had brought the stick not so much for support as to use as a weapon.

"Father, why does the fat man look so angry?" asked Peter, holding Simon's hand. That morning the boy had been in Georg Kaiser's class for the first time, along with three dozen children from the village. Simon hadn't had any chance yet to ask Peter how he'd liked it, as he'd been so busy with the bathhouse.

"The man lost his son," he explained in a whisper. "Something like that makes people angry – mean and angry. They look for someone to blame for what is inexplicable."

"His son was murdered, wasn't he?" Peter asked anxiously.

Simon nodded. He hadn't told Peter exactly what happened, but perhaps he'd heard it from the other children.

It was already past midday. Simon had spent all of yesterday and part of today finding his way around in the bathhouse and treating his first patients. After initial hesitation, more and more Oberammergauers had come to his door. Just as Konrad Faistenmantel had said, the fever had indeed overcome a large number of people in the village.

Simon's predecessor, old Landes, had evidently treated such illnesses with bloodletting and enemas, drastic remedies that Simon strongly opposed. He was actually amazed the patients didn't get sicker or even die from blood loss or exhaustion. Simon instead gave patients a potion of ground cinchona and willow root, which seemed to show initial promise.

Now Simon saw a visibly overtired Georg Kaiser approaching. After his class in the morning he'd held a play rehearsal in the dance hall of the Schwabenwirt tavern, even though he had no idea who would be playing the part of Jesus after the arrest of Hans Göbl.

"Well?" Simon whispered to his friend. "Did you have a good rehearsal?"

Kaiser groaned. "Successful? It was a fiasco." He lowered his voice. "Half the actors didn't even come, and the other half just stood around talking about the murder. What else could you expect? Urban Gabler, the wagon driver playing the part of the apostle Thomas, was impossible. He seemed only half-awake, and the others weren't much better. I'm surprised—"

The priest interrupted his reading from the Bible and cast an angry glance in their direction. Georg Kaiser stopped briefly, then he continued in a whisper. "I'm surprised the Göbls came to the burial now that one of them is in jail as a suspect." He nodded towards a group of men and women standing silently off to one side. "The judge told me they actually found in Göbl's room the page of text Dominik had reported missing – the crucifixion scene, where Christ dies on the cross. No doubt Hans stole the page from his competitor to make trouble for him. Well, the constables took Göbl straight to Ettal and put him in the dungeon."

"Even if Göbl stole part of the text, that still doesn't mean he actually killed Dominik." Simon looked across the graveyard at the assembled Göbl family. "I feel sorry for them. If they come to the burial service, then everyone will say how shameless they are, and if they don't come, people will be even angrier at them, as that would almost amount to a confession of guilt."

"But we would have a more peaceful burial," Kaiser whispered, pointing at Konrad Faistenmantel, who looked like he was about ready to explode. "I can feel it in my old bones . . . There's trouble coming."

"The ways of the Lord are unfathomable," the priest was saying. "None of us knows why the Lord has taken our beloved Dominik from us—"

"But I know how!" Faistenmantel interrupted angrily. "He was vilely murdered by a member of the infamous Göbl clan, and the judge told me they have the proof."

"Please," Father Herele whispered, with a pleading glance. "Didn't we agree there would be decorum, at least here in the cemetery?"

But the chubby financier couldn't be put off. He pointed his walking stick at the Göbls, who had gathered along the wall of the cemetery. "It was those people back there, probably all of them together," he shouted. "They couldn't get over the fact that a Faistenmantel was playing the role of Jesus. Jealousy has poisoned their souls."

"Shut your mouth, Faistenmantel, before I put my foot right through your pasty face," replied Adam Göbl, the oldest man in the family, as Simon had already learned from Georg Kaiser. The tall, burly man, as rough as an unhewn wooden board, advanced towards Faistenmantel with a threatening mien.

"We didn't kill your Dominik – that's slander!" he shouted. "He was so muddled he probably hung himself on the cross. He was crazy and had been hearing voices for a long time."

"How dare you insult my deceased son!" Konrad Faistenmantel roared. "You scum!" He raised his walking stick and charged Adam Göbl, who ducked, put his foot out, and tripped his archenemy. Faistenmantel landed headfirst in a mound of dirt next to a freshly dug grave.

"My dear parishioners, please, I beg you!" the priest wailed, so excited that he forgot himself and reverted to his broad Swabian accent. "It's bad enough when you come to blows on your way back from visiting the taverns, but please control yourselves in the cemetery."

But his pleading was to no avail. The two Faistenmantel brothers came to the aid of their father, and together they all ran towards the Göbls. A wild brawl ensued. Gradually, the other mourners joined in, some taking one side, some the other. Fists flew, curses were flung back and forth, and soon the men, young and old, were battling among the gravestones, while the women and children fled, crying and screaming.

"Stop this! Stop at once!" came the priest's voice again. "God sees us, God is looking down on us. What will He think of us?" But no one was listening.

Simon, Peter, and Georg Kaiser sought shelter behind a gravestone. A few rocks hit the stone, then there was a thud as a heavy body flew against it.

"We've got to do something," Simon gasped, holding his arms protectively around Peter. "They'll bash each other's heads in."

"Oh, this isn't that bad," Kaiser assured him. "I know these folks, and nobody will get killed. We have a brawl like this here at least once a month. On the other hand . . . in the cemetery? And with so many people?" He shook his head as rocks continued to rain down on the gravestone. "I really don't know how I can continue with the rehearsals under these conditions. As long as the Göbl boy is locked up in prison, peace will not return to this place."

Something struck the gravestone again and Simon cringed. He was about to get up and run towards the exit gate when suddenly a sharp voice rang out.

"In the name of the elector, you will stop at once, or I shall have my hangman put you all in chains!"

Simon was stunned. *But that's impossible,* he thought. *How in the world . . .*

He was so astonished he didn't notice that Peter had slipped away and was curiously peeking out from behind the gravestone.

The boy let out a loud cheer. "Grandpa!" he shouted. "I'm so happy to see you here. Now nothing bad can happen to us any more."

And with that he ran towards the new arrivals.

The hangman saw his grandson running towards him and spread out his arms. All around him, the men stopped fighting, fell silent, and stared at the huge broad-shouldered man in the black garb of an executioner as he put his arms around the boy and lifted him up into the air.

"Now that Grandpa is here, everything will be all right," Peter cheered. "Right, Grandpa? If these people give us any trouble, you'll bash their heads in?"

"I'm not going to bash anyone's head in, if he doesn't deserve it," Jakob grumbled and set Peter down gently.

Even if the hangman would never admit it, he was delighted to see Peter again. The boy would never become a good executioner, in contrast to his brother, Paul, as he was much too tender and weak. He was very bright and well read, though, which Jakob almost valued more than a good brawl like the one happening at present.

The Oberammergauers' eyes shifted now to the coach standing in front of the cemetery, its door open. Inside, the Schongau secretary, Johann Lechner, was looking disapprovingly at the brawlers down below.

"What the hell do you think you're doing, brawling in a cemetery?" he shouted. "Do you have no respect for the dead? We've arrived here in this godforsaken town not knowing what to expect, and the first thing we see is a riot."

In the silence that followed, Jakob had a chance to scrutinize the crowd, exhausted by the fight. Some of them had facial abrasions, others were grimacing in pain and holding their hands to their heads, but evidently there were no major injuries. Jakob also discovered Simon, who was still sheltering behind a gravestone and was staring, flabbergasted, at his father-in-law.

"Kuisl!" Simon shouted. "Why—"

"We have no time now for a sentimental family reunion," Lechner interrupted. "You can take care of that later." He brushed from his coat the dirt that had splattered up from the road during their headlong rush in the coach.

They'd made the trip from Schongau to Oberammergau over muddy, rutted roads in just four hours. During their journey, Lechner had sat inside the coach while Jakob and the five guards rode alongside. The secretary's dapple-grey horse was allowed to trot along behind without being saddled. The young lads were visibly uncomfortable to be travelling with an executioner through the lonely, forested region. They hadn't exchanged a word with Kuisl during the entire trip and had turned away when he looked at them.

Now, too, they kept their distance and looked frightened as they observed the seething crowd, all of whom looked ready to put up a fight. Kuisl doubted that his party would last longer than a few sword blows in a fight with these angry mountain folk.

Johann Lechner turned to the crowd, most of whom were looking down in embarrassment. "Who's in charge here?" he demanded in a loud voice.

A huge man stepped forwards, his arms crossed defiantly over his potbelly. He raised his head and stared at Lechner as if to suggest he was unaccustomed to taking orders. "My name is Konrad Faistenmantel," he growled. "I'm chairman of the town council here in Oberammergau."

"The chairman of the town council goes out and picks fights in a cemetery?" Lechner said with a smirk. "I must say, you Oberammergauers are a strange lot."

"And who are you to judge us?" Faistenmantel snapped back.

His opponent did not bat an eye. "I am Johann Lechner, the Schongau secretary," he said in a flat voice. "Representative of the Bavarian elector and investigator of the grisly murder that recently took place in your ill-fated village." Then he pointed to the broad-shouldered hangman still standing with his grandson in the middle of the cemetery. "And this man is the Schongau executioner. Anyone who resists my orders will make his acquaintance."

A murmur went through the crowd, and for a moment even Konrad Faistenmantel seemed intimidated. He quickly pulled himself together, however. "We have no need of Schongauers here," he said. "We have our own judges, and His Excellency Johannes Rieger won't be especially pleased if you start snooping around in his district."

"You can leave that to me. Evidently, His Excellency is not even able to put an end to this tumult in the cemetery." Lechner looked them all in the eye to make sure his point was clear. "In any case, he doesn't seem to be around, and I am thus dissolving this meeting at once."

"But this . . . this is a burial service, Your Excellency," came a hesitant voice from back in the crowd. It was the priest, who until then had remained silent. "Please . . ."

"One that has come to a most inglorious end," Lechner said. "The gravediggers will now close the grave, and everyone else will immediately leave the cemetery." He turned to the crowd. "Go home. And ask the dear Lord to forgive your reprehensible behaviour."

Some of the men muttered and clenched their fists again. "We won't let anyone tell us when to end our burial services," one of them cried out. "And certainly not someone from Schongau." The speaker was a powerfully built young man, a son of the town council chairman, and he now approached Lechner's coach with threatening eyes and a swaying gait. When he reached the gate to the cemetery, he bumped into Jakob Kuisl, who was standing in the way.

"Where are you going in such a hurry, young fellow?" the hangman asked. "Are you coming to see me?"

For a moment, young Faistenmantel seemed to be considering a fight with the Schongau executioner, but then he noticed his huge upper arms that were as large as the trunk of a birch tree and saw the determined look on Jakob's face, and sullenly he lowered his head.

"We'll meet again, hangman," he mumbled.

"My pleasure . . . at the scaffold." Kuisl gave him a light push on the chest, and the young man hurried back to his people. After this confrontation, the locals seemed to give up. One after the other they left the cemetery, though not without casting a few more angry glances at Lechner and Kuisl.

"This is not the end of the matter," Faistenmantel growled. "I'll see to it that the judge and the Ettal abbot learn about this."

Lechner twirled his goatee. "Oh, don't worry, we'll let them know right away. I'm sure we'll soon have a very animated conversation," he said, stretching and yawning, "but first I'd like to rest a bit from this strenuous trip. By the way, I'll be in the Schwabenwirt tavern, across the street from the judge's house. Tell the innkeeper I'm taking the entire top floor . . . and, Kuisl?" Lechner turned to his hangman. "If you wish you can go and look after your family. In an hour we'll leave for Ettal Monastery, where the dear abbot and his judge will graciously receive us – with absolutely no brawling."

With that, the secretary left the astonished Konrad Faistenmantel standing there and climbed back into his coach. The driver cracked his whip, and, rattling and squeaking, the wagon turned into the little lane that led to the tavern.

"Better do what he says," Kuisl said, tapping Faistenmantel on the shoulder. "Believe me, I know what I'm talking about. This guy is tough." He grinned. "If Lechner doesn't get what he wants, he can become a real pain in the backside."

A short time later, Jakob and Simon were sitting in the main room of the bathhouse opposite some shelves containing pickled snakes, salamanders, and toads.

Simon was excitedly telling his father-in-law about everything that had happened recently, while Jakob sat, calmly smoking his pipe. So that they could speak undisturbed, they'd sent Peter into the next room, where he was translating a short text by the ancient doctor Dioscorides from Latin to German – homework that Peter did grudgingly at first, but later with greater and greater enthusiasm.

"A person is crucified just so someone can get a certain role in the Passion play?" Jakob grumbled after Simon had finished. "That seems to me a bit far-fetched, but I suppose the Ammergau judge wants to find a culprit as soon as possible in order to restore order in the village." He was deep in thought, chewing on his pipe stem. "No doubt I should start questioning this Göbl soon."

Simon nodded. "Especially since some sheets with Dominik Faistenmantel's lines in the play were found in his room, and the two had a physical confrontation. Things look pretty bad for Göbl, unless we can find evidence pointing to another culprit." He sighed. "And if I understand correctly, that's exactly what Lechner is expecting of you, even if I don't yet understand why."

Earlier, on their way to the bathhouse, Kuisl had told him about his confrontation with Doctor Ransmayer and how Barbara had been snooping about. Even though Simon was secretly pleased to hear how the obnoxious nobleman had been put in his place, he was sure that Jakob's attack on the doctor presented a grave danger for the entire Kuisl family. Evidently the Schongau secretary had been able to use that to put pressure on the hangman.

"Lechner has an eye on the trusteeship of the Murnau district, to which the Ammer River valley belongs," Jakob Kuisl explained. "If he solves this case, he can count on support from Munich. The abbot of Ettal Monastery will of course attempt to stop him. This area used to be under one jurisdiction, and the abbot and judge will surely try anything they can to restore that power."

Simon groaned. "Isn't that just fine. Either we get on the wrong side of Johann Lechner and have trouble in Schongau, or we anger the abbot of Ettal here in this district where my son attends school." Exhausted, he leaned over, propping his hands on the table where the medications, crucibles, and measuring scoops used in his recent treatments still lay. "What does Lechner expect of you? As a hangman, it's hardly possible for you to go around knocking on doors, asking questions."

Jakob grinned. "No, of course not, but I can think about things and draw my own conclusions. Lechner knows that I've often figured things out that way. Knocking on doors is your job. As the medicus you can keep your ears open, and I'll do the brainwork." His face darkened as he took another drag on his pipe. "Just the same, this case is damned tricky. Nobody could have put Dominik up on the cross by himself, right? So there had to be several people involved."

"Perhaps the whole Göbl family?" Simon suggested. "At least they'd have a motive. They had a blood feud with the Faistenmantels, and it's an established fact that Hans Göbl was trying to steal the part of Jesus Christ from Dominik. Perhaps the rejection was more than they could take?"

"Enough for them to want to nail Dominik to the cross?" The hangman shook his head. "No, a real Oberammergauer slams his archenemy over the head with a beer stein, he doesn't nail him to a cross."

"So was it someone from out of town? But why?" Simon coughed as a cloud from Jakob's pipe enveloped him. He remembered seeing something strange at the cemetery that he couldn't put his finger on, but he was distracted by all the smoke and put the thought aside again.

"There's something strange going on in this valley," he finally continued. "The driver of the wagon that brought us here said he thought there was a curse on the town, and perhaps he's right." Simon paused. "I can't put it into words, but I can feel how these mountains are moving in and crushing the people between them. And then there is this sinister Kofel Mountain with all its gruesome stories. They say a witch lives up there in a cave and bakes little children in his oven."

"Are you a doctor or a superstitious old woman?" Jakob growled. "Stop these silly stories and let's have a look at the facts. Someone has been put to death on a cross – and on a Friday, just like our Saviour. Why?"

"To redeem our sins?" Simon shrugged. "I don't know – tell me."

"Perhaps because this crime is so vile that it distracts us from something. Perhaps someone wants people to be thinking only about this crucifixion, and not about something important."

"And what would that important thing be?"

"That's what we have to find out, but it surely has nothing to do with a mountain, a witch, or other such folderol." Jakob frowned. "I've heard that the Oberammergauers fight all the time, in any case, and not just the Göbls and the Faistenmantels. We have to learn more about this place and its people. Behind every deed, no matter how vile, there are people."

"Oh, I just remembered something," said Simon. "Konrad Faistenmantel threatened the judge during the autopsy. Evidently he had in his hand some incriminating document pertaining to a business deal. Perhaps Dominik knew something about it and had to be silenced? And perhaps the victim himself also had something to hide. I've heard from a number of people that Dominik was saying strange things before he died."

Jakob nodded. "You see, we're starting to put things together. As I said, we've got to learn more about the people here, including the judge, the Faistenmantels, the Göbls, and many others." He stroked his shaggy beard, lost in thought. "At the same time we mustn't forget we've left two women at home who actually need us to look after them."

Simon was startled. In the last two days he'd rarely thought about Magdalena. So much was going on here in Oberammergau. How was she – and Barbara, and little Paul? Jakob had told him that Magdalena was displeased by the news that Simon would be away from home for a while – he expected that. But what he didn't consider was that she was possibly in danger, especially because of Barbara's silly snooping around.

"Do you think the burgomaster and Doctor Ransmayer intend to take revenge on the Kuisls?" Simon asked cautiously.

The hangman thought it over. "Ransmayer swore he would take his revenge on me – that much is clear. But whether Buchner will get involved or not, I can't say. Actually, it's not such a serious matter that the burgomaster would make a big issue of it. Unless . . ." He paused, and took a drag on his long-stemmed pipe, which by then had gone out.

"Unless what?" Simon asked.

"Well, unless Barbara really learned something when she eavesdropped on the two in the church. Then we need to clear up this case here as fast as possible and get back home before the guards come and burn our house down."

The wife of the young wagon driver was screaming like a deranged cow.

Magdalena gently dabbed the sweat from her brow while the midwife Martha Stechlin groped deep down inside the woman for the child. For two weeks Eva Baumgartner had been waiting expectantly for the child to come, and as the pains had got worse and worse recently, Magdalena decided to give the woman a potion made from buttercups to induce the birth. That afternoon she called for Stechlin when the woman's waters finally broke.

Now the two of them cared for young Frau Baumgartner, who was barely eighteen and almost a child herself. Two old women, relatives of the young mother-to-be, sat in a corner of the stuffy room saying their rosaries; the air was thick with the fragrance of incense, sage, and juniper. In accordance with ancient custom, the husband would be permitted back in the house only after the birth. Three times already, Lukas Baumgartner had anxiously and impatiently rapped on the closed shutters, but each time Magdalena had sent him away.

"You're almost there," she whispered into the ear of the screaming Frau Baumgartner. "We can already see the head. It will be over soon . . . Just push hard once more."

In fact, a little head with black, curly locks was appearing between the woman's thighs, and with bloodied hands Martha Stechlin was gradually pulling it out. The young mother screamed at the top of her voice one last time, and the midwife finally took the child in her arms. Martha cut the umbilical cord with a rusty pair of scissors and gave the baby a slap on the back so that it gave its first cry before she finally handed the child to Eva Baumgartner.

"It's a boy," she said. "And he looks strong. I'll pray that the Lord doesn't take him away again this time."

In fact, Eva Baumgartner had already given birth to two children that had both died after a few weeks. At least the priest had baptized the poor little souls in time so they would not spend eternity in limbo, the abode of unbaptized infants.

As Magdalena fetched a bucket to dispose of the afterbirth, she couldn't help thinking of her own child who was on the way. She nearly choked with emotion – would the Lord take this child from her as well, just as He had little Anna-Maria?

In the meantime, Eva Baumgartner had fallen asleep from exhaustion, and the baby had closed its eyes as well. The two old women shuffled out the door to bring the good news to the husband while Magdalena collapsed on a stool next to Martha.

"That's the seventh birth this month," she sighed. "None of them was simple, and now my miserable husband has abandoned me, and it's up to me to run the bathhouse alone, to say nothing of the worries I have because of Barbara's snooping around. If I wasn't so tired I would scream." Once more, anger welled up in her over how Simon had decided so casually to stay in Oberammergau for a while longer. "That's the way it always is: the men take off, and it's up to the women to figure things out as best they can. Curses! There'd have to be three of me to take care of all the work here."

Martha Stechlin smiled. "It's just that people trust you," she said. "Perhaps even more than Simon. And even more than me. Who would believe that you started your training with me just ten years ago?"

Magdalena couldn't help smiling as well. She remembered only too well her first birth as a midwife's helper. Back then, she'd been a young, clumsy kid who, instead of helping Stechlin, got in her way most of the time. Since then, she'd assisted at hundreds of births. A number of mothers had died following childbirth from the fever that was just as mysterious and unavoidable as a curse, but Magdalena had also been able to help many others.

"You have what we midwives call *healing hands*," Stechlin said suddenly in a serious voice.

Magdalena looked at the old woman with surprise. "Healing hands? What do you mean by that?"

"Well, most people think they are saved by medicines." She pointed at the many crucibles with ointments and powders scattered around on the table. "But take this from an old woman: it's not so much medicine that heals, it's faith. By that I don't mean faith in our dear Lord – people believe in *you*, Magdalena. They trust you. You listen to them, and that's what makes you a good healer."

Magdalena silently studied her own calloused hands, still spotted and sticky with blood. In recent years she had in fact become known not just as a good midwife but as a respected bathhouse keeper, respected especially in the poor sections of Schongau – the Tanners' Quarter and down here in the marshlands by the river. Up in the village, on the other hand, many people still thought of her as the dishonourable hangman's daughter – even though she was now over thirty years old. Just the same, well-placed citizens of the town came to her, and to Simon, because they trusted the talents of the bathhouse keepers more than those of the learned doctors. Increasingly, people would even seek

Magdalena's advice about everyday matters – whether they should take a long trip, how to appease an angry husband, or if a contentious engagement could be called off.

"Hmm, healing hands." Magdalena smiled as she looked at her dirty fingernails and the blisters from her work in the garden. "Well, these healing hands still have work to do today."

She arose upon hearing a cautious tapping on the shutter.

"You can come in now, Lukas," she called to him. "Everything went well."

There was a sound of running feet, the door was flung open, and young Lukas Baumgartner rushed in. After kissing the sleeping woman on the forehead, he looked with some embarrassment at the baby wrapped in towels.

"Is it, uh . . ." he started to say.

"Yes, you can rest easy, it's a boy," Stechlin interrupted. "Another one of you drunken, brawling men, as if we didn't already have enough."

Lukas Baumgartner grinned. He was a tall, handsome lad just twenty years old and had been accepted only last autumn as a full member of the wagon drivers' guild. Magdalena had known him when he was still a child who would run after her father, shouting fresh words. Now Lukas had his own family.

Suddenly the young man's gaze darkened. "What do I owe you two?" he asked hesitantly.

"Half a guilder," Martha responded. "I'll give you the mugwort for free. It's just a weed that grows in my garden."

The young man looked down, embarrassed. "I don't have half a guilder. Just this morning a delegation came from the town council to announce a cut in pay for the wagon drivers. The noblemen said they had to do that because there were fewer goods in storage in the Ballenhaus."

"Oh, what a coincidence," Magdalena said sarcastically. "No sooner has Lechner left town than the council cuts the pay, another achievement we can surely credit to our venerable Burgomaster Buchner."

But despite her irony, she knew there had to be something behind the council's decision. Formerly, dozens of shipments every day had passed through Schongau by highway and the port on the Lech, and trade with Venice and Genoa over the Alps had blossomed, bringing prosperity to the town, but for several decades now, business had moved to the northern part of the Reich, where huge ships departed for the New World and returned with silver, spices, and other treasures. Schongau fell on hard times, as did its many raftsmen and wagon drivers.

"When I look at the owner of your wagons, it appears he's not affected by the cut in wages," Stechlin grumbled. "Just this noon, in fact, I saw him sitting fat and happy with Buchner in the Stern Tavern, dining on a roasted goose."

Lukas Baumgartner nodded. "That's right – in recent days those two have been seen together often, and the wagon train supervisors seem to be rather well off. In any case, I haven't heard them complain." He sighed, but suddenly his face brightened. "I can give you an instalment. I've been promised a tidy sum next week."

Stechlin broke out in a dry laugh. "And how are you going to do that? Are you going to attack one of the fat merchants from Augsburg?"

Lukas blushed. "No, no. It's . . . It's actually . . . a little side job. I could pay you five kreuzers now . . ."

Magdalena waved him off. "Just forget it, Lukas. Keep the money and buy a cradle instead, and a christening dress for the boy."

"Really?" The young wagon driver beamed from ear to ear. "That's very kind of you."

"You can pay it back when you're a wagon master yourself," Magdalena replied with a smile. Then she turned to Martha Stechlin. "Now let's clean up quickly and get back home. Since my father left for Oberammergau, I've left Paul in the care of the knacker. I'm afraid he's going to really get on the man's nerves."

A bit later, the women were standing at the landing down by the river, watching as about a half-dozen men tied down some of the day's few deliveries on to a raft. The goods were in large barrels that slipped back and forth dangerously on the tree trunks that had been lashed together to form the raft. Magdalena looked up in surprise at the sun, which was already slipping behind the trees. Usually the river rafts departed in the morning or early afternoon in order to arrive on time in Augsburg, the closest large city. Perhaps this shipment had arrived later than expected.

The supervisor, Michael Eibl, stood on the pier, shouting orders. He was a bull-necked man with a smashed-in nose who had never really cared for Magdalena and visited the doctor up in town when he was ill. When Eibl saw the two women, he glared at them.

"What are you two women doing here?" he barked. "Don't you have anything better to do than to stand around gawking at us?"

"We bring children into the world," Magdalena replied coolly, "something you men can't do. Or do *you* think you could have stopped Frau Baumgartner's bleeding after childbirth?"

The dock boss seemed about to make some uncouth reply, but then he just waved her off. His eyes flitted nervously from Magdalena to the raft that was bobbing in the waves. He seemed to be in a hurry. Finally he jumped from the pier on to the logs that had been lashed together and picked up the long steering pole. Magdalena was surprised. Were the men really going to push off now?

"Let's go," Martha Stechlin grumbled. "I can feel the cold in my bones, and it was a long day. Why should we care what nonsense the men have to say? Half of them I myself helped bring into the world."

She laughed dryly and looked back at the Lech Gate and the way back to town, but Magdalena kept watching as the raft drifted out into the middle of the river and then slowly disappeared behind the willows.

"You're right, why should we care about the men," she mumbled, "as long as we women stick together? I just hope that Barbara hasn't done something stupid again."

She couldn't know that her younger sister had just made the stupidest mistake of her life.

By the light of a candle, Barbara leafed through the pages of a book she was holding in her lap.

She was sitting on the bed in her room, her fingers trembling as her lips silently mouthed the words she was reading. Now and then she stopped and listened to see if Magdalena had returned yet. Her older sister had left around noon to help with a birth and could be back at any moment, but Barbara would surely hear the door closing downstairs and would have enough time to put her secret back in its hiding place.

The secret she was so anxious to keep.

After making sure she could read on undisturbed, she continued – word by word, line by line. For days she'd been worried that Magdalena would learn about her discovery, but the even greater fear was that her older sister would tell Father about it. There had to be a reason why he'd hidden the books in the secret compartment up in the attic.

Barbara had discovered the hiding place when she had been looking for her old slate tablet to give to Peter. The tablet had been way in the back under some old rags and covered with cobwebs. When she finally pulled it out, she spotted a square cut into the wooden wall that looked recent and sounded hollow when she tapped on it. In less than a minute, she discovered how to open it – a simple flap that could be turned. Behind it was a little niche.

Inside there were three books, one of which she was now excitedly holding in her hands.

They were bound in the finest calf's leather, held together by silver fittings, but otherwise they looked old and worn. The mere title of the book, handwritten in large letters on the cover, made Barbara's heart pound.

De Maleficiis Ac Magicis Dictis Liber Auctore Georgio Vulgo Jörg Abriel, Carnifici [Book of Magic Potions and Sayings Recorded by Jörg Abriel, Executioner]

In Barbara's family, Jörg Abriel had always been a sort of legend, an evil spirit that Mother had talked about when the children didn't want to go to bed or were making mischief.

Quiet down now, or Abriel will come along and chop your heads off like little chicks.

Jörg Abriel was Barbara's great-grandfather. During the infamous Schongau witch trials years ago he had beheaded and burned more than sixty women, not without torturing them thoroughly beforehand with fire, tongs, the rack, and millstones. That had been nearly a hundred years ago, but still today horror stories circulated about the hangman in his black robe who had travelled through all of Bavaria with his wagon and helpers, looking for witches. Abriel became famous for his needle test, in which needles had been stuck into suspected witches; if they didn't bleed, they stood convicted.

With Jörg Abriel, no suspect ever bled until later, when they were at the gallows; then they bled profusely. It was said that Abriel could smell a witch's fear from far off, the odour of sulphur emanating from her body, the devil's perfume.

And now Barbara was holding one of his legendary books of magic in her hands! Basically, they were records of the interrogations and confessions of the suspected witches. Abriel had kept careful records of every single session, and taken together they read like one great collection of magical sayings.

Excitedly, Barbara turned to the next page, which described, in hastily scribbled sentences, a curse to bring down fist-sized hailstones on the fields and make trees turn black. Other curses could cause calves to grow two heads; make cows stop giving milk and suddenly fall down dead in the field; or bring scourges of caterpillars, mice, and grasshoppers to destroy the crops. Any evil that man could devise was written down in these books.

It was only last year that Magdalena had told Barbara about the magic books. Evidently they were always passed down in the family to the eldest child. Their uncle Bartholomäus, who was now the executioner in Bamberg, had finally revealed the secret to Magdalena.

Jakob had asserted at the time that he'd burned the books, but that was not the case. For all these years they'd been lying in the dusty little niche until Barbara found them just a few weeks ago.

Since then she hadn't been able to get them out of her mind.

Secretly she'd made inquiries about them and had searched other books among her father's and the midwife Stechlin's collections. Those books referred again and again to Jörg Abriel's books of magic and called them the most valuable books on magic since the *Grimorium Verum*, as they were based on the executioner's innumerable tortures, forcibly extracting knowledge from the presumed witches.

How to make a strong man sick and weak.
How to make lightning strike a house.
How to ride on a broom.
How to let the devil into your house disguised as a black dog, kiss him on the anus, and make him your lover.

Much of that was no doubt nonsense, confessions of poor women hoping to make the pain of torture more bearable – but all of it?

Wasn't it possible that some of these magical incantations really had an effect?

Barbara was ridden with doubt. She felt driven to go back to the books, again and again, to leaf through them. She wished she could ask her father, who surely could tell her more, but the mere attempt, a few days ago, to bring up the matter of her infamous ancestor when she was visiting the retirement house down by the river made her realize the topic was too dangerous. Her father would beat the living daylights out of her if he knew she had the magic books, and even worse, he'd take them away from her.

The question was why he had even kept them at all.

More than once Barbara had toyed with the idea of trying out a few of the curses – to go out to look for the necessary ingredients at the full moon, and to dance and chant just as the magic books prescribed. She knew it was a sin, but perhaps among the chants were some that would make a new life possible for her, that would magically carry her away from this stuffy prison called Schongau, away from the daily cleaning and cooking, the disapproving looks of the townspeople, and also away from her sister, who still treated her like a child.

A pot of gold at the end of the rainbow. A silver coach that will take me to a far-off land. A broom to take me to Nürnberg and back just so the rich people would look up at me in wonder.

Barbara was an inquisitive person, a character trait she shared with all the Kuisls. Perhaps she could start with just a little magic trick – a bolt of lightning hitting an old oak tree, a small thunderstorm, or . . .

She was startled by a knock at the door. Quickly she shoved the books under the bed and walked cautiously over to the top of the stairs. She held her breath – her sister surely wouldn't knock. Was it the constable again? Were they coming to pick her up for her eavesdropping?

"Who is it?" she asked hesitantly.

"It's me, Josef Landthaler. I have a stomachache."

Barbara breathed a sigh of relief. Josef Landthaler was a hard-drinking day labourer who worked down at the docks to make enough for his next trip to the tavern. Barbara couldn't stand him. He was dirty and shifty, but at least he wasn't a constable who'd come to pick her up.

"The bathhouse keeper is not here," she replied. "Come back tomorrow, Josef."

"But by then my stomach will explode," he complained. "I just need a little bloodroot."

"If it's as bad as all that, for God's sake go to see Ransmayer," Barbara said.

"People like us can't afford the doctor. Please open up, or I'm going to go in my pants right here . . ."

"All right, all right." She opened the door with a sigh to see a shamefaced, grinning Josef Landthaler standing on the steps and shifting from one foot to the other, his trousers and shirt wet and dirty from the mud in the river. He was trembling all over and kept rubbing his thin arms; his cheeks were sunken, his face pale, and the few remaining stumps of his teeth as black as tar.

"Well, then come on in," Barbara said, now in a more friendly voice. "I'll see what I can do."

Bowing deeply again and again, Josef Landthaler entered the room. "So kind of you," he murmured, holding out a tarnished kreuzer. "I can pay, too."

Barbara waved him off. "Keep your money. I'll be happy if you just leave again as soon as you can. I'm busy." She pointed towards the bench by the stove. "Sit down and warm yourself, and I'll get the bloodroot for you."

"God bless you," said Landthaler. Visibly relieved, he took a seat by the warm stove. "Take your time."

Barbara hurried off into the next room, where Simon and Jakob kept their medicines. Since the house actually still belonged to Jakob, there were a number of tools here used in executions and torture. There were two chests containing ropes, chains, thumbscrews, and pincers, and next to the chests was the gallows ladder. On the opposite wall stood a huge cabinet with three doors, their so-called pharmacy cabinet, even used by Barbara's grandparents. In it the Kuisls kept books and rolls of parchment, but primarily dried herbs, tinctures, bottles, leather pouches, and vials. It exuded a warm fragrance of summer.

Barbara looked for a while before finding the little drawer containing the ground bloodroot. It always worked best in case of sudden diarrhoea. There wasn't much of it left, but it would be enough for Josef Landthaler. Barbara scraped the remaining bits into a small crucible and returned to the main room.

"Here's your bloodroot," she said. "Pour some water in it and . . ." She stopped short, as something in the room didn't seem quite right to her.

Josef Landthaler was still sitting on the bench by the stove, but Barbara thought she noticed a mischievous grin on his face, and it seemed he'd been sitting closer to the wall before, where the wet coats were hung up to dry. But perhaps she was mistaken.

"Is there something wrong?" she asked cautiously.

Josef Landthaler put on an innocent face. "What could be wrong?" He took the crucible from her. Suddenly he seemed to be in a big hurry. "So thanks then very much, but I've got to return to the dock. We're expecting another shipment from Augsburg today."

He hurried to the door and it seemed to Barbara that he was already looking much better.

Without the medicine.

With a final bow, the worker said goodbye and ran through the garden down to the Lech. Just before he disappeared behind the hedges, Barbara thought she heard a malicious giggle.

She closed the door somewhat uncertainly and went up to her room again. She had suddenly lost interest in the magic books, so she pushed them behind the chamber pot under the bed, where Magdalena certainly wouldn't find them. Then she went into the barn to feed the chickens, the draught horse for the knacker's cart, and the milk cow, which was starting to moo restlessly.

If Barbara had looked around the room a bit more carefully, perhaps she would have noticed that the chest was now standing a bit farther to the right, as if someone had quickly moved it.

But by now she had already forgotten Landthaler's visit.

6

IN THE LIGHT OF THE SETTING SUN, THE WAGON driver Urban Gabler stomped through the marshland between Oberammergau and Ettal Monastery. The last rays surrounded the mountain peaks, bestowing on them a golden wreath that got smaller and smaller until it disappeared and dark shadows crept across the valley.

A slight breeze came up, and Gabler had to hold on to his hat so it wouldn't blow away. Lost in his thoughts, he marched past birch trees, heather, and low bushes whose vague outlines looked like dwarfs and trolls cowering on the ground. Occasionally, pools of black water appeared in his path, which he bypassed in a wide circle. Many an unwary traveller had been pulled to a watery grave in the mossy ground. Urban had known the region since his childhood but didn't want to take any unnecessary risks.

He'd decided against taking the highway but followed the narrow footpath through the moor, as he didn't want to be seen. There were some people in Oberammergau who would strongly disapprove of his mission that day. But Urban Gabler could no longer remain silent. What he knew was something that had to be said.

He was on his way to see the abbot of Ettal Monastery.

For a long time he'd been plagued by a bad conscience, but again and again he'd put it out of his mind. The crucifixion of Dominik Faistenmantel had opened his eyes, however. They were guilty, and now God had sent them their just punishment. Urban Gabler was a man who had been slow to realize the errors of his ways, but now the fire was burning all the brighter within him for that. It made perfect sense that he played the part of the apostle Thomas in the Oberammergau Passion play – the former doubter who had later proclaimed the Good News as far away as distant India. Gabler knew that everything on earth was a sign from heaven, and what greater heavenly sign could there be than a crucifixion?

He prayed silently as he moved through the mountain pines and hawthorn bushes. Truly, this village had been cursed for years. Envy and ill will had been constantly increasing, especially between the longtime residents and the newcomers. In past years the citizens had always come together again at the time of the performance, but now Konrad Faistenmantel ruled the village like a king and had advanced the schedule – and those times were past. The brawl in the cemetery had settled the matter for Gabler. Once and for all there had to be an end to this blasphemous behaviour.

And then there had been the strange carved figurine.

Last night it had suddenly appeared on his windowsill like a present, or rather a curse. The Latin words ET TU were scratched on the bottom of it. Gabler had thought long and hard about who might have put the figurine there. Was it perhaps just a stupid coincidence? By now he'd become convinced it was another sign from God. *You, too, my son* . . .

Lost in thought, he had put the little figurine in his trouser pocket, and it was still there. Urban stopped suddenly and took it out. Its headdress and toga made clear that it represented a Pharisee, one of those Hebrew scribes whom Jesus had condemned as selfish hypocrites. They also had parts in the Oberammergau play. Gabler could hear the ravens circling the rocky cone of Kofel Mountain. It seemed to him as if they had something to say to him.

Confess, Urban, confess, confess . . . Return to the straight and narrow path.

He had pleaded with the others, but they didn't want to hear and called him a superstitious fool. But he wasn't. He had correctly interpreted the signs, and the others were wrong. God would no longer tolerate what they were doing. If they didn't stop, there would surely be further warnings, further deaths. He had to confess – now.

The wind was intensifying, then there was the sound of thunder, and it took a while before Gabler understood it was not a thunderstorm but another avalanche on the mountain. Briefly he thought he saw a flicker of light – perhaps from a torch or a lantern – in the old bear den about a hundred and fifty feet up the rock wall. But who would be up there at this time of day?

Gabler remembered the old legends of the little men from Venice who had once been up to no good in that cave. The light flickered again briefly, then it went out.

That, too, is a sign, he thought, and began walking faster.

Some distance away on his right he could see the outlines of a large structure, and he breathed a sigh of relief. It was the old mill that belonged to the monastery, along the Ammer River. It wasn't much farther, just a few more steps through the bog, and then he would be on firm ground and . . .

He caught his breath and cursed softly as his right foot sank into the dark, gurgling water. He must have been so lost in his thoughts that he'd wandered off the trail. Well, he'd find his way back soon. The mill was in sight, with a warm and homely light shining from the windows.

He pulled on his right leg, but he only sank deeper, with the left leg as well, and now he was standing up to his knees in the cold mud, his boots and trousers sticking to him like a second skin. Nervously he looked around for the safety of a tree or a bush. A willow stood just a few steps away, and its smallest branches were just within his reach. Perhaps he could pull himself out? Without thinking he tossed away the carved figurine he was holding, reached out for the branches, and began pulling.

The branches broke.

Urban Gabler decided that the time had come to shout for help. Both the mill and the road were not all that far off, and surely someone would hear him.

"Hello!" he shouted as loud as he could. "Is somebody there? I'm here, in the moor!"

But nobody answered.

Cursing, Gabler reached out for some stronger branches when suddenly a figure approached, coming from the road. He let go of the branch with relief and waved. Evidently his frantic calls had been heard after all. It was probably a wagon driver coming to see what was the matter. Urban Gabler almost laughed out loud because he'd been so scared he'd almost peed in his pants. What a fool he was. Nothing could happen to him. God was on his side.

"I'm over here!" he cried. "Help me, I'm sinking into the swamp."

The figure came closer. The man was holding something in his hands that Gabler thought at first was a stick, but now, as the stranger drew closer, he could see it was a sword.

A very large sword.

The man in the dark swamp looked almost like the Archangel Gabriel.

"For heaven's sake . . ." Gabler muttered.

The man approached cautiously. Careful not to step into the pool of water, he jumped nimbly from one tuft of grass to the next until he finally reached Gabler.

It was someone Gabler knew.

The man raised the sword with both hands.

"Nooooo! Please don't—" Urban Gabler gasped. The swordsman thrust his blade deep into Gabler's stomach with an ugly sound, and after one last quiver, Gabler toppled forwards into the mud. Red blood mixed with the dark swamp water.

The man drew the sword from the wound and stabbed him again, wiped the blade carefully on the willow leaves, knelt down, and said a short prayer.

Then he went back to where he'd come from.

Rattling and squeaking, the secretary's coach moved along through the moor towards Ettal Monastery, nestled on the south slope of Laber Mountain. Evening had come, and fog rolled over the moor, enveloping the bushes and heather alongside the road.

Jakob Kuisl rode alongside the coach. His horse, an old nag just as grumpy as its rider, trotted past the bushes and willows separating the road from the moor below. Briefly Kuisl thought he heard someone shouting in the distance, but the sound of the rolling coach was too loud to understand anything. No doubt it was just a woodcutter warning his friends of another of the many avalanches that often occurred in this accursed valley.

Jakob looked up sceptically at the summits, which were mostly shrouded in darkness. Only one rock wall, directly above the monastery, was still bathed in the gentle pink light of the setting sun. The hangman did not like the mountains. He could well understand the urge of the young men to scale the mountains in order to escape the narrowness of their villages, but he himself preferred the deep forests and gentle hills of his home.

Evening bells were ringing and brought Jakob's attention back to the sprawling monastery they were now approaching. The road led through fields still spotted with the last of winter's snow, and past orchards and barns. Two Benedictine monks in their typical black tunics and leading a couple of draught horses passed them, greeting them with a nod. The last beer before the summer pause was evidently being brewed in the monastery, and the heavy, sweetish odour of beer mash hung in the air.

The coach entered a large square with a number of inns, shops, and residential buildings around it. Opposite the gate was the most remarkable church Kuisl had ever seen. The building was in the shape of a dodecagon – a polygon with twelve angles and twelve sides – and its roof came to a sharp point, which made it look more like an Oriental temple than a Christian church. To the right of the church stood the bell tower and several ecclesiastical offices. A group of monks was just exiting the church portal, and when they saw the secretary's coach, one of them gathered up his robe and hurried over to one of the opulent buildings. Moments later, two men came out into the court.

Kuisl looked them over carefully in the fading daylight. One had a weasel-like appearance and thinning hair, and was gripping a walking stick – presumably the Ammergau judge, Johannes Rieger, whom Jakob had learned about from Simon. The other man was extremely gaunt, as thin as a stick, but as tall as Jakob. He wore a black Benedictine robe with a white cincture and a silver, jewel-encrusted cross on a chain around his neck, identifying him as the abbot of the monastery. A nervous twitch around his mouth suggested he was struggling to conceal his dislike for the visitors. He observed Johann Lechner suspiciously as the secretary descended from his coach.

"God be with you, Herr Secretary," said Abbot Benedikt Eckart, raising his hand in blessing, a gesture that seemed incompatible with the sour expression on his face. Kuisl thought the gesture looked more like a magical curse to ward off evil spirits. "A most tragic occasion brings you to our valley," the abbot continued in a rasping voice. "I wish it were different. In addition, I've heard there was an unfortunate event in Oberammergau that further delayed your trip." He raised his eyebrow as an expression of his disapproval. "How regrettable."

"I offer you greetings from the city of Schongau," Lechner replied formally as he bowed in recognition of the abbot's high position and kissed his signet ring. "Indeed, there was a confrontation that had to be mediated in the Oberammergau cemetery. My sincere apologies."

"Mediated?" It was the voice of Johannes Rieger, who moved a step closer to Lechner, his eyes flashing. "According to what I heard, you had the cemetery cleared. You had no right to do that."

"Well, unfortunately you were not present, or naturally I would have deferred to you." Lechner grimaced. "Brawling in a cemetery is, frankly, not to my taste. So where were you, Judge?"

"I, uh . . . was busy with other matters in the valley," Rieger replied, raising his finger angrily, "but that certainly doesn't justify your getting involved. Oberammergau is under the jurisdiction of Ettal, for whom only yours truly and the abbot are responsible."

"And Ettal Monastery is under the jurisdiction of Murnau," Lechner replied with a thin smile. "But since that office is vacant at present, Schongau will take over its legal matters." He pulled out a document from under his coat and handed it to the abbot. "The authorization from Munich just arrived in Oberammergau. See for yourself."

Abbot Benedikt reached for his pince-nez, hanging on a silver chain along with the cross, and examined the document, which was hard to read in the fading light. Finally, with a doleful look, he handed it to his judge, who turned pale as a ghost as he read it.

"That's . . . correct, indeed," the abbot finally uttered. "I don't know how you managed this, Lechner, but it looks like you can continue your investigation here."

"For hundreds of years the monastery itself had the right to hold a blood court for crimes committed here," hissed Johannes Rieger as he clutched the parchment roll. "And now we are being told to cede this right to Schongau, of all places. Your Excellency, I beg you."

"You saw the document yourself, Rieger," Abbot Benedikt exclaimed. "Shall I cross swords with the Bavarian elector? Master Lechner can proceed as he sees fit in the investigation of this horrible crime." He shrugged. "I wish we could have solved the case here in the valley, among ourselves. This, uh . . . matter in any case casts a bad light on the monastery and the Oberammergau Passion play. But . . ." He hesitated and pointed at the document. "If you will allow me . . ." The abbot took the document back from Rieger. Once again, he studied the document, this time more closely, and finally a thin smile spread over his face.

"What it says here is that the authorization applies only to the investigation of the case," the abbot said finally. "What follows will depend on the resolution of the case. Well, only our beloved Heavenly Father can know that." Calmly and deliberately he handed the authorization back to the secretary. "Naturally, we will assist in every way we can, as the elector demands, but I'm afraid an abbey doesn't have the same means at its disposal as a city, as much as it grieves me to say so."

Johann Lechner nodded earnestly, though with a slightly derisive look in his eyes. "I completely understand, Your Excellency, and for this reason I have brought along my own people." He pointed at the five young soldiers and Jakob Kuisl, who had remained in the background up until then. "My guards and my hangman. If you will tell us where you have Hans Göbl locked up, we can begin at once with the questioning. As you know, I have the elector's permission to do that."

The abbot's face turned ashen and full of contempt as he stared at Kuisl. He made the sign of the cross and looked away. "I'd heard already that you brought along the Schongau executioner, but I must disappoint you, Master Lechner. For your questioning, we are lacking the necessary . . ." – he shuddered – "instruments. Would you perhaps care to take Göbl back to Schongau and convict him there? Then I'd have sufficient time to speak to the office in Munich."

"Oh, thank you, but that won't be necessary," Lechner replied with a cloyingly sweet smile. "To save you trouble, we've brought the instruments along with us – for torture, interrogation, testing . . . We have it all with us." The secretary turned to the soldiers and to Kuisl, pointing to a few chests stored in the back of the coach. "Unload them," he ordered. "The venerable abbot will surely be happy if we can bring this case to a satisfactory conclusion as soon as possible."

"But this . . ." Abbot Benedikt started to say, nervously fingering his cross, "this is most unusual. A torture in the cloister . . ."

Jakob Kuisl reached for one of the heavy chests and hoisted it in one single flowing motion out of the wagon. As he marched off past the stunned abbot and his judge, a grin spread over his face.

"It won't take long," he promised. "Perhaps in the meanwhile the gentlemen can stand here beating around the bush while our people take care of the dirty work."

Soon thereafter, Jakob stood before a heavy wooden door secured by a bolt. Reluctantly, the monks had guided him to the beer cellar, which consisted of a long corridor illuminated by torches with individual rooms along the side. Most of these rooms were used to store barrels and dried barley, but the one at the very end was usually left empty. There was a tiny grille in the door at eye level, so Kuisl was able to look inside, where a tall lad around twenty years of age with tousled blond hair lay on a dirty pile of straw. Hans Göbl, no doubt. When the young man heard the sound outside the door, he jumped to his feet.

"Accursed papists!" he shouted, rattling the bars. "Let me out. It wasn't me. By God, it wasn't me!"

"I'm here to find that out," Jakob Kuisl replied.

When Hans Göbl heard the deep voice, he stepped back in shock. Kuisl pulled the bolt aside and opened the door. He brought the heavy chest with its iron fittings into the cell while two soldiers stood guard outside the entrance. Then he slid the squeaking bolt behind him, and the two men were alone.

"What . . . is that?" Göbl asked, anxiously pointing at the chest that the hangman had set down in a corner. "And who are you?"

Without saying a word, Jakob opened the chest and spread his instruments out on the dirty stone floor – thumbscrews, pliers, shin bone crushers, long pokers, and a device for holding the jaw open, allowing the torturer to pour urine, rat faeces, and other unpleasant things down the victim's throat.

Hans Göbl understood. His eyes fluttered, his hands trembled uncontrollably, but he struggled to keep his composure.

"My God . . ." he whispered. Slowly, as if in a trance, Göbl slid down the wall to the floor, until he was once again sitting on the pile of straw.

Jakob Kuisl had still not spoken a word. He knew that the best results in an interrogation always came before the torturing began. For this reason, the prisoner was first shown all the instruments, one after the other. The worst torture was often their own imagination.

"In Schongau I have lots more, of course," Kuisl began softly, as he scraped some dried blood off the point of a pincer. "The rack, chains, the Spanish donkey, and the ladder, but I think we can manage with what we have here. Perhaps we won't need anything else, but that's entirely up to you. What do you think?"

Only now did the hangman turn to face the prisoner. Kuisl wore his black gown, his leather breastplate, and, to enhance the effect, a hood covering most of his face so that only his large hooked nose was visible. Kuisl hated this crude farce, but he knew that in this way he could often avoid the thing he hated most about his job – causing anyone unnecessary pain.

The people he tortured in Schongau were for the most part guilty and received their just punishment. He could see that in their eyes, their jerky movements, the sweat on their brow. Often the proof was overwhelming, for example when thieves or burglars were caught red-handed, and the only thing missing was the confession. And the law said that without a confession there could be no guilty verdict.

Each time Kuisl had to torture someone he hoped fervently that the first meeting would be so frightening there wouldn't have to be a second one – and this time it appeared once again that his calculation was working. The prisoner, so haughty just a moment ago, now broke down, hiding his face in his hands and crying. Only now did Kuisl move to the next step.

"You only have to tell me the truth," he grumbled in a sympathetic, almost fatherly tone of voice. "Then no harm can come to you, at least not in this world."

This was the critical moment. If the prisoner opened up now, Kuisl would call for the secretary, Johann Lechner, the confession would be noted, and the interrogation would be over.

In reality, Kuisl knew it wouldn't be that easy.

"But it wasn't me," Göbl sobbed. "I swear by all that is holy."

"The people say differently," Kuisl responded. "They say you and Dominik were quarrelling over the role of Jesus, you even threatened him and stole his text."

"I didn't steal those accursed pages," Hans Göbl said. "God knows how those pieces of paper made it into my room. Suddenly they were just there, among all the other pages of text. And yes, we did quarrel, and I was angry and shouted at him, but as God is my witness, I didn't put anyone on the cross."

"Then help me find out who did," Kuisl replied. "Look, I want to believe in your innocence, but for that to happen, you have to give me something. Did Dominik have any enemies, I mean except for the Göbls?"

Hans Göbl shrugged and he gradually stopped sobbing. Evidently he was reaching for the straw he was being offered.

"Dominik was a good fellow," he said hesitantly. "A bit confused, but very kind. Nobody could really hate him – but he was a Faistenmantel."

"And as a Faistenmantel does one have a lot of enemies?"

Göbl nodded. "Half the woodcarvers in the village work for Konrad Faistenmantel. He sets the prices, and if anyone stands up to him, he's quickly run out of business. Faistenmantel simply makes sure that the troublesome woodcarver can't find any more buyers. He undercuts his prices until the troublemaker gives up, then he buys his shop and gives it to one of the many poor labourers in town."

"Is there anyone Faistenmantel drove out of business in that way recently?" Kuisl asked, stepping closer to the prisoner. He knew the time had come to call Johann Lechner for the interrogation. On the other hand, Göbl seemed forthcoming and had begun to show confidence in the hangman. Confidence that could quickly vanish. Göbl seemed to be hesitating.

Again, Kuisl asked: "Is there anyone Faistenmantel drove out of business recently? Speak up."

Göbl's eyes wandered to the thumbscrews and shin bone crushers, gleaming ominously in the light of the torches. He swallowed hard.

"The . . . Eyrl family," he finally said quietly.

"Who is that? Come on, out with it."

"The Eyrls were once the best-known woodcarvers in town," Göbl replied. "Very talented . . . They sold their carvings to all the large monasteries around – Rottenbuch, Steingaden, even Augsburg. But the accursed Plague carried off most of the family several decades ago, and the only ones remaining were old Johannes Eyrl and his son, Xaver. When Johannes died some time ago, Konrad Faistenmantel gradually drove Xaver out of business. Just last December, Xaver closed his shop and left Oberammergau in the bitter cold of winter. They say that since then he's been travelling around the country with a knapsack as a door-to-door salesman. Some also said they saw him poaching in the mountains. Before he left, he cursed Faistenmantel and the entire village." Hans Göbl sighed. The long story had visibly worn him out. "Xaver is a curmudgeon, stubborn and grim," he finally said, "but I don't think he was capable of doing anything like that."

"Did he ever threaten Dominik?"

Göbl shook his head. "That's the strangest thing. Of all the Faistenmantels, Dominik was the gentlest and kindest. He actually hated his father more than all the rest of us put together. He wanted to get away from his father, absolutely – he talked about going to Venice, or even farther away. Some people even thought he would join Xaver as an itinerant salesman. The two of them used to do lots of things together – Red Xaver was like a big brother to Dominik."

"Red Xaver?"

Göbl shrugged. "He has flaming red hair. Witch's hair, say some people in town who think his real father is the devil himself and not Johannes Eyrl. That's a lot of nonsense, of course, but perhaps now you understand why I didn't want to involve Xaver in this."

Jakob Kuisl remained silent. Lost in thought, he ran his fingers over the cool iron of the poker. After many years' experience, he thought he could tell that Hans Göbl was speaking the truth, but it was like with a beehive – the more you poked around in it, the more came flying out. And that made the matter more complicated.

And Lechner doesn't like it when things are complicated, he said to himself. *He just wants a simple solution, simple and quick. He just wants a confession from Göbl to make him look good to the authorities in Munich. And I've got to bring him this confession, or he'll take it out on my family . . .*

Suddenly the hangman felt very thirsty; an almost irrepressible urge for strong drink came over him.

This young fellow, or my family . . . How I hate this job!

Trembling slightly, almost imperceptibly, he reached for the thumbscrew, a metal ring that could be made smaller with the simple turn of a screw until the blood vessels burst and the ring met the bone. Hans Göbl groaned.

"Please!" he wailed.

"Listen," Kuisl began, "I—" There was a sudden pounding on the door, and he stopped. "What?" he asked gruffly.

"Uh, Master Kuisl, Secretary Lechner has a message for you," said one of the young soldiers. "He wants you to come outside for a moment."

Cursing under his breath, Jakob Kuisl got to his feet, leaving Göbl alone. When he returned a while later, there was a smile of relief on his face.

"It looks like we both have a reprieve," he said, turning to the prisoner.

Hans Göbl was visibly relieved, but he seemed unsure. "Why?" he asked. "What happened?"

"Well, they found another body in the swamp, apparently another actor in your Passion play, run through with a sword." Jakob shrugged and took out his pipe. "The body is still fresh, as rigor mortis hasn't set in yet, so you're obviously not the killer. Who then? Don't worry, I'll find out soon enough. Then they'll let you go."

Drawing on his cold pipe, the hangman left the cell. The door to the dungeon slammed shut, leaving a crying Hans Göbl behind, as a big wet spot spread across his trousers.

7

WHEN MAGDALENA HEARD THE ENERGETIC pounding at the front door, she suspected this day would bring nothing good.

The Schongau church bell had just rung seven o'clock. Magdalena had fed the chickens, milked the cow in the barn, and done some weeding in the garden. Actually, these were all Barbara's jobs, but after the argument with her sister two days ago, Magdalena had decided to try to be kinder to her sister and let her sleep a little longer. She could understand why Barbara was so out of sorts. Magdalena herself had a husband and a purpose in life, but Barbara had not yet found either. Magdalena knew how hard it would be for her younger sister. Their father had tried for a long time to marry off Magdalena to the hangman in Steingaden, though in the end he reluctantly agreed to a marriage with Simon – but even then only after Johann Lechner had approved Simon's appointment as keeper of the Schongau town bathhouse.

Magdalena resolved to have a talk with Barbara that very day. She had really been too mean to her sister. Besides, for some time now she'd had the feeling Barbara was hiding something from her.

She had just prepared some porridge over the hearth in the main room for little Paul, who was working on a wooden figurine he'd been carving since the day before as a present for his grandfather. When he heard the knocking, he put the knife down and looked at his mother hopefully.

"Do you think that's Martha, bringing us a pot of honey, as she promised the last time?"

"I'm afraid not, Paul," Magdalena replied softly.

As if in confirmation, a sharp voice outside bellowed, "Open up! In the name of the town, open the door immediately."

Magdalena's heart began to pound. Had the constables come to pick up her father because of the fight in the street? They had to know that Father was in Oberammergau with Lechner. Then why had they come? Because of Barbara and her foolish snooping?

"Open up, I said," the voice rang out again. "At once, or we'll kick the door down!"

"Very well, I'm coming." Magdalena rushed to the door and pushed the bolt aside. At once the door was pushed open with full force, hitting Magdalena on the forehead. She staggered backwards and at the same moment watched as four town constables stormed into the room. Paul jumped up on to the bench and began to cry.

"Mother, Mother, what are the men doing here?" he asked. "Are they going to hang us?"

"Don't worry, Paul," said his mother, trying to console him by sounding calm and confident. "Nobody is going to be hanged. We haven't done anything wrong."

"We'll see about that," said a voice from outside the door.

Magdalena recognized the voice at once. "Doctor Ransmayer," she said angrily. "Are you behind this break-in?"

With a derisive bow, Melchior Ransmayer entered the house. As usual, he sported his wig and a felt hat with red feathers, which made him look like a nobleman in the simple home. With a look of contempt, his eyes wandered across the scratched table to the somewhat lopsided shelf above it full of crucibles, jars, and a stone mortar that had been in the family for ages.

"Believe me, Frau Fronwieser, I have better things to do with my time than to visit your . . . ahem, abode on a beautiful morning like this," the doctor answered, holding a white lace handkerchief in front of his nose. Magdalena could see he had applied a bit of rouge to his cheeks. "No, I have been sent here, as an advisor, so to speak."

"Advisor for what?" Magdalena asked, somewhat perplexed. "Come on, tell me."

Ransmayer did not reply and remained standing in the doorway, fanning himself. Magdalena had to watch as two of the constables casually opened the crucibles and vials on the shelf and sniffed their contents while the two others went to the next room to inspect the medicine cabinet. There was a sound of breaking glass.

"Hey, be careful!" Magdalena called. "Why are you doing this?" She turned to the youngest of the constables, Andreas, who just two days ago had taken her father to the secretary. "What's going on? Is your tongue tied? Say something."

Andreas looked to one side, embarrassed. "Uh, there are indications that certain forbidden magic substances are being used in your bathhouse," he mumbled. "I'm very sorry, but . . ."

"Quiet!" shouted Melchior Ransmayer. "We don't want to give the suspect a chance to dispose of any evidence."

"Magical substances! Ha!" Magdalena crossed her arms defiantly and stared at Andreas, who was clearly uncomfortable. "And who says so? The honourable Doctor Ransmayer?"

In the meantime, Barbara had come downstairs, looking sleepy. In her haste she had thrown just a threadbare woollen cover over her nightshirt.

"What's the matter here?" she asked, visibly upset.

"Doctor Ransmayer and the constables are paying us a visit because they hope to find some evidence of witchcraft here," Magdalena replied. "They can search all they want, but they won't find any in this house."

"What's this here?" asked the second constable, who had been looking at the coats hanging on a hook next to the oven bench. He cautiously picked up a white object he had pulled out of one of the coat pockets. It had the shape of a dwarf. Ransmayer beckoned to the constable to come over, and he began carefully inspecting the strange item then broke out in a triumphant grin.

"Just look at this – a mandrake root!" he said, gloating. "A witch's implement, evidently used in casting spells. So our informants were right. The devil is indeed at work in this house." He walked over to the coat hook and in disgust held up the coat in which the mandrake root had been concealed. "This is your coat, isn't it?" he asked, turning to Barbara. "I've seen it before. It's the same one you were wearing when your father attacked me."

"But . . . that isn't mine! Someone must have put it in my pocket, and you knew about it." Barbara ran to Doctor Ransmayer and tried to wrest the root from his hands, but he tossed it to the constable, who quickly put it in a bag and made the sign of the cross.

"Burgomaster Matthäus Buchner will certainly be very interested in this," Ransmayer said in a cool voice before turning to Magdalena; she was trying to console Paul, who had broken down in tears. "It doesn't surprise me we've found this work of the devil in your sister's coat pocket. Witnesses have reported that she's been selling expensive love potions to young men in the taverns. Perhaps she intended to sell this mandrake root, as well."

"I know who your witnesses are!" Barbara shouted. "Let me guess: one of them is Josef Landthaler. He was here yesterday and hid this mandrake root in the pocket of my coat." She turned to Magdalena. "I went over to the pharmacy workroom for just a few minutes, enough time for that drunken scum to hide the object in my coat."

"Slander," Ransmayer sneered. "Nothing but slander. Nobody will believe you."

In the meantime, the two other constables had returned from the pharmacy room carrying sacks and bottles that they now handed to the doctor, one after the other. He inspected them and nodded knowingly.

"Hmm, vervain and moonwort, ingredients used by witches in making salves to grease their brooms and make them fly."

"And also used for gout and aching joints," Magdalena retorted. "I'm sure you also have these herbs in your office, Herr Doktor. It's preposterous. Even if people believe your story about the mandrake root, that's nowhere near enough to bring charges against us. At most, they might take the medicines away from us, and it wouldn't be the first time they've done that," she said bitterly.

"Don't get your hopes up too soon, Frau Fronwieser," Ransmayer growled. "Ever since your father started drinking his way through every tavern in town, his support in the town council has been dwindling. Burgomaster Matthäus Buchner is on my side, and so are many other members of the council, and who knows if we might find more witches' tools upstairs."

"Go ahead and have a look." Magdalena stepped aside and pointed up the stairway. "But don't break your neck going up the stairs. Maybe your informer was able to hide something downstairs here, but certainly not in our bedrooms, and I hardly believe Barbara would allow that stinking Landthaler into her room – right, Barbara?"

Magdalena winked confidently at her sister, but she stopped short on noticing Barbara's horrified expression. Her sister had suddenly turned white as a sheet and ran towards the stairway. But Melchior Ransmayer was faster, seizing her by the nightshirt. In response she gave him a swift kick in the shins, the doctor screamed, and his precious feathered hat fell into the dirty reeds on the floor.

"It's upstairs!" Ransmayer called to the guards, his face contorted with pain. "Look in the bedrooms! And keep this witch away from me!"

Barbara kept struggling, but two guards were now holding her so tight she couldn't move.

"Let go of my aunt, or . . . I'll kill you!" Furiously Paul rushed the two constables, but Ransmayer cut him off. "You behave yourself and stay right here, young fellow, or . . . Ah!"

Melchior pulled back on seeing blood trickling down his hand and pointed at Paul, who was still brandishing his little pocketknife.

"He attacked me!" the doctor screamed. "The little bastard attacked me, the damned hangman's brat!"

A third constable now seized Paul, who was fighting and screaming like a stuck pig. Suddenly there was a shout of triumph upstairs.

"I've got something. It was under the bed."

There was a sound of steps on creaking wood, and the fourth constable slowly came down the stairs carrying three books in his arms, which he handed over almost reverently to Ransmayer. "There are such strange signs in them," he whispered. "I think they're books of magic."

Melchior Ransmayer opened one of the books, stopped short, and whistled through his teeth. Finally he turned back to Magdalena, who still had no idea what the constable had found upstairs.

"Are you going to say we planted *this* here, too, Frau Fronwieser?" He held out one of the books to her so she could read the title: *De Maleficiis Ac Magicis Dictis Liber Auctore Georgio Vulgo Jörg Abriel, Carnifici.*

Magdalena was shocked. She recognized the books immediately, though she had never actually seen them. They were the long-lost works of her great-grandfather, the books of magic her father told her about when they were in Bamberg, but he said he'd burned them a long time before. And that's what she'd also told Barbara, who had asked about them a number of times.

But how in the world did they ever show up in our house? she wondered. *And what does it all have to do with Barbara?*

Suddenly Magdalena felt as if the ground were slipping out from beneath her. Alongside her, Paul was still screaming, while her sister just stared at her wide-eyed.

"I'm . . . so terribly sorry," Barbara whispered.

Almost lovingly, Melchior Ransmayer passed his hands over the leather binding of one of the books, then he turned slowly to Magdalena with a smug expression on his face.

"I believe your sister is in real trouble," he said, then turned to the constables.

"Tie her up and take her away. The Schongau Town Council will quickly decide her fate."

"Jesus, Mary, and Joseph! If you don't settle down I'll personally throw all the troublemakers through the window – the closed one."

Konrad Faistenmantel slammed his heavy beer stein on the table so hard that the foam sprayed across the table to where Simon was sitting. The men next to him, who just moments ago had been shouting and grabbing one another by the throat, quieted down, muttering to themselves, and took their seats again. A tense, hostile silence followed that was almost harder to bear than the chaos that had preceded it.

Simon was sitting in the Schwabenwirt tavern along with the schoolteacher Georg Kaiser and around a half-dozen other citizens of Oberammergau and struggling with a bad headache. He had spent the entire evening and half the night in the schoolmaster's house, reminiscing over a couple of steins of strong beer with his old friend, and now his head was pounding and his mouth tasted like damp earth.

"Can we begin finally?" Faistenmantel asked. As he heard no objections, he took a deep slug of his beer and gestured ostentatiously to the Ammergau judge sitting beside him. "Please, you can now open the meeting."

The morning gathering had been announced on short notice after word had got around about Urban Gabler's death the evening before. Almost all the men at the table belonged to the so-called Council of Six, who, along with Judge Johannes Rieger, were responsible for the destiny of every citizen in Oberammergau. Farther back in the room were benches for members of the village council. Most councillors were well over forty years old, all with strong backs, thick, curly beards, and hands like grain scoops, in which they held huge beer steins as if preparing to crush the next person to come along. As soon as the men had taken their seats, the suspicions and insults started flying. The brawl in the cemetery the day before had not been forgotten.

The shifty eyes of the judge flitted back and forth over the assemblage and finally settled on Simon, who was sitting with Georg Kaiser at the far end of the table.

"Before we begin, I would like to know what the gentleman from Schongau is doing here," Rieger said in a gravelly voice. "To my knowledge, strangers have never participated in our council meetings."

"Well, unusual events demand unusual protocols," Konrad Faistenmantel grumbled. "I myself invited the medicus to attend. He examined the corpse of poor Urban Gabler earlier and will present his report to us. Of course, only with the permission of the judge," he quickly added, as if this courtesy due the high official had just occurred to him.

Simon swallowed hard as a half-dozen loutish giants eyed him suspiciously. Only now did he notice that he was the only one in the group with a cup of watered-down wine in front of him, while all the others were holding beer steins. His drinking the night before and the postmortem about an hour ago in the bathhouse had ruined his appetite. Someone had skilfully slit open the man's stomach, then stabbed him straight through the heart. The shepherd who had found the corpse on the moor the evening before first had to drive away the ravens that were feasting on Gabler's guts. The sight did nothing to improve Simon's hangover, and he was glad Kaiser had offered to accompany him to this meeting. For the time being, the school was closed.

After Faistenmantel's remark, the judge was silent and seemed to be considering whether to engage in a power struggle with the council chairman. Johannes Rieger glared at Simon one last time then shrugged and turned to the assembly.

"You've no doubt all heard what happened to Urban Gabler," he began, drumming his fingers on the table. "This meeting has been called by myself and Konrad Faistenmantel in order to . . . ah, dispel certain rumours. There are some who see a connection between the death of young Dominik and this matter in the moor. That's nonsense, naturally. Urban Gabler clearly was killed by someone intent on robbery. He took a shortcut across the moor, where some cutthroat from out of town was waiting for him. Evidently, he was heard screaming, but help came too late. I'm always warning you of all the pedlars who—"

"Rubbish!" shouted Adam Göbl, the father of the imprisoned Hans Göbl. He pounded the table so hard that his stein bounced back almost an inch. "Anyone who can't see a connection between the two murders is a fool. There's a madman prowling around out there, and because of that my innocent son is sitting in the dungeon over there in Ettal. He must be released at once."

There was grumbling all around the table, but some of the men nodded their approval.

"Watch your tongue, Göbl, when you speak with me," Johannes Rieger replied in a piercing tone. "I'm still the judge in Ammergau, and if you can't control yourself, you may soon be keeping your son company in the dungeon." Smugly, he leaned back in his chair, playing with his walking stick. "But I can put your mind to rest. The abbot where he is confined has suspended the interrogation for the time being, though that doesn't mean your son is being released, at least not yet."

"That Göbl gang is responsible for my son's death," Faistenmantel growled. "That's as sure as the amen in the church."

Adam Göbl jumped up, reached for his beer stein, and looked as if he was about to throw it. "Who the hell do you—"

"Silence!" the judge cried. "These accusations don't get us anywhere. Sit down, Göbl, or you'll be sorry. And you, Faistenmantel, certainly should not be throwing stones."

His eyes flashing with anger, Göbl took his seat again, and Simon looked over at Konrad Faistenmantel, who glared back just as angrily.

"Very well," the fat merchant finally mumbled. "For the sake of the play, and peace in the village. I'll pull myself together if he will, too."

"Why is the Schongau secretary meddling in our affairs?" another councilman complained. He had a black walrus moustache and was almost a head taller than most of those present, but his voice sounded high and thin, like that of a woman in a man's body. His name was Franz Würmseer, as Simon had learned from Georg Kaiser, and he was the vice-chairman of the town council.

"Don't we have more than enough foreigners here in town?" Würmseer continued. "Not just the itinerant beggars and pedlars, but especially all the workers and newcomers who have been gathering like flies in the valley since the coming of the Great Plague. It's quite possible that one of them murdered poor Gabler."

Some of the men nodded their approval, and the judge seemed to agree. "The migrant workers are in fact a problem," said Rieger. "More than fifty years ago we also had a large number of poor people, and at that time they were simply driven out of town. Perhaps that's what we should do now. If it turns out that one of the newcomers killed Gabler, that would be our chance to get rid of them. I've said it often enough: this valley is too small to take in any more immigrants."

Once again, Simon could feel how all eyes had turned to him. His headache worsened and he shifted around on his chair, and finally Georg Kaiser, seated beside him, cleared his throat and spoke up.

"Excuse me, Your Honour," Kaiser began cautiously, "but I think I remember years ago we made a point of inviting the foreigners after the Great Plague. We needed the people because so many of our own had died. I have several children of these . . . paupers, as you call them, in my school, and they are poor but decent people. I waive tuition for the poorest of them and in return they do little chores for me. To send them away now would be—"

"Times have changed," Johannes Rieger interrupted. "And how did your council chairman put it earlier? Unusual events require unusual measures." He smiled slightly, as if he'd just thought of the perfect response. "These foreigners have been a thorn in my side for far too long. I'll speak with the abbot about whether we can deport at least some of these families. This dreadful murder gives us a good argument."

Franz Würmseer nodded enthusiastically. "The foreigners hardly pay any taxes and have more children than people like us have, and now it's not even safe any more to walk down the street. If we're not careful, the foreigners will take over the town before long."

"But that's just nonsense," said Georg Kaiser. "They pay their tithes just like the rest of us, and still not one of them has a seat on our council, none of them has—"

"Any further comments?" Rieger snarled.

"I don't know if it's right to place the blame on the foreigners," mumbled an elderly man with long grey hair. His hands were trembling, his eyes reddened and sad-looking. It was the old miller, Augustin Sprenger, on whom Simon had paid a house call just the day before. The poor man was suffering from cataracts. "Perhaps it was just a mistake we made in moving up the schedule for the Passion play, and the dear Lord doesn't like us meddling in His handiwork. Just think of all the avalanches of snow and rock we've already had this spring. God is angry with us. Urban Gabler always warned us that—"

"Please, Augustin!" Konrad Faistenmantel interrupted. "One mustn't speak ill of the dead, but Urban was more religious than the pope and not the brightest star in the firmament. What objection could the Saviour possibly have to our honouring Him four years earlier? And we've always had these avalanches." He smiled self-confidently. "In any case, the play is good for the town. Until now, we have always lost money on the Passion play, but this time I plan to make a handsome profit on it: woodcarvings, statues of saints, crosses . . . The pilgrims will go wild over all the things we have to sell, and our town will be famous everywhere."

"That wasn't the point of the Passion play," Augustin Sprenger grumbled. "Didn't our Saviour Himself chase the money changers from the temple?"

"I believe our council chairman is correct," said the man next to him, a rotund, pleasant-looking fellow with a balding head. This youngest council member, Sebastian Sailer, was a wagon driver and manager of the storage house for goods in transit. He had attracted Simon's attention in the cemetery earlier; he was one of the few who hadn't taken part in the brawl but stood a bit off to one side with Urban Gabler. Now he looked pale and overtired. He was obviously deeply moved by the death of his colleague.

"The last thing in the world we want now is to lose control," Sailer continued, speaking quickly. "The Passion play could be a special blessing for the wagon drivers. You all know how trade has declined on the route through town. More people will come through town because of the play, and more merchants will store their goods here. And that means more profit for us. Anyone who wants to can donate his earnings to the church."

Franz Würmseer nodded. "Sebastian is quite right. For a long time now, we wagon drivers have been slowly going broke, and if there's even less traffic on the roads, we'll be washed up."

A murmur arose, a mixture of anger and agreement, and the judge pounded the table with the pommel of his walking stick. "Quiet, or I'll clear the room!" As the meeting gradually settled down, Johannes Rieger turned to Simon. "Perhaps it's time for our Schongau medicus to tell us more about the deceased," he said, looking at Simon with a malicious smile. "Master Faistenmantel seems to think a lot of you. So . . . wouldn't you agree it was a vile murder by some random vagabond?"

"Eh . . . that's hard to say," Simon replied, slumping down. His mouth suddenly turned dry, and blood pounded in his head. "Unfortunately, the corpse was not in very good shape, but at least I'm sure about the weapon."

"Which is . . . ?" asked the judge.

"Well, the broad, deep cut in the abdomen indicates it was a sword."

"Ah! A sword?" cried Würmseer in his squeaky voice. "Nobody in town has a weapon like that, so it surely was one of the foreigners."

"Or an avenging angel," Augustin Sprenger murmured.

All eyes turned to the old miller, who now rose to his feet, trembling. "A sword," he exclaimed. "Don't you understand what that means? Dominik Faistenmantel was to play the part of Jesus, and he died on the cross. Urban Gabler had the role of the apostle Thomas."

"And that means . . . ?" Konrad Faistenmantel asked uncertainly.

"Well, aren't you infidels familiar with the martyrdom of Saint Thomas?" Sprenger continued, shaking his head. "Saint Thomas went to India, where he was taken prisoner by King Misdai. The apostle was commanded to pray to an idol, but Thomas caused the statue to melt and the high priest then killed him with a sword. With a *sword*!" The old man stared glassy-eyed at the council members, each of whom had an important role in the Passion play. "Jesus on the cross . . . Thomas with the sword. What has to happen for you to realize that God has sent an avenger?"

The men were silent, but their faces had suddenly turned a ghostly white. From far off came a thundering sound as another avalanche rumbled down a mountain into the valley.

It didn't exactly help make Simon's headache any better.

From its rocky throne, the Kofel stared down at the little houses below. A cloud of snow and tiny ice particles flew up as the avalanche finally reached the valley, causing a mere tremor in the interior of the mountain, so faint it could be felt only in the fissures deep within the earth.

The mountain was gradually awakening.

High up on the ridge from the Kofel to the Pürschling and on to the deeply fissured Teufelsstättkopf, a small band of strange little creatures made their way along hidden, snow-covered paths. Their cowls fluttered in the wind and their little legs carried them over the deep snow cover as if they were floating. They were afraid, because in the tunnels and mineshafts the lanterns had swayed and one had even fallen to the ground and gone out with a hiss. The creatures did not know what caused the tremor, but they suspected it was nothing good. The harbinger of a catastrophe that would drag them into the abyss.

The creatures had a mission, and they couldn't stop, couldn't rest, or the disaster would sweep them out of the valley like a cold wind. To conquer their fears they sang the ancient song of the bogeyman. Most of the human men considered it just a funny children's song, but it wasn't, not in its original meaning. It was an incantation about the grim reaper from the dark past, used to keep the spirit of the mountains in check.

The bi-ba-bogeyman, the bogeyman is back . . . He picks up little boys and girls and throws them in his sack.

The little creatures ran and ran, and the mountain watched in wonder.

Only a few hours later, Simon and Jakob Kuisl were walking through the valley of the Laine in the mountains above Oberammergau. Alongside them, the Laine, a mountain brook swollen from the melting snow, now thundered down into the valley as a raging torrent. Branches and whole tree trunks were carried along by the swirling brown water. Higher up on the mountain they could hear the steady chopping of the woodcutters, who were no doubt clearing away debris.

"And these stubborn numbskulls really believe that someone killed the actors in exactly the same way as the *actual* biblical figures?" asked Jakob Kuisl, shaking his head in disbelief as he strode forwards. Simon struggled to keep up with him.

Simon had told him about the controversy in the council that morning. Since the interrogation of Hans Göbl had been postponed,

Lechner had given Jakob some time off, with instructions to stay around and keep his ears open. After a short inspection of the crime scene, the hangman had returned to Oberammergau to pay a visit to his son-in-law. After the binge drinking the night before with his old friend Georg Kaiser, Simon was feeling quite hung-over and had therefore closed the bathhouse until the afternoon. Their walk had finally led them up into the Laine Valley.

"So far it's mostly just the old miller, Augustin Sprenger, who believes that part about the Bible stories," Simon finally responded with a shrug. "But the other council members are at least unsure. They all have roles in the Passion play, after all, and now all of them are wondering what's in store for them."

Kuisl grunted. "If old Sprenger is right, we have bloody times ahead of us. The Bible is a huge horror story. Just think of all the martyrs . . . boiled in oil, burned at the stake, their guts ripped out, bones broken . . . Compared with them, we hangmen are like the kindly Samaritan." He grinned and turned to Simon. "Who has the part of Saint Peter?"

"Eh . . . as far as I know, Konrad Faistenmantel himself."

"Wish him good luck. Petrus was crucified upside down. The apostle Andrew died, as you know, crucified on an X-shaped cross, now called a Saint Andrew's Cross, Bartholomew was flayed alive, Jacob was beheaded, Matthew—"

"Thanks for all the graphic details," interrupted Simon, who suddenly felt sick to his stomach again. "I was only repeating what old Sprenger said. Faistenmantel still believes the Göbls killed his son and that Gabler was killed by some vagrant," he said, scratching his head. "And there are some, like Judge Johannes Rieger or the wagon driver and vice-chairman of the council, Franz Würmseer, who blame the many immigrants and day labourers. It seems the Oberammergauers have trouble with foreigners."

"For those in Oberammergau, foreigners are probably people from Unterammergau, and Schongauers like us are as foreign as if we came from the West Indies." Kuisl spat on the slushy path, which got steeper and steeper. "These narrow-minded damned mountain villagers! Instead of using their reason, they look for a scapegoat. Did any of them ever wonder where Gabler was going at that hour? And why he went alone through the swampland instead of taking the road?"

Simon shook his head. Only now did he realize that he hadn't asked that important question in the meeting, either. "He . . . no doubt was going to the monastery," he said hesitantly, "but why he didn't take the road, I can't begin to say. Perhaps he didn't want anyone to see him."

Kuisl nodded silently. They walked along for a while without speaking, as the Laine foamed and seethed like a satanic slough, cascading over drops large and small on its way into the valley. In an especially wide part of the stream, there was a logjam of trees, apparently carried away by a storm, strewn this way and that, thus forming a pond that threatened to overflow its banks. A dozen or more men with axes were dragging the trunks out of the water and chopping them up. Simon tipped his hat politely, but the men didn't even look up.

"And a good day to you as well," Simon mumbled.

Jakob grinned. "You should be happy they don't throw you in the water when they see your outlandish dress. The Oberammergauers are a stoic people that don't put much stock in appearances."

"Then you probably get along with them just fine," Simon scoffed.

They passed over a narrow wooden bridge and up a winding path towards the top of the mountain, as the sound of chopping gradually faded away. Here, too, some trees felled by the storm had been stripped of their branches and piled together.

"Maybe we're looking in all the wrong places," Jakob said finally. "I questioned Göbl yesterday. He denied everything and said someone had planted the confounded pages in his room. But he did tell me about an old enemy of the Faistenmantels, a certain Xaver Eyrl."

Simon listened intently as his father-in-law told him how the Eyrls had been ruined financially and the son, Xaver, had disappeared.

"And Xaver actually cursed the village?" Simon asked.

Jakob nodded. "It doesn't help that he has flaming red hair. People think of that as a witch's sign."

"Flaming red hair?" Simon stopped short. "That's odd. On my first morning at the Oberammergau bathhouse, a stranger broke in. He got away, but underneath his floppy hat I could see red hair. Georg Kaiser thought it was probably just an itinerant pedlar."

"He's probably right about that," Jakob replied with a shrug.

"Yes, but there's more to it. When I got back to the house, a carved figurine was standing there next to the fireplace, and I'm pretty sure it wasn't there earlier. It looked something like a Hebrew high priest, but I'm not sure who . . ."

Simon stopped short as little stones trickled down on to the path from up on the mountain. When he looked up, he saw a figure that quickly disappeared behind a pile of logs. It was a small person, child-sized, and wearing a cowl with a hood.

"Hey, look! Who's that?" Simon shouted.

The small creature hurried across the path in front of them, disappearing behind a large boulder. The patter of little feet was briefly audible, then silence returned.

"For God's sake, who was that?" asked Simon in astonishment.

Kuisl rubbed his huge nose and looked up at the ridge. "Hmm. Probably just a shepherd boy. Perhaps a cow or a goat got away and he's running after it. Let's think instead of who might be the murderer before—"

At that moment there was a deep, rumbling sound, and Simon thought he felt the ground trembling beneath his feet.

Right after that, the entire mountain began to move.

Bent over like an old woman, wearing an apron and a headscarf tied in a knot, Magdalena scurried through the narrow lanes of Schongau.

She avoided the Münzgasse, the wide main street, as well as the busy squares, in hope of not being recognized as she ran towards the dungeon. Most people were working in their shops or out in the fields, so she encountered only a few people along the way. She turned her face to the side and tried to be as inconspicuous as possible.

All morning she'd been worrying about her little sister, languishing now for several hours in the Schongau dungeon. Magdalena still couldn't figure out how her ancestor's books had showed up under Barbara's bed. She must have found them somewhere – or had the books been planted there by Ransmayer along with the mandrake root? To find out, she had to speak with Barbara.

She had left little Paul with Martha Stechlin. After the attack on Melchior Ransmayer, it took a lot to persuade the guards not to take Paul along, as well. The boy had been so upset he was crying and striking out wildly at anyone who tried to speak to him and had threatened several times to slash open the evil doctor's stomach with his woodcarving knife. Magdalena was shocked by the rage flashing in Paul's eyes. Sometimes she could barely control her younger son.

In the shadow of the buildings she cursed under her breath and crept closer to the dungeon. Rarely had she experienced such a hopeless situation, and she deeply regretted not having spoken to her sister earlier. Melchior Ransmayer and Burgomaster Buchner could put a noose around Barbara's neck because of the mandrake root alone, but especially so because of the books of magic. As it says in the Bible:

For the magicians you shall take their lives . . .

Magdalena's greatest fear was that her sister would be burned at the stake. Then the question was: Who would administer the torture and perform the execution? Certainly not her own father, but an executioner from somewhere else. But there was another problem: if things went badly, her father could be charged with witchcraft along with Magdalena and the rest of the family. Magdalena had heard of trials in which the mere mention of a name during questioning sufficed for a conviction. How long would Barbara hold up under the pain of torture without mentioning everyone who was near and dear to her – her father, her sister, her twin brother, perhaps even her two little nephews?

With hurried steps, Magdalena turned a corner and approached the dungeon, a chunky three-storeyed building clinging like a festering sore to the town wall. Two guards stood in front, holding halberds and staring wearily into space. When Barbara was led away earlier that morning, Magdalena had asked the sympathetic constable Andreas to tell her who was on guard that day in front of the dungeon. At midday two guards she knew well were there, Andreas himself and Johannes, both of whose wives she'd assisted in the birth of their children.

She cautiously approached them, still bent over like an old woman.

"Hey, old woman, get out of here," Andreas growled. "You have no business—" He stopped short on recognizing Magdalena beneath the scarf. He glanced furtively in all directions.

"Come in quickly," he whispered. "If Buchner hears about this, he'll give us hell."

Andreas quickly pulled out a large bunch of keys, then he opened the door while his colleague kept an eye on people passing by. Behind the door was a long, damp corridor with individual cells along the sides. Andreas led Magdalena to the last door on the left, which he opened with another key.

"You have until the next bell rings," he whispered. "Then comes the changing of the guard – so hurry up." Magdalena bent down to enter the low, musty room, and the cell door slammed loudly behind her.

Barbara was huddled against the opposite wall beneath a barred window. Her shaggy black hair hung down into her face, her dress was soiled and torn, and her eyes were fluttering, but at least she appeared uninjured. When she recognized her older sister in the dim light, her tension seemed to melt away.

"Magdalena . . ." she said, hesitantly. Tears rolled down her dirty cheeks. "I'm . . . so sorry . . ."

Magdalena knelt down beside Barbara and ran her hand through her hair just as she used to when her little sister had had a nightmare. All their quarrels were forgotten. "Did they hurt you?" she asked in a gentle voice.

Barbara shook her head. "Ransmayer wanted to tear off my dress. He said he wanted to look for more evidence, but the guards didn't let him." She shivered and wrapped her arms around her knees. "When I heard the door, I thought he . . . he was coming back."

"They won't let him in," said Magdalena, trying to comfort her. "I'll see to that. Nevertheless, you are in deep trouble."

"It was so stupid of me," Barbara said in a hoarse voice. "I've got you all into trouble because of these books that I found in a nook up in the attic. God knows why Father hid them there. I only wish there was some way I could make up for it."

"Indeed, that was a stupid thing you did," Magdalena replied with a sad smile. "Very stupid, even. But that won't help you get out of here. We can only hope the Schongau Council shrugs it off as superstitious nonsense. There are some enlightened men on the council who perhaps—"

"Ransmayer and Burgomaster Buchner want to get rid of me," Barbara interrupted. Unbridled anger flashed in her eyes, suddenly drowning out her fears. "They won't let anything stop them. The two of them are involved in a shady deal, and they know I've figured out what they're up to. That's the reason they planted the mandrake root in the house, and now I have given them another way to get at me." She shook her head sadly. "I could kill myself."

"Don't worry, others will do that for you," Magdalena answered, a little more harshly than she intended. "Especially if you don't put an end to these weird suspicions. That won't . . ." A wave of nausea suddenly came over her as pregnancy made itself felt again. She closed her eyes and struggled against the urge to throw up. "That won't get us anywhere. So just stop with that nonsense." She lowered her voice on hearing footsteps outside the barred window.

"Ransmayer can't hurt us," she continued in a soft voice. "He planted the mandrake root in the house as revenge for the beating Father gave him. But everything else is pure nonsense – dark figures in the cemetery, secret meetings in the church . . . Come on, Barbara! Just tell me why you kept those accursed books under the bed."

"I . . . don't know myself." Barbara slumped down, and in the dim light she was now nothing more than a dark, quivering shadow. "Haven't you ever wished you could perform magic? I thought if I tried those words . . . perhaps there is one that can carry me off to another place – one where I am no longer a hangman's daughter, where no one knows me, where I can begin all over again."

"I'd like to find some magic words that could carry us both off now to another place," Magdalena replied, smiling. "But believe me, I've never in all my life seen any real magic. It doesn't exist. There's just a lot that we can't understand, and we like to think of that as magic."

"Then the women our ancestor executed were not witches?" Barbara asked. "Not even one of them?"

"They were women just like you and me, Barbara. They suffered horrible pain and were made to confess anything their tormenters demanded. And so will you, if something doesn't happen soon." Magdalena straightened up. "I must speak with the council, that's our only chance."

"And how are you going to do that?" Barbara replied despondently. "We are dishonourable. Nobody will listen to us."

"But there is one." Magdalena nodded grimly. "There is one who will do it. He owes a lot to us Kuisls."

"Watch out!"

Simon heard Jakob's voice and at the same moment felt a strong hand on his shoulder. He was yanked back, stumbled, and took a painful fall. In the place he was standing just a moment ago, a huge avalanche of tree trunks and boulders thundered past and down into the valley.

Horrified, Simon looked up. The pile of logs had disappeared, and all that remained was bare black earth. There was a rumbling and crashing as another tree trunk rolled down towards him and Jakob. Simon dived to one side, and the trunk roared past only inches away. A few smaller rocks flew by, then silence returned.

"Thanks," Simon groaned. "That was close."

He got up on shaking legs and brushed off his trousers and jacket. The handsome new jacket he'd bought just recently in Augsburg was badly torn, and his shirt was sprinkled with tiny drops of blood from a cut on his arm. Simon's annoyance at his soiled clothing made him forget his fear of death for a moment, but then it occurred to him that without his father-in-law he would probably now be lying crushed to death down below alongside the Laine. He turned to Jakob. "If you hadn't reacted so quickly . . ."

"My pleasure," Kuisl said with a dismissive wave, but then he pointed down, where shouts and cries of pain could be heard. "It seems we're not the only ones to be surprised by the avalanche. Quick, let's go and see if we can help."

Jakob hurried back along the narrow path that was partially blocked by rocks and fallen trees, and Simon stumbled after him. Finally, when they reached the stream, they found a scene of total devastation. Fallen trees swirled in the churning waters along with a number of the woodsmen, who were desperately trying to avoid being crushed by the logs. The bridge was destroyed, and the nearby shore was strewn with debris and rocks that had rolled down the mountain. Rock dust hung in the air like fog, blinding the men who were groping about in search of their buried comrades. The shouts of pain that Simon and Jakob had heard earlier were now so loud they seemed to drown out everything else.

Jakob ran towards one of the groups of men standing helplessly alongside a huge boulder. A young fellow not even sixteen years old was lying on the ground, pinned under a boulder up to his thighs. His face was white as flour dust and his screams echoed back from the mountain. Behind the almost bestial screams, Simon thought he heard the boy cry for his mother.

"What the hell is going on?" Jakob shouted against the noise.

The men looked up fearfully; they seemed still in shock.

"The rock . . . is too heavy," one of them stammered, pointing at the boulder. "We can't get him out from under it."

"Then, damn it, get a tree trunk! How stupid are you, anyway?"

Without waiting for the reaction of the others, the hangman stomped off and started looking around in the debris, finally locating a birch as thick as a leg that had been knocked over by the avalanche. He grabbed the trunk and carried it like a spear to the scene of the accident.

"Out of my way," he growled.

The woodcutters finally began to understand what the giant stranger in black clothing had in mind. As the lad continued screaming, they all helped shove the tree into a hole under the boulder to lift it up. It moved a bit, just a few inches, then there was a loud crack and the tree snapped in two.

Jakob lunged forwards and pushed to prevent the boulder from falling back down on the youth, but it was like trying to lift a house. The veins stood out on his forehead and one of the sleeves of his shirt burst open, revealing his huge biceps.

"Damn-damn-damn!"

His curses were so loud they even drowned out the screams of the young man. The rock lifted, then suddenly tipped to one side, hit the ground with a loud thump, and finally fell into the surging Laine.

The whole time, Simon had stood off to one side. Earlier he had tried to help the men move the boulder but he'd quickly realized that God had blessed him with other talents. Now he knelt down alongside the lad, who had in the meantime lost consciousness, and inspected his wounds. Except for a few scratches, the right leg seemed fine, but white bone splinters were protruding from the left leg. Blood, stone dust, flesh, and scraps of his trousers mingled in a single mass.

Simon knew what that meant.

As he cleaned the wound superficially to remove the dirt, he turned to the other men.

"Quick, we need to build a litter," he said. "Then take the poor man as fast as possible to the office of the medicus in Oberammergau."

"Who is he?" mumbled one of the woodcutters, regarding Simon suspiciously. "I've never seen this fancy-looking guy before. A foreigner?"

"He's the Schongau medicus who's come to help us for the time being," another woodcutter whispered. "Faistenmantel hired him."

"A Schongauer? Well, I don't know . . ."

"Good God, either you let this Schongauer do his job now, or this boy won't just lose his leg, but his life." Simon was beside himself with anger. "And then be sure to put on his gravestone: 'Murdered by Narrow-Minded Oberammergauers'. Is that what you want?"

The men grumbled, but no one else said a word. Instead, some of them began building a litter from branches lying around, while an elderly man with a shaggy grey beard turned to Simon.

"I want to apologize for my employees," he murmured, patting Simon on the shoulder. "They didn't mean it that way. In a remote area like this, people are a bit reserved towards strangers." He nodded amiably and gave Simon his hand, gripping it like an iron vice. "Alois Mayer. I'm the forester for the Laine Valley."

"Simon Fronwieser, medicus from far-off Schongau," Simon replied between clenched teeth. Then he returned to caring for the injured youth. His anger was still too deep.

"Who's your friend over there?" Mayer asked. "I've hardly ever seen a stronger fellow. He's got the strength of three oxen."

Simon peered over at Jakob, who was now moving other rocks aside to clear their path. He laughed bitterly. "He's Jakob Kuisl, the Schongau hangman, and if your men give me any trouble they'll have to run like hell to get away from him."

Alois looked puzzled for a moment, then he nodded. "I've heard about him. They say he's a wild man, hot-tempered and direct, but as sly as a fox." He broke out in a wide grin. "Damn! If he wasn't a Schongauer, he could easily pass for an Oberammergauer."

For a while, neither spoke as Simon silently dabbed the young man's sweaty forehead, stopping now and then to look up anxiously at the mountain.

"Don't worry," Alois said. "There's nothing more coming, although . . ." He paused as if there was something else on his mind.

"Although what?" Simon asked.

"Well, some of my men think there's something strange behind all these avalanches. I mean, there were avalanches in the spring, but why so many now?" Alois shrugged. "The men say the Venetians are prowling around again."

"The Venetians?" Simon stopped short. "Who the hell are they?"

Alois lowered his voice. "Little people living up here in the mountains since ancient times. They're looking for treasure with the help of secret signs and books. It's possible they're somehow in league with the devil."

Simon laughed softly. "Why does the devil always have to be involved in these matters?" he said, shaking his head. "Couldn't a sudden earthquake also set off an avalanche like this? In any case, the pile of logs up on the mountain didn't look very secure." He shrugged. "Oh, or perhaps the devil stamped his club foot on the ground and set off the avalanche. That must have been it, don't you think?"

Alois Mayer's face darkened. "You can go ahead and make fun of us, foreigner, but we Oberammergauers know that the little men really exist. Recently we have seen more and more of them. They wear hoods and are the size of children. Black dogs and dragons guard the treasures of these mountains, but the Venetians know how to get past them."

"Hoods, you say?" Suddenly Simon felt unsure of himself, remembering the strange figure he and Jakob had seen before the avalanche came rolling down. That figure was also small and wore a hood. "That's peculiar. I myself . . ." Then he stopped short. This superstitious babble drove him crazy. No doubt they'd just seen a child, a shepherd boy, that was all.

Alois looked at him curiously, then waved it off. "What do you flatlanders know about the mountains?"

Simon watched the men who were approaching with a litter made of logs and branches. The woodcutters who had been swept into the raging Laine had all been able to save themselves. Except for the young man, they all seemed to have survived without anything more than a good scare.

"We can take Martin to the village now," said Alois as the men picked up the litter. "He's a good worker and has served me well, even if his parents are only poor immigrant labourers. I will pray a hundred rosaries for him in the church."

Simon sighed. "Add another hundred – he needs it." Once again he looked anxiously up the mountain where he and Jakob had seen the strange little hooded man earlier, then he waved goodbye to his father-in-law and walked alongside the litter back to the village to do his bloody work. He suspected there would be a lot more screams that day.

At around the same time, Magdalena ran down the wide Münzgasse towards the Schongau city hall, where the palatial mansions of the nobility surrounded the square. Colourfully painted walls, balustrades, and stucco figures gave evidence of a time when Schongau was still an important trade centre, but now the stucco was peeling from the walls and the panes of bull's-eye glass were dusty and clouded. Some of the houses were slightly askew, like drunken tavern patrons waiting for better times. Magdalena struggled for breath but ran on without stopping.

The man she was going to visit was her last hope.

Her destination was a three-storey middle-class house on the left that looked a little more inviting than the others. She ran up the few front steps and knocked impatiently on the door, and shortly thereafter a pretty young woman about twenty years old appeared.

"Frau Fronwieser!" she exclaimed. "Are any of our servants ill?"

Magdalena shook her head impatiently. "No, Clara. I must speak with your father on an urgent matter," she gasped. "Is he home?"

"He's sitting upstairs in the library, as he often does," Clara replied hesitantly, clearly noticing how upset Magdalena was. "Come, I'll take you to him right away."

As they ascended the wide spiral staircase, Magdalena scrutinized the elegant patrician's daughter in her close-fitting velvet dress. Clara had been an orphan; she was adopted by the wealthy patrician Jakob Schreevogl and his wife many years ago. Ten winters had passed since the Schongau hangman had saved Clara from the clutches of an evil man. Ever since, the patrician had been a close friend of the Kuisls. Now Schreevogl sat on the town council and, as a deputy burgomaster, had some influence.

On the second floor Clara stopped in front of an oak-panelled door and knocked, then said goodbye with a polite curtsy. "My best wishes to Simon," she said with a smile. "He always used to bring me honey drops."

"I'll do that, too, I promise," Magdalena said hastily, "but now please excuse me, it's very urgent."

She opened the door to the wood-panelled library, where Jakob Schreevogl was sitting in an easy chair, leafing through a book. The tall, gaunt man came from an old family of potters and had invested a significant part of his fortune in this library; Simon always liked to visit him because of this book collection. When Schreevogl noticed Magdalena, he removed the pince-nez from his pointed nose and looked at her earnestly.

"Welcome, Frau Fronwieser," he said, putting down the book. "I think I already know why you are here." He politely offered her a seat. "It's about your sister, isn't it? Half the town is talking about it. Is it true that books of magic were found in her possession?"

Magdalena nodded and quickly told him everything that had happened since that morning. When she had finished, Schreevogl scratched his nose, trying to put his thoughts together.

"I find Ransmayer intolerable as well," he said, frowning. "He's a quack doctor and a bootlick who's making money off people's ignorance, but I'm afraid, unfortunately, I'm the only one on the council who thinks that way. Many of the other patricians go to Doctor Ransmayer when they need some medication, and I wouldn't be surprised if he's trafficking in mandrake roots himself. But these books of magic are, naturally, something else."

"Are you saying you see no possibility of persuading the other council members to change their minds?" Magdalena asked in a weak voice. "You were my last hope."

Schreevogl sighed. "Above all, the problem is Matthäus Buchner. The first burgomaster is not on good terms with your father to begin with, as you know, and this fight with the doctor has certainly not made him any more favourably disposed towards your family." He hesitated briefly before continuing. "In addition, I can imagine that Buchner would like to make an example of your sister."

"What do you mean?"

Jakob Schreevogl lowered his voice as if he feared being overheard even in his own house. "Well, it looks like Buchner wants to take advantage of Johann Lechner's absence to seize control here in Schongau. Lechner, in any case, is overqualified to be a secretary, and Buchner clearly wants to force him out." The patrician leaned forwards and looked at Magdalena with a grim expression. "Usually we have a meeting of the council once a week, but now we meet twice daily, and just this morning the burgomaster signed his first decrees without Lechner in the council – new dress codes, a ban on performances by actors, more stringent curfews . . . I'm afraid our town is facing hard times," he added darkly. "Many of the council members follow Buchner like a dog follows its master, and he will use your sister's case to show again who is the master of the house."

"Do you think you could speak up for my sister in the council?" Magdalena inquired timidly. "Perhaps you could at least convince some of the members to take another look at the case, and that would buy us some time until Lechner and my father return from Oberammergau. You are, after all, the deputy burgomaster."

"A title that sounds much more imposing than it really is," Jakob said dismissively. "Remember there are three deputy burgomasters, and the other two are on Buchner's side. In addition, I'm too young, I don't have the connections. If I could speak with each of the members individually, perhaps we'd have a chance, but as things are now . . ."

"My family has done a lot for this town," Magdalena said. "And for you as well. Remember the terrible murders of children a few years ago, and how your daughter almost died then." It made her furious that her sister's life had apparently become a pawn in a political game. Jakob Schreevogl had been her last hope, a hope that now seemed shattered.

"Simon surely has more medical knowledge in his little finger than Ransmayer has in his whole perverse head," she continued angrily. "And my father has more than once helped these esteemed gentlemen out of a pickle. Still, the patricians turn up their noses when they meet him on the street. Then, after nightfall, their oh-so-refined spouses sneak down to us in the hangman's house for one or another medication. Doesn't any of that matter? Just because of a few dog-eared old books? My ancestor only wrote down what these poor women screamed out to him under torture. Anyone who believes these are real books of magic is a fool."

Without being aware of it, Magdalena had worked herself up into a rage. Jakob Schreevogl looked at her in astonishment and finally nodded.

"That might just work," he said, mulling it over.

"What are you thinking?" Magdalena already regretted losing her temper. Jakob Schreevogl was her last chance, and she couldn't afford losing his support. Then he gave her a wink.

"Perhaps there is a way we can get somewhere with the council, after all, but it will be you, not I, who will present your case."

"Me?" Magdalena said hesitantly. "But I'm just the wife of a simple medicus—"

"Who can speak her mind strongly and confidently, as you've just proven," said Schreevogl, brushing aside her hesitation. "I know it's unusual for a dishonourable person to address the council, but just *because* it's so unusual it might soften the nobles. You've also just given me an idea how we can deal with their objections."

Magdalena listened intently as, in a soft voice, he explained his plan.

"And do you really think the council will listen to me?" she finally asked.

"I can't guarantee anything, but at least I'll try. Our next meeting is this evening, so be ready." He took her hand and squeezed it firmly. "May God help you and your sister, because, if our plan fails, I'm afraid I can't do anything more for your family."

8

Peter was drawing fine lines across a sheet of paper with a charcoal stick.

He was seated against a large rock down by the river, feeling the warmth of the afternoon sun on his face. A pile of papers Georg Kaiser had given him that were blank on the reverse side lay on his knees. Peter was trying to draw from memory a picture he had discovered in Kaiser's library. He'd been working on it for two days and had already rejected a few drafts, but this time he was satisfied. The drawing showed the opened torso of a woman with an unborn child inside that looked like the sleeping Christ Child. Peter smiled, added a few last touches, and his picture was finished. Drawing, sketching, and painting were emotional outlets for him. He could become absorbed in them and forget the harsh world around him.

A world that was rarely kind to him, the son of a simple bathhouse keeper and grandson of a hangman.

He put the drawing aside and looked down at the Ammer, which here, near the bridge to Oberammergau, formed a small concealed cove. Lost in his thoughts, he watched a few linden leaves spinning past in the current as they headed downstream towards his home in Schongau. He clenched his teeth and tried not to cry. Just that morning his father had asked him how he liked school in Oberammergau, and he had avoided answering at first. Just as he was about to tell his father how much he missed his home and his mother, the court official came to pick up Jakob and the schoolteacher Kaiser for a meeting in the tavern. A rumour was spreading in town that another corpse had been found.

Angrily, Peter threw a stone in the water and watched as the circles spread. He'd been so happy when his father told him he'd stay a bit longer with him in Oberammergau, but actually, Father was almost never there. He was always going somewhere with Grandfather because of all the horrible things that had happened here in the village. He couldn't even sleep with Father, because Father wanted him to get accustomed to his new home in Georg Kaiser's house. It wasn't that Peter didn't like it there – the schoolmaster was nice to him, and he could go to the library to get a book whenever he wanted or stay in his room reading, writing, and drawing. Once Kaiser had even given him a private Latin lesson. It was quite different from the school in Schongau, where most of the pupils couldn't even recite the catechism, to say nothing of reading a few lines by the Roman writer Avianus, whose fables Peter loved so much. But one thing was still the same: the grown-ups had no time, and most of the children were mean and teased him because he was different.

Just as back in Schongau.

Another stone landed in the river. Peter remembered the last two mornings he had spent in the village school. First, Georg Kaiser had introduced him and threatened to whip any child who was unkind to the newcomer, then he praised Peter as an outstanding pupil who would go far in life, perhaps even to a university. Nothing could have been worse. Sixty pairs of eyes – some blank and imbecilic, some hate-filled – had stared at Peter, and he already knew that life wouldn't be any easier for him here than it was in Schongau. It would be harder.

Then came a shrill whistle, and Peter was jolted out of his thoughts. He was about to get to his feet and hide the drawing under his shirt when three boys came down the bank to the cove. They were carrying fishing rods and line, and appeared to be looking for a good place to fish. When they noticed Peter, they broke out into loud hoots.

"Look at this! Our smart aleck sunning himself here by the river," shouted one of them, a big fellow who, though only ten years of age, already had a strong back and a huge plump torso. Peter recognized him at once. It was Nepomuk Würmseer, son of the second burgomaster of Oberammergau, Franz Würmseer. Nepomuk had already shouted insults at him in the schoolhouse and tried to trip him up. The two others were Martl and Wastl, who followed Nepomuk everywhere like two little dogs.

As nimble as mountain goats, the boys hopped over the rocks until they got to Peter. Now Nepomuk saw the drawing on Peter's knees and grimaced.

"Ugh, what is that rubbish?" he said, clearly disgusted. "Did Kaiser give you that?"

"No . . . it's mine," Peter answered shyly. "I drew it."

"You drew it?" For a moment Nepomuk seemed genuinely surprised, but then he got control of himself again. "Hand it over." Quickly he ripped it out of Peter's hands.

"Hey, you can't do that!" Peter replied angrily. "That's mine."

"It *was* yours," Nepomuk replied with a grin. He ran his dirty fingers over the pristine white paper as he presented the drawing to his two sneering comrades. "Look at this. What heretical slop. Let's see what the priest has to say about this when we show it to him."

"Give it back!" Peter shouted. In the meantime he'd got to his feet and he tried to tear the paper from Nepomuk's hands, but the big youth held it up high, out of Peter's reach.

"Give it back! Give it back!" the older boy parroted in a falsetto.

Suddenly he gave Peter a shove, sending him flying backwards into the water. For a moment, the cold took his breath away, but fortunately the spot was shallow and the current didn't carry him off. Spluttering, he got up and stomped awkwardly over the sharp stones back to the shore.

"It's just as I thought," Nepomuk jeered. "You're a weakling, like all Schongauers. Have you seen his father?" he asked, turning to his two friends. "He's also a midget, a skinny, creepy-looking guy, a stinking bathhouse keeper who dresses up better than his class."

"And his grandfather's the Schongau hangman who's hanging around Oberammergau now," Wastl added. "My mother told me. She said the whole family is dishonourable, so we'd better watch out for them."

Peter closed his eyes briefly. Actually, it had been clear from the beginning that the other children would soon learn about his notorious family, but he never suspected it would happen so fast.

"My grandfather will slit open your stomachs like fish if you don't leave me alone," Peter replied, his eyes reduced to narrow openings. He was determined not to put up with any more of this. "He's strung up younger fellows than you."

"Your father . . . does-doesn't have any s-say in what happens here," stammered Martl, whose father was on the second council in the village. He had a bad stutter. "Or your Sch-Schongau sec-secretary either. My father thi-thinks we'll be kicking you out of Oberammergau soon, along with all the other riff-riffraff."

"What do you think? Should we show the priest this scribbling?" Nepomuk asked with an innocent expression, waving the paper in front of him. "Hmm. I think this is my lucky day. Do you know what? We won't tell on Peter, we'll just destroy this rubbish." With an ugly smirk, he ripped the drawing in two and then into tinier and tinier pieces.

"No!" shouted Peter. "You mustn't do that."

He watched helplessly as Nepomuk threw the scraps of his beloved drawing into the rushing waters of the Laine, where for a few moments they danced on the surface before finally drifting out of sight like the linden leaves before them. When Peter turned around again, the three boys had moved closer and were eyeing him hostilely.

"And now let's see if the weakling can swim as well as those scraps did," Nepomuk snarled. "If we throw you out far enough, you'll swim at least as far as Unterammergau. You can swim, can't you? Tough luck if you can't." Nepomuk was just about to give him another shove when a commanding voice sounded behind them.

"Leave the boy alone, he hasn't done anything to you."

Nepomuk rolled his eyes, but Peter thought he saw a glitter of fear in them. Two older boys, perhaps eleven or twelve years old, were standing up on the embankment. Peter had seen them in school, but for the most part they'd stayed in the background, and he hadn't seen them at all in school that day. Their clothing was soiled and tattered, their faces thin and gaunt, but for perhaps just that reason they exuded an air of silent strength. Their eyes flashed as if an irrepressible fury was just waiting to be released. They came closer, menacingly.

"Mind your own business, scum," Nepomuk hissed. "This doesn't concern you."

"Oh, but I think it does." The speaker had freckles and wild and woolly red hair. "We've been listening a little to what you were saying. What did you call the kid and his family before? Dishonourable? That's funny, it's just what you always call us. So we're looking after our own people – that's only right."

"It's high time we made it clear to you riffraff who is in charge here in town," Nepomuk berated him. "My father thinks your kind should have never been allowed to come here. There's no place in the valley for lazy scum like you."

"Your father can kiss my arse," the other of the two older boys responded, a dark-haired fellow with an amazingly deep voice for his age. "And now take off before we tell Poxhannes. If we don't beat the crap out of you, he surely will. You know him."

Peter noticed how Nepomuk suddenly blanched. Poxhannes was Georg Kaiser's assistant, a burly fellow about thirty years old who took great pleasure in thrashing troublemakers until they were black and blue. He liked to pick the children up by the ears and hear them scream in pain. Just the morning before, when Georg Kaiser was working again on preparations for the Passion play, Poxhannes had ranted and raved in the classroom.

"All right, then," Nepomuk grumbled after a while. "We only wanted to go fishing anyway." He pointed to Peter, standing alongside him, shivering in his wet clothes. "If you don't think you already have enough troubles, you can saddle yourself with this loser, but I'm telling you one thing," he said, planting himself firmly in front of the boy with the freckles. "The day will come when we Oberammergauers will drive you out of the valley."

He gave a sign to his two companions, and they took off, hopping from one rock in the river to another.

"We're just as much Oberammergauers as you are," the boy with the freckles called after them. "Remember that."

When the sounds of the bullies' footsteps had faded away, the two older boys walked over to Peter, who was shaking with cold. The dark-haired youth with the deep voice took off his jacket and wrapped it around Peter's shoulders.

"Not a good time of year to go swimming," he said with a grin, then looked in astonishment at some of the pages lying around on the ground. "Did you draw these yourself?"

Peter nodded, sniffling, and the boys helped him gather up his soiled pages.

"You're really good at that," said the freckled, red-haired boy, admiring the drawings. "Ha! And not even an Oberammergauer. These people think so much of their woodcarvings and paintings, but there's hardly any other way to make money in this godforsaken valley." He pointed to one of the drawings. "With drawings like these you could easily become a sculpture painter, or later perhaps even a stucco artist. There's more of Oberammergau in you than in all those three little brats together."

"Why do they hate you so much?" Peter asked softly, trying to get his papers together again.

"There's a deep rift in this village," explained the boy with the freckles. "There are the old, established families – and the new arrivals. Most of our families came here after the Great Plague, when the citizens of Oberammergau needed the manpower. Now they think they can just send us back. We do the dirty work, we work in the forest or as cheap labour for the farmers, and we and many of our parents were born in Oberammergau. But God forbid we should call ourselves Oberammergauers. Nepomuk's father and the Ammergau judge as well want to drive us from the village, but we won't let them succeed." He held his hand out to Peter. "My name is Jossi, by the way, and this is Maxl," he added, pointing at the grim-faced dark-haired boy at his side, who gave Peter a friendly wink. "It looks like you can use a few friends, so welcome to our group of dishonourable paupers and labourers. You are one of us." He gave Peter a friendly pat on the shoulder then turned back up the bank. "Come along, we know the best place to catch trout. When Nepomuk and his friends see our catch later, they'll be mad as hell."

Peter smiled and hurried off with the two boys. Perhaps his stay in Oberammergau wouldn't be as bad as he feared after all. For the time being, he'd forgotten how much he missed his parents.

Exhausted, Simon put down the cauterizing iron and wiped the sweat from his brow.

The operation had taken over an hour and had required his full attention. On the table in front of him lay the young man whom Jakob and the woodcutters had pulled from under the boulder in the Laine Valley. His face was pale, as if there were no blood left in his body, but he was breathing regularly and his eyelids fluttered slightly from time to time. Mercifully, the boy had passed out shortly after Simon had started sawing, but until then he had been screaming so loudly that curious neighbours peered in through the window. Jakob, who stood alongside Simon during the entire procedure, glared at them angrily to chase them off, and quiet finally returned.

The hangman continued puffing on his pipe as he applied a fresh dressing to the stump of the boy's leg. The room looked like a slaughterhouse, the floor littered with blood-spattered cloths and flies buzzing around stinking puddles.

"That was a good job," Jakob grumbled. "Your hand was steady, as it should be for every surgeon."

Simon pricked up his ears. "Was that a compliment?" he asked in a weary voice. "It's the first time I've heard anything like that."

"Miracles happen." Jakob grinned, tying the last knot in the dressing. During the operation Jakob had held the boy in a vicelike grip and kept giving him diluted brandy mixed with a henbane potion to drink. Simon had already realized at the accident scene that the lower part of the left leg would have to be amputated. Even if he'd been able to reset the shattered bone with a splint, the boy would have died of gangrene.

Simon first cut through the skin above the knee with a scalpel, then he sawed through the bone. The important thing was to work as quickly as possible, without hesitation, or the pain would become so severe that the brandy and the henbane wouldn't be enough to prevent the patient from dying of shock. The same applied to the final cauterization of the wound to stop the bleeding.

"It's so damn annoying that I don't have my own instruments here," Simon cursed as he settled down on one of the rickety chairs.

"The saw was rusty and dull, and the knife so dirty it looked like the old medicus used it to dig in the garden."

Simon had washed off the scalpel first, even though most of his colleagues thought that was silly, but the cleaning was only superficial, and the rags they used stank of mould and mildew. He pointed with disgust at the jars on the shelves with frogs, salamanders, and cows' eyes floating in them. "Old Landes was a superstitious quack. How can anyone say that a powder made from dried corpses will relieve headaches or the blood of beheaded criminals will cure the falling sickness?"

"Hmm . . . It seems to me I've seen mummy powder in your bathhouse," Jakob answered with a grin. He continued puffing on his pipe.

"Because people believe in it," Simon conceded. "Faith is sometimes the best medicine."

"Faith, love, and hope," Jakob said, pointing at the unconscious boy. "Why isn't someone coming to care for the poor fellow? Doesn't he have a family?"

"That's what we have to find out." Simon groaned and got up from his seat. "I'd better ask Georg Kaiser. He is the village schoolmaster, so he should know all the children and young people here in town. In any case I wanted to go and check up on Peter. School was over long ago."

"Go ahead. After all the brandy and henbane the boy will sleep like a rock for a while." The hangman stretched and walked out into the hallway, ducking under the low doorframe. "Secretary Lechner is expecting a report from me. No doubt he wants me to pick a suspect somewhere out of thin air. He'll have to wait a bit for that."

Without another word, he left, and all that could be heard for a while were his footsteps trailing off into the distance.

Soon afterwards, Simon was ambling through the dirty lanes of Oberammergau, lost in thought, on his way to the schoolmaster's house. The amputation had shown him once again how helpless people were in the face of sickness and injury. If only there were some way to control the pain . . . There were some preparations, like mandrake, henbane, and the sap of the opium poppy, that dulled the pain, but it was always there, like a buried thorn that sooner or later drove the patient mad.

After a while, Simon had reached his friend's house and looked around in the happy anticipation of seeing his son again. The garden in front of the house had been dug up, and a wheelbarrow was standing next to the pile of dirt, suggesting that Kaiser had just been at work. But no one was there, and there was no response when Simon knocked on the door.

"Peter!" His voice echoed through the silent house. "Are you here somewhere?"

He frowned. Perhaps Peter was running errands for Kaiser somewhere in town, or the two were still in the schoolhouse next to the church, but it was already late in the afternoon and school had ended for the day long ago. Simon turned around and headed over to the village church. In the distance he could hear voices in the cemetery, and when he reached the wall he peered over and saw several men standing amid the gravestones. Another group was on the stage, where a long, heavy table was located, along with some chairs.

The rehearsals for the Passion play, Simon thought. He'd completely forgotten about them. *Certainly Peter is there watching.*

At first glance he didn't see his son. Curious, he opened the cemetery gate, and as he approached the group he heard a droning voice coming from the stage. Evidently they were at that very moment rehearsing the famous scene from the Last Supper.

"Uh . . . Take this my body and let it be a . . . remembrance. This is my blood . . ."

"Louder!" cried Georg Kaiser, whom Simon recognized now in the crowd of men. He was holding some tattered manuscript pages in his hand that he glanced at from time to time. "I can hardly understand you, Josef. How will it sound when people are standing here by the hundreds?"

The young bearded man playing the part of Jesus made a deep sigh. Like most of the other actors in the play he wore a long white linen robe. "And I can't even remember my words," he mumbled to himself.

"This is the scene at the Last Supper," Kaiser exclaimed. "Everyone knows these words from the Holy Communion, or weren't you ever in a church? So continue. 'This is my blood, given for you . . . Drink you all of it in remembrance of me . . .'" he prompted the actor, "'so that . . . ?'"

"Good Lord! This is hopeless," said another actor. It was the manager of the warehouse, Sebastian Sailer, whom Simon hadn't recognized at first because of his red wig. In contrast to the others, Sailer wore a yellow robe that identified him as Judas. "This will be a disaster as long as that scatterbrained Josef is playing the part of Christ. A smallholder playing the part of the Saviour? If you had chosen me, we'd be doing much better."

"Aha, so you want fat Judas to play the part of Jesus?" scoffed Konrad Faistenmantel, who had been assigned the role of Peter by Kaiser and the priest. The town council chairman was slouching on one of the chairs at the Communion table. "That would be even better."

"I am not Judas, I just play his part," Sailer replied, visibly exasperated and tired. "But some people seem not to understand the difference."

"How long is the rehearsal going to last?" asked Josef. "I've got to go home to feed the cows and clean out the barn."

"It's going to continue as long as I say," Faistenmantel shouted, "and if you don't stop asking such asinine questions you can take this Communion and stick it you know where."

"Please, please! I don't insist on being Jesus," Josef added, removing his white robe. "Find yourself another jackass to be your Messiah. In any case, it's much too dangerous being in this play."

He jumped down from the stage and disappeared behind the gravestones.

"Josef, Josef, don't leave!" Georg Kaiser called as he started running after the Saviour. "Faistenmantel surely didn't mean it that way."

"Of course he did," whispered one of the apostles. "The old man gives orders and we obey."

"Careful what you say, Mathis," replied Konrad Faistenmantel, who had apparently overheard the remark. "Just make sure the setting for the scene in hell is ready on time," he continued, waving his finger menacingly. "I've paid your carpenters good money for it."

"But how can I finish if every day the priest gives me new instructions on what hell looks like?" he complained. "Moreover, Hans Göbl promised me he'll paint the flames, but pretty soon he's due to get roasted himself."

Faistenmantel was about to reply when Kaiser returned, shaking his head. Evidently, Jesus Christ had quit, at least for the day. Kaiser sighed and turned to the other actors. "I'm afraid there's no point in going on. I'll talk with Josef later, after things have settled down, and we'll meet tomorrow at the same hour."

The others nodded. They, too, seemed relieved that the rehearsal was over for the day. One by one they left the cemetery, until finally Simon and Georg Kaiser were standing there alone.

"We need a miracle if I'm going to put on the Passion play with this crowd in three weeks," Kaiser lamented, as he started picking up the chalice, the plates, and the remaining props from the stage. "I thought Josef was a good fit for the role of Jesus – at least he looks the part with his long hair – but all he can think about is his little farm. I would have given up long ago if Faistenmantel and the priest hadn't insisted we continue." He shook his head and turned to Simon. "I've heard there was an accident up in the Laine Valley. You no doubt have been caring for the injured."

Simon nodded. "The boy's name is Martin. I had to amputate his left leg. I wanted to ask you about him." He told Kaiser what had happened, and the schoolmaster looked troubled.

"I've known Martin for a long time," Kaiser finally replied. "He comes from a poor family of workers who live in a mountain pasture down by the Laber River. Until just a few weeks ago he was a pupil in my school, but now his father has died by a falling tree and his mother is bedridden. Martin is the eldest, and all his younger siblings are able to do is collect windfall in the forest – not enough to support them."

"That's dreadful." Simon went up a staircase on the side of the stage to join his friend. "Can't anyone in the village help them out?"

Kaiser laughed softly. "A starving family of labourers? I give something to Martin now and then, but nobody else gives a thing. You heard it yourself in the council meeting. Most of them just want the poor people to get out."

"And the murder of Gabler comes just at the right time. It's easy to blame everything on people who have nothing. How disgraceful." Simon stopped short, as something else occurred to him. "There's something I wanted to ask you," he began. "The woodcutters said something about little people from Venice who are supposedly roaming about here – not that I believe any nonsense like that. But do you know what there is to it?"

"The Venetians?" Kaiser looked at Simon in surprise and once again a fit of coughing came over him. Gasping, he sat down on a stool on the stage and motioned for Simon to come over. "It's interesting that you bring it up just at this time," he said. "Only yesterday I read again about the Venetians in an old book, and it appears they really were here at one time."

"You mean these dwarfs really existed?" Simon asked suspiciously.

"Oh, no!" Kaiser laughed. "The Venetians weren't dwarfs. They were people prospecting for ore and minerals who came here long ago from across the Alps – from Venice and southern lands. That's where their name comes from."

"And why do people say they were dwarfs?" Simon persisted. He was about to tell his friend about the strange little fellows he and Jakob had seen just before the landslide in the Laine Valley, but then he decided not to, for fear that Kaiser would doubt his enlightened nature.

Georg Kaiser shrugged. "Probably they used smaller people for this work, as it would be easier for them to get through the narrow tunnels. Moreover, people coming from south of the Alps are all a little smaller than we are. At one time the Venetians were here mining cobalt, alum, or manganese used in making the famous Venetian mirror glass."

"And gold, silver, and gemstones as well?"

Georg Kaiser took the chalice used in the Last Supper, which still contained a bit of real wine, and poured himself a cup. He swallowed deeply before continuing.

"I don't believe so, but the people often say that. It's a good story, isn't it? Mysterious little people looking for treasures and protecting the hiding places with magic signs and encrypted books. Who wouldn't want to find a treasure like that and become rich?" Kaiser winked at Simon. "Wouldn't you?"

Simon laughed. "If I had all that money I'd probably not stay in Schongau as a bathhouse owner but go to Augsburg or Venice. I'd be a famous doctor, Magdalena would have the finest clothes and the most valuable jewellery, and my children wouldn't have to go through life as the dishonourable grandsons of a hangman."

"You see? You, too, are starting to dream," the schoolmaster replied with a laugh. "That's what legends are for – they help us to dream. But as far as I know, there haven't been any Venetians in the Ammer Valley for centuries. All that lives on are the stories."

Simon sighed. "I like these little people more than all the rumours about witches and devils in the valley – they're just stories to scare little children, but don't mean anything to . . ." He clapped his hand to his forehead. "Now I remember why I'm actually here. Have you seen Peter? He's obviously not here."

"No doubt he's running around somewhere with the other boys." Kaiser got to his feet. "Be happy he's not always thinking of you. It seems he's found some new friends." He shivered and looked up at the sky, where the sun had already moved far to the west. He coughed again.

Simon was shocked. He had completely forgotten the time. "I've got to go back and check on Martin's injuries," he said. "It would be best for him to spend the night with me in the office, but tomorrow he should be ready to go back home."

Bitterly Simon thought about what *home* meant for this young man with a deathly ill mother and lots of hungry younger siblings. If the Oberammergauers didn't help the family, then he would.

He nodded to his friend then hurried back through the darkening lanes to the bathhouse. Casting one final look back at the cemetery, something there troubled him.

But no matter how long he thought about it, he couldn't figure out what it was.

"I'm really very anxious to know the reason for your unaccustomed visit, Frau Fronwieser, and I hope for your sake it's a good one. I'm very busy."

Burgomaster Matthäus Buchner leaned his fat upper body over the oaken table and eyed Magdalena with a mixture of curiosity and loathing. Finally, he leaned back with a sigh. "Laws must be signed, decrees issued. Now that the honourable secretary is detained in Oberammergau, unfortunately the burden that lies on myself and the council is twice as great."

Evening was approaching. They found themselves in the Schongau Town Council chamber on the second floor of the Ballenhaus, the storage warehouse for goods in transit. A huge U-shaped table stood in the middle. At the table sat the most influential men in Schongau, their chubby hands folded in front of their tight-fitting vests, their eyes directed curiously at Magdalena. It was extremely rare for a simple woman to address the council. The fact that in this case it was the daughter of the Schongau hangman made it even stranger.

It startled Magdalena to see that Melchior Ransmayer was also invited. Though he sat along the back wall where the simple councillors usually took their places, he seemed extremely smug and confident, crossing his legs and playing apathetically with the locks of his full-bottomed wig. She herself had not been offered a seat.

Matthäus Buchner pointed to the right with a smile, where Jakob Schreevogl had taken a place at the far end of the council table and nodded encouragingly to Magdalena. "Our esteemed colleague Schreevogl put in a good word for you," said the burgomaster. "He said you have something to say in defence of your sister. Well then, please begin. We don't have all night."

Magdalena swallowed deeply. She knew that Barbara's life could hang on what she had to say. She had put on her best dress and tied her hair in a modest bun. Just before the meeting she had reviewed her speech thoroughly with Jakob Schreevogl. Now, though, even he couldn't help her. She was all on her own.

"Honourable councilmen, Herr Burgomaster," she began, her eyes wandering over the fat, mostly grey-haired men who determined the fate of the town. Among them were cloth merchants and tavern keepers, builders and potters, all clothed in velvet vests, fustian, and fur-lined cloaks with wide sleeves. The six members of the Inner Council presumably had more money than the whole town put together, but their eyes still sparkled with greed for more wealth.

"The Kuisl family has lived in this city for many centuries," Magdalena began, her voice sounding somewhat uncertain at first, but gaining confidence with each word she spoke. "It has provided the town with executioners who are among the best in the Reich, and made itself useful in other ways as well. Our family's knowledge of herbs and healing is recognized by most doctors. Further, sick people come from far and wide to be treated by our family." She raised her head proudly. "Even here in the council, my father and my husband have assisted a number of esteemed gentlemen with their knowledge."

Magdalena could see some of the council members nodding approvingly. She was on the right track.

"Now my sister is accused of having some things in her possession that look like magic . . ." she continued. "But—"

"'Look like magic'?" Ransmayer hissed from the back row. "Ha! Let's call these things by their right names – evil things – a mandrake root and magic books."

Matthäus Buchner cast a disapproving glance at Ransmayer and drummed his fingers impatiently on the table. "Doctor Ransmayer, please control yourself. You have been invited here only as a witness. When I wish to hear your opinion, I will call on you, do you understand?"

Ransmayer nodded. "Naturally. Excuse me, Your Honour. But such devilish and evil things make me furious."

"The mandrake root is a widely used medicine," Magdalena replied, trying to sound calm and level-headed. "Perhaps its appearance is a bit strange, but actually it's nothing but the root of a mandragora plant. Even the great doctors Hippocrates and Dioscorides praised its healing power. It helps in cases of fever and women's illnesses, and it is furthermore an excellent anaesthetic for surgical procedures." She gave Ransmayer a sideways glance. "It is likely the venerable Doctor Ransmayer himself has mandrake root in his office. But what I actually wanted to say is—"

"The mandrake may indeed be useful as a medication in certain cases, that's correct," Buchner continued with a shrug, "but it's also a substance used in witches' salves and other satanic tinctures and is therefore strictly forbidden in the homes of dishonourable hangmen and midwives. Only doctors and pharmacists are allowed to use them. That is something you should know, Frau Fronwieser." He opened the satchel that had been lying until then inconspicuously on the table alongside him and carefully removed the white root that Magdalena had seen in their living room that morning. With visible revulsion Buchner turned to the other members of the council. "Of course we have seized the evidence and put it in a safe place. See for yourself what this witch has been keeping in her coat pocket. I'm certain we will be able to prove that she used this mandrake root to prepare a salve that would make her broom fly."

"I certainly don't believe that," Magdalena replied dryly, "because this is not a mandrake root."

Buchner looked at her in astonishment, and for the first time he was speechless. "What do you mean, this isn't a mandrake root?" he finally spoke in a hesitant voice.

"That's what I've been trying to tell you all along," Magdalena responded. "This isn't a mandrake, but a gentian root, and the honourable pharmacist Johannson can certainly confirm that."

There was a general murmur of astonishment at the table. After a while, the apothecary Magnus Johannson, a member of the external council, rose to his feet. Leaning on his cane, the elderly white-haired man hobbled towards Buchner, took the suspected mandrake root in his trembling hand, and inspected it carefully. Then he turned to the other members. "Frau Fronwieser is correct," he said with surprise. "This is a gentian root, an excellent medicine for digestive disorders. I myself sell it as an infusion or liqueur almost every day."

"And it is not forbidden," said Magdalena, smiling confidently and hoping the men didn't notice how she was shaking. She had been able to see the plant only briefly when Barbara was arrested and even then the white root looked suspicious to her. Since then, she'd had time to think it over. Her conversation with Jakob Schreevogl had finally strengthened her resolve.

A genuine mandrake root was expensive, since it only grew in southern climates and required special care and harvesting. It was unlikely that Ransmayer would plant such a valuable item on Barbara. It was much more likely to be one of those counterfeits often sold by itinerant pedlars – bryony, bloodroot, plantain, or, in fact, gentian. But that had just been a guess.

Until the apothecary Johannson had examined the plant and made his determination, Magdalena had played a high-stakes game – and won.

"I suspect Barbara got it from a pedlar," Magdalena continued with growing confidence. "We had a few cases of digestive problems recently in the medicus's office on account of people consuming too much fatty food and good wine." She smiled at the gentlemen, most of whom were quite overweight. "A problem no doubt all too familiar to most of you. For that, a gentian root like this can be put to good use. Soaked in brandy it is easily digestible. I'll gladly prepare an infusion for the gentlemen at a reasonable price."

"But it's still magic!" shouted Ransmayer, enraged. He had jumped up from his chair and was pointing at the gentian root. "See for yourself . . . The root has the shape of a little man."

"The radishes in my wife's garden also sometimes have the shape of a little man, sometimes even the shape of a very important part of the male anatomy," said Jakob Schreevogl with a wink from his seat at the end of the table. "Would you accuse my wife of magic, as well?"

Some of the men laughed, and Ransmayer turned crimson. Continuing to stare angrily at Magdalena, he finally took his seat again.

"Let's forget the mandrake, uh, the gentian root for a while," said Buchner, taking control of the questioning again. "Let's turn our attention to this." He reached for the satchel again and this time removed one of the three dog-eared books that the guards had found underneath Barbara's bed. "The contents of these books are so reprehensible that I hesitate even to quote them," he continued, shaking his head. "But I am compelled to, nevertheless." He put on his pince-nez and picked a random page in the book.

"'How to conjure up a hailstorm,'" he began reading. "'Bury the heart of an unborn child under an oak tree in the forest. Wait for the third full moon, when a bush bearing stinking berries will grow out of it. Pick the berries, throw them into the wind, and a hailstorm will come to destroy the fields of your enemies.' Or here . . ." He leafed to another page in the book. "'If you wish to make your neighbour infertile, make a doll from her hair, stick a needle in its belly, and she will bear no more children.'" Buchner looked at Magdalena sternly. "Do you wish to deny that this is about casting magic spells?"

"No," Magdalena responded coolly.

Buchner smiled. "Well, then—"

"Those are magic spells, but this is not a magic book," Magdalena interrupted. "These books once belonged to my great-grandfather, Jörg Abriel, as you know. They are records from an interrogation, nothing more and nothing less, confessions made under duress by women being tortured. You will find similar things in your own city archives." She looked around the table. It all came down to this. It was Jakob Schreevogl's idea to call the magic books nothing but minutes of an interrogation – which they basically were – but it was impossible to know if the council members would accept this argument.

"The honourable Secretary Johann Lechner can confirm this," Magdalena continued, "but unfortunately he is not here. I therefore plead with you, honourable gentlemen, to wait until the Schongau secretary returns from Oberammergau, and in the meantime take your time and think about it."

"These books are the work of the devil," Buchner blurted out, throwing the tattered pages on the floor. "I'm not going to listen to any more of your excuses. Moreover, it's questionable if Johann Lechner is even authorized to search the city archives." He turned to the members of the council and spoke in a booming voice. "I have suggested several times in our meetings that it's time for the city to do a better job of exercising our ancient rights. Lechner is an emissary of the Bavarian elector. For far too long we have allowed him to do as he pleased here. Do we really want our once so proud city to be ruled by Munich?"

Whispered expressions of outrage could be heard all around the table. Some of the council members were conferring individually as Jakob Schreevogl suddenly rose to speak.

"I view the proposal of Frau Fronwieser as quite acceptable," he said so loudly that the others stopped whispering. "Let us wait until the secretary has returned, then surely we can clarify everything."

"We can't wait that long," Matthäus Buchner replied, shaking his head. "People in town are demanding a quick resolution – they want us to act confidently, not like willing vassals of the elector."

"You know yourself that in capital cases you need permission from Munich," Schreevogl added. "We must at least wait until—"

"Do you really think the elector will engage in a power struggle with Schongau just because of a dishonourable hangman's daughter?" Buchner interrupted. He shrugged and then raised his hand for silence. "But please, let us vote. Who is in favour of our beginning the questioning of the accused before Johann Lechner returns from Oberammergau?"

Hesitantly, and one by one, the councilmen raised their hands. Finally, the only one opposed was Jakob Schreevogl. Buchner smiled broadly.

"I believe the matter is decided. I shall at once seek an out-of-town executioner to question the accused. Her father, after all, isn't here, and besides he would refuse to torture his own daughter. The meeting is herewith concluded."

He pounded the table with his mallet, and the councillors rose. Magdalena was stunned. She looked over at Melchior Ransmayer,

who sat on a bench along the wall, smiling slightly. He slowly rose and
walked by her so close she could smell his sickly-sweet breath.

"The game is over, Frau Fronwieser," he whispered in her ear,
"and your sister is just the start. This city no longer needs a medicus, or
his wife. A real doctor would be quite sufficient. Farewell."

With delicate steps and holding his ivory walking stick, he
sauntered towards the exit.

A short time later, Magdalena was sitting on a crate downstairs, staring
into the darkness. There was an odour of cinnamon, nutmeg, clove,
and many other spices in the crates and sacks waiting to be forwarded,
but Magdalena smelled nothing, felt nothing – the only thing she could
think of was that all hope was lost. The Schongau Town Council had
decided to torture her little sister, and the pain would be so extreme that
Barbara would confess to everything she was accused of.

Her execution was now just a question of time.

The guards had cast furtive glances at Magdalena, some of them
compassionate, and they had allowed her to remain down here alone
for a while. At one time or another, the mostly young guards had sought
her help, and the Kuisl family had much support among the common
people. Jakob Kuisl, Simon, and Magdalena had set many broken bones
for them, removed warts, or made them medicines to cure constipation.
She had helped to bring their much-longed-for children into the world
– and aborted unwanted ones. And now these same guards would drag
her little sister, only seventeen years old, through the city, torture her
with glowing tongs, and finally burn her at the stake. And there was
nothing Magdalena could do about it.

For the first time in her life she broke down and cried bitterly. Her
body, weakened by the onset of her pregnancy, trembled. The vigour
she had shown during the council meeting had dissipated, and all that
remained were sorrow and emptiness.

She was still crying when she felt a hand give her shoulder a tender squeeze. It was Jakob Schreevogl. Evidently he had been waiting for her outside the entire time.

"You did well, Frau Fronwieser," he said softly. "Very well, even, but as I had feared, Buchner wants to make an example of your family." He shook his head slowly. "Still, it's strange how important this trial appears to be for him – it's as if he is afraid of something."

Suddenly, Magdalena remembered what Barbara said about the burgomaster and Doctor Ransmayer.

The two of them are involved in a shady deal, and they know I've figured out what they're up to.

Was there perhaps something to her sister's claims, after all?

"Barbara noticed some strange things going on," she said hesitantly, turning to Schreevogl. "And Matthäus Buchner played a role in at least one of them. She may have exaggerated a bit, but perhaps there is something to it." She told Schreevogl what Barbara had said about the secret meeting between Buchner and Doctor Ransmayer, and Schreevogl frowned.

"Well, that is indeed remarkable, and it fits in nicely with what I have observed myself," he replied after a short pause. "I never thought anything of it, but now I'm no longer so sure. Something strange is going on here." He sighed and settled down alongside her on a sack of pungent spices. "Before you arrived at the council meeting, Buchner pushed through another resolution. He's betting on the injured pride of our citizens – Schongauers want to be important again, just as they used to be." He laughed softly. "The people don't notice how Buchner is lining his own pockets with each resolution. He stands to make thousands of guilders just from the renovation of the church that he pushed through – he earns a percentage of every sack of mortar sold."

Magdalena wiped away her tears and stared defiantly at Schreevogl. "Someone had better warn Johann Lechner what this man is doing in his absence, and perhaps then the secretary can intervene." She nodded emphatically. "We need to send a messenger to Oberammergau."

"Do you think I haven't already thought of that?" Schreevogl whispered, looking around cautiously. "But Buchner is not stupid – he and his friends on the council have given strict orders to intercept any messenger heading for Oberammergau. For some days now, the city gates have been closely watched and guards are patrolling the streets. Buchner knows that not everyone in town agrees with what he is doing. On Pentecost he is supposed to hand over his position as chairman to one of the three other burgomasters, and he intends to fight to keep his seat. He's sitting in his cleverly spun web like a big fat spider."

"But can't you go to Oberammergau yourself and warn Lechner?" Magdalena suggested. "The ruling burgomaster certainly can't arrest one of his representatives."

"Don't be so sure," Schreevogl replied glumly. "Judging from the mood of the council, he will be able to turn the other council members against me. He has probably already bought off the two other burgomasters, old Hardenberg and the cloth merchant Josef Seiler, judging from how meek and lamb-like they were in the meeting. The two gentlemen were as quiet as mice." Schreevogl frowned. "In any case, Buchner won't let me go – and even if I go secretly, he'll notice my absence in the next daily meeting of the council, become suspicious, and try to stop me."

Magdalena thought it all over in silence for a while, as the church bells outside rang the eighth hour of the evening. The intoxicating aroma of the spices helped her start thinking clearly again. "He probably won't let you go," she replied finally, "and would stop a messenger on horseback as well, but how about a harmless old woman with a scarf over her head who's just heading out to visit one of the local markets?"

Schreevogl looked at her in astonishment. "You mean . . ."

"Buchner can't possibly lock all the city gates," Magdalena replied, taking the patrician's hand firmly. "Give me a letter for His Excellency

Secretary Lechner," she pleaded, "and I swear I'll pursue this mission with just as much passion as I did in the town council."

"I have no doubt about that, but have you stopped to think what will happen when they notice your absence? Buchner and Ransmayer will at once become suspicious."

Magdalena sighed. "You're right, but they'll still have to delay Barbara's questioning until the other executioner arrives – I probably have two or three days, enough time to find Lechner and bring him back."

"But if you come back too late . . ." Schreevogl stopped short and stared into the darkness. "Buchner's vengeance will be dreadful."

"I won't be too late, not when it's a matter of my sister's life. Do you see any other possibility?"

The patrician shrugged. "Unfortunately, no, but—"

"Then write this accursed letter for me, and tomorrow, before dawn, I'll set out for Oberammergau." Magdalena got up from the crate she was sitting on and walked with determined steps towards the door, visible as a grey patch amid the bales and crates. "I'll be back on time with Johann Lechner, I swear. You know my father, and so you also know that we Kuisls are a rather stubborn bunch."

Under a starry sky, Jakob Kuisl stomped through the moor, heading for Oberammergau. Out here in nature, removed from the noise and chatter of people, he could think clearly. The moon provided the needed light for him to find his way along the narrow paths and deer trails. He heard the cries of barn owls that always put his mind to rest, but this time he could find no inner peace.

The conversation with Johann Lechner had not gone well. The Schongau secretary reminded him they had to find a culprit – and that it was Jakob's job to find this culprit as soon as possible. Lechner didn't even need to say anything about the trouble awaiting Jakob after they got back to Schongau. Jakob knew.

The secretary has me right where he wants me because of that stupid fight with the doctor. I have to dance to his tune whether I want to or not – or my son, Georg, will never come back from Bamberg . . .

And if there was one thing Jakob hated more than anything else, it was to dance to someone else's tune.

In addition, he was still convinced that the imprisoned Hans Göbl was innocent: he couldn't possibly have set up the cross all by himself, and it seemed very unlikely that the Göbls had all ganged up to kill young Dominik Faistenmantel. Then there was the murder of Urban Gabler, which Hans Göbl could not possibly have had anything to do with, as he'd been imprisoned in the dungeon at Ettal when it happened. Nevertheless, Jakob would probably have to torture the poor fellow soon, because those were Lechner's orders. It was driving him crazy.

On a whim, Jakob took the path through the moor instead of the main road – the same one poor Gabler had taken before him. After a while, he passed the scene of the crime that he'd examined earlier that day. In the moonlight he could see the shadowy footprints of many men, and twigs that had broken off the bushes all around. There was no sign that until recently a dead man had been lying there in his own blood.

He was about to move on when he heard a cracking sound under his shoe, as if he'd stepped on a nutshell. Puzzled, he leaned down and picked up from the ground an object about as long as a finger and broken in two. It had been lying in the mud, and it took a while before Jakob realized what it was. He stopped short.

What in the world?

It was probably just an accident, but he decided to keep the little object. Lost in thought, he put the two parts in his pocket and continued walking past the gurgling pools of water and low-hanging trees on his way to Oberammergau. A gentle wind tugged at his hat.

At least he'd persuaded Lechner to let him go back to Simon's house for the night instead of staying in the monastery, telling the secretary it would be better for his investigations to be closer to the scene of the crime. The actual reason, however, was that Jakob could no longer tolerate the sour faces of the abbot and his priests. Every time they walked by him they made the sign of the cross and ran into the church to pray, as if he were the devil himself. The hangman grinned. It wasn't the worst of all possible things to be regarded as a devil. At least they'd leave him alone. After half an hour Jakob finally reached Oberammergau. In contrast with Schongau and other cities and towns, there was no town gate here, no city wall, and no night watchman. Here and there along the main street, light could be seen through closed shutters, but otherwise it was pitch-dark. On the right was the tall steeple of the church, and somewhere in the distance a cow was mooing.

Despite the darkness, Jakob decided to take a shortcut. He turned left into a muddy lane that led down to the rushing waters of the Ammer. Somewhere down there along the shore was the bathhouse. As he walked along he couldn't help noticing the many sprigs of St John's wort still hanging on the doors; Simon had told him about them. Grimly, Jakob looked towards the dark outlines of the mountains looming on the horizon. So far, the sprigs had done little to drive evil from the valley.

As he was about to turn towards the bathhouse he noticed a figure about twenty paces away. Suspicious, he stopped. It wasn't so much the fact that someone was still roaming the streets at this late hour that aroused his suspicions, it was the cautious way the figure was moving, sneaking along like a thief in the night, as if he didn't want to be seen.

Who the devil is that? That's not the way a farmer walks when he's on his way home from the tavern. It's more like a person with something to hide.

He decided to follow the suspicious figure at a distance, carefully scurrying from house to house, occasionally ducking into small alleys ankle-deep in rubbish. By now, Jakob had seen enough to say the figure was young, broad-shouldered, wearing a black cloak and a floppy hat, and holding a sack over his shoulder. He was stooping down as he approached the main street in the village, where the home of the judge as well as the warehouse was located. On the wide street it was harder for Jakob to follow the stranger without being seen, so he leaned against a wall and waited a while.

When he stepped out into the street again, the man had vanished.

Damn!

He looked around frantically, but no one was there. He was about to give up when he heard a clatter in a side street that sounded like a barrel falling over. Quietly he crept closer, stopped . . . and grinned. The stranger had evidently used an empty beer barrel to climb up to the second floor of a house, but the barrel had fallen over, and now the man was clinging to the windowsill above him, swinging back and forth like a pendulum.

And soon he'll fall down and I can harvest him like a rotten apple . . .

Jakob was convinced that the stranger was just an ordinary burglar, probably one of these itinerant pedlars being discussed in the town council and everywhere else. Though he wasn't really looking for people like that, he couldn't allow any random gallows bird to break into other people's houses. Perhaps an arrest would help him win over the stubborn Oberammergauers.

The man was still dangling beneath the window, but Jakob hesitated, suddenly realizing whose house it was – it was the back of the stately mansion of Konrad Faistenmantel and his family, one of the finest homes on the square. The burglar definitely had good taste.

To Jakob's surprise, the stranger was actually succeeding in pulling himself up to the window – the fellow, evidently, was strong as an ox. Instinctively, Jakob cracked his knuckles and ran out into the street.

It was time to act.

He ran towards the man, and before he could slip out of reach, pulled him by the feet. With a loud shout, the man tumbled to the ground. For a moment he was stunned and just lay there, but then he got control of himself again and got to his feet. Instead of fleeing, however, he attacked the hangman, who was taken by surprise and fell over backwards.

"Damn!"

Cursing, Jakob flailed about with his arms like an out-of-control windmill. Arresting this man had turned out to be far more difficult than he'd expected. The hangman was going on sixty now, and even though he was a bear of a man and a skilful fighter, it was a long time since he'd fought in the Great War, where he was feared as a master of the longsword. Nowadays Jakob could feel pain in every bone in his body while standing up, bending down, walking long distances, and above all in dirty brawls like this one. If he was going to win this fight, he'd have to be fast.

The hangman feinted to the right then landed a blow with his left fist, catching his opponent off guard. Jakob struck him hard on the cheek, and the man uttered a sound of surprise. But then he prepared to attack and pummelled Jakob with a hail of blows.

His opponent was strong, and Jakob couldn't dodge all the blows, but he clenched his teeth and concentrated completely on his own next move. The hangman let his guard fall, which left him open to a few more painful blows, but he managed to straight-arm his opponent like a battering ram.

Jakob's opponent took a direct hit to the chin, groaned softly, then fell to the side like a rock landing in the muddy alley. As he fell, his hat fell off, and for the first time Jakob was able to see his face. It was actually a young fellow with prominent facial features and bushy eyebrows. Though he was perhaps only twenty, he seemed as massive as a stone monument.

And he had fiery red hair.

The man's eyelids fluttered and he kept turning his head from side to side, moaning. Presumably he would soon wake up again. When Jakob leaned over him for a better look, he noticed a sack the man had been carrying lying next to him on the ground. It had flown open and some small objects had fallen out. Reaching down in the darkness, he could feel the sharp corners of carved wooden figurines. The moon shone on a number of dainty statuettes about as long as a finger.

They all represented a man in clerical garb.

"Good heavens! That's . . . Xaver!"

The voice came from one of the windows overhead, where an old maid had opened the shutter and was looking down at the unconscious man. "What is Xaver doing here? I thought he was long gone – to the West Indies, or God knows where."

Now the shutter of another window opened – the one the burglar had been trying to break into – and the massive figure of Konrad Faistenmantel appeared, dressed in a thin nightshirt and nightcap and looking very tired and very angry.

"What the hell . . ." he started to say, but then he discovered the young man with the fiery red hair lying unconscious below, and his eyes flashed with anger.

"Xaver Eyrl!" he hissed. "Haven't I told you to stay away from us Faistenmantels? You have some explaining to do." Then he looked in astonishment at Jakob Kuisl, whom he obviously had just recognized. An evil smile passed over the face of the town council chairman. "What a pleasant surprise. I see, Xaver, you have brought your executioner along. Now I hope we'll find an explanation for some of the things happening in town."

9

JOHANN LECHNER'S FINGERS PLAYED WITH THE wooden chess piece as he pondered a brilliant move. His nails dug into the finely whittled lindenwood figurine, over the veiled headpiece and robe of the finger-sized Pharisee – so finely carved that even the folds in the robe were visible. Lechner carefully placed the figurine back on the table alongside the others, all of them identical. There were seven.

A subtle smile spread over his face as he leaned down towards Xaver Eyrl, who sat in a chair opposite him.

"Good work," Lechner said approvingly. "There are not many people who can carve something like that – especially not seven of them that so resemble each other." He pointed at the other figurines. "Why seven, Eyrl? What did you intend to do with them?"

The young carver shrugged and remained silent. His hands and feet were in chains, and around his neck was an iron ring fastened to the wall by another chain. He stared at Lechner grimly. The secretary, the abbot of Ettal, and the Ammergau judge were sitting at a rough-hewn table brought down from the main floor into the basement of the monastery just for this purpose. The morning sun was already shining over Ettal, but none of that penetrated down here into the dark dungeon, where the only light came from a smoking oil lamp on the wall.

At the side of the table stood Jakob Kuisl, his arms folded over his broad chest and a black hood drawn down over his face. The hangman knew that he was expected to put on a dramatic presentation – and part of that was this damned hood that itched and scratched like the fur of a mangy wolf. Concealed under the hood, Jakob studied the accused, visibly scarred by the previous night's brawl.

Eyrl's left eye was black and blue and his lip so swollen it looked like a fat caterpillar. He had fought tooth and nail when he was arrested the night before, and it had taken four men to tie him up and get him into a cart bound for Ettal Monastery. Now, early the next morning, he seemed to have calmed down a bit.

But Jakob suspected he would be a hard nut to crack. The hangman's gaze wandered over to the instruments of torture lined up neatly along the wall and gleaming, cold and metallic, in the light of the oil lamp. A sharp odour rose from the pan of glowing embers standing in the corner.

"I'll ask again," said Lechner after a while. "What were you doing with those little figurines?"

"They are woodcarvings," Eyrl replied curtly. "I sell them in the villages."

"Aha! And you wanted to sell one to Faistenmantel, as well, and for that reason were trying to climb through his window?" Lechner asked. "Didn't he hear you knocking at the door, hmm?"

Eyrl remained silent, defiant, but Jakob could see him eyeing the torture instruments out of the corner of his eye – the thumbscrews, the hot poker, the jaw-expander . . .

He's wondering which instrument I'll use first, Jakob thought, *and how long he'll be able to keep silent. In any case, he's a tougher nut than Göbl.*

At daybreak, Lechner had released Hans Göbl, the first suspect, with instructions not to leave the valley. The once proud sculpture painter was so overwhelmed he burst out crying and collapsed, and when his family arrived to pick him up at the gates to the monastery, he was still trembling. It was not the first time Jakob had seen how strong, upright men could react under the fear of torture.

The judge, Johannes Rieger, shifted back and forth on his chair and cleared his throat. "Well, I believe the matter is clear," he began, drumming his fingers on the table where the ink, quill pen, and documents were located. "Eyrl was trying to break into Konrad Faistenmantel's house, and in the process he dropped this sack of figurines. That's all there is to it," he said, turning his ferret-like face towards Johann Lechner. "I don't know the point of your questions, except that—"

"*ET TU*," Lechner interrupted sharply. Rieger blinked. "What do you think that means, *ET TU*? These two Latin words are engraved into the base of each of these figurines." Lechner turned over one of the Pharisee figurines and handed it to Rieger. "You too . . . What does it mean, and why the seven statuettes of Pharisees, Jewish scholars, not beautiful figurines of the Madonna that would sell very well?"

The judge frowned and leaned back, his arms folded. "That's something you'll have to ask the accused, not me."

"That's just what I was going to do before you interrupted." Lechner pointed at Jakob and his torture instruments. "I brought my hangman along not just to put down stupid brawls in the Oberammergau cemetery. Eyrl will talk – if not now, then tomorrow or the day after." He pounded the table with his fist and glared at his two colleagues. "As you know, I have permission from Munich to pursue this investigation, wherever it takes us, and with all means at my disposal, whether you like it or not."

"Torture in a monastery," hissed Abbot Benedikt, sitting beside him. "That's . . . blasphemy."

"To crucify a man is also blasphemy," Lechner replied dryly. "I'll find the culprit, you can count on it, and I'll also find out what it has to do with these statuettes."

"Don't you think you're getting ahead of yourself?" Johannes Rieger asked sarcastically. He pointed at Xaver Eyrl, who stared ahead with a grim look on his face. "This man is an outlaw, a burglar, there's no question about that. He left the village some time ago and since then has been drifting around the area. When he ran out of money, he came back and tried to burgle Konrad Faistenmantel because he thought that's where the money was. He'll pay the price for that, but your assumptions concerning these statuettes are simply ridiculous. We should have continued questioning Göbl – this is a dead end."

"He didn't just try to break into Faistenmantel's house," Jakob grumbled softly. "He wanted to take revenge on him. Good God, is that so hard to understand?"

The three inquisitors spun around.

"What are you saying, fellow?" Rieger snarled.

The abbot laughed scornfully. "Has it gone so far that the hangman now takes part in the questioning in a burglary? This dishonourable fellow has to keep his mouth shut and only speak when he is asked."

"Eh, you're right," Lechner replied, glaring at Jakob. "My hangman is sometimes a bit . . . impertinent. But he speaks the truth. He told me all about it yesterday. The initial investigation of Hans Göbl revealed that there is deep hostility between the Eyrls and the Faistenmantels. Konrad Faistenmantel brought financial ruin down on Xaver Eyrl's family. There is therefore ample reason to suspect that Xaver killed young Dominik Faistenmantel and now has designs on Dominik's father." Lechner glared at Rieger and the abbot. "It's interesting that neither of you two gentlemen mentioned this hostility, which must be general knowledge here. So why didn't anyone tell me about it? Why do I have to learn about this from my hangman?"

"Are you trying to say we're impeding your investigation?" Abbot Benedikt burst out.

"I don't give a damn what you think," whispered Lechner. "I only know that I'm going to solve this case, with or without your help." Suddenly he clapped his hands loudly and rose to his feet. "Since the accused refuses to speak, we will continue the questioning tomorrow with the use of the first level." He pointed at the torture instruments. "I think we'll use the thumbscrews and pincers first, and if Eyrl continues to be stubborn, we'll continue with fire and sulphur. Those usually make people talk. For today, the meeting is concluded."

Lechner got up and gave Rieger and the abbot a sickly-sweet smile. "I would be pleased to have the esteemed gentlemen at my side tomorrow as witnesses. Believe me, the Schongau hangman is a tough fellow, and in three days at the latest this case will be solved and I can send my report to Munich." Johann Lechner eyed the abbot suspiciously. "I'm sure Your Excellencies will welcome this outcome, won't you?"

"Naturally," Abbot Benedikt responded, his lips tightly pursed as he nodded to the Schongau secretary. "We all pray that the case can be solved as soon as possible. You will excuse us, morning mass calls." Then he gathered up his robe and hastily left the cell with Johannes Rieger.

A while later, Jakob stood alone in the dungeon, which smelled of smoke and mould, and cleaned his torture instruments one by one with a filthy rag. The tongs had become badly rusted, the pokers had a black gleam like polished basalt, and suspicious red spots were still visible here and there on the thumbscrews. Many years ago, Jakob's grandfather Jörg Abriel had wrested confessions from alleged witches with these tools. Afterwards, they were passed down to Johannes Kuisl, Jakob's father, and finally to Jakob. He had always hated them.

The hangman sighed deeply and continued cleaning the tools. His mouth felt dry and he longed for a tankard of strong brown beer.

Tomorrow it would begin again, the crushing and tearing, the shouting, howling, and crying. How he detested it. Perhaps Eyrl would weaken and confess, but Jakob doubted it. The young woodcarver looked strong and, above all, very stubborn, reminding Jakob in a certain way of how he was in his younger years.

But now I'm standing on the other side . . .

In the meantime, the guards had taken Xaver Eyrl to his cell, where, amid old wine barrels and mouldy grain sacks, he could think about the pain awaiting him the following day. This was the reason Lechner had called off the questioning so abruptly. That fear could be a terrifying weapon, especially when darkness fell, with its sombre dreams and the cold damp breath of loneliness in one's face.

Jakob heard a door squeaking behind him, and when he turned around he saw Johann Lechner standing in the cell. The secretary had appeared suddenly, like a ghost.

"We must talk, hangman," he said, lost in his thoughts and stroking his beard.

Carefully, Jakob set the instruments aside. "If it's about the questioning tomorrow, Your Excellency, may I say—"

"I swear, if you exceed your authority again and embarrass me in front of the abbot, I'll see to it that your family is run out of town like a pack of wolves," Lechner hissed. "And your son will never – I repeat *never* – be allowed inside the gates of Schongau. Have I expressed myself clearly enough, hangman?"

Jakob was silent, then he nodded and said, "I understand. Please allow your loyal servant to continue his work now."

"Jakob, Jakob." Lechner sighed deeply, collapsing on the chair the accused had occupied earlier and shaking his head. "How long have we known one another? Twenty years? Thirty? Believe me, I value your work. And further, I not only admire your work, I admire *you*, Jakob, above all your intelligence." The secretary frowned. "It's really a disgrace that high officials are sometimes as dumb as sheep and that those of lesser birth are blessed with the intelligence of rulers. But that's just how it is. And just because you are so intelligent you should understand we won't achieve anything here if you embarrass me." He pointed to one of the armchairs for the observers, but the hangman remained standing, his arms crossed. Lechner shrugged.

"As you will. I only want you to understand that our fates are linked together. You want your son, Georg, to come back from Bamberg someday, and I want the trusteeship over Murnau, which I can obtain only if I can demonstrate a success in this accursed village." Lechner rubbed his hands. Despite the embers still burning in the pan, it was unpleasantly cold.

"The Ettal abbot and his judge will always try to put a spoke in my wheel," he continued. "The monastery will do everything to keep the jurisdiction from being transferred to Schongau. If word gets around that the Schongau hangman is making his secretary look foolish, they will use that against me. Do you understand?"

Jakob grinned. "As you said yourself, I'm not stupid. On the other hand, you want me to help you. What's in it for me if I keep silent?"

"Don't be so impudent." Lechner leaned forwards curiously. "I noticed before that you know something, so spit it out, now that we're alone."

The hangman bared his teeth. Lechner and he had in fact known one another for years, and he was sure the secretary would understand his message and come to visit him later.

"It's about these figurines with the strange inscription," Jakob said in a low voice. "Your suspicion is completely justified. Simon told me that there's one like that in the house of the deceased bathhouse owner, too. A stranger with red hair broke into the house and left it there."

"Xaver Eyrl. Hmm, that sounds possible." Lechner nodded, mulling it over. "But why?"

"It must have something to do with these two Latin words, *ET TU*. It sounds almost like a warning. Perhaps Dominik Faistenmantel also found a figurine like that at home."

The secretary frowned. "You think Eyrl gives these figurines to certain people and afterwards he kills them? But according to what I've heard, the old bathhouse keeper died of a fever and not through some act of violence."

"Well, Eyrl had been away from Oberammergau for a long time and couldn't know that old Landes was already dead. He placed the statuette in his house and only later learned of his death." Jakob took out his pipe and lighted it from the pan of embers as little clouds of smoke rose towards the ceiling.

"Hmm, I don't know." Lechner rubbed his nose, thinking it all over. "If you're right, and you looked in Urban Gabler's house, you'd also have to—"

He stopped short on hearing a little click and something falling into his lap. Surprised, the secretary held up a wooden statuette, broken in two.

It was a Pharisee, and it looked just like the other wooden figurines that had just been standing on the table. On the base were the words *ET TU*.

"Where did you get that?" Lechner asked in surprise.

"It was lying near the place where Urban Gabler was murdered. I found it there in the mud. As I said, it was perhaps meant as a warning." Jakob turned around and went back to working on his tools. "Look for another figurine like this either at Dominik Faistenmantel's house or in the cemetery where he was murdered. If you find one there, then we have our connection between the murders. Three dead men, three figurines, and then perhaps Eyrl will confess before I have to torture him."

Johann Lechner smiled, stood up, and carefully slipped the broken statuette into his coat pocket. "Damned smart, hangman," he said approvingly. "I wasn't mistaken about you, and if you're right, you can expect a reward. In any case I'll immediately send out the guards to look for other statuettes like this, and perhaps we'll find out whether to expect other victims."

His face suddenly hardened. "Tomorrow morning we'll continue the interrogation with all the consequences, just as the statutes provide. This fellow looks like a tough customer, and blood will have to flow." Lechner nodded with determination. "So we'll need a doctor or a medicus, as is customary in such inquisitions. Finally, we won't want Eyrl to die before he confesses."

"Do you mean . . ." Jakob started to say.

"Naturally. Your son-in-law, Simon Fronwieser, must be here for the torturing. He's the only one around, isn't he?" Lechner was already heading towards the door. "The fellow is too sensitive – a good doctor, but just too sensitive. It's time he learned that sometimes it's necessary not just to relieve pain, but to inflict it."

The door slammed shut and once again Kuisl was alone in the room. Deep in thought, the hangman puffed on his pipe as his thirst got stronger and stronger.

He couldn't imagine his son-in-law would be especially fond of Lechner's plans.

Once more, Magdalena checked the knot in her headscarf as the line of people ahead of her gradually moved towards the checkpoint on the bridge. Horses whinnied, drivers grumbled and cursed, and down below at the Schongau landing another raft cast off heading for Augsburg. She could smell the slightly mouldy odour of the river. The Tanners' Quarter wasn't far away, and there the stinking waste and animal remains were dumped into the steep streets around the bend and washed into the river the next time it rained.

Magdalena was standing at the western end of the wide bridge spanning the Lech that led to the small towns of Peiting, Rottenbuch, and Soyen on the other side. From there the old trade route headed south into the Ammer Valley towards the Alps. Once, huge caravans of merchants with their goods travelled the road, but the flow had gradually declined. The road ran along the river a way, a dusty brown thoroughfare, finally disappearing behind the hills. At this time of year the Lech had overflowed its banks and flooded the meadowlands on both sides, leaving the bridge the only way to cross.

Magdalena raised her trembling hand to her bodice, beneath which Jakob Schreevogl's letter was concealed. Yesterday evening the patrician had written and sealed a long letter addressed exclusively to Johann Lechner. Schreevogl had strongly enjoined Magdalena to make certain the letter did not fall into the wrong hands; Burgomaster Matthäus Buchner would surely deal harshly with a traitor in his own ranks. Magdalena had left her son Paul temporarily in the care of Martha Stechlin. Barbara would receive a short message from her, as she had no time to waste. She estimated it would take at most two days before word got around that she was no longer in Schongau and Buchner got wind of it.

She had two days to find Lechner, warn him of what was happening, and convince him that Barbara was innocent and in great danger.

All around her she heard the grumbling of many small traders and farmers who were on their way to Ammergau that morning. The wooden beams of the bridge groaned under the weight of the carts and wagons. Ordinarily travellers were simply waved through the checkpoint, but today the guards were being scrupulous.

And I know why, Magdalena thought to herself.

"What's the matter with the guards?" an old farmer alongside her grumbled. "Are they asleep? If I'm not in Peiting by noon, there's no point in my trying to sell my carrots any more. I will miss the market."

"It took just as long yesterday," a shabbily dressed wood collector chimed in. He was wearing a knapsack loaded to the top with wood and pinecones he'd picked up in the forest. "Evidently they're looking for someone," he whispered conspiratorially. "It probably has something to do with the young Kuisl girl who was found to have those books of magic. Did you hear about it? Perhaps she has already broken out of the dungeon."

In the darkest possible colours, the wood collector told his listeners about the dangerous powers these magic books conferred on their owner. "If they hadn't caught the girl, she would surely have let loose an army of mice on our fields," he said in a hushed tone. "Just like a few years ago, when the mice swarmed all over and ate everything. The priest had to walk up and down the fields three times with the staff of Saint Magnus in order to drive the pests away."

"I'm not sure," said the old farmer alongside him. "These Kuisls may indeed be dishonourable, but I know of no one better when it comes to healing. Just last year I went to the hangman with a dislocated shoulder, and I must say . . ."

Magdalena carefully stepped back a few paces in order not to be recognized by the old man. She was wearing a headscarf, just like yesterday, and had rubbed some soot on her face, and with a basket in her hand and a crooked cane she looked at first glance like a travelling merchant. But Magdalena had no illusions. Anyone who knew her even slightly wouldn't be fooled for long by this disguise. That was the reason she hadn't set out at sunrise, as originally planned. The guards on duty at this hour came from neighbouring Altenstadt and only knew her by name.

But even that was no protection against accidental discovery.

After waiting a while, she finally found herself standing in front of the two guards, who regarded her casually.

"So, woman, where are you headed for today?" the fatter of the guards wanted to know. He was poorly shaven and there was a bright yellow boil under his nose.

"To the market, in Soyen," Magdalena answered quickly in a slightly disguised voice. "I sell my garlic there." She reached into her basket and pulled out a few mouldy, stinking samples. "Would you like to have a few, young man? They're very good for festering infections, also on one's nose . . ."

The guard turned away in disgust. "Get out of here with that stuff, old woman. You stink like a whole field of them. If that's all you have to sell, people will give you a wide berth, I promise."

"I have nothing else," Magdalena said, looking down with a guilty look so the man wouldn't see the smirk on her face. It was for just that reason she had decided on bringing the old garlic.

"Fine, now move along." The guard waved her through and Magdalena stepped out on to the wide bridge. Other itinerant pedlars, farmers with handcarts, and also wagons and men on horseback went clattering past her. Jakob Schreevogl had offered Magdalena a horse for the trip, but a woman on horseback, especially one in simple clothing, would have been much too conspicuous. It was about a day's march to Oberammergau, and Magdalena hoped to arrive before nightfall. Then she'd have enough time to warn Lechner, take her son Peter briefly in her arms, and return home.

At best, with her father and Simon.

Magdalena was still angry at her husband for simply abandoning her. At least she wished he'd given her a better explanation, perhaps even made a short visit back to Schongau to talk things over – anything but just that brief message. But there were no two ways about it, Simon was a coward. By this evening at the latest she'd give him a good dressing-down. Basically, though, her anger was nothing compared to her worry about Barbara. Glumly, she went over in her mind the many little quarrels she'd had with Barbara recently. How insignificant that all seemed now. She absolutely had to be back before the hangman arrived from out of town and started going about his work.

The wooden planks creaked as Magdalena walked the final yards across the bridge, finally arriving at the road to Peiting, where there was also a guardhouse and a toll station. The sun came out from behind the clouds and a silent hope began to stir within her. She tucked the basket under her arm and strode towards the wooded hills separating Schongau from the next town. A narrow, determined smile crossed her face. Yes, she would return with Johann Lechner. Perhaps Barbara would be facing a trial, but certainly not torture or execution. Lechner would put this burgomaster and the filthy doctor back in their places. She once again touched the valuable letter under her bodice and breathed a sigh of relief.

Everything would be fine.

"Credo . . . in . . . in uno . . . Deum Patrem omin . . . omni . . ."

"'Omnipotentem!' God, it can't really be that hard!" Georg Kaiser pounded his lectern with his book and looked out at the rows of school benches. The children glared back at him, blank-eyed. The fat boy, Nepomuk, was struggling with the first sentence of the Apostolic Creed, and despite the cold temperature in the schoolhouse, sweat poured down from his brow. As so often, there was a faint odour of decay in the room that came from the neighbouring cemetery.

"Nobody is expecting you to recite the entire catechism by heart," Kaiser scolded, "but it must be possible to fit a little Latin in between the work in the stables. Peter, can you help Nepomuk?"

Peter shuddered when the schoolmaster turned to him with an indulgent smile. Surely Kaiser only meant well, but he couldn't suspect the burden Peter felt in being the only one to know any Latin in a class of almost sixty lazy, stubborn village children. Peter could already feel the eyes of the others boring into him like needles.

"'Credo in Deum Patrem omnipotentem, Creatorem caeli et terrae,'" he whispered.

Kaiser sighed gratefully. "Well, you see, it's not so hard. Take Peter as your example – he'll amount to something. And now—"

Church bells sounded the noon hour and the end of school. Cheering, the children jumped up from their worn benches and ran towards the exit. As he walked by, Nepomuk bumped into Peter, knocking his slate tablet to the floor.

"See you outside, smart guy," whispered the fat boy, who was almost a head taller than Peter. "It's hard to speak Latin when your teeth are broken." But at that moment, the schoolmaster approached, and Nepomuk took off. The schoolmaster ran his finger through Peter's hair in a friendly way. Evidently he hadn't heard a word of Nepomuk's threat.

"Progress here in the classroom must seem very slow to you," Kaiser said. "But we are just a little village school and have to consider the less intelligent ones. Besides, Nepomuk's father donates almost half the wood for the schoolhouse stove." He coughed dryly, pointing at the small, rusty stove standing in the corner; the room was still bitterly cold in May. Wind whistled through the cracks in the walls of the former stable, the few benches were cobbled together from spruce wood full of knotholes, and half the children had no seat at all and had to sit on the cold hard-packed dirt floor.

Kaiser smiled at Peter. "If you like, you can come to my room tonight, and we'll study Catullus. Something more befitting your intelligence. Shall we say around six o'clock?"

Peter nodded hesitantly. "Uh, fine." He packed up his things and headed towards the door. "But now I have to—"

"And Peter" – Kaiser put his hand on Peter's shoulder – "don't be intimidated by the dolts here. They're just jealous of you. As I said, someday you'll amount to something."

"If . . . if you say so," Peter replied, "but now I really have to go. The others . . ."

"The other children are waiting for you? Very well, if you have already found friends, all the better." Laughing, he gave Peter a final friendly pat on the shoulder and left. "Until this evening."

Peter ran outside, where Jossi and Maxl were waiting impatiently for him in front of the schoolhouse.

"We suspected that Kaiser would have you recite the whole stupid catechism," said black-haired Maxl in his deep voice, shaking his head. "Where did you learn all that Latin? That's weird."

"I don't know," Peter replied with a shrug. "I just know it. It's sort of like a game."

"A game?" Jossi laughed. "I can show you some better games — catch, marbles, and hide-and-seek, for example. You're really a bit strange. And then there are your drawings!"

Peter cast his eyes to the ground. "I'm sorry if I—"

Maxl patted him on the shoulder. "Oh, think nothing of it. At least someday I can say I've known a real scholar. Now come along before Poxhannes catches us." He pointed furtively behind them, where Kaiser's assistant was splitting wood in the yard with an axe.

Hannes was big and broad-shouldered, and his bulging muscles were visible beneath his sweaty shirt. His face was covered with scars that were probably due to an earlier case of smallpox, leading to his nickname, Poxhannes. The schoolhouse assistant chopped wood with the same grim determination that he often showed when handling disobedient children in school, and in less than half an hour Peter had learned to hate him. He was surprised that a friendly man like Georg Kaiser had taken on such a boor as an assistant. Poxhannes couldn't read any better than most of his pupils, and in Latin he had just barely learned to recite the Lord's Prayer, but perhaps it was simply impossible to find a more capable school assistant in Oberammergau.

At that moment, Hannes looked up and wiped the sweat from his forehead. The boys ducked down, but it was too late.

"Hey!" he called out, and motioned to them to come. "Quit staring and help me with the firewood. Hurry up and get over here."

"Keep moving," Jossi whispered. "Act as if we haven't heard him, or we'll never get out of here."

They ran off as Hannes kept shouting after them. "I'll remember you, you brats!" he yelled. "Don't think I'll let you get away with this. When I catch you, you'll be working your arses off all night."

"What does Poxhannes want you to do?" Peter asked as they ran. "Work all night? What the hell have you done?"

"It's not that," red-haired Jossi panted. "It's just that he always has something for us working-class kids to do." He put on a gloomy face. "Especially now. But save your breath for running – keep going!"

Stooped over, they ran alongside the cemetery wall and through the narrow streets towards the Ammer bridge. Peter's heart was pounding. Yesterday his two new friends had shown him some good places to catch trout, and today they were going to tell him a secret. All morning Peter had shifted around restlessly on his chair in school, and during break outside he'd pestered Jossi and Maxl with questions, but they just wouldn't tell him – yet. Now he'd learn.

"Where are we running to?" he asked, completely out of breath, but Jossi just giggled and ran on.

"Be surprised. Your eyes will pop out." After they'd passed the Ammer bridge they continued across the fields, still partially covered with snow, towards the dark forest of pines directly below Kofel Mountain. As soon as the three boys entered the forest it became noticeably darker and cooler. Rugged, deeply fissured boulders lay strewn all around as if cast in anger by a mountain giant, and a narrow pathway wound through them.

After a while they came to a huge boulder with a smooth rock face more than twenty feet high. Peter stopped in amazement on recognizing some strange characters etched into the rock – among them a pentagram, a chalice, and a more than life-sized head of a knight in armour.

"What in the world is that?" he asked.

"We call this the Wall of Evil," Maxl declared in a conspiratorial voice. "The drawings are reputed to be ancient. Hidden messages and defensive magic against evil spirits." He pointed to the path ahead. "There are similar places here all along the foot of the Kofel, and because of this the region is considered cursed. Only very rarely do men go up this path." He grinned. "And that's lucky for us."

Peter looked more closely at the symbols. "A pentagram!" he said excitedly. "And this here looks like a lion's head or a double-headed eagle."

"When the two-headed eagle utters its cry, stay on the narrow path in the shadow of the mountain," Jossi whispered.

Peter stared at him in confusion. "What do you mean?"

"Well, some people think that mythical little men from Venice—"

"Hey! Hurry up," Maxl interrupted, casting an admonishing glance at his friend. "Or maybe another woodcutter will come along and kick us out. This is a private forest for avalanche protection and belongs to the monastery. We actually shouldn't even be here."

Sure-footed as a mountain goat, Maxl clambered up one side of the boulder and disappeared into a crevice, then Jossi and Peter followed. Even while he was climbing up, Peter pondered the meaning of the strange signs and wished he knew more about these mythical little men from Venice. Perhaps there would be a chance later to ask a few questions.

They crawled through a slippery crevice, around the boulder, and over fallen trees, which made their progress difficult. Suddenly Jossi stopped, folded his arms, and gave them a strange look.

"Before we go on, you must swear you'll tell no one about this place," he declared solemnly.

Peter nodded excitedly. "I swear."

"Swear on the life of your mother and the Holy Trinity," Maxl demanded.

"By the life of my mother and the Holy Trinity."

Jossi grinned broadly. "Well, then come along." He took Peter by the hand and led him a few steps forwards until they found themselves on the opposite side of the boulder. "Welcome to the Malenstein, the hideout of the dishonourable children," Jossi exclaimed, making a stiff bow. "Make yourself at home."

Peter's jaw dropped in astonishment. On this side, the imposing boulder formed a kind of slanting roof over the entrance to a cave about as large as the schoolroom. Off to the right was another chamber, with flat rocks arranged along the walls like chairs. In the middle was a hearth and next to it an almost waist-high disc cut from the trunk of an oak tree. Evidently the disc served as a table, since even in the dim light Peter was able to make out earthenware cups and a few stained copper plates.

"This . . . is a palace," Peter finally stuttered.

Jossi laughed. "Well, perhaps not exactly a palace, but still a very pleasant hangout, especially when Poxhannes is out looking for us."

Together with Maxl he climbed down into the rocky chamber and gave Peter a sign to follow them. "If you break an oath, you'll be sorry," said Jossi threateningly. "We'll hang you upside down over an anthill so they'll eat you alive. Do you understand?"

"Under . . . understood," Peter gulped. "Who knows about this hiding place?"

"In addition to us, around a dozen," replied Maxl, and started counting on his fingers. "John, Wastl, Lilli, Joseffa . . . all children of dirty dishonourable labourers and immigrants." He grinned. "The people that Nepomuk and his ilk call worthless riffraff, and now you're one of us. People from Oberammergau avoid this area, so we have our peace and quiet here." He sat down in the moss and pulled out a pouch from under a flat rock. With a patronizing look, he handed it to Peter.

"Help yourself. They're dried berries and nuts that we gathered. In the autumn, we'll even make apple cider."

Peter put some of the delicious berries in his mouth, enjoying the sweet taste. He leaned back, feeling comfortable and happy. A warm feeling infused him – the feeling of finally belonging to a group. In Schongau he had always been simply the grandson of the dishonourable hangman.

"If so many children know about this place, why aren't they here?" he finally asked, after swallowing a mouthful. "Don't they have any time today?"

Silence reigned for a while, while the two older boys looked at each other in embarrassment. Then Jossi spoke up.

"They're not here because in the afternoon they have to work for Poxhannes," he answered darkly. "Their parents haven't paid tuition, so they labour for him, in the field and in the forest." He pointed at Maxl and himself. "The two of us will have to report to him, too, within the hour. We only hope his mood will be better then than it was a while ago."

"But that's unfair," Peter exclaimed angrily. "Some of them don't know a single sentence in Latin, yet they can lie around in front of the stove in the afternoon, while others have to do hard labour."

"Our parents are happy that in this way we can at least go to school." Maxl shrugged. "That's how it is. We children of the labourers have no rights, and now they want to expel us from the valley."

He fell silent on hearing a noise outside. There was a sound of footsteps, and someone walked by very close to the cave. Jossi held his finger to his lips and looked at Peter conspiratorially. When the sound had finally died away, the older boy turned to the two younger ones.

"Let's check and see who that was," Jossi whispered. "There's hardly ever anyone wandering around in these woods."

"Oh, God, don't let it be Poxhannes," Maxl moaned. "If he finds our hiding place, it's all over."

Jossi walked over to the front part of the rocky chamber and cautiously stepped outside. After looking around, he beckoned to the others. "There's someone else here," he whispered. "Come!"

Quickly Jossi and Maxl climbed up to the top of the boulder, while Peter followed them, anxiously, slipping a few times on the mossy stone, but finally reaching the top, where the two other boys were waiting impatiently for him. As silently as possible they crawled over to the edge, where they could still hear the sound of steps below.

Very slowly, Peter stuck out his head to see a stocky man with a black moustache down below, at the foot of the wall. It was clearly not Poxhannes – and yet he somehow seemed familiar to Peter.

"I just don't understand – it's Franz Würmseer," Jossi whispered. "Nepomuk's father. What's he doing here?"

And indeed, the man down below looked a lot like fat Nepomuk. He was kneeling on the ground near the rock wall, stooped over so Peter couldn't see exactly what he was doing. After a while Würmseer stood up again and hurried away. On the ground lay a few white pebbles and sticks of wood in a strange configuration. It took Peter a while to remember where he'd seen this sign before.

The wayside cross, he suddenly remembered. *The day we arrived.*

It was during their trip to Oberammergau, while he was sitting with his father in the wagon. They'd stopped at the wayside shrine as they entered the Ammer River valley and saw twigs and pebbles like those lying at the foot of the cross. What in heaven's name did it mean?

"Würmseer has left," Maxl whispered. "Let's go down and see what he did there."

In a flash they climbed down over another boulder and arrived at the foot of their hiding spot. From up close the sign on the ground seemed even stranger and weirder.

Like the mark of Satan.

Jossi kicked it, and the branches and pebbles flew off in all directions. "Franz Würmseer is a dirty bastard just like his son," he cursed. "No matter what it was, now it's gone." He was shivering and rubbing his arms. "For some reason I'm no longer happy here by our cave. Let's go home."

Peter nodded – he also wanted to go home, but above all he wanted to tell his father about Franz Würmseer's strange behaviour. Could he perhaps help his father and his grandfather in their search for the murderer? His father would certainly be grateful, and maybe he'd pay more attention to Peter if he told him about his remarkable find.

These signs couldn't be good, whatever they meant.

"You want me to do *what*?"

Simon stared at Jakob as if he were a ghost. He was wearier than he'd been in years, and bleary-eyed. The night before he'd stopped by briefly at Kaiser's house to visit Peter and put him to bed. The boy was excited to tell his father about the new friends he'd made that day, but Simon was only half listening. His thoughts were still with Martin, the badly injured young man who so desperately needed his help. The woodcutter had been running a temperature all night and was shouting in his sleep. In addition, the stump of his leg had become infected and the wound had to be freshly dressed. Earlier that morning it had been difficult finding a few helpers to take the poor fellow back to his home on the Alpine pasture below the Laber River.

After that, Simon had to make a few house calls, visiting some old, sick people in the valley who were homebound. Finally, after many difficult hours, he arrived back in the bathhouse only to meet his father-in-law with the latest disturbing news.

"You understood me," Jakob said. "Lechner expects you at Ettal Monastery tomorrow morning to assist with the cross-examination."

"That's not cross-examination, it's just torture," Simon said. "How long will men continue to revert to this barbarity instead of using their reason?"

Simon collapsed on a chair in the living room and brooded silently. He'd always been afraid that someday he'd be called upon to do this. A doctor always had to be present during a cross-examination so that the suspect didn't suddenly collapse or even die. In Schongau that had been done either by Simon's father or the bathhouse keeper and medicus at the time, and later Melchior Ransmayer, who was happy to pocket the money without the slightest scruple and wasn't much concerned with the suspect's wounds. Simon viewed torture as a relic of a dark time in the past, but he stood more or less alone in his views, unfortunately.

"Perhaps we won't even get that far," said Jakob, trying to reassure him. "The evidence is so clear that Eyrl will probably confess without all that. Perhaps all we'll have to do is show him the instruments."

Jakob told Simon about the strange wooden figurines in Eyrl's bag, one of which was found near the corpse of Urban Gabler.

"The figurine is identical to the one you found here in the Oberammergau bathhouse," Jakob explained, pointing at the carved figurine of the Pharisee now standing on a shelf next to the pickled cow eyes and salamanders. "If we can find a similar figurine in Faistenmantel's house, then we have our connection. Eyrl was trying to take revenge on selected members of the community. First he sent each of them a statuette as a warning, and then he killed them." Jakob crossed his arms in front of his chest and leaned back on the bench, which was much too small for him. "I caught Xaver just as he was about to attack old Faistenmantel. He had his bag of carvings with him."

"I don't know." Simon scratched his head. "You might be right in your suspicion of the Faistenmantels – after all, they ruined Xaver's family financially, and the fellow has a reason to strike back. But then what did Urban Gabler and the old bathhouse owner have to do with it?"

Jakob shrugged. "Gabler was on the town council, and old Landes, who ran the bathhouse and served as the medicus, certainly had influence in town. It's quite possible the two of them helped to drive the Eyrls out of town."

"And then he takes revenge by first planting these figurines on them?" Simon walked over to the shelves and returned with the little wooden figurine, turning it over and pointing to the inscription on the bottom. "But what's the meaning of this ET TU?"

"How do I know?" Jakob looked more and more defiant. "The figurines are in any case from Xaver Eyrl – there's no doubt about that. He had a sack of them."

"Didn't you tell me yourself that Xaver and young Dominik Faistenmantel were good friends?" Simon said. "Then why would he kill him? Because he was the son of his archenemy? That just doesn't make any sense."

"What does it matter whether or not it makes sense?" Jakob asked. "Xaver is the best suspect we have and Lechner wants to wrap up this case as soon as possible."

"As do you," Simon said softly.

"Good Lord, don't you understand?" Jakob pounded the table so hard that the glass jars of salamander eyes trembled in the shelves. "Lechner has got me and my family in a corner. If I don't help him solve this case, he will make my life hell in Schongau."

Simon sighed. "Well, you did punch Ransmayer in the face, so you and perhaps our whole family are already in a lot of trouble, but even then we can't allow innocent people—"

"But that's not all," Jakob interrupted. "Lechner told me straight out that if I don't help him, he'll never allow Georg to return to Schongau. My son's banishment will become permanent." He turned away and began looking in his pouch for a few last crumbs of tobacco for his pipe. His fingers trembled slightly and an awkward silence came over the room.

Simon bit his lip. "I . . . understand," he finally said.

"You don't understand a damn thing." Jakob had put down his pipe. Grimly he peered out through the shutters at the Ammer River rushing by, and in moments like this Simon realized how old his father-in-law had become. The many strokes of fate had caused deep rings to form under his eyes. The hangman was still as strong as a bear, but to Simon it seemed like he was shrinking more and more beneath his firm shell, like a snail plucked out of the water. His excessive drinking had reddened his face and eyes, and his large aquiline nose was covered with a network of fine veins.

"I can empathize," Simon murmured eventually. "It's also hard for me to let Peter go. The very thought that he might never be able to return to me would break my heart." He hesitated a while, then he went on in a firm voice. "But I have always valued you as a man of principle. You know this case is not as simple as it appears."

"I still want to get all this quickly behind me, though," Jakob said. "You are right, I've become weak, but by God, I can't always carry the load. It's time for others to pull the wagon out of the mud; I'm too old." He turned to Simon, and his eyes narrowed to little slits. Once again Jakob Kuisl looked invincible; his moment of weakness was past.

"So tomorrow I'll torture this Eyrl fellow," he continued firmly. "I'll do it well, and I'll do it fast, and you're going to help me. And then we'll both go back to where we are needed, to our families."

For a long time neither of them said anything; the only sound was the rushing water of the Ammer.

At that moment, hasty footsteps could be heard approaching the house, the door opened, and Peter walked in. His brow was sweaty and he was clearly excited.

"Father, there's . . . something I just have to tell you," he began breathlessly. "We discovered a hiding place in the forest and—"

"Peter, tell me about that some other time," Simon interrupted. "Your grandfather and I have important things to discuss."

"But Father, I just want to tell you that—"

"Not now!" Simon said angrily, motioning for him to leave. "We're discussing a matter of life and death, do you understand? So enough of your children's stories, I have no time for you now. There's an important interrogation coming up, and your father has to prepare for that."

Peter stood in the doorway, his hands trembling and tears of anger in his eyes. "You always have something to do," he said in a quavering voice. "Yesterday you had no time and had to go back to visit the boy."

"That boy lost his leg," Simon said. "And I had to take care of him so he wouldn't die."

"And what about me?" Peter shouted. "Someone has to take care of me, too!"

Simon sighed. "It's very selfish of you to think only of yourself when we're dealing with such a tragedy," he scolded. "You are healthy and have a father. This boy's father is dead, and the boy will never be able to walk again. You should be thankful and happy that you have friends here and can go to school."

Peter looked down, embarrassed. "I'm sorry," he murmured.

"Do what your father says, Peter," said Jakob, echoing his son-in-law. "This is a conversation for the adults. After noon tomorrow your father will have all the time in the world."

Simon nodded. "Definitely, that would be better, Peter," he said in a softer voice, trying to calm him down. "And tonight I'll read you a few stories, I promise." He tried to smile, while in the back of his mind he was already sorting through the medications and instruments he would need to take along for the torturing.

Cloth to bandage up the wounds, marigold ointment for burns, opium poppies to dull the worst pain . . .

"Why don't you go to . . . uh . . . see Kaiser in his library . . . or draw something else?" he suggested. "You can show me the picture in the morning. Perhaps a figure study, or a pretty picture of Oberammergau, if you like?" With a cheerful wink he glanced briefly at Peter again, but didn't wait for a reply, turning instead to stare grimly at all the medicines on the shelf.

My father-in-law tortures, and I heal the wounds, then it begins all over again. It is so senseless . . .

Simon was so lost in his thoughts that he didn't even notice that his son, softly and with tears in his eyes, left the room and disappeared.

Barbara stared up at the little barred window that allowed only a thin shaft of light to penetrate into the dungeon.

She had already been locked up a day and a night in the Schongau dungeon. She could hear far-off sounds – the shouting of merchants, the lowing of cattle, the anxious squeaking of pigs just before they were slaughtered. So it had to be market day, probably just before the noon church bells. Time passed slowly. She'd already spent hours cursing herself for her stupidity. Why had she spent so much time leafing through those accursed books of magic? Why had she removed them from their hiding place? They were bloody books, and the next blood they claimed would probably be her own.

Suddenly this whole magic thing seemed ludicrous to her. Her sister was probably right: there were no such things as witches. If they really existed, why hadn't they magically freed themselves from their dungeon back during the Schongau witch trials? Why didn't they jump on their brooms and fly away? Why hadn't they struck down their persecutors with bolts of lightning? Now Barbara felt as they must have as they were carried away, crying and trembling, to await their first torture by the executioner.

Now she was a witch like them.

Someone hurried past just outside her window, and for a moment Barbara's heart beat faster in the hope that it might be Magdalena coming to visit her, but it was just some passer-by, and the steps soon faded away. Barbara had heard nothing from her older sister since the day before. In any case, she didn't think that Magdalena's plan to ask their friend Jakob Schreevogl for help would be successful. The anxious waiting played on her nerves so much that she'd scarcely slept a wink that night.

Groaning, she got up and walked a few steps back and forth. Her back ached from lying so long on the ice-cold stone floor, and once again a rat scurried through the dirty straw and disappeared in a corner of the cell. Up to now the guards had been very polite to her, even bringing her fresh bread and barley soup. She no longer had any appetite, however, and the rats gorged themselves on the food.

Over and over, the same thoughts raced through her mind. Had Magdalena perhaps had some success with Schreevogl? What other possibility was there for her to escape her fate?

A soft whistling interrupted her thoughts. She looked up at the window and recognized a familiar little face. Her heart beat faster.

"Paul!" she whispered. "It's so good to see you here. Where is Mother?"

Paul had knelt down in front of the bars; he looked down at her and made a face. "Mama went away. I'm staying with Stechlin, but she's very strict with me. She doesn't let me play with the cat, even though I only pulled its tail once." He looked around carefully, then took a little folded sheet of paper from under his shirt.

"Mama asked me to give this to you," he said quietly. "She said I mustn't get caught or there would be trouble." Paul reached through the bars with his little fingers. Barbara stood to take the note. She hastily unfolded it, quickly read the few lines, then sank back against the wall and closed her eyes.

It was just as she'd feared. Magdalena's conversation with Jakob Schreevogl had got nowhere, Burgomaster Buchner showed no sign of granting clemency, and her older sister was now on her way to Oberammergau to ask Johann Lechner for help. But how could the wife of a simple bathhouse owner convince such an important man as the Schongau secretary to come back home? Nevertheless, Magdalena's mission was no doubt Barbara's last chance – a thin thread of hope that might save her from torture and a hanging.

"Th-Thanks," she stammered as she turned to Paul, who was still staring down at her curiously. "It's probably best for you to hurry back to Martha Stechlin's house before the guards catch you. No one is allowed to speak with me, you know."

Paul's face darkened, and angrily he shook the bars to the dungeon. "They can't lock you up here," he protested. "You didn't do anything wrong. I'm going to get you out of here, and soon."

Barbara smiled sadly. "That's very kind of you, Paul, but I'm afraid it's not all that easy."

"I don't care, I have a knife, I'll cut through the bars, and then—"

"Hey, kid!" came a loud voice from the street. "What are you doing there? Get out of here! Aren't there any guards here to stop this?"

Barbara flinched on recognizing the voice. It was Melchior Ransmayer. She quickly shoved Magdalena's message under her bodice.

"Run, Paul," she whispered. "You mustn't let that bad man catch you. Come back tonight."

Paul snarled like a wild animal, then scurried away as Ransmayer shouted at the guards.

"I'll have to report to the burgomaster that the prisoner can chat with people here just as she could in the marketplace. It's a scandal!"

"I'm sorry, Doctor," mumbled young Andreas, who was on duty at the main gate, "but it's just a little boy . . ."

"He's the nephew of this witch. He should be put away in the dungeon, too, along with his mother and the whole family." There was a rustling of paper. "I have to check the prisoner to see if she is prepared for the coming interrogation. Here's the document. Let me in."

"Yes, sir, Herr Doktor."

Barbara closed her eyes briefly in preparation for the confrontation with Ransmayer. She was gripped with nausea and fear, for she had an idea what was going to happen. The examination of the suspect was officially the job of the executioner, and the fact that Ransmayer took on this function was a bad sign.

She heard footsteps, first in front of the building and then in the hallway, and finally the door opened and Ransmayer stepped in. He turned around to the guards once again. "Leave me alone for a moment with the accused," he said in a rasping voice.

The door closed and the doctor looked Barbara over from head to foot, undressing her with his eyes. Then he spread his arms out as if in greeting.

"It's really sad we two must meet here in the dungeon," he said with a sigh as he came towards Barbara, smiling. "Don't you agree? Why didn't you accept my little offer back then, in the street? We could have had a lot of fun together."

"I'd have sex with my neighbour's sheep before I'd let you touch me," she snarled. "You're a disgusting lecher and a bootlick. Also, you stink like an old billy goat."

Angrily, Ransmayer stepped back. "You'd better watch what you say," he said in a low voice. "Your life is in my hands, and if I decide now that you're fit for torture, we can begin tomorrow."

"Tomorrow? So soon?" Barbara tried to keep her composure but couldn't suppress a slight trembling. "But . . ."

Ransmayer smiled on noticing her uncertainty. "Burgomaster Buchner has already looked around for a suitable executioner and has asked Master Hans from Weilheim for help." The doctor shrugged. "The man isn't cheap, but he's said to be an excellent executioner. He's perhaps a bit overzealous, but, oh well . . ."

His voice trailed off, and he gloated over the look of horror in Barbara's face. Her legs suddenly felt like two little twigs, and she had to hold herself up on the wall so she wouldn't fall over. Master Hans was considered one of the most unscrupulous hangmen in all of Bavaria. Since torturing was generally well paid, the executioner from

Weilheim did everything he could to draw out the torture as long as possible. Hans had never forgiven Jakob Kuisl for taking a prisoner from him some years ago, and Barbara suspected that was the reason Hans agreed to take on a prisoner outside his district. It wasn't every day that one could torture the daughter of a competitor.

"I've been told that it makes no difference to Master Hans whether he is torturing a man or a woman," Ransmayer continued, toying casually with a lock of his wig. "He has even put children on the rack. For him, all people, well . . . are just raw material. He once pulled out every fingernail of a young witch, one by one. Then he started on the teeth, and finally—"

"Filthy swine . . ." Barbara whispered, almost inaudibly.

"As a doctor, you surely know, my job is to examine the body of the accused," Ransmayer declared, impassibly. "It all depends on whether witches' marks can be found on you. Moles can assume suspicious shapes." He went over to her and passed his hand over her dirty, tattered dress. "Witches' marks can be found in the oddest places – in the crook of the neck, on the breast, indeed sometimes also in the crotch . . ."

Barbara froze. She was choked not just with disgust but the fear Ransmayer might find Magdalena's message in his search. If he learned that her sister was on the way to Oberammergau, then it was all over. When the doctor's fingers reached her navel, she couldn't stand it any more. She kicked Ransmayer in the groin with more force than the time they'd met near the cemetery.

Melchior Ransmayer collapsed and rolled around on the floor. Barbara knew she'd made a bad mistake, but she was overcome by a fury not unlike that of an approaching thunderstorm. She bent down to whisper in Ransmayer's ear.

"What's up between you and Buchner?" she asked. "What were you talking about in the church?" She kicked him again. "Who did you meet in the cemetery? If I have to die, then at least tell me why first."

The doctor groaned, then he struggled back to his knees and glared at her. Despite his pain, he had a wolfish, evil smile. "You would like to know, wouldn't you, you hussy? But you never will. Soon I'm going to know every one of your little secrets, though. Everyone breaks down on the rack."

Barbara spat in his face. "Before that happens, before you see me crying and whimpering, I'll hang myself in the dungeon."

"Guards!" Ransmayer suddenly screamed in a high, effeminate voice. "I'm being attacked! Help me!"

The bar in the door was pushed back and Andreas stuck his head inside.

"What's going on here?" the guard asked when he saw Ransmayer kneeling on the floor.

"A sudden stomachache, probably," Barbara replied, still trembling with rage. "The doctor is not well. He needs a doctor himself."

"She . . . struck me," Ransmayer moaned, bending over again suddenly like a whipped dog. "Watch out for her."

"This weak young girl beat you? Hmm, I don't know . . ." Andreas scratched his head, and his eyes sparkled sarcastically. "Are you sure it isn't a stomachache, after all?"

"Damn it! You'll pay for this. All of you." Ransmayer got to his feet and limped towards the door. On the threshold he turned around again to Barbara. "You have just spoken your death sentence," he hissed. "I'll pay Master Hans ten guilders extra to make it last a long time."

The door slammed shut and Barbara was alone again.

The anger subsided and all that remained was naked fear.

10

$\mathfrak{L}$ONG AFTER JAKOB HAD LEFT, SIMON SAT AT
the table in the house of the Oberammergau medicus, brooding and
staring into space.

In front of him stood all the drugs he would need to treat the
tortured prisoner the following day. Along with the marigold
ointment and dried yarrow, he had found opium capsules and
henbane seeds in the jars belonging to the old medicus, and he'd
crushed them in the mortar to make a few pills. Perhaps he'd be
able to give some of them to Xaver Eyrl secretly in order to relieve at
least the worst of the pain. Simon knew that an accused person who
was able to survive the various degrees of torture without confessing
would be released. Even if the wounds healed, however, as a medicus
he knew that these people were usually broken – they lived, though
they were already dead. Simon had often seen it, and now, for the first
time, he would also take part.

Exhausted from the long day, he rubbed his eyes and tried to
think, but no matter how hard he tried, he could find no solution. If
he refused to help with the torture, Johann Lechner would probably
take away his permission to run the bathhouse, and his family would
be ruined. The only thing that could help him now was a miracle.

He thought of Jakob, who had recently revealed a moment of weakness for the first time. The hangman had returned to Ettal to prepare everything for the torture the next morning. Torturing was also hard for Jakob, though, unlike Simon, he had learned to live with it. But at what price? In the last two years Simon's father-in-law had become increasingly sullen and had often sought refuge in alcohol. And now Lechner was also threatening to banish Jakob's son, Georg, from the town forever. What if his own son—

Peter! He suddenly remembered.

He shuddered as if he'd just awoken from a bad dream. Absorbed in his gloomy thoughts, he had completely forgotten his own son. Simon felt a twinge of guilt for being so harsh with his son earlier, but Peter had to understand that his father now had more important things to do than listen to some wild adventure stories. So many people here needed his help, and now this accursed torturing . . . When Peter was older, he would surely understand. And that evening, Simon resolved, he would tell him a few stories, leaf through some old picture books with him, and be a good father.

Even if it would be hard for him not to think about the next day.

Someone outside knocked on the shutter, and Simon cringed, as if the guards were coming to summon him to his own torture. He cursed under his breath.

Oh, if only I hadn't taken the place of the medicus here and got involved in all of this, he thought. But now it was too late.

"Yes?" he asked impatiently. "Who is it?"

"It's me, Alois Mayer from the Laine Valley."

Simon stood up with a sigh and opened the shutter. Blinded by the bright afternoon light coming through the window, he rubbed his eyes and finally recognized the old woodcutter he'd met after the accident in the Laine Valley. Alois grinned at him affably with his stumps of teeth.

"You look pale, Herr Fronwieser," he said. "You university folks don't get out enough in the sun."

"A good day to you as well," Simon replied with a thin-lipped smile. "What's going on?"

Alois suddenly took on a grim expression. "It's about Martin, whose leg you took off. His mother sent me, as his fever is getting worse. The lad is shouting nonsense and thrashing around. Was a curse put on him?"

"By your little men from Venice, I suppose."

The woodcutter looked angrily at Simon. "Do not mock something you do not understand, city man. In this valley, strange things happen. Men on horseback, black as the night, have been seen, and children have vanished without a trace." He stopped short. "But why am I telling you that? I've come to plead with you to visit the lad in the mountain pasture once again. Farewell."

He turned around and stomped off.

"Hey, aren't you going to take me there?" Simon called after him. "I don't even know where this damned pasture is."

"Careful what you say. God curses those who curse." With a stern gaze, Alois turned around again. "The mountain pasture is just below the Laber Mountain trail – just follow the Laine, and shortly before the Laine Valley the path branches off to the right. You'll find the cabin – after all, you're a smart university man, aren't you?" Without another word the old man turned the corner and was gone.

Simon stood there, cursing softly. These Oberammergauers were even more pigheaded and tight-lipped than his father-in-law. Simon wondered if perhaps the whole Kuisl family had once come from the Ammer Valley. He paused, wondering if he should just refuse to visit the crippled man, but he felt sorry for him, and the little trip would be a welcome diversion. Otherwise he would no doubt sit there all day thinking about the grim scene that would unfold the next morning in the torture chamber.

Quickly he packed his medical bag, closed the door behind him, and set out for Laber Mountain, which, like a mute brother of the Kofel, towered over the other side of the valley.

After less than half an hour, Simon had reached the turn-off that Alois Mayer had described.

A narrow muddy path led up Laber Mountain from the Laine River, which rushed past down here in the valley, seething and swirling. Dark firs blocked the view, making it difficult for Simon to see the steep mountain peaks partly shrouded in mist. The path, still covered in last winter's snow, zigzagged its way up the mountain.

Simon slung his bag over his shoulder and started the steep climb. Soon beads of sweat appeared on his forehead, and his breathing came hard and fast. He couldn't help thinking that those who dwelled in the mountain pasture probably had to hike this trail several times a day, and until yesterday, Martin had also taken it. Now the boy was condemned to life as a cripple up on the mountain. *If he doesn't die of gangrene in the next few days,* Simon thought gloomily.

He heard cawing, and a murder of crows rose up from the treetops, fluttering noisily down into the valley over Simon's head, as if mocking the little medicus. An eerie feeling came over him, as though he was being observed from behind the branches of the thick undergrowth, but whenever he turned around, he saw nothing but dark firs and snowfields. He shivered, astonished at how long the winter lasted up here in the mountains.

After another half-hour he came to a clearing, and a gently sloping Alpine meadow appeared, free of trees and bushes. The meadow was swampy and shone yellow with buttercups and primroses, and a few skinny goats were drinking water out of a hollowed-out tree stump.

Not far away stood a tumbledown cabin cobbled together from unfinished tree trunks, with two children in threadbare dresses playing with a dog in the slushy snow. When they saw Simon, they ran anxiously behind the house while the dog barked furiously at the stranger.

After a while, the door opened a crack and the mongrel stopped barking. An old woman clothed in a tattered woollen coat with a shawl made of pieces of wolf pelts that had been stitched together stared suspiciously at Simon. Her face was worn and her cheeks fallen. Suddenly she smiled, revealing an almost toothless mouth.

"Ah, you are surely the new medicus who helped our Martin," she said in a feeble voice. "Thank you for making the long trip to visit us." She shook with a dry cough.

When her coughing finally stopped, she waved for Simon to enter the house. "Martin is dying before my eyes, and there is nothing I can do," she murmured as she shuffled along, stooped over. "Perhaps there is some way you can help."

Simon ducked down as he entered the low-ceilinged cabin, which consisted of only one room. A sharp odour was in the air, perhaps coming from the adjacent goat shed, and a small fire sputtered in one corner. The smoke had trouble escaping through the small hole in the roof, making tears well up in Simon's eyes, and it took a while before he was able to see his surroundings. Five children from three to ten years of age were crouched down on the hard dirt floor, staring at him fearfully. There was a wobbly table with a few empty bowls standing on it, and one large bed piled high with rags and furs. From it came a heart-rending moan.

Simon approached the trembling pile, pushed some covers aside, and bent down to Martin. Fat beads of sweat stood on his forehead, and he thrashed back and forth in the bed, mumbling incoherently.

"So hot . . ." he whispered. "The . . . the fire . . . take the lantern away . . ."

"How long has he been like this?" Simon asked, dabbing the cold sweat from Martin's brow.

"Since the men from the village brought him here this morning." The woman rubbed her thin fingers together, trying to keep warm. With her toothless mouth and grey, stringy hair she looked to be about sixty, but Simon guessed she was thirty-five at the most.

"Martin is my eldest," she said in a soft voice. "My dear Josef, God bless his soul, was killed last year by a falling tree. At that time Martin was still in school, but since the accident he has had to take over as the man of the house. He earns the little money we need to live on, working for Mayer over in the Laine Valley. And now . . ." Tears ran down her wrinkled face. "He'll die, won't he?" she asked finally.

"That's something only God knows," Simon replied, "but I'll do everything I can to save him." He pushed the covers aside and looked at the stump of Martin's leg – and recoiled in horror. The bandage had been removed, and he could see that new pus had formed in the dirty wound.

"Who did that?" Simon asked angrily. "Who took the bandage off?"

"It was . . . Mayer, and his assistant," she replied anxiously. "They poured holy water over it and spat on it, then Mayer spoke some magic words. They said that would appease the spirits of the mountain."

"Mountain spirits and magic words!" Simon was so angry he could hardly contain himself. "Have you all gone crazy? There are no spirits, just incredible stupidity. Only I can remove this bandage and replace it, is that clear?"

The woman nodded silently and Simon began to clean the festering wound, which was already full of dirt and filth. Finally the medicus took a jar of honey from his pocket and smeared it liberally over the wound.

"What are you doing there?" the woman asked.

"I am trying to extract the pus from the wound with honey. If that doesn't work, we'll try mouldy bread."

"Honey? Mouldy bread?" The woman stared at him in astonishment. "That sounds like magic to me."

"It's your murmured words and holy water that are magic," Simon retorted. "Honey and mould, on the other hand, are proven to relieve infected wounds. Believe me, even old Dioscorides—"

He stopped short as Martin started to mumble again hysterically. "The . . . the cliffs are falling . . . the lantern . . . Markus . . . Marie . . ." the boy gasped.

"Who is he talking about?" Simon asked.

The woman frowned. "He's been going on like that all day, but I have no idea why he's talking about Markus and Marie, two children who disappeared from around here a few years ago. Back then, after it happened, Martin went for days without talking. They were good friends of his."

"The children simply disappeared?" Simon stopped working for a minute. He remembered that Alois Mayer had also hinted about children going missing recently.

The woman nodded. "The rumour was that the Kofel took them," she whispered. "The Kofel is an evil man who now and then needs his sacrifices, and then he sends an avalanche of snow or rock that makes the whole valley shake."

"Woman," Simon interrupted, "what nonsense are you talking? Haven't I just told you there is no such thing as magic?"

But the woman persisted. "Believe me, when I was a child the ground once shook so much that two houses in the village collapsed. And can't you feel how the earth has been trembling more and more recently? I'm telling you, the mountain is awakening."

"For the last time, that's—" Simon stopped short. He suddenly remembered that he himself had felt a strange trembling just yesterday, shortly before the rock avalanche descended into the Laine Valley. Perhaps that had been a small earthquake. He'd never experienced one before, but he knew that such quakes frequently

occurred in the Alpine foothills. Years ago, near Peiting, a whole
castle collapsed, and still today people told of that horrible night.

"Very well, the earth trembles," he said, trying to calm her down.
"That happens now and then even where I live in Schongau, but it's
nonsense to believe you can pacify the mountain with sacrifices."

The woman laughed softly. "That's something you wouldn't
understand, stranger. For thousands of years our people have lived
in this valley and we have always made sacrifices to the Kofel." She
pointed towards the window, which was covered with dirty rags, and
through the tears in the cloth Simon could see the conical mountain
on the other side of the valley. The woman pointed to a flat, cleared
area on one side of the mountain.

"Over there, atop the accursed Döttenbichl, in ancient times
they sacrificed first men, then later treasures, tools, and weapons.
Nowadays people go up there to leave a bouquet of flowers or a cup
of milk for the mountain spirits. But sometimes the spirits come down
again to take a child." Her voice broke. "And now, my Martin. By
God, he is not the first, nor will he be the last. And they are always
the children of us poor people and labourers."

"How often do I have to repeat that . . ." Simon started to say. But
then, with a sigh, he gave up. He'd never be able to convince these
stubborn mountain people. Silently he treated the wound with honey
and applied a new bandage. The children and the grieving mother
watched, as if he were a magician performing a trick.

A brown-feathered mountain eagle circled over the top of the Kofel.
With a shrill cry it spiralled up and then glided over to the cliff that
plunged nearly five hundred feet down into the valley. In a rapid
descent it approached the moor, ready to seize its prey.

The eagle's sharp eyes had discovered a mouse poking its
little head out of its burrow, its whiskers trembling and snub nose

quivering nervously back and forth. Just as the eagle was about to dive, it discovered a second mouse not far away, then many others, dozens in all that had left their burrows and were scurrying through the brush, heading towards the Graswang Valley.

And they were not the only creatures on the move.

A blindworm had awakened early from its winter sleep and, still numb and lazy from the cold, was slithering over the smooth stones along the shore of the Ammer. Beetles joined in, crawling by the hundreds through the heather. Many foundered in the snowfields or drowned in the icy pools, but the rest moved on tirelessly, sometimes climbing over the bodies of the dying ones. A black cloud of bats poured out of a crack in the rock face and fluttered excitedly over the valley. Cows lowed in their barns, and horses whinnied and pounded the walls of their stables with their hooves.

One last time the eagle circled over the Ammer Valley, then it flew away with a warning cry.

The mountain was awakening, and the animals sensed it.

Magdalena wiped the dirt of the road from her brow and looked down into the gorge, where the raging Ammer made its way between the rocks.

Four hours ago she'd set out from Schongau at a fast pace and she had not yet paused. Several wagons had passed her, but she hadn't asked any of the drivers for a ride. Local wagon drivers were engaged on the portion of the trip from Schongau to the gorge in Echelsbach, and Magdalena felt the danger of being recognized by one of them was too great. In addition, she was fearful that the burgomaster Matthäus Buchner might have sent out guards to patrol the road. Once, a horseman clad in black had dashed past her, and she was afraid she'd been discovered. For that reason Magdalena had kept her disguise as an old woman and had moved along quickly with her headscarf and basket. A half-hour ago she'd passed the monastery at Rottenbuch and had thus made it about halfway.

She was feeling slightly faint and had to hold on to the cattle fence separating the roadway from the deep gorge and the river that flowed almost two hundred feet below. She'd already missed her menstrual period three times, and this forced march was certainly a risk for her pregnancy, but she had no choice. Her trip to Oberammergau was perhaps her last chance to save Barbara from the torture chamber. She took a long drink of water from the leather pouch she kept in her basket, then started down into the valley.

Down below she saw the bridge spanning the Ammer. The Echelsbach Gorge was the only way across the raging river for miles around. Farmers in the area earned a good living assisting the wagons entering and leaving the gorge. On the other side Magdalena saw three wagons being pulled up the steep road by a half-dozen horses each. On her side, a few donkeys trotted calmly down the winding road. Each of them wore a hundred-pound salt ring around its neck, and a farmer urged them on with shouts and a whip. One of the restive donkeys kicked, stumbled, and nearly fell into the river. Once again, a numb feeling came over Magdalena as she looked down at the rushing waters. Her mouth was dry even though she'd had some water just a few minutes ago.

After a few sharp curves, she'd finally reached the bottom of the gorge and faced the rickety wooden bridge leading to the other side. It was rotted and old, and it groaned when the wagons rumbled over it one by one. Magdalena hurried past the wagons to the other side and was climbing up out of the gorge when sickness suddenly hit her like a hammer. She broke out in a cold sweat and was just able to get behind a boulder, where she threw up what little breakfast she'd eaten. She stood up, pale and trembling, and at that very moment another wagon from Schongau drove past. In the coachbox sat a man Magdalena knew and really hadn't expected to see here.

It was the young wagon driver, Lukas Baumgartner, whose child she'd just helped bring into the world a few days ago. He appeared as surprised at this chance meeting as she was.

"Frau . . . Fronwieser," he stuttered in surprise and brought his wagon to a stop. "What are you doing here?"

"I need a few glass vials for our medicines," she replied, straightening up even though her feeling of nausea had not yet passed. "Unfortunately I can get them only from the merchant in Soyen. If I'd known you were coming this way I would have asked you to bring them back for me." She smiled amiably. Actually, she had no reason to fear that Lukas would betray her and report her to Buchner and his men. Nevertheless, just to be safe, she carefully avoided telling him where she was going.

"I was probably walking too fast, and my feet gave out on me down by the river," she said with a shrug. "Would you care to take me along?"

Lukas nodded, but Magdalena sensed it made him a bit uneasy.

"We'll have to wait for the farmers to hitch the extra draught horses to the front of my wagon, to get it up the hill," he said, "and that can take a while."

"I don't mind – I need a rest, anyway."

Magdalena sat down on a mossy rock and watched the men at work. She still felt a bit queasy and rubbed her belly. She was angry that she had to play such a dirty trick on her unborn child. Nonetheless, she took a deep breath and smiled amiably at the wagon driver, who turned away sullenly and continued hitching up the horses. Magdalena assumed that Lukas had a bad conscience because he really should be at home with his wife and newborn child. On the other hand, the poor fellow had to earn money for his family, and didn't he say he'd be coming into some money soon? Perhaps this load had something to do with the expected windfall he'd mentioned a few days ago.

When the horses were finally hitched up, Magdalena took a seat on the coachbox while Lukas walked alongside with the farmers and held the reins. Someone cracked a whip and the wagon rumbled forwards. Curiously Magdalena looked back at the flat cargo area behind her, where a few barrels were tied down. The ropes were tied loosely, and the barrels swayed back and forth precariously.

"What are you carrying?" she asked Lukas with a wink. "Hopefully nothing too heavy, or pretty soon it will all roll down into the Ammer."

"It's wine," he mumbled. "I'm taking it to Soyen." Grimly he pulled at the reins, as though the work were especially strenuous.

The farmers shouted, cursed, and whipped the strong draught horses, and finally they reached the top of the gorge and unhitched the animals. From here, Lukas's route took them over gently rolling hills, through a small town, and on to the village of Soyen. Lukas remained silent the whole time, and even when Magdalena inquired amiably about how his wife was doing, he was evasive.

What's got into him? she wondered. *The fellow is acting almost as if he had something to hide.*

Instinctively she reached under her bodice to make sure Jakob Schreevogl's letter was still there. Was Lukas working for Burgomaster Buchner perhaps? Was this his extra job – to be an informant? She glanced at him furtively, but the young wagon driver just stared straight ahead.

The first houses in Soyen now appeared in front of them. The quaint little village lay on an old trade route that led from Augsburg through Schongau all the way to Venice. In the north another road branched off to the salt road, so that the little town earned good money from the many travelling merchants, pilgrims, and wagon drivers. There were a handful of taverns, some blacksmiths, and also a well-supplied general store. Wheels of salt packed in cloth were for sale in an open barn. Some children were playing with spinning tops

on the wide, dusty main road; a boy threw a piece of horse dung at one
of the wagon drivers, who threatened him angrily with a clenched
fist. The clinking sounds from a nearby blacksmith shop echoed
through the entire village.

"You can let me out here," Magdalena said, pointing to the
general store. "And thanks very much."

Lukas Baumgartner stopped and let her off. With a brief nod he
said farewell, cracked the whip, and drove a bit past her. Magdalena
headed towards the general store but then ducked into a niche in
the side of a wall where she could keep an eye on the street. Lukas's
strange behaviour had made her curious. If he was really a spy for
the burgomaster, she'd have to learn more in order to avoid trouble.

The young wagon driver stopped in front of a tavern on the
right; over the entrance hung a metal sign depicting a two-headed
eagle. He tied up the horses alongside a fountain and quickly started
removing the ropes from the barrels. Magdalena assumed the wine
barrels were intended for the tavern and breathed a sigh of relief.
Everything appeared to be in order. As she was about to turn away,
though, something else attracted her attention.

Lukas Baumgartner took one of the barrels, lifted it up with both
arms, and took it into an alley alongside the tavern.

It took Magdalena a few moments to see what was actually so
strange. She stopped short.

How could Lukas lift the heavy wine barrel all by himself?

The barrel was more than waist high. If it really was filled with
wine, as Lukas had said earlier, it surely would have taken two men to
carry it, but the wagon driver had lifted the heavy drum as if it were
a basket of wheat. Now she realized why the barrels had bounced
around so much in the wagon. They were empty. But why had Lukas
lied?

He had just disappeared around the corner with another
barrel. Magdalena still felt a bit nauseated. She'd intended to have a

refreshing drink at the fountain and then continue her journey. Now she decided to wait a bit.

She slipped out of the recess in the wall, crossed the busy street, and followed Lukas. A narrow lane strewn with rubbish led between two houses to a shed whose door was wide open. Magdalena approached cautiously and peered inside. The building had evidently been a horse stable at one time, and there was a strong stench of horse manure inside and rotted harnesses still hung on nails in the wall. But the stalls once intended for horses now held dozens of wine barrels instead, to which Lukas added the one he was carrying. Then he went over to a corner, where a man was just emerging from a stairway that went down into a cellar. The man had a beard and was wearing the tall, bell-shaped Stopselhut that was traditional in the high Alps and Bavaria. When Magdalena saw him, a distant, buried memory suddenly stirred, but she was too excited to give it any further thought.

"Leave the other barrels on the wagon," the Tyrolean said in his harsh dialect. "The plan has changed. The situation is too hot right now. We'll make just one more delivery."

Visibly startled, Lukas turned to the man.

"What do you mean, the plan has changed?" he asked. "I was told—"

"Save your breath, little fellow," the Tyrolean interrupted. "You'll get your money, and the rest is none of your business. I've just learned that the Master has arrived."

"And what shall I tell my people?" Lukas moaned. "I'm doing this for the first time, and they'll think I failed."

"The Master will explain everything to you. He's over in the tavern now, paying the innkeeper so he'll keep his mouth shut. He'll be right back."

Magdalena was shocked.

He'll be right back . . .

Suddenly she heard footsteps behind her. She spun around, and someone gave her a violent slap in the face, and then something hit her hard on the back of the head. Her whole world turned dark, she fell, and the last thing she heard were the voices of the men hovering over her.

"Just how stupid are you?" someone said. "The bitch overheard us, and now she'll turn us in."

"No she won't," replied the Tyrolean calmly. "It would be best to just cut her throat right now. Dead people don't talk."

At that moment it occurred to Magdalena why the man speaking in the harsh Tyrolean dialect sounded so familiar.

It was late in the afternoon when Simon finally left the meadow on Laber Mountain. Before he left he sternly reminded Martin's mother again to leave the bandage on and to refrain from trying to help her son with magic spells or sacrificial gifts. He doubted that she really understood him. It was hard enough trying to eradicate superstition in Schongau; here in the mountains it seemed impossible.

The children followed him for a while, darting through the forest alongside the path like anxious little fawns, then Simon was alone. The descent was steep and often wet and mushy, and he had to watch carefully where he stepped. Nonetheless, he made good progress, and after about half an hour he had reached the Laine at the point where it plunged thunderously into the valley below.

Simon wiped the sweat from his brow and looked around. To his left, behind the mountains, lay Ettal Monastery, where his father-in-law was presumably still preparing for the torture the next morning. The Kofel that Martin's mother had spoken so much about rose up ahead.

The Kofel, and the legendary Döttenbichl where, in ancient times, people had been offered as sacrifices.

On a whim, Simon decided to hike the short distance to the other peak. The sun wouldn't set for a while, and he would have plenty of time later for his son. Besides, he was tempted by the chance to visit this apparently pre-Christian sacrificial site. Up to now, the oldest place he'd ever visited was the church of the Knights Templar in Altenstadt, near Schongau, where he and Jakob Kuisl had made a strange discovery some years ago. So he made a detour around Oberammergau and headed for the place the woman had pointed out. A rickety, rotted hanging bridge spanned the Ammer at this point, and beyond it there were meadows and, finally, directly at the foot of the Kofel, a green hill.

The accursed Döttenbichl, Simon thought.

In the twilight he could well imagine that sacrifices were made here in early times. The hill was cleared except for several oaks forming a small grove on the top. A number of moss-covered boulders were scattered around the base, and a beaten path wound its way up the short distance from the swampy meadow to the top. At the place where the path branched off from the main trail something lying in the grass caught Simon's eye.

It was a small circle of white pebbles with a few twigs protruding from the centre like the spokes of a wheel.

Simon remembered seeing such a marker at a roadside shrine during their trip to Oberammergau. Was this circle perhaps some sort of pagan symbol? The wagon driver had certainly acted very strangely. After his conversation with Martin's mother, Simon could well imagine there were people in this valley who believed there was power in pebbles and birch twigs.

After hesitating briefly, he started climbing the hill to get a closer look at the grove of trees. Earlier, Martin's mother had asserted that gifts were still left here for the spirits of the mountain, so there had to be an altar or something similar, and perhaps that would help explain the strange circle of stones. Simon quickened his steps and had soon reached the top and the grove of oaks. There was no altar to be seen, only a row of clefts in the rock about three feet deep and so narrow he could just barely get his hand inside. He stooped down and in fact discovered little sprigs of dried St John's wort and Easter roses in some of the clefts and even a stained copper bowl glittering in one of the deeper fissures.

Simon could not suppress a smile. These people really believed they could pacify the Kofel with their little gifts. On the other hand, were these sacrifices much different from the blessing of the Easter ham or the lights in the window celebrating the Feast of St Lucia in December? Did he really have a right to ridicule the faith of these people?

He was about to turn around when his foot struck something on the ground. There was a snapping sound, and something white emerged from under last autumn's dried oak leaves. With the tip of his boot he pushed the mouldy leaves aside and was startled to see that what he'd stepped on was a shoulder blade, actually nothing unusual in a forest. Judging by its size, Simon guessed it belonged to a goat or sheep, though it was not so much the bone that gave him pause, but rather what was adhering to it.

A scrap of cloth.

Surprised, he bent down and took a closer look at the bone and the scrap of cloth stuck to it. It had lost some of its colour but was still quite recognizable as clothing. He dropped the bone in disgust, knelt down, and examined the area.

In a rock crevice nearby he finally found what he was looking for.

There was a leg bone, apparently chewed on by wild animals, two upper arm bones, another shoulder blade, and, finally, a human skull.

A very small human skull.

What the woman up on the meadow had said to him flashed through his mind.

The Kofel is an evil man who now and then needs his sacrifices . . .

Was it possible that people were being offered up as sacrifices in this valley? Even children?

Once again Simon picked up the shoulder blade with the piece of cloth attached to it. It was impossible to say how long the bone had been lying there. Perhaps it had just recently been pulled out of the fissure by wild animals. Had it perhaps belonged to Markus or Marie, those children of whom Martin had been speaking in his delirium and who had disappeared without a trace in the mountains?

A dreadful suspicion rose in Simon's mind.

At that moment he heard the whinnying of a horse coming from the direction of the meadow. It sounded nearby, as if the rider had just turned into the path towards the Döttenbichl. Startled, Simon dropped the bone and ducked behind a large boulder, where, in the fading light, he could make out the shape of a rider clothed in black on a black horse. At the foot of the hill the man abruptly reined in his horse, dismounted, knelt in the grass, and inspected something on the ground.

Simon knew at once what it was. The man on horseback inspected the circle of stones and twigs that Simon had seen just moments earlier.

Then something strange occurred. The man did not mount his horse again, but led the animal some distance away to a small group of trees, evidently trying to make as little sound as possible. Did he intend to hide there? Simon held his breath in expectation and waited. And indeed, the man did not return. What in God's name was the meaning of this? *Who was he lying in wait for?*

Simon wondered if he should announce himself but decided against it. He was overcome with anxiety. The children's bones, the strange stone circle, the rider in black . . .

The black riders!

Hadn't Alois Mayer spoken of black riders prowling around the valley? He remembered now that, shortly before his arrival in

Oberammergau, he had seen such a rider – and now there was one very close by and behaving strangely.

He decided to descend the hill at once on the side opposite from the rider's hideout to avoid being seen.

As quietly as possible, Simon slipped from one boulder to the next, finally dashing down the hill so fast he got tangled in some raspberry bushes and ripped his clothes. He stumbled, fell, then struggled to his feet again and continued running, gasping for breath, until finally he had reached the hanging bridge. Only now did he feel relatively safe and slowed his pace. The rushing waters of the river calmed his nerves.

Simon shook his head. What had come over him? A strange rider and a pagan stone circle had scared him off like a little boy confronted by a ghost. But then he remembered the child's bones. They were genuine and, indeed, threatening.

Someone had buried the child's corpse in an unholy place.

Simon hurried across the bridge and turned right, towards Ettal. Peter would have to wait a bit longer for his goodnight story.

The medicus needed to visit his father-in-law that very night.

11

THE MOMENT JAKOB KUISL ENTERED THE TAVERN in Ettal, he could feel the hostile stares of the other guests. Conversations stopped, the laughter and singing died away, and everyone stared at him as if he were a ghost, a dangerous creature to be avoided at all costs. Finally they looked away, leaning over and whispering to each other for a while before turning back to their mundane conversations. But the mood remained subdued. People didn't like to drink when the hangman was sitting at the next table.

This behaviour was nothing new to Jakob; he'd seen it many times at taverns in Schongau. He'd hoped no one would recognize him here, but thanks to the brawl in the Oberammergau cemetery, he'd been recognized right away in the tavern. Many people, after looking into the eyes of this broad-shouldered colossus with the hook nose and grim gaze who was dressed in black from head to toe, crossed themselves or ran off. The gaze of a hangman was said to bring misfortune, if not death.

All afternoon Jakob had been sharpening, polishing, and wiping bloodstains from his torturing tools. The monotonous work always helped him think. What was going on in this valley? Who was behind all these strange events, these murders? Why had Xaver

Eyrl gone around secretively, distributing carved figurines to some residents of the village?

But what tormented Jakob the most was the expression on his son-in-law's face. During their last conversation, Simon had got a quick glimpse into Jakob's inner thoughts and had seen the truth. Yes, he had grown old and weak. His curiosity, sharpness of mind, and sense of justice – everything that had once driven the feared Schongau executioner – seemed to have faded away. Now all he wanted was peace and quiet. But – damn it! – what was wrong about just wanting to live life like everyone else? If he had to torture this Eyrl fellow to obtain it, then so be it. Jakob could feel that this fellow was some sort of troublemaker. He wasn't torturing an innocent man.

But is he really a murderer? Did he kill young Faistenmantel and Urban Gabler?

His inner voice had been troubling him more and more in the last few hours – and Jakob knew only one way to silence it.

A tall brown beer, or perhaps two.

The hangman finally put down his tools and went over to the monastery's tavern, where he now sat at a table in the corner, stuffing his pipe and waiting for the tavern keeper to bring him a tankard. It took a while, but finally a young maid approached him anxiously with a foaming mug. Jakob put it to his lips and emptied it in one gulp. It was good strong Märzen beer, and it helped clear his head. He sighed happily and pushed the mug back across the table to the barmaid, who was standing by, trembling. "One more," he said.

He drank the second beer more slowly as he puffed on his pipe, disappearing behind the clouds of smoke. After a while a degree of calmness came over him. But despite all these efforts, he still heard a voice in his head:

You're torturing an innocent man . . .

Jakob thought of the old midwife, Martha Stechlin, whom he'd had to torture more than ten years ago. Back then, he was convinced of her innocence and had set out to find the real culprit. His drive for justice kept moving him to postpone the torture again and again. And this time? This time his son-in-law had to help him torture a possibly innocent man. Jakob saw no way out.

It will take a miracle, he thought.

But clearly he attended church too rarely to expect that.

"So here you are! I've been looking for you everywhere."

A high-pitched, excited voice roused him from his musings. Jakob rubbed his eyes and through the clouds of smoke recognized Simon taking a seat at the table. The little medicus was completely out of breath. It looked like he'd run the entire way from Oberammergau.

"I've discovered something new," Simon told him in a muted voice, "something that has to do with our murders. Apparently children have been disappearing in this valley in the last few years, and it's quite possible someone killed them."

Jakob listened closely as his son-in-law told him about his conversation with Martin's mother, the strange discovery on the Döttenbichl, and the black rider who had appeared there so suddenly.

"The woodcutter Alois Mayer also mentioned children who had disappeared," Simon quickly added. "And the child's bones aren't the only thing. There's also a strange circle of stones there; I saw one like it when we arrived in the Ammer Valley. The black rider seemed to be very interested in it. We'd be a lot further along if we knew who's making these stone circles." He looked around cautiously and continued in an even softer voice. "On my way here I asked some farmers about it. Their behaviour was very suspicious – they avoided my questions, almost as if they were afraid. But I've no doubt they know about the stone circles."

"The secretiveness in this valley is really getting on my nerves," Jakob said. "Torturing that woodcarver, Eyrl, is more than I can take. I'm completely at a loss."

He took another gulp of the strong Märzen beer and tried to think clearly, but as so often recently, his thoughts blurred just as he thought he'd started to focus. Alcohol was a good friend, but it was also jealous and would tolerate no competition. Simon stared at him expectantly, as if thinking his father-in-law could solve all these riddles.

But this time, Jakob had no answer. "My mug is empty" was all he could say.

He held the mug up in the air and waved it in the direction of the bar, but the tavern keeper had vanished. Jakob finally noticed him by the front door, standing alongside Judge Johannes Rieger, who was clothed in black and had apparently just entered the monastery tavern. The tavern keeper was pointing to Jakob and Simon and whispering something to Rieger, who now, with a determined look on his face, headed for their table.

"I am an honoured guest of this tavern," he said in a sharp tone, "and I must tell you officially that we don't allow any dishonourable riffraff in here."

"But the work of a medicus is—" Simon started to say angrily.

Rieger waved him off and pointed at Jakob. "I am speaking not about you but about this man here. A hangman has no business in a monastery tavern. It's enough that I have to see him tomorrow morning during the questioning." Now, for the first time, Rieger looked Jakob right in the face. "Get out, scum," he ordered.

Jakob Kuisl closed his eyes briefly. It was so often like that – they made him do the dirty work and treated him like a dog. There was no end to it.

"Get out, I said," Rieger repeated in an even sharper voice. "Or must I call a guard?"

Slowly, almost as if in a trance, Jakob rose to his feet. His strong, sinewy fingers clenched the mug; he felt the cold earthenware against his skin and knew that if he exerted just a bit more force, the mug would shatter, just like the skull of the rat-faced judge. A wave of anger swept over him, he raised the mug, and . . .

At that moment there was a sound of something shattering nearby.

The tables shook and tottered back and forth, as if an invisible force were tugging at them, and then the first tankards fell to the floor, where the beer flowed out in sweet-smelling puddles. Jakob could feel the earth trembling under his feet. A beam in the ceiling came loose and crashed down on the bar. People ran around screaming, knelt down, prayed to God, or ran in a panic towards the exit. Simon had jumped up as well. The judge pulled up his robe and raced through the wild crowd as plaster fluttered down from the ceiling like snow.

Only Jakob had settled back down again comfortably, sitting at his place like a rock and staring at the empty mug in his hand – the same mug he was about to use moments ago to smash the judge's skull.

"An earthquake!" shouted Johannes Rieger, who was one of the first to make his way through the narrow exit. "God sent an earthquake. Move aside, make way for your judge."

A miracle, Jakob thought.

Then he pushed the mug away and started walking calmly towards the door while all around him the world seemed to be collapsing.

Simon rushed out into the square in front of the tavern, where some people were already standing, staring up at the Kofel, as if expecting it to give them an answer to this inexplicable catastrophe. It was almost dark, and a final pink glow of sunlight shone on the highest peaks. The tremors had passed as quickly as they had come, but Simon could hear women crying in fear and men cursing and praying loudly. Judging by what he could see in the dim light, however, no one was injured, and even though some shingles had come off rooftops, none of the buildings in the monastery had collapsed.

Simon couldn't help but think of Martin's mother, up in the Laber meadow, who had spoken of such an earthquake just that afternoon. Evidently her warning was correct – there had been omens that Simon also had noticed over in the Laine Valley. Though he was uninjured, he trembled all over and his pulse was racing. He'd never experienced anything like this. Back when he was at the university in Ingolstadt he'd read about how storms and winds raged in subterranean caves and chasms, thus setting off earthquakes. But who really knew why they happened? Now at least Simon could understand why ancient chronicles always spoke of earthquakes as the anger of God. It was as if the fist of the Creator Himself had shaken this valley.

"Why is the Kofel punishing us?" wailed an elderly farmer who had walked over from the stables, clinging uncertainly to his pitchfork. "What have we done wrong?"

The people standing around joined in his lament or continued mumbling their prayers. Simon also made a hasty sign of the cross. He didn't think an angry mountain had sent them this earthquake, but a bit of Christian piety couldn't hurt. A rafter in the tavern had fallen to the floor just a few steps from where he had been seated. He shuddered. If he had been running just a bit slower towards the exit, he'd be lying inside there now with a shattered skull.

And my son would have lost a parent, just as Martin's mother could lose her son . . .

Shocked, he suddenly remembered his son, who was probably lying in bed in Oberammergau. The quake had not been especially strong, but who could say whether any buildings in the neighbouring village might have collapsed.

"What blasphemous nonsense do I hear?" a loud voice suddenly cried out. "You ignorant oafs. It's not the Kofel but God who is punishing you and trying to lead you back on to the path of righteousness."

Simon turned to the side and saw the Ettal abbot running over the short distance from the monastery. Benedikt Eckart had spread out his arms as if he were about to ascend into the pulpit and preach. Alongside him, the judge clutched his walking stick and struggled to radiate the authority expected of his high office. Simon remembered how just a short while ago he'd pulled up his robes like an anxious old woman and fled from the tavern. In the meantime some of the monks had also gathered in the courtyard.

"Yes, God is angered because of your sins," the abbot continued accusingly. "For far too long He has looked down on this valley with compassion, but now He has raised His thundering voice!" As if to underline his point, the bells of the monastery began to ring at this moment and the monks fell to their knees and started to pray.

"Bad things have happened in the Ammer Valley because you have not prayed enough," Abbot Benedikt admonished them. "I'm telling you to go home and pray to God for forgiveness. We shall hold a mass tomorrow morning and ask the Lord to show mercy."

The people in front of the tavern seemed uncertain. They whispered and put their heads together, and finally the old farmer spoke up again.

"When I was a child, God was angry with us and made the earth tremble," he said anxiously. "Who can say we won't be surprised again in our beds by another quake?"

"There will be no more earthquakes," Johannes Rieger assured them, but his anxious gaze as he looked over at the walls of the monastery revealed he wasn't so sure.

"Uh . . . You can go home without concern, but this evening, each of you must say a few rosaries," the abbot added. "Just to be sure."

"Bah! What nonsense. When the earth shakes, it shakes. A man should make sure instead that his roof beams are solid, or perhaps when he's praying one will fall on his head and he'll be dead as a doornail, even if he is holding rosary beads in his hands!"

It was Jakob Kuisl who now appeared behind Simon. In contrast to the frantic people in the courtyard, the hangman appeared calm and composed. His composure seemed odd in this chaotic environment.

Now Johannes Rieger also had discovered the hangman and glared at him angrily. "Perhaps God is angry because we still haven't found the perpetrator of these two dreadful murders," he cried loudly, pointing at Jakob. "The Schongau secretary sent us his hangman, but neither he nor the venerable secretary has been able to find anything. Instead, they drink our beer. I wonder why we need help from outside our valley, and why the help of a dishonourable hangman? Haven't we always settled matters among ourselves?"

People grumbled and turned around to look at Simon and Jakob. A few of the farmers still held the pitchforks and hoes they'd been using in the fields, and they clenched them firmly now, as if they were halberds and spears.

"I think it's time to get out of here," Simon whispered to Jakob, "before they start looking for a scapegoat for the earthquake."

The hangman nodded. "For once you're right. There's no point wasting our time fighting with these fools."

Slowly they retreated. Some of the farmers followed them, their grim faces full of menace, but when Jakob stared back at them just as menacingly the men finally stopped and let them leave. They passed the open gate to the monastery, inside which there seemed to be a great commotion.

Men ran around everywhere. Some of the monks held torches and were checking the buildings one by one for damage. Suddenly loud warning shouts could be heard from the tavern, and Simon stopped on seeing a fiery glimmer coming from one of the houses. An anxious servant had evidently left a lantern in one of the sheds, and it had fallen over. Thick smoke poured out of a window and soon flames were rising from the roof. A chain of men quickly assembled to carry buckets of water from a nearby well.

Simon hesitated. He really wanted to get back to Oberammergau as soon as possible to see if Peter was all right, but on the other hand, such a fire was very dangerous and demanded the services of every single man. If the fire couldn't be stopped in time, the whole village could go up in flames. Or the monastery.

Simon was still agonizing over what to do when Jakob came running past him through the gate and grabbed several buckets. A few men at the well nodded their thanks.

When a fire breaks out, even the hangman is much sought after, Simon thought, hurrying after his father-in-law. Simon's dear friend Georg Kaiser would surely take care of Peter. Lives were in danger here.

Filling the buckets and passing them down the line actually calmed Simon's nerves. The church bells were still ringing in the steeple, and a muted echo came back from the rock faces of the mountains. It appeared that the fire could be brought under control if everyone joined in the effort.

Simon had just taken another bucket of water from the well when he caught sight of someone up on the roof of the tavern. The man was running along the ridge towards the northeast, the side of the monastery closest to the mountains, and for a brief moment Simon had a good view of him in the glow from the fire. He looked big and strong and his clothing was soiled and torn . . .

And he had fiery red hair.

"Xaver Eyrl!" Simon gasped, tapping his father-in-law on the shoulder. Surreptitiously he pointed up to direct the hangman's attention to the man running along the roof. Jakob just nodded silently and looked around cautiously, but evidently no one else had seen the fugitive.

"Perhaps the door to the dungeon collapsed," Simon whispered. "Or the guards with him fled in a panic when the earthquake hit."

"Perhaps he even set the fire himself in order to flee in the commotion," Jakob grumbled.

"What should we do now?"

"What should we do?" A broad grin appeared on Jakob's face and he started to snort. After a while Simon realized that the hangman was laughing.

"Nothing, of course, you idiot," the hangman said after a while. "Neither of us wanted to torture him, and now we're spared that by divine providence." His face turned serious as he continued in a solemn tone: "The Lord God has sent us a miracle. We should accept that gratefully and let Eyrl go."

Simon stared at Jakob as if he were a ghost. He'd never heard his father-in-law speak like this.

"Since when do you believe in miracles?" he asked in astonishment. "You used to say the holy rosary was just nonsense."

"Oh, just forget it." All of Jakob's solemnity vanished. "Whether or not it's a miracle, just let the fellow go. Tomorrow I swear we'll start figuring out what's going on with your stone circles, the vanished children, and all the other stories. We'll figure out what's at the bottom of this accursed riddle, or my name's not Jakob Kuisl." He stared at his son-in-law. "And don't ask me ever again if I believe in miracles or you'll be sorry."

The hangman ran with four buckets at once and threw them on the flames with a loud splash.

It was almost three more hours before Simon finally got to his son's bedside.

Actually, he'd hoped to find Peter still wide awake, as he'd wanted to apologize for being so rude to him that day in the bathhouse. It wasn't the boy's fault that this valley had gone crazy. He wished he'd kept the promise he'd made that afternoon to tell his son a bedtime story. But Peter was already fast asleep. His breathing was regular, but his pale face looked even more serious than it did when he was awake. Simon was tempted to lie down beside him – he was so tired, so dreadfully tired. The whole day had been one long nightmare. First the hallucinations of the boy whose leg he'd amputated, then the earthquake and the fire at the monastery in Ettal.

He gently stroked his son's cheek as he thought about the events of the day. They had finally got the fire under control, largely because of Jakob's help. Simon hadn't dared to ask his father-in-law again about his solemn words, but something in his behaviour had seemed to change. Evidently the hangman really regarded Eyrl's escape as divine intervention.

He's just getting old, thought Simon. *Perhaps he'll still find his way to religion.*

But no matter how hard he tried, he couldn't imagine the Schongau hangman in a hair shirt, flagellating himself, a pious smile on his lips.

He heard a creaking sound, turned around, and saw Georg Kaiser, stooping to enter the low-ceilinged attic. Simon had learned from his friend that the quake was felt in Oberammergau as well. A few windows had broken and many old people had sought protection in the village church, where the priest had sung and prayed with them. Here, too, the quake had been of short duration, but people were already beginning to describe it in the blackest possible tones.

Georg smiled at Simon and pointed to Peter with a vague nod of his head. "You love him very much, don't you?" he said softly. "You can be proud of him. He's a clever lad and will amount to something."

"I should have been with him during the earthquake," Simon whispered.

"He was brave and didn't cry, if that's what you mean. My maid, dear old Anni, made some hot milk for him, and he asked about you a few times, but I told him you surely were detained by work. Then he fell asleep right away." Kaiser shrugged and seemed just as tired and overwrought as Simon. He was still suffering from his hacking cough.

"It really seems like this valley is under an evil spell," said Simon, shaking his head. "There are so many stories and legends, and they all seem to have something to do with these strange events and murders. Now even the earth is shuddering."

Kaiser gave a dry laugh. "You're as bad as the superstitious old women in the village. They take everything that happens and spin it into a legend, though it rarely has anything to do with them. In any case, I'm curious what this earthquake means for our Passion play. It looks like the Lord God is directing the play this time. There surely will be a meeting tomorrow about where we go from here." He ducked to go through the doorway. "Well, I'll gladly accept whatever they decide – then maybe I won't have to struggle with a group of untalented farmers and woodcarvers. I have enough to do, anyway."

Coughing softly, he shuffled out the door. A short time later Simon heard the door to the main room close and a chair scrape across the floor. Evidently Kaiser still had a lot of work to do on the new text for the play, though perhaps this work was no longer necessary, as God had now sent another sign of his displeasure.

One last time, Simon looked out the window to check for fire here as there had been in Ettal, but all was quiet and dark outside. He was about to turn away when he noticed a flash of light up in the mountains near the Kofel. Could there be someone up there at this hour? He couldn't help but think of the Venetians – the little men said to wear hoods down over their faces, carrying lighted lanterns in their hands and picks over their shoulders, who came to search for treasure in the mountains.

So many stories . . .

No, surely it was just a single woodsman sitting by a fire to warm himself. It must be rather lonely up there in the mountains. On the other hand, you were far away from trouble and human suffering.

Shivering, Simon closed the shutters and looked at his son, who lay sleeping in his bed like an angel. Once this was all over, he'd have lots to make up for – to him, but also to Paul and Magdalena, who were waiting for him in Schongau.

Simon kissed his son's forehead, then he left for his lodgings.

Once outside he could hear the steady scratching of Georg Kaiser's quill pen coming from a lighted room above.

12

ACCORDING TO THE MEDICUS, THERE WERE A half-dozen broken church windows, five runaway cows, and three cases of old women fainting, and a number of shingles fell from the roof – but no severe consequences. Ah yes, and farmer Pärtl's old barn collapsed, but he had been planning to tear that down, anyway." Konrad Faistenmantel looked up from the list he held in his hands and turned to the other council members seated with him at a table in the Schwabenwirt tavern. It was early in the morning, but each of the men already had a mug of strong Märzen beer in front of him.

"All in all, we've been pretty lucky," the Oberammergau council chairman continued. "Also, the fire over in the monastery was extinguished."

"Still, it's a sign from God," mumbled the old miller, Augustin Sprenger. "First a crucifixion, then what looks like a martyr's death, and now an earthquake. God is angry at us, and we all know why."

"What nonsense, Augustin." Faistenmantel took a long drink then slammed his mug back down on the table. "It was an earthquake – that's all there is to it. My father, God bless his soul, told me about earthquakes, that they just happen for no special reason, so don't start on again with how we shouldn't have rescheduled the Passion play."

"'*We*'?" Sprenger practically spat out his reply to the council chairman. "*You* wanted to have the play four years early, because all you think about is making money!"

With a threatening look, Faistenmantel got up from his seat. "How dare you . . ."

"Silence!" cried Johannes Rieger, the Ammergau judge, who was accustomed to giving orders. "If you want to fight, please wait till the next village fair. This is an official meeting." He glared sternly at the two adversaries. "The majority of the council has decided in favour of advancing the schedule of the Passion play, and now only the council can decide our further course of action. The views of each individual on this council have always been respected." He sighed. "Unfortunately. But that's the law – so?" Rieger looked all around, awaiting a reply. "Who's in favour of our performing the Passion play despite the recent events?"

The members of the council began to discuss the issue quietly among themselves. Simon sat with Georg Kaiser at the far corner of the large table, anxiously awaiting the result of the vote. Kaiser had asked him to come along again, as the council wanted a report on any possible injuries during the earthquake, but Simon got the impression his friend was also happy to have an enlightened soul at his side. The earthquake had made people in the village even more suspicious of one another.

After a while, the judge pounded the floor with his walking stick. "And how does the council decide? Those in favour of performing the Passion play this Pentecost, raise your hands."

Konrad Faistenmantel agreed, as well as the vice council chairman, Franz Würmseer, who had just returned from a trip on the road. Old Augustin Sprenger and the sculpture painter Adam Göbl, on the other hand, leaned back and folded their arms over their chests defiantly. Now all eyes were on Sebastian Sailer, manager of the Ballenhaus. Given the death of the sixth council member, Urban Gabler, everything now depended on his vote. Usually very congenial, Sailer was now nervous, pale, and unshaven, and he fumbled with his collar as if he felt too hot.

"What's wrong, Sebastian?" Faistenmantel asked. "You said yourself that the Passion play makes good money for us. If we want to revive the old trade route, the play is our only chance, and it must be now, not in four years."

"You are right," Sailer replied softly, "but events recently have been, uh . . . very strange. Perhaps there's something to the idea that God is angered. Urban also—"

"Urban was a superstitious fool," snarled Würmseer. "One mustn't speak ill of the dead, but for Urban if there were two hailstorms in June, one after the other, that was a sign from God." Then in a more soothing tone: "We'll find his killer, I promise you, Sebastian. But now get hold of yourself and don't let us down. The future of the village is at stake."

"If I may say something . . ." Kaiser spoke up cautiously. He was allowed to speak even though he was a non-voting member of the council. "We are behind schedule in our rehearsals. Actually, we were supposed to have one today, but nothing came of it. The actors lack confidence when they read their lines, and I'm not so sure that—"

"The delays are also caused by your revising the text almost every day," Würmseer interrupted. "I still don't know exactly what my Caiaphas is supposed to say when Judas appears before the council of the Jewish high priests. Perhaps it's easier for you if the play is put off!"

"Don't forget that I am first of all the schoolmaster in the village," Kaiser answered between clenched teeth. "If this work demands more of me than expected, that's certainly because of your son, who can't learn simple multiplication!"

Würmseer leaned his massive body across the table and waved his finger in Kaiser's face. "Watch what you say, teacher. Who are you going to get your firewood from, eh? Maybe from the worthless labourers' children you like so much?"

"Silence!" Rieger ordered, banging his walking stick on the table. "Can't we just *once* have a meeting without fighting with each other? We're off topic." He looked at Sailer impatiently. "So what is your decision? For or against the Passion play?"

Sailer swallowed hard and Simon noticed how angrily Würmseer was looking at the young administrator. "Until now, you've only been Judas in the play," Würmseer said so softly that it was almost inaudible. "Take care that you don't really become one."

Trembling, Sailer raised his hand.

"Then the matter is settled," the judge said with relief, "and the play will be performed at Pentecost. But now, to another matter." His face darkened. "I've just learned from the abbot of Ettal that Eyrl escaped from the dungeon yesterday, evidently taking advantage of the chaos after the earthquake."

There was angry murmuring around the table. The men took a few deep gulps of beer, as if they could quench their anger along with their thirst.

"How is that possible?" Faistenmantel finally asked. "This pompous Schongau secretary comes to our valley with soldiers and an executioner, and they just let the prisoner get away?"

"That's exactly the way I feel," the judge replied. "It's a disgrace – Eyrl would surely have confessed today. That's what you get when a Schongauer meddles in our laws. Well, there's one thing good about it. Eyrl's escape will certainly convince the elector that Master Lechner is not capable of taking jurisdiction over our beautiful Ammergau."

"Xaver Eyrl is no doubt still out there somewhere," said Faistenmantel gloomily. "Who knows which of us he will crucify or slit open next? In any case, we should send out all available men to hunt him down. Eyrl won't escape us."

Simon frowned. Until just recently, Faistenmantel was firmly convinced that one of the Göbls had killed his son. Evidently the council chairman was quick to change his opinion – as long as the play was performed soon.

"Don't be so sure that Red Xaver will run right into our net," said Würmseer, turning to Faistenmantel. "The fellow has a lot of cronies among the labourers and tramps in the valley. If he takes cover in one of their miserable hovels, it will be difficult." Then he turned to the judge. "Were you able to speak to the abbot about finally doing something about this riffraff?"

Rieger nodded. "His Excellency is thinking of expelling at least some of the labourers by force, if necessary."

"If he doesn't, we'll have to take the matter into our own hands," Würmseer growled. "For ages we've lived here as a proud people. We drove off the Romans, and after them so many other intruders. We've asserted our rights against every feudal lord, and we won't let ourselves be squeezed out by these homeless vagabonds. The valley is full."

Johannes Rieger leaned forwards and shook his finger. "Even though I can understand your anger, Würmseer, beware of taking the law into your own hands. The ruler in this district is still the abbot of Ettal."

"Ha! Or the Schongau secretary," Faistenmantel sneered. "At present in Oberammergau we're not quite sure."

A bit later, Simon and Georg Kaiser were standing alone outside the tavern. The meeting had ended without any further action, and all the men had returned to their work. At least they had agreed on a few extra rehearsals for the Passion play.

"I would have been quite happy if we'd just cancelled the play," Kaiser said with a sigh. "Würmseer is right – I have quite a lot going on at present, and in addition there's this dreadful cough."

As if to prove it, he was shaken by a new fit of coughing, and Simon looked at him with concern.

"Shall I give you a few herbs?" he asked. "Thyme, masterwort, or—"

Kaiser waved him off. "Don't bother, I'm going to be all right." He laughed. "Tell me instead the horror stories you heard in the village yesterday. You look so glum – like you've had a bad dream."

"For good reason," Simon replied. "It's not every day that you come across children's skeletons."

"Children's skeletons?" Kaiser quickly turned serious again. "What do you mean?"

Simon told him of his horrible discovery on the Döttenbichl, the circles of stones, and the black rider. After the earthquake the day before, things had happened so fast he was only just now getting around to telling Kaiser about it.

"That sounds very strange indeed," Kaiser said finally, apparently trying to figure out what it all meant. After a long silence he continued. "Martin's mother was right, by the way. Markus and Marie disappeared several years ago, though that was before I came to Oberammergau." He lowered his voice. "There are people who say their disappearance had something to do with the hatred of the foreign workers. Both children came from poor families. Perhaps they were caught stealing and quickly put away."

"You mean they were sacrificed, the way the pagans used to do?" Simon gasped.

"Well, these stone circles certainly are not Christian, and you've just heard yourself from the mouth of Franz Würmseer how great the hatred is for foreigners and immigrants."

Simon scratched his head. "It's possible the bones are older and have nothing to do with the two children. It's hard to say – I only got a brief look at them. In any case they deserve a Christian burial."

"I'd wait a while before doing that," Kaiser warned him. "People are so riled up now I could imagine Würmseer trying to blame the labourers for those murders."

"You're probably right. There's no problem in waiting a few days." Simon shuddered. "Who would do something like that . . . kill little children? Do you really think they were sacrificed?"

Kaiser shrugged. "I have no idea. Perhaps you've infected me with your horror stories. I no longer know what to believe . . ." He paused and looked disturbed.

"What's the matter?" Simon asked.

"Well, I'm thinking about the sword that was supposedly used to kill Gabler. It may be a coincidence, but I was looking around last night in the chest that holds the props for the play. There's the scene on the Mount of Olives in which Peter cuts an ear off the servant of the high priest. We use a real sword for that scene in the play – it looks better than those painted swords made of scrap wood. It's rather old and rusty, but for our purposes it's good enough." He cleared his throat. "That sword . . . well, it's missing."

Simon stared in disbelief. "Do you think someone took the sword from the chest of props and killed Gabler with it?"

Kaiser simply shrugged. "During rehearsals all the players have access to the chest. Anyone could have taken it."

"But . . . why didn't you mention that in the meeting?"

"Don't you understand?" Kaiser lowered his voice. "Because it could have been *any* of them. Every member of the council has a part in the play, and any of them could be the murderer – Faistenmantel, Sailer, old Sprenger, Franz Würmseer . . ."

"Everyone except Xaver Eyrl," Simon mused, "the one they all suspect."

Kaiser nodded. "I thought it best the murderer didn't know about my discovery, at least not for now. I'm only the village schoolteacher." He smiled mischievously. "In any case, I've got to go over to the school. My assistant, Hannes, has been teaching the children while I was at the meeting. They don't especially like him, but at least he maintains discipline." He patted Simon on the shoulder and left.

Simon remained standing there a long time, thinking about what Kaiser had just said.

Any of them could be the murderer . . .

Perhaps there was some connection between these ghastly discoveries and the recent murders.

Still deep in thought, Simon finally started back to the bathhouse. Once again he wondered if it had been a good idea to send Peter to the Oberammergau school.

Magdalena opened her eyes and was blind.

She was seized with panic, tried to move, but couldn't do that either. Was she dead? Was this what purgatory looked like? If so, then purgatory had a strong odour of wine. Carefully she stretched out her fingers and felt damp wood. Her back ached because she was squeezed into some kind of container.

A barrel. They shoved me inside one of the wine barrels!

Her relief at knowing she wasn't dead yet gave way to anxiety about what lay ahead. Slowly, her memory returned. In Soyen, she'd followed Lukas Baumgartner into an old stable with empty barrels standing all around. There was someone else, evidently a man from Tyrol, inside, and then suddenly a third man came up from behind her and struck her down. Was he the Master that the two others had been speaking of? The Tyrolean man had insisted they kill her, so the fact that she was still alive was promising.

Her head was pounding as hard as if she had drunk all the wine in the barrel. The more she thought about it, the worse the pain became. In addition, she had no idea how long she'd been there – for an hour, or many?

Magdalena tried to get control of her breathing and calculate her chance of survival. Clearly she was on to something, or someone, and was going to be eliminated for knowing too much, but why hadn't they killed her already?

Because they don't want to get their hands dirty, she realized. *They're just going to let me suffocate in here and rot away.*

Magdalena shouted so loud her ears rang, but she couldn't hear anything outside. Again she groped around the interior of the barrel to see if she could find a crack in the staves or a thin spot she could break through, but all she could feel was wet wood and some sort of sand that stuck to her fingers.

Desperate, she started rocking violently back and forth and actually made the barrel totter and, after a while, tip over. It fell with a loud crash. She felt the impact all through her body, but the barrel didn't break as she had hoped. Now she tumbled around inside several times as the barrel began to roll, then it crashed against some obstacle, where it came to rest.

"Hey! What's going on there?"

She could hear a muffled voice, then a door squeaking as it was opened. Her heart was pounding. Was it a possible rescuer? Was she imprisoned in the cellar of the tavern, and had the innkeeper come to see what was going on?

"Help!" she cried at the top of her voice. "Help! I'm inside here, in the barrel. Please . . ."

She heard a malicious laugh, which made her shudder, as she knew now it was no rescuer but one of her tormenters.

"Well, just look at that," said the man with the Tyrolean accent. "The woman actually knocked over the barrel. I thought she'd suffocate and spare us the rest, but now we must actually do something. Lukas!"

Someone sighed deeply as footsteps approached, and Magdalena heard someone speaking, softly and in an anxious tone – it was the voice of young Lukas Baumgartner.

"This isn't what we meant to do. We only said we'll keep her here and—"

"If you'd paid better attention yesterday to who was following you, we wouldn't be in this mess, young fellow," the Tyrolean interrupted. "You heard what the Master from Oberammergau said. She saw us, and so we have to get rid of her. The barrel is the best solution."

Magdalena froze. The Tyrolean had just said she'd followed Lukas *yesterday*. Had she really been unconscious all night? Perhaps the men had drugged her to keep her silent for a bit longer.

"I know the woman," Lukas responded hesitantly. "She's the wife of the Schongau medicus, the daughter of the executioner."

"Ha! Then hardly anyone except her father will miss her." The Tyrolean gave a dirty, throaty laugh. "I'll tell you what we're going to do," he continued. "We'll put this barrel in the wagon along with the others being shipped to Schongau, and down by the Echelsbach Gorge we will unfortunately lose it. It will fall into the Ammer and our beautiful hangman's daughter will then be just another unfortunate suicide, a poor, lovesick girl who hanged herself and was tossed into the river. That happens all the time, and no one will be suspicious."

Magdalena was shocked. In fact, people who killed themselves were often stuffed in a barrel that was nailed shut and thrown into the river. Their corpses brought bad luck, and nobody wanted to bury them. Magdalena once saw such a mangled cadaver that had been washed down the river from Füssen and was washed ashore in Schongau, where the barrel split apart. For many long nights she had not been able to get the sight out of her mind.

"Lukas!" she shouted anxiously. "You can't let that happen. I helped birth your children, I—"

"Hold your tongue, woman," the Tyrolean snarled, "or I'll cut your head off right now."

Magdalena fell silent, and for a while all she could hear was Lukas sobbing softly.

"Hmm, she's alive and kicking," the Tyrolean said. "That could be a problem when we pass through Soyen. Damn, why couldn't she have just stayed unconscious and suffocated? Now we'll have to get our hands dirty, after all. I really don't want to open this damned wine barrel again and . . ." He hesitated. Finally he let out a loud laugh. "Ha! I've got it. I know what we'll do. What a beautiful way to die. Count yourself lucky, girl." Magdalena heard a rumbling, then someone groaning with exertion, then she felt the barrel being set upright again. Something popped and finally a tiny ray of light shone in from the top of the barrel.

The Tyrolean had opened the bunghole.

Shortly after that, a cold liquid poured in and down over her head. She almost passed out from the strong odour of alcohol.

"Drink up, girl, drink up!" the Tyrolean bellowed. "Swim in the wine until it comes out your ears."

Magdalena pounded her fists against the staves of the barrel as it slowly filled with wine.

When Simon returned to the bathhouse, Jakob was already sitting at the table and smoking his long-stemmed pipe. The hangman had spent the night in the old bathhouse owner's room and had been waiting impatiently for the arrival of his son-in-law. In contrast to Simon, Jakob evidently had no problem sleeping in the bed of someone recently deceased. He appeared well rested and ready to get to work.

"It's about time," he grumbled. "I thought you'd never stop talking back at the tavern. What do you do all day? Drink?"

"Eh, there were some things to discuss with the council because of the earthquake, and also the play," Simon responded, looking a bit surprised. He hadn't expected to find Jakob here. "Shouldn't you be with Lechner about now?" he added.

Kuisl waved him off and grinned. "We had a very quick meeting. Lechner is about to have a fit because of Eyrl. His only possible suspect has got away, and Lechner suspects the abbot and the judge let Eyrl out just to get back at him."

"Hmm. This suspicion is not completely unjustified, is it?" replied Simon. "After all, the abbot is doing everything he can to keep Lechner from getting jurisdiction over the valley."

"You may be right, but Eyrl isn't our murderer anyway."

Simon smiled. "Why are you so sure? Yesterday you seemed to be singing a different tune."

"Forget about what I said yesterday." His pipe had almost gone out and he drew on it morosely. Nevertheless, Simon thought he seemed extremely alert.

"Xaver Eyrl did not murder Dominik Faistenmantel," Jakob continued. "They were good friends. Although it's possible he killed Urban Gabler."

"I don't think that is the case," Simon said. "There's some new evidence that Gabler's killer was one of the actors in the play." He told his father-in-law about the missing sword from the chest holding the props.

"Why didn't those idiots use a wooden sword for their play? That wouldn't have made such a mess!" Jakob grinned. "But your news basically confirms my suspicions. The murderer comes from Oberammergau, he's one of the actors, and perhaps even a member of the council. Nevertheless, Lechner sent his soldiers off into the forests and mountains to find Eyrl. That will take a long time, and these pimply-faced city guards will just get lost in the woods."

"Faistenmantel also intends to send citizens out. That will be a wild chase." Simon sighed and sat down at the table next to Jakob. "I really have no idea what to believe any more in this valley. My head is spinning with all the weird stories."

"Then let's bring you back down to earth. While you were drinking in the tavern, I've been thinking." Jakob reached into the soiled canvas pouch on the bench and took out a few simple wooden figurines. They all represented shepherds.

"Where did you get those?" Simon asked in surprise.

"Bought them from a travelling salesman for a few kreuzers," Jakob answered curtly. "They are poorly made and partly broken, but they'll help us get our thoughts together."

Simon watched as the hangman cleared the table and put all the figurines in a corner. In contrast to their last meeting, his father-in-law now seemed quite focused.

Simon couldn't help wondering if this had anything to do with Jakob's epiphany the night before. *He's changed, somehow,* he thought. *But whatever it was, now he's back to his old self, thank God.*

"That's Xaver Eyrl," Jakob said, pushing a worn figurine to the other side of the table. "An outcast, the black sheep in town. Old Faistenmantel ruined Eyrl's family. Xaver had to leave Oberammergau, comes back. and distributes little carved figurines to some people in town – but not just any figurine, only the Pharisees."

"We know that already," Simon interjected.

"Shut your mouth, sonny boy, I'm not finished yet." He looked at Simon impatiently. "You ought to read your Bible more, then you'd know that Pharisees have long been considered the embodiment of hypocrisy. The Hebrew scribes made sure the laws were enforced but they didn't live by them themselves." The hangman shook his finger like a schoolmaster. "That's why the Bible tells us that if your justice is not far greater than that of the scribes and Pharisees, you will not enter the Kingdom of Heaven."

Simon couldn't suppress a smile. "I had no idea you were so well versed in the Bible, hangman."

This time Jakob just gave him a stern look and continued. "Eyrl is distributing these figurines to people because he wants to tell them something. He's saying they are god-damned hypocrites. And that explains also the inscription on the bottom of the statuette – *ET TU. You, too, are a hypocrite*, he's saying."

"But why are they hypocrites?" Simon asked. He looked over at the figurine of the Pharisee with its toga and headdress that the old bathhouse operator, Landes, had received after his death. It still stood on a shelf alongside the mummy powder and pickled salamanders.

"Because they've all done something wrong. Urban Gabler, old Landes, Faistenmantel . . ." Jakob placed three more carved figurines next to the one of Xaver Eyrl. "They all received a Pharisee from Xaver."

"But young Dominik Faistenmantel—"

"Exactly, clever lad." Jakob interrupted Simon and nodded impatiently. "He evidently did not receive one, or at least if he did, we haven't found it yet. If I execute someone so cruelly, on the cross, that means I want to show the world something. Believe me, if Eyrl had murdered Dominik Faistenmantel, he would have placed the figurine right alongside the cross. There was none there, and that's why I don't think Red Xaver is our murderer."

"But . . . who is?" Simon asked.

"Well, let's look at the other townsfolk." Jakob tapped his huge hooked nose. "My beak tells me again that it's someone who lives here in town, someone with a huge grudge. It couldn't be anyone from out of town. Someone is trying to say: this is what you're in for if you cross swords with me." Jakob pulled a few figurines from the pouch and held them up, one by one. "This one is Hans Göbl, our first suspect. He's jealous of Dominik because of his role in the play. But would he nail him to the cross just for that? I don't know . . ." He pushed the figurine away to the side of the table. "Likewise, we can probably rule out the victim's own father, even if he wasn't especially fond of his son and has been cold and behaving oddly. But what about all the others? A member of the council, for example?" Jakob took a long puff on his pipe and studied the figurines through the smoke.

"Isn't it possible that Dominik knew something about shady dealings here in the valley?" he finally mused, almost as if he were speaking to himself. "Maybe he learned of it from his friend Xaver? And for that reason they had to silence him, and do it in such a ghastly fashion that everyone would know what would be in store for them if they talked?"

"Hmm. So a troublesome person who knows too much has to be eliminated." Simon scratched his head. "Before his death, Urban Gabler must have been a very anxious man. Perhaps he was about to talk as well . . ."

"And he had to be eliminated as well, just like pretty-boy Dominik. But by whom?" Jakob set down an especially rough-cut figurine in the middle of the table. "Here's your man. The mystery man from Oberammergau, a man who wants to keep something hidden, something that now only Eyrl knows." Lost in thought, he placed Eyrl's figurine alongside the other in the middle of the table. "We must find Eyrl before our mystery man finds him and kills him, too. So, as fast as we can, let's—"

He stopped short on hearing a soft scratching against the closed shutters. Jakob cast a wary glance at Simon and continued speaking calmly as he slowly moved towards the window. "Hmm. Let's go for a quick walk in the mountains and see what's going on there. Who knows, perhaps we'll find a shy deer trying to hide from us and . . . *Caught you!*" He threw open the shutter and reached down. There was a cry of surprise, then someone was wriggling around in Jakob's huge hands.

Someone Simon knew all too well.

"Peter!" he cried out in surprise. "What are you doing at the window? Were you eavesdropping?"

"Of course he was," Jakob growled, yanking the boy into the room. He stared angrily at his grandson, still holding him by the scruff of his neck about a foot above the floor. "If your father doesn't give you a good beating for that, I'll be glad to."

Peter struggled to hold back his tears. "I just wanted to talk to Father," he wailed. "When I heard voices behind the shutter, at first I didn't know who it was, so I did listen a bit."

"Let him go now," Simon pleaded with his father-in-law. More than anything, he was glad to see Peter again. He still had a bad conscience for having neglected his son the last two days. Jakob set Peter down on the bench roughly.

"Aren't you supposed to be in school?" Simon asked the boy, shaking his finger. "I hope you're not skipping your classes."

Peter shook his head. "School was over early today. Poxhannes, the schoolmaster's assistant, needs the workers' children to help him do something in the forest. The rest of us were given homework, but all we have to do is memorize a few Bible verses," he said, shrugging. "I finished that long ago."

"And then you thought you'd come and listen at our door," Jakob grumbled.

"I really just wanted to see Father," Peter replied, teary-eyed.

Simon walked over to Peter and hugged him. "Of course," he said in a soothing voice. "And I'm glad you're here. Just the same, you must keep to yourself whatever you heard here. I don't want you dragged into this, too."

Peter nodded earnestly. "I only heard that you're looking for someone in the village . . . a murderer . . . and that you still don't know who it is."

Simon ran his hands through Peter's hair. "That's correct, and the biggest favour you can do for us is to let us figure it out."

"Perhaps I can help," Peter said.

"And how would you do that?" Simon smiled. "Did you see the murderer with your own eyes, hmm? Or perhaps one of those dwarfs people say are lurking around here making trouble?"

"No, not that." Peter looked down in embarrassment. "I wanted to tell you yesterday, but then you sent me away, and at night there was that awful earthquake, and you didn't have any time then, either."

"Then speak up and tell us what you know," Jakob grumbled, "and then go out and play."

"I went out into the woods with Jossi and Maxl and watched a man making strange stone circles on the ground."

Suddenly the hair on the back of Simon's neck stood on end.

Strange stone circles . . .

"And who was it?" he finally asked. Peter told him.

And Jakob moved another figurine on the table.

"Stop! I can't do this." Magdalena could hear Lukas Baumgartner's muffled voice through the wall of the barrel. "Stop it, or I'm going to leave and tell the first person I see what's going on here!"

Wine poured in through the bunghole and over Magdalena as the barrel slowly filled. The cold liquid had already reached her waist, and she shouted and pounded in desperation against the side, but her tormenter just poured it in faster. Then suddenly it stopped and just a few drops followed.

"So what do you want to do with her?" the Tyrolean asked in a threatening voice.

"This woman was one of the midwives when my child was born," Lukas said, his voice cracking. "I've known her since I was a child, and I can't let her drown like a rat. I'd rather see us all get caught."

"Oh, just go ahead," the other snarled. "And I swear I'll make sure your wife, and your child as well, are nailed up in a barrel just like her."

"Oh God, please don't!" Lukas sobbed. "I didn't want this to happen, I just wanted to make a few extra guilders so my family would have a better life. As God is my witness, I didn't want this to happen."

"She saw us, young fellow," the Tyrolean said. "If we release her, she'll go straight to the village judge in Soyen and report us, and your child will never see his father again, because you'll be on some galley heading for the West Indies. So don't be so stupid!"

"If you drown this woman, I swear I'll turn you all in." Lukas's voice suddenly sounded firm and determined. "That's my final word. I can't live with guilt like that no matter what happens to me."

"I won't report you," cried Magdalena, pounding against the side of the barrel. In the half-full barrel of wine her voice sounded strangely muffled, like a voice from the grave. "I don't even know what you—"

"Hold your tongue, woman!" the Tyrolean snapped, hitting the bunghole with his fist and closing it. "I've got to think about this," he said, and it seemed the young man's threat had worked. Silence returned.

"Very well, lad," the Tyrolean said in a gentler voice. "No more wine – too bad it was all wasted. I tell you what we'll do: we'll take the woman out of Soyen before anyone here gets suspicious. I know of an old goat shed far from the main road where we can lock her up until this whole thing has blown over. What do you think of that?"

Tears of relief ran down Magdalena's cheeks, mixing with the wine in the barrel. Although she was trembling all over, it appeared her life had been spared. It was easy to see why the Tyrolean would want to silence her, but for now she at least had a chance to think about what to do next. Fate had granted her a reprieve.

"Very well," said Lukas, who also sounded relieved. "We'll lock her up, and later we'll let her go if she promises not to squeal on us."

"You have my word," Magdalena gasped.

The Tyrolean laughed. "The word of a hangman's daughter. Just great. Well, it will have to suffice. In a few days I'll be back in Tyrol, anyway."

Now Magdalena finally realized why the man's voice had sounded so familiar to her even the last time. She remembered that Barbara had told her a Tyrolean man in a Stopselhut had met Melchior Ransmayer in the old cemetery in Schongau. Barbara's stories had always sounded far-fetched to Magdalena, but now Magdalena wondered if the man who had just been planning to drown her was the same man as Barbara's Tyrolean. And there was something else going through her mind: the Tyrolean had spoken earlier about a Master from Oberammergau. That was evidently the man who had knocked her out.

What's going on here, for God's sake? Who are these people and what is this plot?

"So we can now finally head back to Schongau?" Lukas asked hopefully.

"Not yet," the Tyrolean replied. "Our people say the route is not yet safe. There are too many black riders along the way. We'll probably have to wait until nightfall."

"But we've been stuck here since yesterday. I must get home to my wife – she'll be terribly worried."

"This is my last word – we're waiting until nightfall."

Magdalena was shocked by the Tyrolean's words.

Until nightfall . . .

Magdalena had already been held here since yesterday, and now more endless hours would follow. It was possible that Burgomaster Buchner had already discovered she was no longer in Schongau. He'd certainly be suspicious. Her time was running out.

"Let's take her out of the barrel," Lukas suggested. "If we gag her, she can't cry for help."

"Do whatever you think you must," the Tyrolean responded, "but just so you understand, later we'll have to put her back in the barrel. We can't risk anything."

Magdalena heard pounding, then she saw a beam of light shining into the dark barrel. Lukas's powerful hands pulled Magdalena up, and she gasped for air as if she'd been pulled up from the bottom of a lake. Her dress was soaking wet, she stank of wine, and every muscle in her body ached, along with the back of her head where she'd been struck earlier.

But I am alive. At least for now, she thought.

"Thank you," she croaked as Lukas lifted her out of the barrel.

"I'm so sorry, Frau Fronwieser," the young wagon driver whispered in her ear. "This is all a big misunderstanding, believe me." He glanced over at the Tyrolean, who was leaning listlessly against a barrel, sipping from a bottle of wine. "I had no idea what I was getting myself into." He shook his head. "Somebody is going to pay for this when it's all over."

"Who?" Magdalena whispered, almost unconscious. "Who is behind this?"

But Lukas didn't answer as he grabbed her under the arms and dragged her to a corner of the basement. She hardly noticed that the Tyrolean tied her up after that, and gagged her.

Her final conscious thoughts were of her little sister, whose rescue was looking more and more unlikely.

13

So YOU BOYS WATCHED AS FRANZ WÜRMSEER made a circle of pebbles on the path over by the Malenstein?" Simon asked his son again.

They were seated with Jakob at the table in the old medicus's bathhouse. As Peter recounted what he had seen, the hangman's pipe gradually went out, and he picked up a chip of wood to light it again.

Peter nodded emphatically, clearly happy that the grown-ups were finally listening to him. "I was trying to tell you yesterday, but you wouldn't listen," he said, turning to his father. "It looked just like the circle of pebbles we saw on our trip here to Oberammergau. If Herr Würmseer is even half as mean as his son, then he's a very bad man. Besides, Jossi says he hates the labourers."

Simon remembered how Franz Würmseer had behaved in the council meeting earlier that day. He hated the immigrants. *So much that . . .*

Suddenly a horrible thought crossed his mind. *The murdered children on the Döttenbichl . . . the circle of stones . . . the black rider . . .*

The idea was so horrible that he rejected it out of hand. It couldn't be possible, could it? But in any case it was strange that the second burgomaster of a village would be making pagan symbols in the forest – strange enough to warrant looking into.

"We need to keep an eye on Würmseer," said Simon, turning to Jakob. "I can't tolerate him anyway – always attacking foreigners, and now this. He's up to something."

"And what do you think that might be?" Jakob asked gruffly. "I've got to get back to Lechner in a while, and you'll be staying here as the medicus. You could make a house call to Würmseer and snoop around a little, though, unfortunately, he looks fit as a fiddle."

"Of course, you're right," Simon replied. "That won't work. We need someone who—"

"We can do it," Peter interrupted.

Simon looked at him in surprise. "Who is *we?*"

"I told you about my new friends," Peter said excitedly. "Jossi, Maxl, and many others. They are all children of labourers and can't stand Würmseer, and even less his son, fat Nepomuk. I could ask them to keep a close eye on Würmseer, and so would I."

Jakob snorted. "You can forget that idea. How old are you? Seven? If you're as clever at spying on people as you were just a while ago eavesdropping at our window, Würmseer will whip your arse so bad you won't be able to walk for a week!"

"Hmm. I'm not sure – the children could at least try," Simon said. He was glad that Peter had made friends so quickly in Oberammergau. In Schongau, where he was just the dishonourable hangman's grandson, he'd never been able to do that. In addition, after all the disappointments of recent days, he wanted to do something for his son, and when he saw the spark of enthusiasm in Peter's eyes, he continued: "If you get caught we can just say it's mischievous kids, fooling around. What do we have to lose? In any case, it's better than if we stalk Würmseer ourselves. He'd immediately become suspicious."

"Well, then it's all right with me." Jakob raised his massive arms in surrender and he sighed. "We'll let a bunch of toddlers help us find the murderer. It's all worth it if we can finally solve this riddle."

Noisy steps could be heard coming down the hall in the Schongau dungeon.

Barbara, startled, straightened her tousled hair. Up to now she'd been able to face the guards who brought her a skimpy meal twice a day with defiance and her head held high. She didn't want them to notice her fear, her racing heart, and the gloomy thoughts plaguing her mind as she sat alone there in the dungeon. The last message that Paul had brought her from Magdalena was almost a night and two days old, and by now her sister should have arrived in Oberammergau. Had Johann Lechner agreed to see her? Barbara was still hiding the message underneath her bodice, but now and then she took out the crumpled piece of paper and silently mouthed the words.

I'm going to get help . . . Hold on . . .

Most of the time she dozed, trying not to think of what was awaiting her.

The first level of torture . . . then the burning, stretching, and pulling . . . the indescribable pain of finally being burned alive at the stake, all because of some stupid mistake.

Her only diversion was when Paul appeared at the window from time to time and told her about his latest pranks – but the guards always quickly shooed him off. At least Melchior Ransmayer hadn't appeared again. She still felt sick to her stomach thinking of the doctor's spindly fingers on her body. His hateful words had convinced her that her suspicion was justified; Ransmayer and Burgomaster Buchner were up to something.

But what?

The loud steps outside did not augur well. Ransmayer had threatened that the torture might begin that very day. Had the time come? Every muscle in her body tensed as the bolt squeaked and was pushed aside.

When the door opened, she suppressed a scream.

"Good day, Barbara," Master Hans said, ducking through the doorway. "I see you've grown up since the last time I saw you."

Barbara tried to stay calm, but she couldn't control the faint trembling that gradually came over her. She had seen the Weilheim executioner only once before in her life, at a meeting of Bavarian hangmen that her father and her brother had taken her to in Nürnberg. She was only nine years old then, and the sight of the huge, cruel man had followed her in her dreams for weeks afterwards.

Master Hans had long snow-white hair even though he was at least ten years younger than her own father, and his skin, too, was a faded white like bleached, flaking stucco. But what made him look so menacing were his eyes.

They were blood-red like a rat's.

The eyes of the devil, she thought.

There were rumours about Master Hans, horrible stories people whispered to one another that had made the Weilheim executioner famous and infamous in all of Bavaria. Some considered him the son of Satan, others said he was the child of a reformed witch, which explained why he was so cruel to heretics. His speciality was the pulling of fingernails and toenails, and he always got his confession. At the gallows, Hans tied the knot in such a way that the victim struggled and writhed an especially long time, much to the amusement of the onlookers.

During the execution he passed his hat around to the spectators, and the kreuzers, hellers, and pennies kept coming as long as the writhing continued.

Master Hans leaned against the opposite wall of the cell and stared at Barbara, who cowered in a corner like a wild animal brought to bay.

It seemed to her he was trying to determine how much pain she could tolerate. Suddenly a thin smile appeared on his face.

"It's a bad thing you got yourself into," he whispered in a voice that was both strangely tender and hoarse. It sounded to Barbara like the rustling of dried leaves. "Hiding magic books. How stupid of you." He shook his head sadly. "You might just as well have set fire to yourself, girl."

"You know that the books belonged to my great-grandfather Jörg Abriel," Barbara replied, trying hard to sound calm. "He was a hangman, just like you."

"God knows he was the best hangman that ever lived," Hans replied, nodding respectfully. "I worshipped him – in contrast, by the way, to your father, whom I consider far too gentle. It's hard to believe he's Abriel's grandson." He shook his finger playfully. "I still won't forgive Jakob for taking that ugly fellow away from me in the Weilheim dungeon a few years ago. I lost a lot of money because of that."

The huge man walked over to Barbara and sat down beside her. He put a friendly arm around her shoulder, but it felt cold, as if winter had returned.

"I like you, Barbara," he began in a soft voice, winking at her with his red, rat-like eyes. "You were just a little tomboy in Nürnberg. I'd be really sad if I had to pull out your fingernails one by one. That's not nice, but that's what the higher-ups want me to do, especially now that your sister, the beautiful Magdalena, has disappeared. She hasn't been seen in Schongau since yesterday, and the bathhouse is empty. Strange, isn't it?" He squeezed Barbara's shoulder harder. "You don't happen to know where she went, do you? Malicious gossip has it that she wanted to attack the Schongau burgomaster. Would she perhaps be crying on

Lechner's shoulder in Oberammergau? Is it true, Barbara? Tell me – is that true?"

"I . . . really don't know," Barbara replied in a hoarse voice. "You may have forgotten that I've been locked up inside here. Why don't you ask Buchner? Everyone out there knows more than I do."

"Do you really think your sister has abandoned you? That she's taken off for some market, even leaving her little son behind with the midwife?" There was sincere regret in Hans's eyes. "And what's even worse – do you think *I* believe that?" The Weilheim hangman's fingers suddenly dug like fangs into Barbara's neck. A stabbing, almost paralyzing pain shot through her, and she let out a muted cry. Hans brought his lips up close to her ear.

"Don't think I'm stupid, Barbara," he whispered. "Where is your sister? Buchner wants to know. He'll pay good money for that, and won't rest until you tell me."

"I . . . just . . . don't . . . know," Barbara gasped, as tears welled up in her eyes. The pain was so great that she almost screamed like a lunatic.

Suddenly the pressure eased off. Hans patted her shoulder and pulled a few dirty pieces of straw from his jacket. "Too bad, then . . . You could have saved yourself a lot of trouble. But you have time to think it over. The council decided not to begin torture until tomorrow morning, as your father took most of his torturing tools with him to Oberammergau, and what he left behind is in bad condition." Master Hans shook his head sadly. "Dried blood is sticking to the thumbscrews, the Spanish boots are rusted, and the ashes in the brazier are as hard as rock. I'll have to send for my own instruments."

"If I confess," Barbara whispered, "will you let me go?"

"Do you mean if you admit to practising witchcraft and also tell me where your sister is?" Hans scratched his head as if he were actually thinking it over, then he chuckled softly. "Ah, Barbara, you're a hangman's daughter, and you know how it goes. You'll be put to the stake, one way or the other. But I can ease your pain before that, and even more . . ." He patted her again on the shoulder to cheer her up. "When the smoke gets thick, I can step behind you without anyone noticing, wrap a thin hemp rope around your neck, give it a firm tug, and it will all happen so fast you won't even have time for an Ave Maria. What do you say to that?"

Barbara stared in horror at the Weilheim executioner, who winked cheerily at her, his red rat eyes sparkling as if he'd just told a good joke. It seemed he really considered his suggestion to be a humane gesture.

"Master Hans?" she said.

The Weilheim hangman regarded her expectantly. "Yes?"

"Go to the devil, and kiss his arse."

Hans smiled sadly. "Still a real tomboy, eh? You haven't changed a bit, Barbara."

He stood up, brushed the dirt from his black trousers, and headed towards the exit, where he turned around.

"I'll see you tomorrow, Barbara," he said. "Sleep well. You'll need your strength for tomorrow."

The door closed, and only then did Barbara start to cry softly. How she wished she had her big sister at her side, but here in the dungeon, her sister was as far away as the moon.

As night fell, a cart rolled down the main road in Soyen. Music and laughter could be heard in the taverns, and narrow shafts of light escaped into the dark through cracks in closed shutters. The road, so crowded during the day with innumerable merchants, pilgrims, and wagons, now was deserted. The manager of the general store was just closing his shop, and he watched in surprise as the wagon loaded with barrels left the village and disappeared into the Echelsbach Gorge in the gathering darkness. It was strange for a wagon driver to begin his trip at this time of day.

It was even stranger for a woman to be hidden in one of the barrels, but that was something the merchant couldn't see.

Inside the barrel Magdalena fought against the feeling of claustrophobia that swept over her again and again and took her breath away. Her heart began to race and again she felt the urge to throw up. Her lower body was squeezed like a wet, crumpled rag, and her stomach was churning.

I must not lose my baby. Oh, Saint Margaret, patron saint of the pregnant, help the two of us survive this horror.

About half an hour earlier, when the Tyrolean and Lukas had put her back in the barrel, she was seized with panic. She had done everything she could to calm herself down, as the gag alone made breathing very difficult. The Tyrolean had spoken of taking her to a goat shed somewhere out of town, but he hadn't said how far it was, and she still didn't know what this was all about. Evidently the Tyrolean was afraid she would find out and say something – but she didn't have the slightest idea what was going on. It had to have something to do with what Lukas was transporting in the wagon. The roads weren't safe during the day, the Tyrolean had said, and he'd spoken of riders and a Master from Oberammergau. What were the men carrying in the barrels that absolutely had to be protected from prying eyes?

Magdalena listened to the sounds outside. The noise and laughter of the town had long ago died away, and now all she heard were the squeaking wheels and the occasional snorting of the horses. The men up front were silent. It seemed to Magdalena they must have arrived at the turn-off to Schongau some time ago. By now Burgomaster Buchner must have become suspicious of her absence. And Barbara? Had the Schongau Town Council already found an executioner to torture her? But all that was secondary now – first she had to save herself.

For the hundredth time Magdalena shifted around, looking for a halfway comfortable position. There were some sandy dregs at the bottom of the barrel, and fine dust fluttered down from the underside of the cover and fell in her eyes, causing tears to run down her cheeks. After what seemed like an eternity she suddenly heard the astonished voice of Lukas.

"Hey, stop!" she heard the young man shout. "We just passed the last farmhouse where we could ask about an extra team of horses. How are you going to climb back up the gorge on the other side?"

"The horses can manage that by themselves," the Tyrolean replied. "We didn't load as many barrels as usual."

"You forget our prisoner – she weighs something, too, and you can't expect her to get out and help us shove the wagon up the other side."

"Damn it! I said the horses can manage, so just shut your mouth."

He cracked the whip, and the trip continued. Soon the barrels started rattling back and forth alarmingly, and Magdalena could sense they were descending into the gorge. The men applied brake shoes to the wheels to slow their descent, but the wagon kept going faster and faster, and Magdalena feared she'd fall into the gorge along with the barrels and wagon. The men cursed and whipped the horses as the rushing waters of the Ammer got louder and louder.

Finally they had reached the bottom of the gorge, and the clattering sound told Magdalena they were crossing the wooden bridge. Suddenly, however, the wagon stopped.

"What's the matter?" Lukas asked.

"We've got to remove the brake shoe at the front of the wagon before we move ahead," the Tyrolean replied. "Come and help me."

The two got out again, and Magdalena could hear the muffled sounds of wheezing, heavy steps, and angry shouting. She shuddered.

The two men were fighting.

There was another muted cry, and it was unmistakably the voice of young Lukas. Down below them, something splashed into the water. Then silence.

"Go to hell, you blue-eyed idiot," the Tyrolean snarled after a while. He panted, and finally uttered a dry laugh. "Did you really think you could threaten me? Greetings to the fish if you see any along your way."

Now Magdalena heard steps approaching the wagon. She could feel the tailgate of the wagon being lowered, then her barrel shook and tottered, finally tipping over and landing with a hard thud on the ground. She wanted to shout, but the gag allowed only a muffled gurgling.

Below her, the Ammer rushed by.

"I never should have tried doing business with children," the Tyrolean growled. "That's what I told them in Schongau, but they wouldn't listen, they just sent me this whining kid who almost blabbed out the whole story. Well, this is what he gets for it."

Very slowly he started rolling the barrel across the bridge.

"It's nothing personal, you understand?" the Tyrolean continued in a voice that sounded almost friendly. "You're pretty, too. If I'd met you in a tavern I would have danced with you, no doubt, and taken you to bed. You were just in the wrong place at the wrong time."

The barrel rolled faster, and Magdalena tried to scream despite the gag.

"You'll be a good-looking corpse; now say your last prayers," the Tyrolean said.

Suddenly the rumbling stopped, and it seemed to Magdalena that time was standing still, as if she were flying, like in a dream. The splashing and thundering of the river got louder and louder.

Then, with a loud crash, the barrel hit the water.

The impact was so sudden that it took Magdalena's breath away. In the next moment, the barrel began to spin wildly as if caught in a whirlpool, and the thundering of the water was deafening. There was a bump as the barrel hit a tree trunk or a rock, and the sound of the rushing water was muted.

I'm underwater! Magdalena thought. *The barrel is sinking!*

In the next moment it evidently shot back to the surface, where waves splashed against it. Rocking softly from side to side, the floating coffin continued on its way down the river.

The impact had caused the gag to slip, however, and now she could breathe easier and also cry for help. After shouting several times with no response, she gave up. Who would ever hear her, out here in the darkness, and even if someone happened to be travelling along the slope of the steep gorge, how could they help her in the rushing waters? The melting snow had turned the Ammer into a raging monster.

To her horror, Magdalena noticed how the barrel was gradually filling with water. The staves were evidently too old to seal properly. In a few moments the barrel would be full and then she would drown inside it like a cat in a sack.

Cold black river water streamed in through the cracks. Whenever the barrel turned over she took water in through her nose and mouth and tried to spit it out, all the while struggling to breathe. Every breath could be her last.

Magdalena kicked and pounded the staves, but they wouldn't move – they were old but not yet weak. Again the water sloshed over her, and this time she swallowed some and desperately shook her head from side to side, trying to breathe. The water now completely engulfed her, and she closed her eyes as if trying to wish herself away to some distant, secure place.

I don't want to die. I don't want—

There was a crash as the barrel was thrown against a boulder, the staves splintered, and the cold, dark water surged over her.

Then the Ammer claimed its victim.

With a knotted whip in his hand, Sebastian Sailer stood before his Creator and begged for forgiveness, but there was no reply.

The manager of the Ballenhaus, the Oberammergau storage depot, groaned and fell to his knees before the high altar in the Sacred Blood Chapel. Above him hung the monstrance containing the physical blood of Christ – a religious relic so potent that he could feel the power flowing from it. But even the blood of Christ could not help him now.

"Mea culpa. Mea culpa. Mea maxima culpa!" he mumbled over and over, lashing his back each time with the rope whip.

For half a day Sailer had been wandering through the valley in despair, looking for a way out, a way to save his soul, but when he suddenly found himself standing in front of the chapel at the edge of the village of Unterammergau, he knew what he had to do. Not far from the chapel, near a cattle trough, he had found the rope, like an ultimate sign, and since then he had been agonizing and praying.

Sailer bowed his head humbly, for he had sinned, greatly, and what was even worse, God was punishing not just him, but the entire valley. They never should have become involved in this. He realized too late that God had been sending them signs all along – first avalanches, then the crucifixion, and finally this earthquake – telling them they had gone astray. It was like the seven plagues, and he himself had been the devil's henchman.

Nervously he wrapped the hemp rope around his hands until they appeared fettered, like the hands of a martyr. The carved figures on the side altars that had been illuminated earlier by the setting sun now were completely engulfed in darkness, but Sailer could sense nevertheless the gaze of the sacred figures; they were whispering something to him.

Judas . . . Judas . . .

Sailer laughed in despair, because this was his role in the Passion play. How fitting. First he had betrayed God, and now he had betrayed one of his closest friends. Sebastian Sailer closed his eyes and prayed.

"Lord, I am not worthy to receive you, but only say the word and I shall be healed."

But the Lord spoke not a single word; He remained silent.

The good man Urban Gabler had been right – after the crucifixion they should have stopped, but their greed had been too great and the lot had finally fallen to him. And so he did what was commanded of him. In his left trouser pocket he still had the little wooden piece that had made him a murderer. Since then he had been plagued by nightmares, and screaming demons had flown over his bed, thrusting their lances at him. The earthquake had been the last sign. What would follow now? A flood? Swarms of locusts? The death of every firstborn in the village?

Sebastian Sailer reached for the little figurine in his pocket along with the piece of wood. He, too, had received a Pharisee from Xaver, this stubborn dog. The corners and edges of the carved figurine pressed against his skin and reminded him of what they had done.

It all started with Xaver Eyrl. It hadn't been right to ruin the family and force them to leave the valley. But why were these Eyrls such stubborn know-alls, setting themselves up as upholders of morality? Couldn't they have simply kept their mouths shut? That's when the sinning had begun.

Now it was time to answer for it.

Sailer took a length of rope, threw it over a heavy beam in the nave that supported the gallery, then climbed up on a pew and closed his eyes again. He murmured one last prayer.

"Say just one word, a single word . . ."

The Lord did not answer.

Sailer kicked away from the pew, and his feet danced and wriggled to a tune only he could hear.

They wriggled for a long, long time.

14

𝔉ATHER, IF THOU BE WILLING, TAKE THIS bitter cup from me." Jesus Christ knelt down and raised his hand imploringly towards heaven, his voice echoing far across the Oberammergau cemetery. "But if this be not possible . . ."

"Indeed, but perhaps it's possible for the Saviour to speak a little faster," Konrad Faistenmantel growled, lying on the ground with old Augustin Sprenger and the carpenter Mathis between a few pots of Alpine roses. "I'm an old man, and my bones are freezing. It isn't nice and warm here like in Palestine."

With a grin, Simon looked up from the text that Georg Kaiser had handed him earlier. The schoolteacher had asked him that morning to come to the rehearsal along with the priest Tobias Herele to serve as a prompter. All morning they'd been rehearsing the famous scene on the Mount of Olives in which the apostles Peter, Jacob, and John slept while Jesus agonized over his fate. Many of the other actors had been summoned by the council chairman to search for Eyrl in the forests and the moors around Ammergau.

"But that's not what it says here in the text," said Simon, turning to Konrad Faistenmantel with feigned severity. "It should say—"

"Damn, I know myself that's not what it says," Faistenmantel groaned as he got to his feet, snorting and brushing the dirt from his brown apostle's robe. "But Göbl is dragging the speech out on purpose so we'll have to sit here and freeze our arses off."

"This is the scene on the Mount of Olives," Göbl replied with a thin smile. "Jesus talks, but Peter is sleeping, that's what it says in the text."

"Dear actors, please!" Father Tobias wailed. "We can't make any progress like this."

Simon anxiously looked at Georg Kaiser, who just shrugged helplessly. After Hans Göbl's release from prison, his father had insisted his son be given the role of Jesus again. Farmer Nikolaus, who had temporarily been given the role, was all too happy to be reassigned as a stand-in. Since then, Hans Göbl had used every opportunity to get back at Faistenmantel. After all, Faistenmantel had been the first to express his suspicion that Göbl could have been Dominik's murderer.

Simon was still astonished at how quickly the council chairman had got over the loss of his youngest son, but then he remembered how much money Konrad Faistenmantel had already put into the play. The play had to be a success, or he would probably be facing financial ruin. Until the performance was over, nothing else was important. Now, too, Faistenmantel bit his lip and controlled himself.

"Very well," he grumbled. "But is it essential for us to just lie here during the rehearsal?" he said, glaring at Göbl and rising to his feet. "The backdrop of the Mount of Olives is still missing, and the painters – all of them Göbls – should have finished that long ago."

"You forget that part of the family was in prison," Hans replied bitterly. "Falsely accused by the Faistenmantels."

"And you, you little chicken, no doubt forget that I lost a son." Konrad Faistenmantel turned red in the face. "Damn, if this play weren't so important, I'd . . ." His voice broke.

"Let's continue with our text," Georg Kaiser pleaded. "We have lots to do today because we are so far behind due to the delays in recent days." He pointed at Göbl. "So continue."

Again, Hans Göbl raised his hands heavenward and his face looked transfigured. "I'll drink it . . . Thy will, not mine, be done," he lamented. He stopped suddenly and pointed at the three bored-looking apostles. "Now I must shake them and wake them up, but they're already awake."

"Good Lord! How is it possible to put on a Passion play with a troupe of peasants like this?" Tobias Herele exclaimed, pulling his hair. "It's like throwing pearls before swine."

"We have to wait for Judas anyway," said Mathis, a young carpenter playing the part of John. "He should have been here long ago. In just a moment we get to the famous scene with the Judas kiss."

"Sebastian acted so strange in the meeting yesterday," Sprenger said, with a worried expression. "Do you remember? He was pale and sweating all over. Maybe it's the fever going around." He put on a gloomy face and crossed himself. "Or something else," he added ominously.

Simon shrugged. "He didn't come to see me in the bathhouse."

For a while the men waited silently, then suddenly Konrad Faistenmantel kicked one of the gravestones. "It's always the same with Sailer," he exclaimed. "You can't count on him. Damn! Time is running out on us and Sailer is probably sleeping off his hangover somewhere."

Young Mathis scratched his nose, trying to think. "I'll go over to the storage house," he finally suggested. "Maybe he just forgot the rehearsal." Dressed in the simple cotton garb of an apostle, he ran past the gravestones to the cemetery gate, then down the street towards the village.

"Sprenger is right," the priest said after a while. "Sebastian has been behaving strangely of late, actually ever since poor Gabler was found dead. I mean, naturally we're all troubled by his death, but in Sebastian's case there's something more to it, even though they weren't very close friends."

In the meantime, Hans Göbl continued declaiming his lines. "Oh, Father, I am in such great fear," he said. "Now I am in the clutches of death . . ."

"Can't you just cut that out!" Faistenmantel shouted. "You're driving me crazy." He seemed unusually restless and kept looking over at the cemetery gate.

"Ah, does this worthy gentleman find the words of our Saviour hard to accept?" Göbl said sarcastically. "If I'm going to play the part of Jesus, I've got to learn the text." He loudly continued while the council chairman glared at him. "Oh, Father, help me bear this burden, or I shall surely despair. Fear makes me bitter, and so—" He stopped short as suddenly loud cries rose from the street outside the cemetery. Shortly thereafter Mathis returned, followed by some old wailing women.

"What is it?" Georg Kaiser called out in surprise. "Is the guardhouse burning? Has there been another earthquake? What's happened now?"

Mathis didn't stop running until he arrived, panting and struggling for breath, before the group. As he clung to a gravestone for support, he finally burst out, "Seb-Sebastian . . . he . . ."

"Well, speak up," Faistenmantel demanded impatiently. "What happened?"

"Sebastian hanged himself," Mathis finally burst out. "In the village pilgrimage church in Unterammergau. The sexton just brought us the news."

"Oh, my God!" Father Tobias put his hand to his mouth. "That's dreadful. But why?"

Now everyone began shouting at the same time – there were appeals to the saints and prayers to God, but above the tumult, finally standing out above all the others, came the rasping voice of old Sprenger.

"Have I not told you?" he shouted. "The Lord is judging us, just as it says in the Bible. First Jesus dies on the cross, then Thomas by the sword, and now Judas has hanged himself. The end is near."

The old women who had entered the cemetery with Mathis fell to their knees, whimpering and praying. After a while they got to their feet and hurried back to the gate, wringing their hands, to bring the horrifying news of Sebastian Sailer's death to the villagers.

"We have brought down the anger of the Lord upon us," the priest now wailed. "What crime has this village committed that brings the wrath of God upon us like this?"

I'd be interested to know that, too, Simon thought to himself, looking at the actors one by one. They all looked horrified except for Konrad Faistenmantel, who was staring blankly into space, his face as white as a sheet.

"This is the end," he mumbled. "The end of the Passion play, my life's work . . ."

"You'd better have a closer look at Sailer," Georg Kaiser whispered to Simon. "Perhaps you can find the reason for this suicide."

Simon nodded resolutely. "I shall, but this time I want to take someone along who really knows something about hangings."

The stick came down, and little Basti groaned softly with pain. Beads of sweat covered his forehead, but he didn't shout. The seven-year-old leaned over a bench in the Oberammergau village school with his trousers down as Poxhannes flailed him as he would a horse.

"Twelve, thirteen, fourteen . . ." Poxhannes counted aloud. The other children cowered down stoically in their places, relief showing in their eyes that someone else got caught this time, and not them. Peter was sitting in the first row, quivering with each blow. He was familiar with beatings in the Schongau school, but Poxhannes thrashed away with a special vengeance. For some time Peter had wanted to tell the workers' children of his plan to observe and follow Franz Würmseer, but then Georg Kaiser was suddenly called away for a rehearsal, and the assistant had to take the class. Since then, talking or planning what to do had been out of the question, so Peter had asked the others to come to the cave in the Malenstein after school.

"Fifteen, sixteen . . ." said Poxhannes loudly between blows. By now, Basti's naked bottom was covered with welts, but he still didn't cry.

"He's going to beat the poor boy to death," Peter whispered to Jossi, who was sitting next to him, but Jossi waved him off.

"Oh, no he won't. He still needs Basti. Who else is going to do the dirty work?"

"What dirty work?" Peter asked. Jossi was silent. Instead, his eyes wandered over to fat Nepomuk, who was clearly enjoying the punishment of the slender boy. A faint smile passed over his lips, and he seemed to be counting along softly.

"Nineteen, and twenty," Poxhannes panted, out of breath from the whipping. He put the stick aside, rolled down his sleeves again, and put on his stained vest, as if he'd just been in a tavern brawl.

"Let that be a lesson to you not to sleep during class," he said. "Now let's continue with the catechism."

He gave little Basti a strong push, and the boy stumbled back to his seat. Moments later the children resumed reciting the Latin catechism.

"Dirty pig," Jossi snarled softly. "Hannes makes us working-class kids slave away until we're ready to drop, and when we doze off, we get whipped."

"Do you mean Basti had to work for Hannes last night, too?" Peter whispered.

Jossi nodded as he continued silently mouthing the words of the catechism. Only now did Peter notice that one of the working-class children was missing. It was the pretty, freckled Joseffa, who shared with them the secret of the Malenstein cave. It was not unusual for children to be absent from school, especially the poor children who had to lend a hand at home. But it was nine-year-old Joseffa's turn today to get the firewood, and neither Hannes nor Georg Kaiser would tolerate any excuses.

"Where is Joseffa?" Peter asked as quietly as possible.

Jossi hesitated, and at first it appeared he wouldn't answer, but then he pulled himself together. "There was an accident last night," he said darkly. "Something bad, and honestly, I don't know if Joseffa will ever come back."

"Do you mean . . . she's dying?" Peter gasped. He saw how pale Jossi looked. Jossi had dark rings under his eyes, as if he'd hardly got any sleep. Maxl, sitting alongside him, also looked exhausted.

"Who cares about a worker's child?" Jossi whispered. "If we can't work any more, then nobody will need us. But that's not your business. It would be better—"

"Aha, it seems we have someone else here who needs to learn how to behave," Poxhannes suddenly exclaimed. Seemingly out of nowhere he appeared alongside Jossi and Peter and slapped his stick on the table. He pointed menacingly at Jossi. "Take your trousers down and bend over. For you we'll probably need thirty lashes, you fresh, obstinate rascal."

"That . . . was my fault," Peter spoke up. "I asked Jossi something."

The words just came gushing out instinctively. Hannes glared at him in surprise, and Peter began to tremble. The assistant tapped Peter's hair with his stick and grinned maliciously, making the red and partially inflamed pockmarks on his face stand out. It reminded Peter of a piece of raw meat.

"Aha! Here we have a little hero who wants to spare his new friend a beating – but it won't work," he said, slamming the stick on the table. "Take your trousers down right now, both of you. Each of you rascals will get thirty blows so you don't forget who's in charge here."

Peter's heart was pounding. He'd just seen how badly Hannes had beaten little Basti and doubted he'd be able to hold back the tears like Basti had, especially as he was supposed to get thirty blows. He could feel bile rising in his throat and he choked with anger.

"Now the smarty-pants is finally getting what he deserves," Nepomuk whispered, and a few other children, among them Nepomuk's friends Martl and Wastl, started giggling.

I mustn't cry, Peter thought. *I mustn't cry, I mustn't* . . .

Very slowly, Jossi stood up alongside him, his face pale but determined. "It's true, Peter asked me something," he said quietly.

"Ah, so you admit it!" Hannes exclaimed.

Jossi's voice was so soft that only Poxhannes and Peter could hear him. "He asked me where Joseffa is," he whispered. "Could you perhaps tell him, Herr Teacher's Assistant?"

Hannes lowered his stick and glared at Jossi. For a long while he stared right into the eyes of the boy standing before him, who returned the look defiantly. To Peter it looked as if the two were engaged in a silent duel. Finally, Poxhannes smiled at Peter, but his eyes remained cold. "Oh, yes, poor Joseffa," he finally said in a cloyingly sweet tone. "She had a little accident while collecting pinecones in the forest. I hear that a tree fell on her. Life in the mountains is hard, and some people die there if they're careless." As he spoke these last words, his voice suddenly became as sharp as a knife. Then he returned to the front of the room and turned around to the class.

"Because Peter is a good pupil, and also the favourite of the schoolmaster, we will dispense with the whipping for once." Hannes grinned on hearing angry hissing from some of Nepomuk's friends and held up his hand for them to be quiet. "I think instead the two will copy the entire catechism, pages five to twenty . . . three times by tomorrow morning. That will teach them not to chatter during class. Now we shall continue."

"But—" fat Nepomuk started to say, evidently disappointed that Peter had been spared a whipping.

"Hold your tongue," Hannes barked, "or I'll regret my kindness and whip you next, you fat little toad."

Nepomuk fell silent, and all the children continued reciting the catechism. Peter was so relieved that for a moment he couldn't say a thing. The punishment was still severe, but nothing compared to the beating that he and Jossi had been facing.

After two more long, agonizing hours the church bell rang, and the children hurried out the door. Along with Jossi, Maxl, and the other workers' children, Peter ran across the Ammer River bridge into the neighbouring forest, where they finally took shelter in the cave behind the Malenstein. After they'd all taken a chunk of hard bread and had a gulp of well water from a battered jug, Peter turned sympathetically to little Basti, who couldn't sit because of his pain.

"My father is a medicus and could probably give you some ointment," Peter suggested, but Basti just clenched his teeth and shook his head.

"It will be all right. I've had worse beatings from Poxhannes. Besides, ointment just costs money, and if I tell my mother, she'll just give me another whipping."

"But you can't just let Hannes beat you like that," said Peter, turning to the others. "Can't you go to Georg Kaiser and tell him?"

"You think we should tattle?" Jossi shook his head and laughed bitterly. "That will just make it worse. You're really smart, but that's something you still don't understand. We're the children of workers, and nobody cares about us."

"I think I do understand," Peter persisted. "Don't forget I'm the grandson of a dishonourable hangman."

For a while, they all just chewed on their pieces of hard bread and kept silent. Once more Peter noticed the careworn faces of the children and the dark rings under their eyes. The youngest ones lay down on the hard stone seats or huddled down in the dirty straw strewn all around.

"You were going to tell us something," Maxl finally said to Peter, shaking his curly black locks. "So tell us, what are you hiding?"

"I think . . . actually my father and grandfather believe that Franz Würmseer is involved in some shady deal," Peter began. "Something that may be connected with these murders, and I thought we could—"

"Did you hear the news?" said Bartl, the crippled boy who lived alone with his father in a charcoal-burner's cabin in the forest. "There was another murder. I just heard it on my way over here. Sailer, the manager of the storage building, was found hanged to death in the pilgrimage church in Unterammergau. Some say Red Xaver did it – you know, the one everybody's looking for? Other people say it was a curse from God, and we will all die, one after the other."

The children whispered excitedly to one another until Jossi finally called for silence. "First let Peter tell us what he knows," he said. "Perhaps he can tell us something more about it."

Peter was confused and for a moment couldn't speak. The fact that there was a new victim was also news to him. Finally, he told the children in a hesitant voice about the strange circles of stone, and the suspicion of his father and grandfather that Franz Würmseer might have something to do with recent events.

"Jossi and Maxl are my witnesses," he said. "Würmseer also made such a circle of stones here at the Malenstein, so I thought we could keep an eye on him to see what's behind it all."

"I've seen circles like that," Basti said. "And strange black riders were also seen around here. One of them almost ran me down when

I was on my way down to the Graswang Valley. That was about two weeks ago."

"Then you're with us?" Peter asked excitedly.

The children looked silently down at the ground, embarrassed. They all seemed tired, and their wrinkled, fallen cheeks reminded Peter of little old men. Finally Jossi cleared his throat.

"Listen, boy," he said. "Life is hard on us here in the valley, and no one wants to make trouble. Everyone knows that the Oberammergau council as well as the abbot of Ettal wants us workers to leave. Things are getting worse and worse for us; it's almost as bad as it was more than a hundred years ago, when foreigners were expelled. Many of us fear that our families will suffer the same fate."

The others nodded anxiously.

"Würmseer is a powerful man in Oberammergau," Maxl added gloomily. "Nobody wants to pick a fight with him – that would be dangerous."

Peter could almost smell their fear. Suddenly he had a dreadful thought. He remembered Jossi's dogged silence when he asked about Joseffa, and he also remembered the two dead children his father had spoken of.

"Does Joseffa's accident have anything to do with your being so cautious?" he asked hesitantly.

Once again there was nothing but silence, and none of them looked up at him.

"What's wrong with Joseffa?" Peter asked, now even more insistently. "What happened?"

"It would be better if you didn't ask. It wouldn't be good for you – or for us. Sometimes too much knowledge just leads to disaster. Here's a suggestion, Peter. Maxl and I will help you with your plan, we'll keep an eye on Würmseer, but you must leave the others out of it, it's not worth it." Jossi moved towards the entrance of the cave, where he turned around again to Peter. "Now let's go home. Many

of us have to help our parents in the field or in the forest, and the two
of us have a long homework assignment."

"I really have no idea what that fellow is doing here. I mean, a
hangman in a church . . . a church containing the blood of our Saviour
– one of the most sacred religious relics in all of Christendom?"

Crimson with rage, Judge Johannes Rieger stood at the entrance
of the Sacred Blood Chapel in Unterammergau, pointing at Jakob
Kuisl, who was just coming up the steep path from the village with
Simon. The ancient pilgrimage church was set in a blooming, rolling
meadow above Unterammergau, about half an hour's walk from
Oberammergau. Many pilgrims on their way to Ettal stopped here
to pray to the blood of the Saviour, which had been mixed with soil
and preserved in a silver monstrance.

"According to what I've heard, the church has already been
sufficiently desecrated by a hanged man dangling from the balcony,"
Jakob said. "The presence of a hangman here doesn't make much
difference."

Jakob had learned of Sebastian Sailer's death just an hour before.
He'd been in the bathhouse, leafing through the small number of
medical books that had belonged to the deceased medicus, brooding
over the carved figurines on the table, and had already lit his third
pipeful of tobacco that day. Ever since Xaver Eyrl had fled from the
dungeon in Ettal, there was nothing more for Jakob to do in the
monastery, so he'd taken temporary quarters with Simon, who had
brought him along on this short walk.

"I asked the hangman to come, because hanging is his, uh . . .
special field," Simon said hastily. "It's possible he can figure out
exactly what happened in the chapel."

Johannes Rieger managed a thin smile. "I tend to doubt that," he
replied, pointing to a bald-headed man who had just appeared behind

him in the entrance portal and was nervously rubbing his hands. "The Unterammergau sacristan found Sailer and cut him down from the balcony. The poor devil hanged himself, and that's all there is to it. Your visit is in vain."

"I probably forgot to lock the side door," the sacristan admitted sheepishly. "I didn't notice until early this morning, and that's when I found Sailer dead, hanging from the balcony."

"Hmm. It seems he strung himself up with a calving rope," Jakob said.

Rieger looked at him, bewildered. "What calving rope?"

"Well, the one that was hanging here recently alongside the trough on a rusty ring." The hangman walked the few steps over to the trough next to the sacristan's house and pointed to a short piece of rope still tied to the ring. "The rope was just recently cut off. Didn't any of you learned gentlemen notice that?"

"Hmm. Sailer actually did hang himself on a calving rope," Rieger mumbled. Then he shrugged. "But what does that tell us?"

"It tells us that Sailer didn't decide to kill himself until he got here," Jakob replied. "He hadn't been planning it for a long time, and so no one helped him."

"Nonsense, I'm sure Xaver Eyrl did it," said a third man, who evidently had been waiting inside the church and now walked back towards them at the portal. It was Franz Würmseer, staring coldly at the hangman and Simon. "It sounds like him. The fellow was evidently insane. He killed poor Sebastian and then hanged him up here."

Jakob stopped short. He'd expected to see the Ammergau judge here, but not Franz Würmseer. Clearly the two knew one another better than he thought.

"May we enter the church, or not?" Simon asked.

Rieger seemed undecided, but finally he wearily raised his hands. "Oh, all right, but only because you're the medicus." He nodded disparagingly at the hangman. "See to it that the dishonourable fellow doesn't accidently touch the holy monstrance." He stepped aside, and Jakob and Simon entered the Unterammergau Sacred Blood Chapel.

The church consisted of one long nave with a choir and apse at the east end and niches along the sides containing painted wooden figures. On the high altar stood a silver monstrance, gleaming almost ethereally in the sunlight falling through the windows. On the stone floor directly beneath the loft lay Sebastian Sailer, his head twisted to the side. The rope hadn't yet been removed and still hung from his neck like a dog's leash.

Johannes Rieger pointed at the carvings in the loft behind them, where another piece of knotted rope dangled. "This is where he hanged himself. The sacristan found him this morning before lauds and cut him down. Since then, no one has touched him. Hey! I said no one—"

Without paying attention to Rieger's protests, Jakob walked over to the dead man and bent down. Sebastian Sailer's dead eyes stared back at him; his blue tongue hung from his lips like a garden slug. There was a purple ring around his neck where the rope had been. Jakob Kuisl had seen hanged men so often he was not shocked, and went about examining the corpse with a professional eye – like a butcher looking at a dead calf. He palpated the corpse, thinking.

"There's no sign of a struggle," he murmured finally. "No blow to the back of his head. This man went willingly, without any help." He examined the knot directly behind the neck. "This is the way suicidal people tie the rope," he said. "They don't know the knot has to be behind the ear for the neck to break quickly. This way it lasts much longer." He bent down even closer to the corpse and began sniffing with his huge hooked nose.

"What's he doing there?" asked Franz Würmseer in disgust.

"Ah . . . he's smelling the corpse," Simon replied. "Perhaps it looks a bit unusual, but it tells us a lot."

"It looks bizarre, damn it," Rieger said. "Tell him to stop."

"Sailer died here yesterday," Jakob said suddenly, getting to his feet. "I would say in the evening, after the sacristan left. Rigor mortis and decomposition have already set in. He was sober – one or two beers at the most – and . . ." He looked through Sailer's pockets, finally pulling out a small wooden object from his left trouser pocket. "Well, look at this," he mumbled, "here's our old friend again."

"The damned Pharisee." Franz Würmseer suddenly turned very pale and ran his hand nervously through his hair. "Will there be no end to this?"

"Ha! If we need any more proof that Eyrl is involved in this, here it is," Rieger hissed.

"He must be involved in it somehow," Simon replied, "but how? That's still a mystery. Eyrl might have—"

Loud footsteps could suddenly be heard outside the church portal, and shortly afterwards the door was yanked open and an angry Schongau secretary appeared in the nave. Johann Lechner was trembling with rage.

"How dare you not inform me immediately about this!" he shouted at the Ettal judge. "I had to learn from some farmers I just happened upon that there's another corpse."

"I would have told you in time, Your Excellency," Rieger replied through pursed lips. He pointed to Jakob Kuisl. "But in any case your hangman is already here, and we thought he'd inform you," he added haughtily. "Didn't he?"

Only then did Lechner notice the hangman and Simon. His eyes contracted to narrow slits.

"You haven't heard the end of this, Kuisl," Lechner threatened. "We'll talk this afternoon over in the monastery. Now leave me alone with these people for a while." He pointed at Simon. "You, too, out with you both."

Jakob bowed. As he walked past Franz Würmseer he casually handed him the carved figurine. "Here, as a remembrance of your colleague. Put it over your fireplace, perhaps along with your own." Würmseer dropped the carving as if it had stung him.

Without another word, Jakob and Simon left the church and found three of the Schongau soldiers standing outside around the trough next to the sacristan's house, talking quietly. As the hangman approached, they fell silent.

"What's the meaning of this?" Simon asked angrily. "Why did Lechner send us out? We could have given him some information about the deceased."

"I can do that this afternoon," Jakob replied. "The important thing is what we discovered."

"Discovered?" Simon looked at him sceptically. "Do you think Sailer was given one of these Pharisees before he hanged himself? Honestly, I'd always suspected that."

"No, that's not it, you idiot. What's much more interesting is that Würmseer recognized the little figurine right away." Jakob grinned. "If I recall correctly, only Rieger, the abbot, and Secretary Lechner knew about the figurines – they were the only ones present during Xaver's questioning."

"Maybe Rieger told Würmseer about them," Simon replied, but Jakob waved his hand dismissively.

"It was dark in the church. Franz Würmseer was standing some distance from the corpse, yet he knew right away what he saw. That can only mean one thing, namely—"

"Namely, that he himself got a figurine just like it," Simon gasped, "and that's why he turned so pale."

"One more reason to have a closer look at him."

Once again Jakob turned around to look at the church, which stood like a white pearl in the midst of the rolling meadows. He clung tightly to the other object, about as long as a finger, that he'd found next to the Pharisee in the dead man's pocket.

A chip of wood with a clean break in it.

Jakob's mind was working feverishly, as he knew even the smallest clue often was of great importance – little stones in a mosaic that would eventually come together to form a complete picture. He enjoyed this intense reflection – it helped him forget his mundane worries and also his yearning for alcohol.

The hangman was back.

Barbara closed her eyes and thought of all the wonderful things that had happened in her life over the last few years.

A flowering meadow in May . . . The dance at the county fair with Jockel Leidinger . . . The smell of hay after a night in the barn . . . The sweet smell of tobacco smoke when Father sits happily with the family at the table . . . The handsome boy Matheo in Bamberg . . . Picking woodruff with Magdalena . . .

The memories helped her calm down a bit. Nevertheless, fear kept crawling back into her subconscious like a spider. She'd hardly slept a wink since last evening in the Schongau dungeon, thinking that Master Hans could come at any minute and take her off to the torture chamber. Now it was almost midday and the hangman still hadn't appeared. What was going on? Was it part of the torture that the prisoner was kept waiting and wondering whether Hans would pull out their fingernails first or their toenails?

In the last few hours she'd started to wonder what was happening outside her cell. A few times she'd heard the guards at the door whispering to one another, and now and then someone hurried past her barred window. In addition, Paul had visited her that morning and thrown a folded note down the airshaft. The brief message was from Martha Stechlin.

Courage! It said. *Help is coming soon.*

Was it possible that Magdalena had returned from Oberammergau with Lechner? Had Burgomaster Buchner already been deposed? But if so, why was she still here in the dungeon?

Once again she heard steps, the pattering steps of a child, and soon between the bars she could see Paul's dirty little face peering down the airshaft.

"Paul!" she called out in relief. "What's going on outside there? Is Mama back yet?"

Paul shook his head sadly. "No, she's away." But suddenly a wide grin spread across his face. "But Stechlin wants me to tell you to be ready. And she wants me to pester the guards." Triumphantly he pulled a slingshot from his trouser pocket and loaded it with a rock the size of a plum. "This one is for fat Karl."

"Be ready? What do you mean by that, Paul? Wait . . ."

But Paul had already disappeared. Shortly afterwards, Barbara heard an angry cry of pain.

"You just wait, boy!" shouted the man, apparently fat Karl. "I'll beat you black and blue for that. If your mother ever comes back, she won't recognize you."

There were the sounds of heavy boots running down the street, along with Paul's taunts, which had made many other people furious, not least of all his own family.

"Paul!" she cried softly, even though she knew her nephew could no longer hear her, then she whispered a curse. There was so much she wanted to ask Paul, and now he was running down the street with the guards in pursuit. If they got their hands on him, it was possible they'd throw him in the dungeon as well. He'd done too much in recent days to anger them.

She was so lost in thought she realized someone was at the door only after it had swung open with a loud creaking sound. Her heart started pounding – her time had come. Master Hans had come to take her away. Whatever happened she'd try to maintain her dignity as long as possible. Her lips tightly pressed, she turned around and . . . cried out loud with surprise.

In the doorway stood Martha Stechlin and Jakob Schreevogl, the deputy burgomaster.

"We don't have much time," the patrician whispered. "The guard will soon give up trying to catch Paul and return. Right now we need to escape."

Barbara was at a loss for words. "You . . . mean I am . . ." she stammered.

"Come now, girl," Stechlin urged. "There's no time to talk. We'll explain everything once we've escaped."

She tugged at Barbara's sleeve and the girl stumbled after her, dazed. Outside in the corridor young Andreas was standing and waving impatiently.

"Fat Karl could come back at any moment," he whispered. "He doesn't know I'm here. I told him before I had a stomachache and had to go out to the privy." He smiled at Barbara. "Your father and your sister were always good to me and my family. You saved my little Annie when she had a bad fever and the priest had already come to give her the last rites. My family will always remember the Kuisls for that. You still have many friends in Schongau. Now, let's go!"

"Thank you," Barbara whispered as Stechlin pulled her out the door, where Jakob Schreevogl was waiting. The tall patrician looked around nervously, then threw a dirty blanket over her and put a bell in her hand that people with infectious illnesses had to carry around with them. "Here, take this," he ordered. "I would rather have waited until nightfall, but then it might be too late. Anyway perhaps you can help us."

"Help?" Barbara was completely confused. Things were getting stranger and stranger. First she was escaping from the dungeon and the torture chamber with the help of the deputy Schongau burgomaster, and now the patrician was saying he needed her help. What was this all about?

Martha Stechlin grinned at her with her four remaining teeth. "Just keep ringing," she said, pointing at the bell. "We don't want to infect anyone, do we?"

Luckily the fortress stood close to the city wall and a number of small, almost deserted lanes. The three of them hurried down the street. Jakob Schreevogl walked ahead and Martha Stechlin came along behind him, holding Barbara by the elbow as if she were a deathly ill old woman, and Barbara kept ringing her bell. At an intersection near St Sebastian Cemetery they met two young women drawing water from a fountain who looked at the strange group curiously.

"Yes, yes, a bad thing, this smallpox," Martha wailed loudly. "Comes faster than the wind. The dear old woman only wanted to care for her sick husband, but the illness doesn't spare even good Christian souls, does it?"

The two women didn't answer but quickly ran off.

Twice again they met passers-by, but people always fled when they saw the midwife with the supposedly infectious patient and heard the bell.

After a while Barbara heard shouts coming from the fortress. Evidently the second guard had returned and found the door to the dungeon open. Jakob Schreevogl walked faster. "We'll be at Martha's soon," he said, breathing heavily, "and then we can catch our breath."

Soon thereafter they arrived at the house, which bordered directly on the city wall and was surrounded by a wild herb garden. It was a small, rickety old place that Barbara had known since early childhood. Martha Stechlin pushed her inside and quickly closed the door behind her and Jakob Schreevogl. Paul, who was in the main room crouched down in front of the stove, jumped up and embraced his aunt warmly.

"You look like a witch," he said, laughing and pulling on the blanket.

"Cut that out," Stechlin scolded him. "Tell me where the guard is."

"Ha! I hit fat Karl right in the middle of the forehead." Paul smirked. "He'll have a bump as big as a ram's horn."

"Did he see which way you went?" Jakob Schreevogl asked impatiently.

Paul shook his head and grinned. "I climbed up on to a roof, then I jumped across the street. Karl just snorted and shook his fist."

"Well done." Schreevogl nodded with relief, then he pointed to a bench in one corner. "Have a seat," he said to Barbara, pushing aside a stone mortar and a few jars filled with herbs. "We have some things to discuss."

Barbara put down the dirty, stinking blanket and sat down while Martha brought a jug of diluted wine, a loaf of bread, and some cheese. Only now did Barbara realize how hungry she was. Fear of torture had robbed her of her appetite since the day before. She eagerly broke off a piece from the warm, steaming loaf and put it in her mouth.

"I think they'll soon be here to search the house," Jakob Schreevogl ventured. "After all, dear Martha is an old friend of the Kuisl family. We don't have much time, so I'll be brief." He leaned forwards and squeezed Barbara's hands. "From now on my fate and yours are closely linked. I hope very much that I won't wind up on the torture rack and come to regret this, but by God, what could I do? Your father saved the life of my daughter, Clara, years ago. Now I'll pay him back and save the life of his daughter." He made a fist. "How did it get to this? The town is going to hell!"

"What happened?" asked Barbara after washing down the bread and cheese with some wine. In the meantime Paul had crouched back down again in front of the stove and was playing with Martha Stechlin's cat.

"Buchner is going to dissolve the council," Schreevogl said with a grim look. "He intends to rule as a dictator with only the help of the two councilmen who remain loyal to him. Lechner will be removed from office." The patrician's voice had lowered to a whisper. "I know that from reliable sources. Tomorrow evening, in a final council meeting, he intends to separate the wheat from the chaff. Anyone siding with Buchner will be spared, and the rest will be thrown in the dungeon. That's the real reason the burgomaster called for Master Hans – to pressure the few remaining councillors to sell the city to the bishop of Augsburg, an outrageous lie in order to accuse us of high treason, but it gives Buchner the chance to set himself up as the town's saviour."

"But how about Johann Lechner?" Barbara asked. "Someone should warn him that he could—"

"Ha! Do you think no one has tried?" Martha interrupted, filling Barbara's cup with fresh wine. "Buchner has locked the city down like a mousetrap. Your sister already left two days ago, but we're afraid something has happened to her, since she hasn't returned yet with Lechner."

Schreevogl nodded earnestly. "I gave her a letter for Lechner, but unfortunately we still haven't heard from her. I don't think she was caught by Buchner's henchmen, or they would have found my traitorous note and I would have been tossed into the dungeon with Barbara." He drummed his fingers nervously on the tabletop. "In any case, Buchner knows he doesn't have much more time, and that's the reason for hastily calling a council meeting."

Barbara turned pale. "My God," she moaned. "Isn't there anyone in town to stand up to him?"

"I'm afraid there are very few in the council, in any case." Jakob Schreevogl sighed. "Yours truly and a few of the young patricians. Buchner bribed some of the older members just to be sure, and the others are simply afraid or hope to benefit from the changes. For a long time, the town's dependence on Munich has been a thorn in the flesh of many council members. After all, we were once a great imperial city." He frowned. "If it comes to a vote, Buchner's people will probably win. The constables are already instructed to immediately remove any troublemakers from the council. Unless . . ." He paused and poured himself a cup of wine as well.

"Unless what?" Barbara asked excitedly.

The patrician took a long drink before continuing. "Unless we can prove by tomorrow that Buchner is acting contrary to the best interests of the town – then, perhaps, the council might change its mind. I know that Buchner is planning something outrageous, and I suspect Doctor Ransmayer also has a part in it. There are witnesses, but none of them can tell me exactly what the two are planning."

"I observed the two of them together," Barbara interrupted, "in the parish church, and they were discussing something secret."

Schreevogl nodded. "Magdalena told me about that, so, as you see, maybe you can help us. Exactly what did you see? It's important, Barbara. Perhaps we still have a chance to stop Buchner."

"Actually, there were two meetings," she answered hesitantly. "The first time I saw Ransmayer with that odd Tyrolean in the hat in the parish cemetery, and then later Buchner and the doctor upstairs in the bell tower."

"Can you remember any details of their conversation?"

Barbara closed her eyes, trying to concentrate. "At the first meeting, the Tyrolean told Ransmayer to be ready. Later, in the bell tower, the doctor demanded more money from Buchner – but for what, I don't know."

"Curses!" Schreevogl pounded the table. "That's nowhere near enough. I thought you might have overheard something that would help us, but now . . ."

"That stupid doctor was there in the cemetery again yesterday," Paul said suddenly from his seat in front of the stove. "And he was there before, too. I've seen him often."

Everyone turned to look at Paul. "What are you saying?" Schreevogl asked with surprise.

"Well, I like to play around the building site. I climb around on the sacks of mortar for the new steeple." He petted the purring cat, looking a bit embarrassed. "I know I'm not allowed to do that, but—"

Barbara jumped up and held him firmly by his two little hands. "Paul, that doesn't matter now. What exactly did you see?"

"The doctor sometimes looked into the bags, then the wagon drivers came by, he spoke with them, and the men loaded the sacks on the wagon. Fat old Buchner was sometimes there, too."

"This is our chance," Schreevogl whispered. "I knew the two were up to something. We've got to find out as fast as we can what Ransmayer and Buchner were doing in the old cemetery – and it must have something to do with those sacks."

"That won't help if we can't catch them in the act," Martha interjected. "Even if those sacks were full of gold and jewels, they'd just deny everything."

Barbara nodded. "I'm afraid you're right. We need someone to . . ." She stopped and smiled. "Paul?" she said, turning to her nephew. "I think your aunt will let you go and play on the building site once more. Would you like to?"

Paul nodded enthusiastically. "Definitely. Can I take my slingshot along?"

"Indeed, and this time you can bring some extra large stones."

Anxiously, Jakob Kuisl made his way through the moor towards Ettal Monastery, whose dome shone red and white like a huge jewel in the rugged mountains. It was a sunny afternoon. In the distance a woodpecker was hammering and little thrushes fluttered back and forth excitedly between the branches, but the hangman took no notice of all this. He stomped along determinedly, his boots sinking deep into the mire.

He was restless, because he didn't know what Lechner planned to do with him. Clearly he had angered the secretary earlier in the Unterammergau church. Would he send him back to Schongau now that Eyrl had fled from the dungeon? Until recently, Jakob would have been all too happy to leave, but lately he'd been overcome, as often before in his life, with a burning curiosity. He had to figure out what was going on in this valley. In addition, he suspected he would never see his son, Georg, again unless Lechner was happy with him.

Only now did Jakob notice how much he'd succumbed to grief and his bad temper in recent years. The death of his beloved wife, the departure of his son, and the gruesome dreariness of his work had driven him into a despair that he'd tried to overcome with beer, wine, and hard liquor.

Just like my father, the old drunk, Jakob mused. *Is this the fate of our family?*

The hangman was not an especially pious man, but the earthquake the day before had actually seemed to him like a sign from God. He had prayed for a miracle, and it came.

The earthquake had awakened him from his torpor.

Still, he damn well wasn't going to admit it to his son-in-law. His innermost thoughts weren't anyone's business except his own and the Almighty's, before whom he'd stand someday, with all his sins.

After Jakob had left the Sacred Blood Chapel in Unterammergau with Simon, they had first taken a high mountain trail back to Oberammergau. The many crosses and roadside shrines had reminded them that the Lord was keeping a very close eye on this valley. Twice they met a group of armed hunters and forest workers looking for Xaver Eyrl, but it seemed the woodcarver had disappeared from the face of the earth, and Jakob doubted the men would ever find him.

The valleys and the mountains offered many places to hide, and Eyrl was presumably long gone.

While Simon stayed behind in Oberammergau, Jakob started out on the path of penance to Ettal Monastery. As he entered through the main gate, he saw some Benedictine monks busy tearing down the shed damaged by fire during the earthquake. They were looking down as if they were absorbed in their work, but Jakob suspected they just wanted to avoid eye contact with him, a hangman, a bringer of misfortune. The collegial atmosphere he had felt when extinguishing the fire had disappeared.

"Ah! Behold, the executioner honours the monastery with another visit."

Jakob turned, saw the abbot descending from the main building, and bowed slightly as he waited for him at the bottom of the stairs.

"Word has got around that you are a master at showing up where a hangman has no business being," said the abbot in a sardonic tone. "First came the brawl at the Oberammergau cemetery, then you appeared at the monastery tavern during the earthquake, and now you are even snooping around in the Sacred Blood Chapel."

"Someone was murdered," Jakob replied curtly. "The medicus wanted my opinion."

"The medicus who just happens to be your son-in-law. They say you ask questions about things that don't concern you."

Jakob shrugged. "The venerable secretary gave me his permission to ask any question I wanted to." That was a lie, but the hangman assumed that Lechner and the abbot didn't waste much time talking about a dishonourable underling. "As you already know, Sailer hanged himself in the chapel," Jakob said. "He's the third Oberammergauer in just a week to die under questionable circumstances. Surely, officials at the monastery must hope there are no more such incidents."

"This matter is no longer a worldly concern," the abbot snapped. "Ever since the earthquake it must be perfectly clear that we have angered our Lord. We never should have tried to reschedule the Passion play. Only faith can save us now." His face twisted into an evil smile. "In any case, it appears that your superior, the Schongau secretary, is overwhelmed by these events. I shall write a letter to Munich and ask that the investigation be put back in the hands of the ecclesiastical court here at the monastery. And oh, by the way . . ." Abbot Benedikt stopped as if something trivial had just crossed his mind. "The secretary has been waiting for some time to see you. It seems he's not very happy with his hangman, or so I hear."

Jakob frowned and looked around. The secretary's splendid dapple-grey horse was hitched up outside one of the sheds, but he himself was nowhere to be seen. "Where can I find him?"

The abbot pointed up the steep mountainside behind the monastery. "He has gone for a walk up the trail into the mountains. You should go and join him immediately. And now run along. I have to pray for all the lost souls in this valley. And for yours, as well."

His robe swishing, Abbot Benedikt hurried away, leaving the puzzled hangman standing alone in the courtyard. Jakob had been surprised by the abbot's words. Why, for God's sake, was Lechner waiting for him up in the mountains and not here in the monastery? Well, no doubt only the secretary himself could give him the answer, so he left the monastery through a low-beamed side door and headed towards the back of the building. From there, a muddy path led first through fields and mountain pastures and finally along a brook and into the monastery's forest. At regular intervals, Jakob passed little shrines representing the stations of the cross in the Saviour's journey from His sentencing by Pontius Pilate to the crucifixion site. Jakob couldn't help thinking of the three victims, all of them actors in the Passion play.

Who will be next? he wondered as he strode up the way of the cross. *Matthew, John, or perhaps the venerable Peter?*

Little beads of sweat stood out on his forehead. The path was not especially steep, but it was a warm day and he was still wearing his thick woollen coat. Briefly, he considered taking it off, but he didn't want Lechner to see him looking like some random peasant in his sweaty shirt. He was, damn it all, the Schongau hangman. And he wasn't accustomed to marching up some way of the cross only because his superior wanted him to.

It's time for me to retire . . .

After about a quarter mile, the path led out of the forest, ending in a hill behind the monastery. A final devotional plaque showed the Mount of Calvary and three crucified men. Next to it was a bench where Johann Lechner sat, looking very relaxed. The secretary was alone. He had closed his eyes, stretched out his legs, and was clearly enjoying the afternoon sun.

"You are late, hangman," he said, without opening his eyes.

"I'm a simple man without a horse or a coach," Jakob grumbled, as he wiped the sweat from his brow with his dirty shirtsleeve. "It takes a bit longer for folks like us to get here from Unterammergau, and I also stopped at each station of the path to say a prayer for the honourable secretary."

Lechner laughed softly. "Always in a joking mood, our Schongau hangman." He pointed to the bench. "Take a seat."

Kuisl settled down, and for a brief moment they were just two old men resting in the mountains and enjoying the sun. They looked at the monastery below, in the midst of blooming meadows and surrounded by mountains. The sight was so breathtakingly beautiful that for a moment Jakob actually forgot why he was there.

"Pretty spot," Lechner said after a while. "So peaceful and undisturbed, with no nosy eavesdroppers."

"Is there any reason we should fear eavesdroppers?" Jakob asked.

The secretary smiled. "If there's one thing I've learned in the last few days, it's that you can't trust a soul in this accursed valley – not the abbot, not the judge, and above all not these stubborn mountain people who don't seem to live by any laws or rules." For the first time, Lechner turned to look at Jakob. "The same is true for these cramped, mouldy chapels where a private conversation is almost impossible. So, what have you learned, hangman?"

Jakob froze. He'd expected a severe tongue-lashing because he'd been snooping around without telling Lechner first, but evidently Lechner's angry outburst in the chapel had just been an act.

The secretary winked at him as if he'd guessed what Jakob was thinking. "You are my dog, hangman," he said. "I've taken you off your leash so you can sniff around, but I don't want anyone to know I'm the one who let you go. And now, speak up and tell me what you know."

Jakob cleared his throat. "Sailer hanged himself, there's nothing secret about that, but I found one of the Pharisees in his pocket, too. I assume that Franz Würmseer also received a figurine like it." Then he told Lechner how Würmseer had immediately recognized the figurine even in the semi-darkness of the chapel. He didn't mention the broken piece of wood in Sailer's pocket, even though it raised questions in his mind.

After he'd finished, Lechner nodded approvingly. "Good sniffing, executioner. That all fits together with what I've been thinking."

"Sailer got the figurine as a reminder from someone," Jakob speculated, "and shortly afterwards he hanged himself. But why? Why does anyone kill himself just because he was given a carved Pharisee? It must have something to do with greed and hypocrisy."

"Yes, this Xaver Eyrl could probably have told us what that was, but he escaped, unfortunately." Again Lechner closed his eyes, as if he just wanted to sit there and enjoy the sunshine.

"So it's Würmseer," he said finally. "Well, you see, you really helped me."

"But there's something else," Jakob said. "Simon told me about some strange happenings here in the valley." He told Lechner about the children's bones, the black rider, and the stone circles. When he got to the last one, Lechner suddenly pricked up his ears and sat up on the bench as if he'd been stung by a wasp.

"Where did Simon see these stone circles?" he asked sharply.

"Beside the old Roman highway near Unterammergau, and then there's one alongside the Malenstein and one up on the Döttenbichl, too."

"Three stations, then," Lechner mumbled, partly to himself. Then he continued: "Have you talked with anyone else about this?"

Jakob shook his head. "Not that I can remember." But he didn't mention that little Peter probably had already talked about it with some of the children, and Georg Kaiser most likely knew about it, as well.

Lechner looked at Jakob very sternly. His calm expression vanished and he seemed very concerned. "Listen, from now on I want you and Simon to stay out of this. You can go home. I don't need you here any longer."

"I beg your pardon?" asked Jakob.

"I said you can go home to Schongau before you stir up things any more here. You have helped me very much – thank you."

"But . . ."

"You can go." Lechner motioned impatiently. "Now let me sit here a while by myself. I have to think."

"And so do I," the hangman responded grimly. "About lots of things – especially about sniffing dogs released from their chains," he added quietly.

He got up from the bench and walked back down to the monastery. He was so furious he'd forgotten to say goodbye to the secretary.

But Johann Lechner had already closed his eyes again, as if listening to a melody only he could hear.

Magdalena was dead.

She lay in a mouldy coffin, her limbs cold and stiff. She could feel the coolness of the metal coins placed on her eyes as an offering to Charon, the ferryman of Hades, who carries the newly deceased across the river from the world of the living to the world of the dead. From far off, muffled by the thick lid of her casket, she could hear the deep, sad singing of the faithful assembled for her burial service. Magdalena wished she could cry, but she was dead, after all.

Suddenly she heard a loud rushing, and her legs felt wet.

The water, she thought. *The water.*

Cold dark water rushed into her coffin, from her legs to her hips, then to her shoulders, and finally a wave passed over her face, taking her breath away. She struggled to stay above the water, but no matter how hard she tried, she kept banging her forehead against the lid of the casket. All that remained was a tiny bubble of precious air, and then that, too, was gone. The water flowed up her nose, into her mouth, into her entire body, and it tasted salty, like . . . *blood?*

Magdalena wanted to scream, but more and more salty liquid poured down her throat.

She was bathing in her own blood.

"Water, water!" she gasped.

She felt a warm, comforting hand on her forehead. "All is well," said a deep, muffled voice. "The Lord is with you."

Suddenly she felt something warm on her lips, a salty liquid just like the one she was coughing up and spitting out in her dream just seconds ago.

"It's too bad to waste the good potion," someone grumbled. "Sleep, girl, sleep . . . Sleep is the best medicine now."

"Barbara . . ." Magdalena mumbled. "The Master . . . I . . . must get to Oberammergau . . ."

"You must sleep now and get better."

Again she felt a hand on her sweaty forehead and heard someone speaking reassuring words in Latin that sounded like a prayer. She smelled a mild fragrance of burned herbs that made her feel infinitely tired.

"Sleep, girl."

Her lips still tasted salty from the liquid she had been given, salty like the blood that had come pouring over her in the dream. Just before she passed out again she could feel clearly that this dream was meant to tell her something.

Blood . . . water . . .

But she was too exhausted to think about it any more.

15

ℙONTIUS PILATE WASHED HIS TREMBLING hands in the bowl of water and looked around uncertainly at the crowd of Jews standing among the gravestones in the Oberammergau cemetery. Everyone was waiting impatiently for the Roman governor to find the right words.

"You . . . Pharisees, I wash my hands of the blood . . . of this innocent man . . ." Pilate stopped and stared into the crowd like a calf just before slaughter. Sweat poured down his brow.

"Who suffers . . ." whispered Simon, standing at the edge of the stage and serving again as a prompter.

"Who suffers this *horrribble* indignity," Pilate proclaimed.

"*Horrible* . . . More passion – and pronounce it correctly!" Father Herele shouted, stamping his foot. Wedged between two bearded woodcutters dressed in yellow robes, the priest had been silent until then, intensely watching the events on the stage. Now he came forwards, shaking his finger threateningly. "Didn't anyone teach you peasants proper German in school? What will the pilgrims think, after coming from far and wide only to hear this gibberish?"

"That's not gibberish, it's Bavarian dialect," exclaimed Pontius Pilate, who was actually the woodcutter Alois Mayer. "Where we live we don't say *horrible*, but *horrribble*, just as we call death here *boandkramer* and the king is a *kini*."

"Aha! I see. Do you think here in Oberammergau we should inscribe KINI OF THE JEWS on the cross?" the priest asked irritably.

"That's all right by me," snarled Jesus Christ, alias Hans Göbl, who was dressed in a white robe and stood alongside Pontius Pilate. "Nobody talks in pompous words like the ones in this play – except for our venerable priest, of course. But after all, he comes from Swabia!"

"Please," Georg Kaiser begged, raising his hands and trying to calm everyone down. "I know everyone here is a bundle of nerves, but let's continue – at least until noon."

"I've got to be back in the barn by the noon church bells at the latest, or my Resl will scratch my eyes out," grumbled one of the peasants, dressed in his costume and leaning wearily on a wooden cross. "This crap has been dragging on since early this morning."

"And anyway, God doesn't want us to put on the play this year," a second one said. "Every ten years – that's what our ancestors promised back then. And now this fatheaded Faistenmantel comes along and thinks we can do it all differently. Well, you can see what comes of that."

Simon sighed and turned to the next page while his gaze wandered over the Oberammergau cemetery. Almost the entire village had shown up to rehearse the famous scene in which the crowd demands the death of Jesus, and Pontius Pilate washes his hands in innocence before finally delivering him up to the crowd to be crucified. Ever since Sebastian Sailer had been found dead the morning before in the Unterammergau Sacred Blood Chapel, the villagers had become increasingly restless, especially as the suspect, Xaver Eyrl, was still on the loose.

Father Tobias Herele had decided to rehearse the famous crowd scene in hopes of reviving a certain sense of community, but just the opposite occurred. People cursed, cried, and wailed; many couldn't help wondering aloud who would be struck down next by this sinister curse that had already taken the lives of three men. But there were also some citizens, primarily confidants of Konrad Faistenmantel, who continued to support the accelerated schedule for the production.

"Please continue," Georg Kaiser pleaded in a loud voice, turning to the crowd. "The people cry out *'Crucify him'*."

"Away with him, crucify him," mumbled the crowd. Indecisively they stood amid the gravestones in their homemade robes, appearing to Simon like a group of foreign pilgrims who had got lost.

This action doesn't really take place on the stage, he thought. *But either way it's a Passion play, a story about human suffering.*

The medicus admired the fine filigree of the painted backdrops that had been set up behind the stage before rehearsal with a block and tackle. Their depiction of houses, synagogues, and palm trees was so artistic that the audience might imagine that they had been transported to Jerusalem. Simon grinned. The Oberammergauers might be stubborn, angry people, but they were also artists, woodcarvers, painters, actors . . .

A really unusual place, he thought, *in every respect.*

"Can't you speak a bit louder?" Georg Kaiser called to the crowd. "Come on, we want to hear you everywhere in the valley!"

"Crucify this man. Crucify him, for he has done much evil," they called a bit louder, but they still sounded more like a grumbling crowd of drunken taverngoers than an enraged mob in the streets of Jerusalem.

"What's the point of all this?" Pontius Pilate mumbled, drying his hands on his filthy toga. "We have no Judas any more . . . Who's going to betray the Saviour?"

"Don't worry, we'll find another Judas," Georg Kaiser said, trying to calm him down.

Mayer snorted. "I don't think so, after everything that happened here last week. This curse is going to—"

Astonished shouts could be heard coming from the area near the cemetery's entrance. Moments later Simon saw Judge Johannes Rieger striding solemnly through the crowd, waving his walking stick and heading towards the stairway leading to the stage. After climbing up, he turned towards the men and women who were watching him anxiously. His earnest expression suggested he had a very important announcement.

"Dear citizens of Oberammergau, hear me," he began sombrely, banging his stick on the floor of the stage. "I have just returned from a visit with the abbot of Ettal and have bad news for you, news that some of you may have been fearing for a long time." He paused dramatically before continuing. "The play has been cancelled. There will be no more rehearsals, and you can therefore all go back to your work, as is pleasing to God."

The uproar now was quite a bit louder than the grumbling of the unwilling actors. Rieger raised his hand, and the crowd fell silent.

"The abbot is of the opinion that it was wrong to schedule an earlier performance, and all the dreadful events of recent days have shown we no longer have God's blessing. We must now do everything we can to regain His favour."

"A just decision," cried the miller Augustin Sprenger. "The Passion play was cursed, and one of us would have been taken next."

Some in the crowd loudly applauded him, but there were also objections.

"What are we going to do with all the backdrops and costumes we've made?" asked a young woman who came from a family of seamstresses. "Shall we throw them all in the Ammer?"

"They'll be put in storage for the production that's scheduled in four years," Rieger responded. "Just as we've always done. I'll repeat . . . It was a mistake to move up the schedule for the play, and God has punished us for that."

"But we had expenses," an old shoemaker protested. "Who's going to repay us?"

Johannes Rieger grinned and pointed at Konrad Faistenmantel, who was standing in stunned silence amid the quarrelling crowd. "The chairman of the town council will pay for everything, as promised. That's the monastery's irrevocable decision."

Konrad Faistenmantel was stunned at Rieger's words. The blood drained from his face, and suddenly he looked very vulnerable. Simon remembered that the fat, blustering merchant had just lost his youngest son a week earlier. The Passion play had sustained him since then, but now Faistenmantel slumped over.

"But . . . but . . ." he gasped. "How is this possible? I had figured on income from the play, and if it is cancelled now, then . . ."

"Why should we give a damn?" one of the woodcarvers cried. "For years, you've forced us to buy wood at exorbitant prices, and paid us far too little for our carvings. Now it's finally your turn to pay the piper."

The crowd shouted their approval. A circle of angry villagers started to close in around Faistenmantel.

"I built the cross!" Alois Mayer shouted.

"And we painted the backdrops," the younger Göbl brothers chimed in. "He promised us five guilders for that."

"Pay up! Pay up!" they all started shouting.

"You're getting nothing, you riffraff!"

Konrad Faistenmantel had evidently regained his old self-confidence. He glared at his creditors, his arms folded across his chest and a vein bulging out on his forehead.

"You have not yet heard the last of this," he snarled. "I'll speak with the abbot, and who knows . . ." His eyes narrowed to tiny slits. "Perhaps I know a thing or two that will displease His Excellency and make him change his mind."

Franz Würmseer had remained in the background until then, but now he ran forwards and seized Faistenmantel by the shirt collar. "You dog! What do you know? You . . . you know nothing!" He shook the fat council chairman, who was evidently surprised by the attack.

"Don't push your luck, Franz," gasped Faistenmantel as Würmseer kept a firm grip on him. "Nothing matters to me now."

With a clenched fist, Faistenmantel took a swing at Würmseer, knocking him to the ground, but at the next moment the two younger Göbl brothers jumped up and started pummelling the council chairman furiously.

"Wait for me!" shouted Jesus Christ from up on the stage. "That bastard has it coming to him."

Hans Göbl jumped down and joined in the fray. Even Pontius Pilate didn't seem to want to wash his hands in innocence that day. Dressed in his gold-trimmed Roman toga, Alois Mayer pushed his way through the crowd, swinging his fists, until he got to Konrad Faistenmantel, who was now flanked by his two remaining sons. Together, the three Faistenmantels flailed in all directions.

"I built the damn cross," Mayer shouted again, as if it were a battle cry. "Expensive, solid oak. The bastard owes me eight guilders."

Johannes Rieger was still standing on the stage, staring in disbelief at the raging mob that, for the second time in a week, was now brawling in the cemetery.

"I hate these Oberammergauers," he groaned, finally. "Why did I ever let them transfer me to this valley?"

"What did Faistenmantel mean when he said he knew a thing or two?" Simon asked. He ducked as a fist-sized clod of dirt came flying towards the stage.

Rieger stared at him angrily. "How should I know? Don't always be poking your nose into things that don't concern you, Herr Fronwieser. I warn you, that can have dire consequences," he added menacingly.

Down below, the priest was still struggling to get the angry crowd under control, which was proving to be difficult. The only one standing above the fray, it seemed, was Georg Kaiser. The director had taken a seat on what was supposed to be the throne of Pontius Pilate, calmly observing the altercation, with a look of extreme relief on his face.

"So this is the end of this madness," he said softly. "I probably wouldn't have finished my revisions to the text by Pentecost, anyway."

"Probably not even by the Last Judgement," Simon answered, dodging a rusty helmet that landed on the stage.

Kaiser shrugged. "Some things just take time."

Simon was about to reply when he stopped short. The melee was still continuing down below, but one of the participants had disappeared. Carefully, Simon looked around the cemetery, but he couldn't find him anywhere.

Franz Würmseer had vanished.

Magdalena opened her eyes and found herself looking up into the branches of a willow that had grown together to form a sort of roof overhead. It took her a while to comprehend she was not lying under a tree but inside a simple hut. Outside, not far away, she could hear a monotonous rumbling, and it took her a while to figure out what it was. There was also the sound of rushing water, and she assumed it was the Ammer.

The Ammer . . . All of a sudden the memories came rushing back. The Tyrolean and young Lukas had spirited her out of Soyen in a barrel, then a fight had broken out on the bridge – a fight that Lukas lost. His sympathy for Magdalena had presumably cost him his life. Finally, the Tyrolean had thrown the barrel, with her inside, into the river. The barrel had finally burst, and sunk.

And now she was here.

Where am I?

Carefully, she sat up and looked around the sparsely furnished, dome-shaped hut. She was lying on a mat of rushes spread over a bare hard-packed dirt floor. Crab traps and mended nets hung on the walls, which, like the ceiling, were also made of willow branches.

Magdalena's head still hurt, presumably from the blow she'd received in the shed in Soyen. She had a dry cough, and her limbs were as limp as swamp grass. She was probably running a fever, which would be no surprise since she'd almost drowned in the cold waters of the Ammer. But someone must have saved her. She remembered the gentle voice in her dreams as well as the water, the taste of salty blood, and her own burial . . .

Magdalena frowned. Something in the dream rang a bell.

Water and salty blood . . .

"Ah! You are already looking better," said a muffled voice behind her.

Magdalena turned towards the entrance and cried in terror on seeing a horrible, positively nightmarish figure. The creature was wearing a thick woollen robe that almost looked like a suit of armour, but instead of a head, a sort of fuzzy sausage grew out of his shoulders, ending in a smooth protruding disc. It looked like a beheaded monster. Now the disc spoke again, once more in the strange, muffled voice.

"Oh, excuse me, I forgot I'm still wearing my beekeeper's hat. How clumsy of me."

Leather gloves tugged at the felt, and a friendly, very wrinkled face appeared. The head looked much too small atop the strange body in the heavy black uniform.

"I just returned from caring for my bees," the man explained with a friendly smile. He had a monk's tonsure and was probably going on seventy years of age. "We have a new queen, and there's a lot of excitement," he continued genially. "My little friends are not always especially kind to me." He grimaced, pointing to his right ear, which had swollen to twice its normal size.

Magdalena couldn't help laughing. "Excuse me," she said, "but I briefly thought a monster . . ." she started to say before breaking out in a coughing fit.

The old man looked concerned and came forwards to lay a hand on her forehead. "You still have a fever," he murmured. "I'll give you some of my honey – that will help at least with the coughing – and perhaps a potion made from willow bark."

The deep voice seemed out of place coming from the delicate little man, but it had a calming effect on her. It sounded like the same voice she'd heard in her dreams. "Where am I?" she finally asked.

The old man looked surprised. "Oh, didn't I say? You're near the Augustinian monastery in Rottenbuch. I'm Brother Konstantin, in charge of caring for the bees, and occasionally I go fishing, too." He shook his head slowly from side to side. "It's lucky for you I was down at the river yesterday morning checking my traps."

"*Yesterday* morning?" Magdalena was shocked. "And so . . . I've been here since then?"

"Yes, almost two days. Most of the time you were sleeping, but several times you spoke in your dreams. 'The water, the water,' you kept saying. It appears you almost drowned." Brother Konstantin smiled sheepishly. "I had to kiss you in order to bring you back from the dead – the first kiss I ever gave a woman, and probably my last. The life of an ascetic monk can sometimes be very lonely."

Magdalena struggled to sit up. "I've got to go to Oberammergau," she said. "If it isn't already too late."

Brother Konstantin gently pushed her back down on to the reed mat. "You'll go nowhere, at least not yet. You've got a fever, girl. You should thank God and all the saints that they saved you from the raging river."

"With your help," Magdalena replied weakly.

The monk shrugged. "I was only the tool. You were caught in my traps like a fish with especially beautiful scales, and I was sure you were dead. But you were still breathing, so I brought you back to my fisherman's shack, dressed you, and—"

Magdalena was shocked. "I was naked?"

"Well, your clothes were soaked, and you needed something dry to wear." Brother Konstantin winked. "Have no fear. I'm a monk, firm in the faith, and besides already quite old, so that the Lord has freed me from the desires of the flesh. All I needed was the kiss."

Only now did Magdalena realize she was wearing a rough monk's robe instead of her dress. It was black, made of heavy wool, and, even though it was scratchy, very warm. But it didn't have any pockets, and . . .

The letter!

She suddenly remembered the message Jakob Schreevogl had given her. If she'd lost it in the river, then she was done for. Lechner would never believe her.

"Is this what you're looking for?" Brother Konstantin asked, holding the folded and sealed paper in his hand. Evidently he had correctly guessed why she looked so shocked. "It got wet, but the parchment isn't damaged, and surely the letter is still legible." He smiled mischievously. "And as you can see, I haven't broken the seal."

"I'm deeply indebted to you," said Magdalena, hiding the letter under the robe, "but I have to leave as soon as possible. It's a matter of life and death. My sister is in grave danger, and if I can't help her in time, she will have to suffer great pain and die – if she isn't dead already . . ." she added in a broken voice.

Brother Konstantin looked at her sympathetically. "And you don't want to tell me anything more? Not even why you almost drowned, or what the letter is all about?"

Magdalena hesitated. If she told Brother Konstantin the reason for her trip, he might pass the news on to the Rottenbuch abbot. Rottenbuch and Schongau had a number of commercial ties, and perhaps the abbot here was even aware of the plans of the Schongau burgomaster Buchner. With a sigh, she finally answered, "I'm afraid that's all a bit complicated. To the best of my—"

She stopped short as another dizzy spell came over her. She had to think of her unborn child. Was the child still alive? Or had it perhaps died inside her in the cold water or during her long spell of unconsciousness? Instinctively, she reached down to touch her abdomen.

"You're pregnant," said the monk. "The slight rounding was evident, but you did not have any bleeding, so you needn't worry about that."

Magdalena looked sceptical. "For a celibate monk you know a lot about women."

"Well, even if we have to live without women, we can at least read about them." Brother Konstantin grinned, revealing a few crooked remaining teeth. "Everybody has such secrets."

Again, Magdalena struggled to sit up. "Brother, I absolutely must get to Oberammergau today. Please . . ."

"That's at least four hours away by foot, and with the fever you have, you'd never make it."

"Then let me have a horse. I promise to return it to you. And I . . . I'll pray for you every day."

Brother Konstantin laughed softly. "How can I do that? I'm just a poor old hermit and have no horse – and the monastery certainly won't give one to a nameless girl who doesn't even want to tell why she needs to go to Oberammergau." He shook his head. "It's not possible. It would be best for you to wait here until you feel better, and then go by foot."

Magdalena sank back on her bed of rushes. She felt weaker and more worn out than ever before. All the excitement of the last several days – the worry about Barbara, her fear of death in the barrel, the struggle in the water – overwhelmed her. "Then all is lost," she whispered, as tears welled up in her eyes. The monk sighed.

"Don't cry," he said. "First the kiss, and now this. It's almost as if we're married." He hesitated. "Perhaps I have a solution."

Magdalena's heart beat faster. "What are you thinking?"

"Well, I have an old, stubborn donkey. His name is Franziskus, but unfortunately he's not as gentle as his human patron saint. Perhaps he could take you to Oberammergau." He winked at her. "If he wants to. Franziskus loves to lick on salt-stone, and if you give him enough, perhaps he'll let you ride him."

Magdalena laughed with relief. "By all the saints! I'll treat him like the Saviour's donkey on His entrance to Jerusalem."

Cautiously and with unsteady steps she let Brother Konstantin lead her outside, where bees buzzed excitedly over the riverbank. The sun had already passed its highest point and Magdalena's legs threatened to buckle at every step, but she walked upright down the narrow path leading to the monastery.

She could only hope it wasn't too late to save Barbara.

"You're supposed to go *home*?"

Simon stared wide-eyed at his father-in-law. He'd just returned from Georg Kaiser's house, where the two old friends had gone after the disastrous and apparently last rehearsal of the Passion play. Simon and Jakob ate their meal together silently, each absorbed in his own thoughts. Even the last of Simon's coffee couldn't change the atmosphere. But Jakob's announcement that he'd have to return to Schongau tore Simon from his dark musings.

"Lechner doesn't want me to snoop around here any more," Jakob continued. He settled down comfortably on the bench alongside the stove, where he'd also spent the previous night, his feet on the table and his pipe dangling from the corner of his mouth. "He wants me to pack my things and stay out of this from now on. Yesterday afternoon he fired me."

"And you waited until now to tell me?"

Jakob took a deep drag on his pipe. "I had to think about it; besides, how would it have changed anything if I'd told you? In any case, as you see, I'm still here, and all Lechner can do is throw a fit."

"But why does he want you to leave?" Simon asked, puzzled. "I mean, Johann Lechner brought you along specifically to find out more about the murders."

"Perhaps we've found out too much," said Jakob, pointing the long stem of his pipe at Simon. "The order to stop snooping around applies to you, as well, so perhaps you can soon return again to my charming daughter." He grinned. "That's what you want, isn't it?"

Simon cringed. In fact, ever since the events in Oberammergau had got out of hand, he hadn't thought very much about Magdalena and could only hope that she and Paul were well. Probably Magdalena was still angry at him because he'd decided to accept Faistenmantel's lucrative offer and stay a while with Peter. In any case, he hadn't received any letter from Schongau so far, which wasn't exactly the best sign.

"Konrad Faistenmantel is paying me a king's ransom to work for a few weeks as the bathhouse keeper and medicus," Simon replied as he sat down alongside his father-in-law at the table. "I can't just up and leave, even if Lechner orders me to. Besides, I don't like being pushed around like a pawn in a chess game. We're close to solving this riddle, I can feel it." He sighed. It was driving him crazy . . . If he went home now, everything they'd learned would be in vain, and he'd never receive the money he needed so badly from Faistenmantel. If he refused to leave, he'd be crossing swords with none less than the Schongau secretary. "But everything has changed," he added gloomily, "now that the abbot has cancelled the play."

Jakob frowned. "Cancelled?"

Simon told his father-in-law about everything that had happened at the final rehearsal. Jakob listened silently, and only when Simon mentioned the disappearance of Franz Würmseer did the hangman suddenly prick up his ears.

"Do you know where Würmseer might have gone?" he asked.

"Well, he didn't go home. I went there looking for him, and his wife was very upset. I think she was telling me the truth. She said her husband had been acting very strange recently."

"Hmm. And you said Konrad Faistenmantel said some strange things earlier?"

Simon nodded. "He said he knew something that wouldn't please the abbot, and then Würmseer attacked Faistenmantel like a madman. That's how the whole melee got started."

"Damn!" said Jakob, slamming his fist down on the table. "Everyone in this place seems to know more than the two of us do. Don't we look like fools? And now I'm beginning to think even Lechner knows more than he's letting on. But I'm not going to let them make a fool out of me any longer," he said, pointing his pipe stem at Simon. "Tell your son that he and his friends need to keep an eye out for Würmseer. If he even breaks wind, I want to know about it. And in the meantime, you go and have a talk with Faistenmantel. By God, those two councillors know something that can lead us to the murderer, I can smell it, as sure as I am the hangman of Schongau." He tapped his huge hooked nose. "I'll get hold of Xaver Eyrl. He's the third one who knows something, and if he's somewhere here in the valley, I'll find him."

"And how are you going to do that if Lechner sends you home?" Simon asked.

Jakob grinned mischievously. "Oh, but I left a long time ago, didn't I? I said goodbye to you, then headed back to Schongau. It was this afternoon." He stood up and walked out into the hall, where a long coat, a knapsack, and a floppy hat with a wide brim hung on a hook. "These things only belong to the old pedlar who wanders through the Ammer Valley. It's possible he'll be coming to your door tonight." He nodded grimly. "A Kuisl can't be bossed around that easily, as many have learned."

Just a few hundred paces away, Konrad Faistenmantel started up the path into the forest at the foot of the Kofel that protected the village from erosion and avalanches. Crumpled up in his hand was the letter he'd just received in his workshop at home. One of the young journeymen had handed it to him without comment, but Faistenmantel knew who it was from. He'd been expecting this for days. There was a lot to discuss, and the village tavern was surely not the right place for that. But he couldn't quite figure out why the meeting had to be in that accursed region atop the Kofel. There were other out-of-the-way places that weren't so forbidding.

Sullenly he stomped over the Ammer bridge, then down a narrow cow-path, past the meadows, towards the dark forest. It was late afternoon, the shadows were getting longer, and the Kofel stretched its black fingers out towards the valley. In the dense pine forest, darkness had already fallen.

Anger began to rise again in Konrad Faistenmantel as he pushed his way through the dry branches. The abbot had cancelled the play. Did this arrogant half-wit have any idea how much money, time, and work he, the Oberammergau Town Council chairman, had put into this production? The early scheduling would have given the Oberammergauers the money the village needed so urgently. The town coffers were empty and the trade route, in former times so busy, was in dreadful shape. They urgently needed the money – now – or the town would go to the dogs.

But Faistenmantel wasn't driven just by the money. In fact, the merchant wished to present the Passion as a gift to the Lord, because he too carried the burden of much guilt in his life. He had ruined his competitors; he had sold them bad wood; and he had paid his colleagues poorly for their carvings, then sold them for outrageous prices in Augsburg and Venice. He had always been the strongest one and had swallowed up the others. For this reason – and because he knew they disliked him and in fact were afraid of him – he'd allowed them to play their little games behind his back. He'd guided this village with a carrot on a stick. But now they'd gone too far. What were suspicions at first had turned into a certainty for him. He couldn't go on like this. And as far as the play was concerned, the last word had not yet been heard. Faistenmantel wouldn't give up that easily.

Somewhere in the dense pine forest he could hear a cuckoo announcing the long-awaited summer. A second cuckoo answered, and Konrad Faistenmantel was surprised that he'd heard two of them almost at the same time. It was almost as if they were talking to each other.

Just like people, he thought.

For a moment he thought about his youngest son, Dominik, who had died such a gruesome death. He had also been a strange bird, and Faistenmantel had always suspected that the sensitive boy, in contrast to his strong, strapping brothers, was illegitimate. Last year, when his wife confessed to him on her deathbed that she'd had an affair with an itinerant law student, he wasn't surprised. His grief at the loss of the strange alleged son was therefore restrained. But now other faithful citizens of the town had died, and he had to put an end to it. He would put his foot down, and then this miserable Schongau secretary and his crony the hangman would finally stop snooping around. No matter what some fellow townsmen might have done, they didn't need any out-of-towners here to put things in order.

Again he heard the cry of a cuckoo, now much closer. Konrad Faistenmantel pushed another branch aside and found himself facing a steep rock wall directly below the summit in a dark forest of firs. Following the directions in the message, he turned left and was soon at the specified meeting place: a shell-shaped hollow known for its deep rock crevices.

Here, too, just as at the Malenstein, the children's hiding spot in the forest, there were ancient drawings in the rock, magical symbols and representations of pagan gods. Among the moss and lichen was a sneering devil's face along with some numbers and letters. For this reason, the place was called Devil's Rock and was, for the most part, avoided, as were the Malenstein and the Döttenbichl, neither of which was far away.

Konrad Faistenmantel passed his fat fingers over the shallowly engraved images and had the impression that some of the figures hadn't been there on his last visit. Perhaps children had added to them – or would grown-ups possibly do things like that?

From far off he could hear bells ringing in the Oberammergau church steeple – three rings, the prearranged signal. He leaned against the cold rock wall and waited. Water dripped on to his bald head from higher up on the mountain, and as he wiped his forehead, he heard a trickling of small stones nearby.

Again he heard the cuckoo, this time directly overhead, and suddenly he was sure it was not a bird but a human voice.

As he looked up, something suddenly grabbed him by the feet, and with a surprised shout he fell hard into the dirt. Only now did he realize there had been a snare on the ground in front of the opening that was suddenly pulled tight. The fat merchant struggled like a rabbit in a trap.

"Hey, what's going on?" he shouted. "Get your dirty fingers off—"

He was silenced as a fist-sized stone struck him on the forehead and, with a groan, his bloodied head tipped to one side.

Quick hands bound him by his arms and legs so tightly that he almost looked like a well-tied bale of rags, then someone pushed a gag into his mouth in case he regained consciousness too soon.

Strong hands marked by hard work lifted him up and carried him through the forest to the place where the great sacrifice had been prepared. If Faistenmantel hadn't been unconscious, he would have seen the imposing cross made of oak beams erected there for him.

Mercifully, he was spared the sight.

With fast, skilful movements Peter sketched the strange stone circle from memory and stared at it, wondering. He wished he knew the meaning of the lines that Würmseer had made with the stones and twigs – if only to impress his father. But no matter how hard he thought, he couldn't make any sense of it. Discouraged, he crumpled up the drawing and threw it into a corner of the cave.

He was sitting with Jossi and Maxl in their hiding place behind the Malenstein. All morning the three boys had been looking for Franz Würmseer. They'd even gone down to Unterammergau, but the wagon driver had seemingly vanished from the face of the earth. Eventually they'd decided to go back to the cave and discuss what to do next. They'd heard noises outside a while ago, and it sounded like a large group of people was walking by, but now silence had returned. The entire time they'd remained silent, carving little figurines and occasionally chewing on their hard crusts of bread.

Peter, at least, had finished the homework Poxhannes had given him the day before as a punishment, and he'd been able to help Jossi, who hadn't got very far in Latin beyond memorizing the Ave Maria and the Lord's Prayer. Strangely, Hannes hadn't seemed very interested in their progress, and Peter assumed he didn't know much more Latin than Jossi. Otherwise, even though the teacher's assistant had whipped a few pupils in school that day, he had seemed distracted, his thoughts elsewhere.

Jossi and Maxl seemed distracted, as well, possibly because Joseffa still hadn't returned to school. There were rumours she'd been badly injured in the forest, and some said she was dying.

"I told my father about Joseffa," Peter said finally, in order to break the silence in the cave and cheer the boys up a bit. He was proud his father was able to cure people. "He said he'd go have a look today."

Jossi looked at him in astonishment. "You did *what?*"

"Well, my father is a medicus, and I thought I could—"

"How many times do we have to tell you not to meddle in our affairs?" Jossi interrupted angrily. "You're just going to make it worse."

"But I just wanted to help," Peter whined. Tears ran down his face and, once again, he felt that he didn't belong.

Maxl sighed. "But you don't understand," he said gently, putting his arm around Peter's shoulder. "You meant well, but nobody can help us, we are . . ." He struggled for words.

"Cursed," Jossi said darkly. He stared towards the cave entrance, where the first shadows of the afternoon were settling over the dark firs. A breeze had come up, shaking the branches as if it wanted to reach in to the children in the cave. "God knows, we are cursed."

"By the way, starting tomorrow you'll have to get along without me," Maxl said after a while. Then he cleared his throat. "My father needs me to help with the logging over on the Laber. He'll give me hell if I don't go along."

"It's the same for me, I'm afraid," Jossi added, trying to sound a bit calmer. "If not my parents, then certainly Poxhannes will need me. We can't always escape him. Just this morning he ordered the others to be ready, starting at four o'clock. No doubt he's going to be furious again." He scratched his head. "Even though I don't think he's going to send us off to work in this weather. There's something brewing up there on the Kofel." He smiled sadly at Peter. The older boy looked pale again, just as he had yesterday, and there were still dark rings under his eyes. "Perhaps some other time, all right?"

Angry and confused, Peter tossed a stone towards the back of the cave. Just that morning his father had asked him to keep his eyes and ears open. Würmseer had disappeared during the rehearsal for the play and was now nowhere to be found. Peter was happy his father had put so much trust in him, and now he'd have to disappoint him again.

"Würmseer is up to some mischief," he grumbled, "or we would have found him. I'm telling you, he's hiding somewhere and planning to make trouble. It wouldn't surprise me if he was out to get you workers."

"Perhaps he even left our area and is in Graswang Valley or Tyrol, or God knows where," Maxl replied. "In any case, I'm not sorry he's gone, and I wish he'd taken his fat son along, too – then we'd finally have a little peace around here." He laughed bitterly, then got up from his rocky seat and addressed the others. "Let's go home. It'll be dark soon and we won't be able to look any more."

Jossi, too, stood up. With an apologetic look, he turned to Peter. "We really tried, Peter. Don't be sad. We've taken some risks because of you, and we just can't do anything more." Along with Maxl he squeezed his way out through the small hole in the back of the cave. Peter followed, struggling with tears. For a brief time, he thought he'd finally found a group of friends, but now everything seemed to be falling apart. Moreover, he had the feeling that Jossi and Maxl were hiding something from him. Sometimes they would glance furtively at one another or whisper behind his back with the other workers' children. No doubt they wanted to keep their distance from him, the dishonourable grandson of the Schongau executioner. How could he know if the story about having to work for their parents or Poxhannes was really true or if they got together to play secretly without him?

The boys were just climbing over a boulder alongside the Malenstein down to the path, when they suddenly heard steps coming up the trail from the south. Jossi grabbed Peter by the collar and yanked him back behind the rock, and when Peter was about to object, Maxl put his finger to his lips.

"It's possible Poxhannes is snooping around, looking for us," he whispered, fear showing in his face. "He likes to wander around in the forest. Let's have a look at who it is."

As they waited, the sound of the footsteps drew closer, and soon the footsteps were right in front of their hiding place. Peter held his breath, but there was no reason to be afraid. Whoever was coming up the path was in a hurry and ran on past them. Curiously, Peter peeked over the top of the rock – and froze.

There, just a few yards in front of him, Franz Würmseer was jogging up the trail. Soon he disappeared behind a clump of trees.

"Come on, let's see where he's going," whispered Jossi, who had clearly smelled blood.

They followed the trail, scurrying over moss-covered boulders and fallen tree trunks, trying not to lose sight of Würmseer. Once or twice Peter stepped on a dry branch and cringed, fearing that Würmseer might have heard it, but the wagon driver seemed completely wrapped up in his thoughts. He was running so fast that they lost sight of him a few times, but he stayed on the path and each time they were able to catch up.

After a while the path led out of the forest and back to the country road. Franz Würmseer was now just a tiny figure with a coat fluttering behind him as he hurried back to Oberammergau. An icy wind swept down the mountain, and Peter was freezing cold. High above, the clouds gathered in dark masses, and he had to squint to protect his eyes from the gusts of wind.

When he opened them again, Würmseer had disappeared.

"Damn! That's not possible," Maxl muttered. "He can't have just vanished in thin air – it's almost like black magic."

"I think it's a lot simpler than that," Jossi answered. "Follow me."

As fast as their feet could carry them, the boys ran across the muddy fields strewn with cow droppings and towards the road. Now that they'd lost sight of Würmseer, they threw caution to the wind and had soon reached the road, which here, just outside of Oberammergau, was full of ruts and puddles. The ancient flagstones had shattered or were missing completely. At this point the road ran atop a slightly elevated embankment through the moor.

"Now you must be very quiet," Jossi whispered, "and I'll show you how Würmseer was able to disappear."

They scurried along the road through the bushes and heather until Jossi suddenly stopped and pointed downwards excitedly. A ramp led down from the road to a cattle trough with a stone shrine and a bench alongside it.

And in fact, Franz Würmseer was sitting there.

In the hollow he would be invisible from the forest. Two black horses bathed in sweat were there, drinking from the trough, and behind them stood a wagon like the ones wagon drivers used. At that moment a man with a shaggy beard and wearing a battered floppy hat stepped out from behind the wagon. He had been lashing the barrels and sacks together on the wagon, and now he appeared to be very annoyed.

Jossi motioned to the other boys, and they crouched down behind a stunted mountain pine to see what would happen.

"We've got to stop this, it's becoming too dangerous," the man said as he tightened the ropes around a chest. "The Tyrolean thinks so, too." He looked up nervously at the sky, where black storm clouds were gathering.

"Not if you do exactly what I say," Würmseer said, his voice oddly soft and high-pitched. "We've already taken this too far, and there's no going back, and that goes for you, too."

"That Schongau hangman will put you on the rack when they find out," the other man answered angrily. "And before that he'll yank your guts out and feed them to the dogs. I don't want to end up on the scaffold like you, Franz, not for all the money in the world."

"Nobody is going to end up on the scaffold," Würmseer reassured him. "Believe me, all this nonsense concerning the Passion play can only benefit us. People fear the anger of God more than anything else, and that fear is our best defence. I'm sure the Schongau secretary has no idea what's going on. Remember, I sit on the council."

Spellbound, the three boys hunkered down behind the mountain pine to listen. Peter had no idea what they were talking about, but he suspected it was connected somehow with the terrible murders. Was this unscrupulous wagon driver perhaps the murderer everyone was looking for? Or was it Franz Würmseer? He stuck his head out a bit farther to get a better look. Suddenly, a duck came out of a bush nearby, quacking and fluttering its wings, and Würmseer looked up. In the last split-second, Peter pulled his head back in again.

"What was that?" Würmseer asked in an undertone.

"You saw it yourself – it was a duck," the other man answered with a shrug. He made a little quacking sound and laughed. "You're so anxious."

"Rightly so. This is too important, and we can't be careless. If anyone hears us and reports it, we're finished. We'd better not stay here any longer." Würmseer got to his feet. "I'll see you tonight after sundown on the Döttenbichl, right?"

The other man sighed. "Very well, if that's the end of it." He sniggered diabolically. "But you're right, it's all worth it just to have a chance to spit in that fat bastard's face again."

The bearded stranger led the horses away from the trough and started hitching them up again while Franz Würmseer walked up the ramp to the road.

He was walking straight towards the three boys.

Peter put his hand to his mouth in horror, as the crippled pine was not a very good hiding place. Even if the boys could have disappeared down a rabbit hole, Würmseer would still see them.

He came closer and closer, three paces, two paces, one . . .

"Hey, Franz!" the man called at that moment from down below. "These damn animals are refusing to move again, they won't let me hitch them up. Come on, I need your help."

Cursing, Würmseer turned on his heels and walked back down again to the trough. The children used this chance to run to the other side of the road, down the embankment where they couldn't be seen, and back to Oberammergau.

"That was damn close," Maxl panted as they ran along. "I don't know what they would have done if they'd found us, but it would certainly be more than a spanking."

"They would have killed us," Jossi replied simply. "Did you recognize the wagon driver? That was the knacker Paul who sometimes drives for Würmseer. He's a gloomy character who lives alone out on the moor, and they say he's robbed people's coaches and slit the drivers' throats."

Now they were running along the road again atop the embankment. In front of them they saw the Ammer River bridge, behind which the first houses of Oberammergau were visible.

"Was this knacker Paul perhaps the one who crucified the son of your council chairman?" Peter whispered, slowing down with exhaustion.

"I wouldn't put it past him," Jossi replied. "I'm just happy we—"

He stopped short on seeing a figure that appeared as if out of nowhere on the bridge in front of them. Evidently the person had been waiting down along the river and had jumped up over the railing like an angry spirit.

It was Poxhannes.

In his hand he clutched a switch made of fresh walnut, the kind he always used in class. It whistled as he swung it through the air while he grinned triumphantly.

"Ha! I knew you little brats would come back from playing in the forest sooner or later," he said, bending the switch into a U as if testing its strength. "You had to come back over the bridge, didn't you? There's no other way back." His face darkened. "Didn't I tell you to be back by the four o'clock bell? We have work to do tonight, and the others are waiting."

Maxl's face was as white as a sheet. He pointed up at the sky, where dark clouds were gathering. "But it looks like we'll have a thunderstorm today," he replied hesitantly. "In this weather, do we really want to—"

"Shut your fresh mouth," Hannes snarled, and drew the whip across his neck in an unambiguous gesture. His pockmarks turned a fiery red. Impatiently he pointed at Peter. "You, brat, beat it, or I'll whip your arse so hard you won't be able to walk for a week. And you other two, come with me. Get moving." Maxl screamed as Hannes grabbed him by the hair and dragged him across the bridge and towards the moor. Jossi hesitated briefly, then followed the two, his head bowed. He turned around one last time and looked sadly at his friend. Silently, Peter mouthed a single word.

Why?

But Jossi didn't answer. He turned and ran after Maxl and Poxhannes through the moor and into the mountains, where threatening clouds hovered overhead like giant black mushrooms.

The wind tugged at the shutters in the village, making them rattle like little goblins.

Simon hurried down the deserted street, where gusts of wind stirred up dust and leaves. Somewhere an open garden gate squeaked, while from far off came the groaning of the pine trees swaying back and forth in the gathering storm. He looked up at the black clouds as he clutched his hat tightly, ducked down, and continued running.

Simon was still undecided if it was right to disobey the orders of Johann Lechner and stay in Oberammergau. On the other hand, people here needed him. He'd just returned from a quick visit to the

Weidingers, a family of poor workers living outside the village. Peter had told him a little girl lived there who had been badly injured in an accident in the forest. In order not to disappoint his son again, he'd hurried there at once, but when he arrived, all they told him was that the girl was doing much better and she was outside playing with the other children. Strangely, the expressions on their pale faces said something different. The parents looked worried and anxious.

Simon wondered if Jakob Kuisl had really gone out looking for Xaver Eyrl in this weather. Perhaps the hangman was already back in the bathhouse waiting for him. He had decided to pay a visit to the council chairman, Konrad Faistenmantel. After the cancellation of the play, there were some things that had to be discussed – after all, Simon was expected to stay on as the bathhouse keeper and medicus only until the performance. His work was actually finished, and perhaps he could pick up at least part of his pay. In addition, Simon hoped to learn more about Faistenmantel's threat at the rehearsal that morning.

He turned on to the main road, which looked just as deserted as the other streets in the village. Darkness was falling, and Simon assumed that most people had sought shelter in their homes in this weather. The little bunches of St John's wort on the doors swayed in the wind, and a few sprays of the dried herb had been torn off and were blown away over the roofs. One could only hope the storm wouldn't bring hail that would destroy the fields and bring starvation to these poor farmers.

There was no light in the tavern. Apparently the innkeeper had decided to close for the day. Simon turned down a side street and soon stood before the house of the Faistenmantels, where light was visible behind the bull's-eye windows. Hesitantly, he knocked on the door. He heard hasty steps approaching, and the door swung open. Kaspar, the elder of the two living sons, looked at Simon in surprise.

"Oh, it's just you," he said after a brief pause, with visible disappointment. "I thought Father had finally come back."

"That's a shame, I actually wanted to speak with him," Simon replied. "Do you know where he is?"

Kaspar shook his head. The young, powerfully built man looked genuinely concerned. "We don't know. This afternoon he apparently got a message from someone, and then he left abruptly."

Simon stopped short. "Your father got a message? From whom?"

"The journeyman thought it was from a woodcarver's assistant, but he was just the messenger, and we have no idea who the message was from. We're getting worried." Kaspar looked up at the dark sky. "It's not just that he's up in the mountains in this weather."

"He didn't say anything?"

"Hey, are you listening to me?" Kaspar looked Simon up and down with growing annoyance. "No he didn't. Anyway, I don't know what business that is of yours, stranger."

"Well, I'm waiting for my pay. That ought to—"

The door slammed shut and Simon was standing out in the street, his mouth wide open. For a moment he was tempted to bang angrily on the door again, but then he changed his mind. It was pointless trying to argue with these stubborn Oberammergauers – all it would get him was a bloody nose. In any case, it was interesting that Konrad Faistenmantel had got an anonymous message so soon after he'd issued his threats. Had something happened to him? Then again, why should he be interested in the quarrels of these angry little mountain people? Why not just let them bash each other's heads in? Maybe it was better for him simply to pack his things and go home to Schongau – to Magdalena, Barbara, and little Paul. He scratched his head. He'd have to talk with Peter about that tonight. At least the boy was in good hands with Georg Kaiser. He could only hope he wasn't out playing in the forest in this weather. If the wind got any stronger, one could easily be killed by a falling branch.

Wrapped up in his thoughts, Simon was wandering through the little streets towards the bathhouse when he heard a familiar voice. It was Peter, running towards him excitedly. Evidently he'd been playing out there after all.

"For crying out loud," Simon said, shaking his finger at him. "In this weather you'd better get—"

"Father, I've been looking for you everywhere," Peter blurted out. "We . . . we found Würmseer. And he said that . . . that . . ." He was so out of breath he couldn't speak any more.

Simon smiled and took Peter in his arms. "Calm down first – you're completely out of breath, child." For a few moments he was just happy to hug his son and feel his little heart pounding. When this was all over, the two of them would take a long hike in the mountains, go fishing in the Ammer, practise shooting with a bow and arrow, and do all the things that fathers did with their sons.

And certainly not send them out as spies to look for a killer, Simon thought. *But that's just it – we're not a normal family.*

"So," he finally asked. "What did you see?"

Excitedly, Peter told him about Franz Würmseer and his meeting with the strange wagon driver. "They're going to meet after sundown on the Döttenbichl," he concluded, his voice cracking. "And they acted very secretively – they said nobody should find out about it."

Simon looked over at the Kofel. Its summit already lay in darkness, and a first flash of lightning announced the coming storm. "It will be dark soon," he mumbled, trying to get his thoughts together. "What did Würmseer say they would be doing there?"

Peter shook his head, but then something occurred to him and his face brightened. "The other man said he's looking forward to spitting in the fat bastard's face."

"The fat bastard?" Simon sucked the air in between his teeth, and a sudden chill ran over him. "Damn! I have a suspicion who this fat bastard could be."

He struggled to think. If the bastard they'd spoken of was actually Konrad Faistenmantel, he was in grave danger, if not already dead.

Somebody had to go up there and check, but who could he trust in the village? Actually there was no one except his old friend Georg Kaiser and, naturally, his father-in-law, but Kaiser was a sick old man and Jakob Kuisl was out somewhere in the valley. He couldn't wait for him to come back, because then it might be too late. Brushing aside his doubts about remaining in the Ammer Valley, he realized he'd have to climb the Döttenbichl alone, like it or not. A human being possibly needed his help there – and besides, Simon was more than curious what this meeting was all about. He suspected he'd find the key to at least part of the riddle there.

"Where are your friends?" he asked Peter.

Peter put on an anxious face. "Poxhannes took them away with him, out on to the moor. I don't know what they're doing there, but—"

"Peter, I don't have any time for a long story," Simon interrupted. "If your friends aren't here, I'll take you to Georg Kaiser. I don't want you playing out here by yourself. After everything that's happened, it's too dangerous, especially with the storm coming."

"But . . . but . . . I wanted to go up to the Döttenbichl with you," Peter said angrily as the sound of thunder drew nearer.

"Out of the question," said Simon, shaking his head. "This is not a thing for children, so come now, we've got to hurry. It's going to start raining soon, and it's bad enough that I'll get soaked."

He grabbed Peter by the arm and started dragging him off to the schoolhouse.

"You . . . you are so mean!" Peter shouted. "I helped you."

"And I'm grateful to you for that, but I can't take you along. If everything goes well, I'll be back soon and we'll look at some books together, all right?"

"I don't want to look at any books, I want to go to the Döttenbichl."

Peter protested loudly as Simon dragged him down the road, past the cemetery and the school, until they were finally standing in front of the schoolmaster's house. They knocked, and an astonished Georg

Kaiser answered almost immediately, holding a quill pen in his hand. Evidently he had been hard at work.

"Well, why the uproar?" he asked calmly. "Has Peter got into some mischief?"

"No, it's not that," Simon replied, trying to catch his breath after struggling with his son. "Actually, he helped me, but now it would be a good idea for him to stay indoors with you."

He briefly told his friend what he'd learned from Peter, and Kaiser frowned. He tucked his quill pen into the pocket of his housecoat and started polishing his pince-nez, lost in thought.

"And you're sure you don't want to take anyone from Oberammergau along with you?" he finally asked. "Not even a clerk or the judge?"

"My father-in-law hasn't returned yet, and by the time I tell Lechner it may be too late," Simon replied. "I really just want to see what this meeting is about. Perhaps it's something quite innocent, and if not, I can still have someone go and get Lechner." He shrugged. "Aside from him, to tell you the truth, I don't trust anyone, least of all the judge."

Georg Kaiser laughed bitterly. "I understand you all too well. Sometimes this village is one huge snake pit." He leaned down and ran his hand paternalistically through Peter's hair. "Well, then, come along with me," he said in a soothing voice. "I'll ask my maid to make you some sweet porridge before I send her home, and I have a few nice books with illustrations from the Old Testament as well as a book about local legends that we can look at together. Well, what do you say?"

Peter cried softly, but he gave Kaiser his hand and followed him into the main room. It almost broke Simon's heart to see his son being led away looking so sad and forlorn, but he knew it was the best solution for the boy.

"I'll be back soon," he said.

Again there was a rumble of thunder and a bolt of lightning flashed above the Kofel.

"Thank you," Simon said to his old friend as they left. "I know that with you he's in good hands."

Georg Kaiser turned and smiled. "I always wanted children myself, but God never granted my wish. Now at least I try to be a good substitute for a grandfather."

"It was maybe too easy for us," Simon replied, a little more glibly than he intended. He waved to them one last time, then turned away and ran down the deserted street to the Ammer bridge.

The approaching storm whipped up little whitecaps on the river.

"You stubborn beast! This way, not over there. Can't you ever listen?"

Magdalena kept lashing out at Franziskus with her hazel whip, but the old donkey was unmoved by her entreaties and kept turning off the path towards a little brook trickling through the moss. The last rays of the sun fell on the houses of Unterammergau, and then night descended. In addition, a violent thunderstorm was approaching, and they still hadn't arrived at their destination.

Magdalena had been riding along for more than four hours on the donkey Father Konstantin had kindly lent her, and more than once she had wondered if she couldn't have made faster progress on foot. But she was still weak, had a fever, had lost her appetite, and felt sick to her stomach, which was probably due to her pregnancy. As she pulled the donkey behind her, now and then her legs would give out and she'd have to take a seat on the animal. Along the side of the road she'd picked watercress and veronica for her cough, but it hadn't got much better.

Travellers she encountered from time to time on the old trade route stared at her wide-eyed. She still wore the black monk's robe that Brother Konstantin had put on her while she was unconscious. Her unworldly appearance riding on a donkey like a pilgrim was reinforced by her pale, exhausted face and matted hair. People gave her a wide berth, possibly thinking that anyone looking like that would stink three miles against the wind. But perhaps it was just the grim, determined look on her face.

Magdalena had only one goal – to get to Oberammergau and give Lechner the letter from the patrician Jakob Schreevogl. The secretary had to be informed about what was going on in Schongau! This was perhaps her last chance to save Barbara from torture and certain death at the stake.

If it's not already too late, she thought. More than three days had passed since she left Schongau, and it was likely the torturing had already begun.

Courage, Barbara! Courage!

Cursing loudly, Magdalena dismounted and tried to push Franziskus back on to the road with both hands. But the animal just looked at her and brayed. To Magdalena's ears it sounded like mockery. Then the donkey sauntered over the embankment and down to the brook.

"You stupid beast," Magdalena cursed, settling down exhausted on a tree trunk covered with mushrooms. Now she understood why *ass* was such a popular swearword. These animals could drive you crazy with their stubbornness. In an odd way the behaviour of the old donkey reminded her of her father.

With trembling hands, she pushed the hood of the robe over her head. She was freezing, and it wasn't all because of her fever. In the last hour, a cold wind had risen, black clouds loomed up over the mountaintops, and there was a smell of rain in the air. Impatiently she watched the donkey, which had now descended to the edge of the brook, and suddenly realized what the animal was looking for so stubbornly. A rotted, dilapidated trough was standing there on a flat bed of gravel. Someone had hung a little ring of salt there on a nail, no doubt for the cows and goats in the area. Franziskus began to lick it contentedly.

Magdalena couldn't help smiling. The animal loved salt just like little children love candy. The few lumps of salt that Brother Konstantin had given her were used up before they were even halfway there. Now at least she knew how to get Franziskus to move along towards Oberammergau.

Slowly she got up and walked the few steps down to the trough. The nail was rusty and loose, and when she grabbed it, Franziskus licked the back of her hand with his long, warm tongue. She finally managed to pull off the crumbling white ring.

"Come now, good fellow," she said, walking backwards with the ring of salt up to the street. "Here's your candy."

Franziskus followed her like a loyal servant and soon she was sitting atop the donkey again. She leaned forwards, holding the ring of salt in front of his nose, and soon he was trotting along. That wasn't a very comfortable position, but at least they were moving towards Oberammergau much faster now. She thought she could already make out the steeples of the town at the far end of the moor.

While the donkey trotted along, Magdalena pondered the dreadful events of the last few days. Evidently she'd accidentally crossed paths with people planning a crime – and it had to be a big one, as a young Schongau wagon driver had already been killed, and she, too, had narrowly escaped death. She still had no idea what was behind it all. There were hints that it involved the Tyrolean who'd tried to kill her, the same Tyrolean Barbara had seen in Schongau. In addition, the man had spoken about a Master in Oberammergau.

The Oberammergau that now lay only a quarter mile away.

Schongau, Soyen, Oberammergau . . .

The names rang a bell, but whenever Magdalena reached out for it, the thought vanished.

Schongau, Soyen, Oberammergau . . . Schongau, Soyen, Oberammergau . . .

Magdalena gave the donkey one more slap on the side, which didn't seem to make much of an impression on him. A thin white crust of salt had formed on her hand, and she licked it. It seemed to help, as she'd perspired a lot recently. But at the same time it brought back the memory of that horrible dream in which she was drowning in the barrel as if in a coffin and at the end there was a taste of a salty fluid like blood.

Instinctively, she shuddered.

Like blood . . .

She let out a muffled cry. The taste in her mouth had set in motion a chain of thought that shot through her in a fraction of a second. Glances, scraps of conversation, faint smells and tastes instantly came together like stones of a mosaic.

Salty like blood . . .

And suddenly Magdalena knew why she was marked for death, why Lukas Baumgartner had been silenced, and what the Tyrolean was doing in the basement in Soyen. And everything Barbara had seen in Schongau, as well as the identity of the strange Master from Oberammergau, made sense.

"Hey, Franziskus, what the hell do I have to do to make you run faster?"

She spurred the donkey on so forcefully that it was shocked, brayed loudly, and started to run. Magdalena leaned far down over its back and hung on for dear life. Ahead of her, the mountains came together to form a narrow valley with Oberammergau at the other end beneath the low-lying clouds.

The solution to the riddle lay right in front of her.

16

THE FIRST RAINDROPS WERE FALLING AS SIMON
set out for the Döttenbichl. The drops were icy and stung his face
like needles, and the wind had become so cold that the medicus was
freezing in his thin overcoat. Was winter returning again now, so late
in the spring? On the other hand, Simon had heard it could snow
in the mountains as late as June. Once again he missed his home in
Schongau, which, though only twenty miles away, felt to him like a
very different, far more congenial place.

He hadn't met a soul on his way across the Ammer River bridge,
nor on the path along the pasture, which didn't surprise him, as
no sensible person would leave their house in such weather. *Only
someone with evil plans . . .* A gust of wind blew Simon's felt hat off,
and it swirled through the air like a bundle of straw as he cursed and
staggered across the muddy field, chasing it. When the hat finally
came down, it landed right in a stinking pile of cow manure. Simon
carefully picked it up and brushed it off. The hat, which he'd acquired
in Augsburg, was of the highest-quality felt with a red rooster feather
– the only valuable article of clothing he'd taken along on his trip to
Oberammergau. Strangely, the mishap angered him more than all the
other misfortunes of the day. It felt more normal to get riled about

something that wasn't as strange and inexplicable as the black riders, the stone circles, strange figurines, and murdered apostles.

After a superficial cleaning, Simon replaced the hat more securely and continued stomping ahead through the cold rain. Soon he entered the forest and followed the familiar path along the flank of the Kofel. Simon knew he'd soon come to the sloping meadow adjacent to the little hill with a clearing on top that the Oberammergauers called the Döttenbichl. He still couldn't figure out why Franz Würmseer wanted to meet anyone in a place like this. He remembered the children's bones he'd found there and the stories from the woman up on the Alpine meadow over the Laber.

Over there on the accursed Döttenbichl in ancient times they sacrificed men . . .

Even though the sun had set just minutes ago, it was already almost as dark as the dead of night. Thunder rumbled across the high peaks, and the rain gradually turned into wet snowflakes that clung to Simon's coat and skin. His teeth chattered.

In the darkness, the medicus could make out some flickering lights on the hill, presumably torches. Evidently, the meeting had already started. Simon began to count, then he stopped in astonishment. This was no meeting of a few men in the forest, it was a large group. More than a dozen figures were up on the hill, and from somewhere out there in the wet snow and sleet came a deep, muffled murmuring and hissing. Simon took cover behind one of the boulders at the edge of the clearing to observe the activity at a safe distance. Only then did he notice flickering lights on the other side of the hill, as well. It was an entire sea of lights.

Who in the world are all these people?

Despite the rain and the cold, the medicus got down on his knees and crawled closer through the wet grass, hardly noticing that cow dung was soiling all his clothes. He was much too concerned about staying out of sight to think about the sweetish stench of decomposing manure.

Gradually he was able to make out individual figures moving slowly towards the Döttenbichl, and to his astonishment and horror he noticed not just men but women and a few children among them. The strange murmuring and hissing that he'd heard came from these people, who were all looking up at the hill, where a strange structure was being raised. Simon gasped as he recognized the shape in the flickering light.

It was a cross.

And hanging on the cross, upside down, was a fat man, too far away to recognize, though Simon had no doubt who it was.

Faistenmantel! They are crucifying Konrad Faistenmantel!

The hill, the cross, all the people . . . Simon had to put his hand in front of his mouth to keep from screaming. The sight was like a perverse variation of the Passion – as if the devil had decided to write his own play.

And only now did he realize what this huge gathering meant.

The murderer is . . . the entire village.

It seemed like the entire population of Oberammergau had gathered on the Döttenbichl to sacrifice the hated council chairman to some dark power.

About a mile away, Jakob Kuisl plodded through snow and freezing rain towards Oberammergau, where only a few lights were visible in the gathering darkness. From a distance, the village looked strangely lifeless, as if it had been abandoned in a time of war and no one had yet come back to resettle there.

Jakob pressed his floppy hat far down over his face and leaned down to protect himself from the biting wind and lashing rain. Behind him in the Graswang Valley, flashes of lightning bathed the

Kofel in an eerie light, and distant thunder could be heard rumbling like a huge beast reluctantly backing away.

Some time ago, Jakob had angrily tossed the knapsack he'd been using as a disguise in a ditch. He'd spent half the day looking for Xaver Eyrl, a hopeless undertaking, as he had to admit to himself now. The valley and surrounding mountains offered enough hiding places for a whole army, and not one of the pedlars and other dubious characters he'd questioned between Unterammergau and Ettal had seen Eyrl.

Nevertheless Jakob was quite sure the young woodcarver was somewhere nearby. His job wasn't finished, as six of the ten Pharisee figurines had not yet been handed out.

Who were they meant for?

And why?

Back then in the dungeon, Jakob had looked into Eyrl's eyes and had seen an almost maniacal gleam. This man was driven and wouldn't rest until he'd reached his goal. However, it made no sense to continue searching in the snow and sleet – there was just one reason Jakob hadn't stopped searching earlier.

In the darkness, he could look for a light.

It was wet and cold, and if Eyrl was somewhere out there, he'd certainly light a campfire, and even if it was a very small one, Jakob would see it. The hangman could rely on his sight almost as much as his famous sense of smell.

And, fellow, you're finally going to tell me what's going on in the village.

Until now, though, Jakob hadn't spotted any light, not even in Oberammergau, which seemed increasingly strange to him.

Where are they all? Are these stupid mountain people already sleeping?

Well, no matter what was going on, it was damned cold and he urgently wanted his pipe. As he hurried back, he looked up and saw a glint of light in the mountains about a quarter mile away, just above a meadow. At first he thought it was another flash of lightning, but the light didn't go out, and it moved.

Jakob put his hand up to his forehead to shield his eyes from the rain and get a better view. It was either a woodcutter with a lantern, which was improbable in this weather, or it was Eyrl moving to another hiding place.

Lost in thought, the hangman stroked his beard, now partly encrusted with ice. To find out the truth he'd have to go up there in the maelstrom – a rather unappealing and above all dangerous undertaking.

"Damn, Eyrl, if it's really you, I'll skin you alive just for making me do that."

Cursing, Jakob turned off the road and headed back towards the mountains.

Lying on his belly in a cold pile of cow dung, Simon could feel the wet seeping in through his coat and then his shirt underneath. Snowflakes danced before his eyes, but he didn't feel the cold – he was much too horrified and confused to even notice. The sight was so gruesome that he instinctively tried to huddle down even deeper into the grass and mud.

He shut his eyes, then opened them again, but that cross still towered above the Döttenbichl with Konrad Faistenmantel hanging upside down on it. Simon shuddered, thinking of the similarity.

Like Saint Peter, who died the same martyr's death in Rome . . . Faistenmantel wanted to take the part of Saint Peter, and now he's taking it on more literally than he expected.

It was now pitch-black, but in the light of the torches Simon thought he saw blood dripping down from Faistenmantel's temples.

The councillor didn't move and was probably unconscious, if not already dead.

The view got better when a great fire was lit up on the hill. Flames crackled and shot up into the dark night sky, and Simon could see Franz Würmseer standing alongside the cross with a dark and determined look on his face. He crossed his arms and looked down at the crowd, which had formed a narrow semicircle around the hill, their faces glowing in the light from the fire. Simon was shocked to see a number of people that he recognized.

My God, how is this possible?

The superstitious woodsman Alois Mayer was in the crowd, as were Adam Göbl and his sons. Simon saw some of the patients he had visited in just the last few days, as well as some of the familiar actors in the Passion play, such as the young carpenter Mathis, and Josef, the farmer. Among the female players, Mary was there, as was the young Mary Magdalene, holding her two children by the hand. They were picking their noses and curiously observing the activity on the Döttenbichl. Other children sat on their parents' shoulders to get a better view. The people looked curious and expectant. Some appeared a bit reserved, but nowhere could Simon see a trace of sympathy for the crucified man. Simon was relieved to see that Georg Kaiser was not among the spectators, and he couldn't find the priest or the judge, either.

Nevertheless, it appeared that a large number of Oberammergauers had gathered there in the meadow – faithful, good people who went to church on Sunday and gave their tithes to the Ettal abbot, and who were now here to witness a real-life crucifixion.

"Dear friends!" Franz Würmseer announced in a resounding voice while holding up his hand to plead for silence. "I'm pleased to see so many of you here tonight. Some have come because I sent word to you, and others are here perhaps out of curiosity or justified anger. But the one thing uniting us all is concern for our village." He made a dramatic pause and looked down into the crowd below as if trying to look each person in the eye. "Oberammergau has seen bad times. For years, throngs of pilgrims and merchants passed through our town. Our numbers were few, but we all were of old, honourable lineage with certified, documented rights bestowed on us by none less than the German kaiser himself. And today?" His shrill voice rose in a crescendo like the tirade of a ranting priest. "Filthy labourers have settled in our valley like ticks and bugs. They come from far away because they've heard of our beautiful valley, but they don't fit in here – they speak differently, dance other dances, sing other songs. But above all, they are lazy and bring evil into our valley. What has happened recently should serve as a warning to us all."

The crowd began to grumble loudly, and some of the spectators who had evidently come from their work in the fields held up their rakes and hoes like weapons.

"Damned foreigners!" someone shouted. "The devil take them all, and also Faistenmantel, the greedy traitor."

Franz Würmseer nodded approvingly. "In earlier times these filthy, dishonourable immigrants were simply expelled from the country," he added in a loud voice. "They were chained to wagons, hauled down to the Loisach, and put on river rafts. Today the law is much too lenient in these matters, and we can only hope all that will soon change. But until then, we must defend ourselves."

This time there was a loud murmur of approval. Würmseer raised his hands again, and the crowd immediately fell silent.

"Many of you know we have tried everything to stop the decline of our valley," he continued. "We were making progress, even if we broke certain laws. What else could we do if these laws limited our ancient, guaranteed rights? But just as our success seemed at hand, envious people arose who wanted to report us to the authorities because they feared the loss of their own benefits. You all know who I am speaking of." Würmseer pointed at Konrad Faistenmantel, who was still hanging on the cross upside down, lifeless. "Some of you may have sympathy for the fat merchant, but I ask you, hasn't he bullied you and sucked you dry for all these years? Tell me yourself, hasn't your venerable council chairman got fatter and fatter while we suffer want and deprivation? You were all at the last rehearsal, and you heard how he threatened us. So shall we continue to bow down and humble ourselves before him?"

"Never!" roared old Adam Göbl, raising his fist. "We'll put an end to that. The fellow had my son locked up in a dungeon, and now he will pay for that, and for everything else, too. Let's show that greedy dog no mercy – he has tormented us long enough."

Franz Würmseer lowered his hands to quiet the crowd. "We all have various reasons to hate Konrad Faistenmantel, it's not just this last stupid threat. Some of us were bought out, some were paid far too little for our carvings, and still others were cheated in cattle trading or in a thousand other ways." Würmseer's voice lowered almost to a whisper, but with an even more urgent tone. "In ancient times, sacrifices were made here on the Döttenbichl. Some of us still observe this practice in the form of food or precious little objects. But I fear in dark times like these, a greater sacrifice is called for . . ." Again the second burgomaster paused dramatically. Simon could see how all eyes sparkled with anticipation in the light of the torches.

They're really going to kill the old man.

Simon's thoughts were racing. It was probable that here, in this very place, the two immigrant children, Markus and Marie, were sacrificed by Würmseer and some other xenophobic madmen. Konrad Faistenmantel had probably been a witness then and had threatened to expose those responsible. And for that reason he had to die. Simon wondered if young Dominik and Urban Gabler had been murdered for the same reason. Had Sebastian Sailer killed himself because he could no longer live with the guilt?

"We citizens of Oberammergau were always a free and proud people who took orders from no one," Würmseer continued. "We always made our decisions together, and that's what we will do this time. All who agree that Konrad Faistenmantel deserves the death sentence and wish to ward off further trouble, raise your hands."

First hesitantly, then in increasing numbers, hands shot up in the air.

"Kill him!" someone shouted. Another joined in. "Kill!" And then as if in a demonic chorus, "Kill, kill, kill!"

Franz Würmseer raised his hand again to quiet the crowd, then he nodded solemnly. "So shall it be." He pulled out a long dagger and slowly approached the cross.

At that moment there was a faint sound behind Simon. Trembling, he turned around and saw Judge Johannes Rieger along with four of his guards coming out of the forest and striding towards him.

"Jesus, Mary, and Joseph! Thank God you've come," Simon gasped. A wave of relief came over him. Apparently the judge had learned of the horrible plan at the last moment and was coming now to stop it. There was law and order in this valley, after all.

"This wild mob is about to sacrifice Konrad Faistenmantel," he whispered as Rieger stepped up to him. "It seems that Würmseer and a few others have done something dreadful to the immigrant children and the council chairman knew about it. You must immediately—"

"There's a spy here!" Rieger shouted, pointing his walking stick at the astonished Simon. "The fellow was hiding and heard everything. I knew it was a good idea to post guards around the forest." With a thin smile, the judge turned to his guards. "Well done, men – now take the fellow up the hill. It appears the Kofel will have yet another sacrifice today."

Rieger leaned down to Simon, who was frozen with fear. The judge's voice was soft, almost apologetic. "I told you not to get involved in things that are none of your business, Herr Fronwieser. Now it's too late."

Simon shouted as the guards seized him and dragged him up the front as the crowd parted, leaving a path for them. His hat fell off and was trampled in the mud by the mob. The guards pulled the defenceless medicus up the hill, like a sheep to the slaughter, towards the crackling flames and the cross bearing the bloody Konrad Faistenmantel, hanging head down.

Würmseer was still standing at the top, holding the long dagger in his hand.

"Friends! I'm afraid we'll have to vote again," he shouted.

Simon closed his eyes. *This is a nightmare,* he thought. *Dear God, let me wake up!*

As he opened his eyes again briefly, hands were starting to rise.

He could guess what the vote would be.

When Magdalena finally arrived in Oberammergau, it was snowing hard, as if it were again the middle of winter. A thin white layer covered the houses and roads, and the wind howled down from the mountains. She was still holding the ring of salt in front of Franziskus's nose, and he was snapping at it with increasing impatience.

In the last half-hour, Magdalena had got increasingly annoyed by her own stupidity. She really should have figured out much earlier what was going on in that shed in Soyen. Her fear of death had obviously clouded her thinking, but this awareness made no change in her present situation. She had to find Johann Lechner as fast as possible – that was all that counted. She had to save Barbara. At present she had no idea where the secretary was, except that he'd gone to Oberammergau with her father. Now surely Simon could help her find him. She was still angry at him for having extended his stay without discussing it with her, but she felt a deep longing nevertheless to see her husband again – him, and her elder son, Peter, and perhaps there would be an opportunity soon to tell them about her pregnancy. She ran her hand over her abdomen, and her face darkened.

Hopefully Brother Konstantin was right and nothing happened to the child while I was unconscious, she thought. *At least there was no bleeding.*

Magdalena looked around the dark street covered with drifts of snow in hopes of finding someone she could ask about Simon, but there wasn't a soul in sight. Strangely, there were no lights in any of the houses, and the large tavern on the right appeared closed. Had all the Oberammergauers gone to evening mass? Magdalena decided to ride over to the church, whose steeple stood out darkly in the gathering gloom. Here, too, everything seemed forsaken. In the cemetery stood some strange scaffolding and beneath it a sort of stage. Only one man was there, his hands folded in prayer, walking back and forth through the drifting snow.

"Hey! You there!" Magdalena called, waving to him from atop her donkey. "Can you hear me?"

The man looked up, shocked. Magdalena recognized him now by his robe as the village priest.

"Good Lord in heaven," the priest gasped, falling to his knees. "The Saviour has come to Oberammergau."

"I'm not—" Magdalena started to say, but the man interrupted her.

"Oh, I know I have sinned," he whined. "I never should have permitted it. I'm weak, O Lord, and was fearful for my own wretched life. O Lord, forgive me!"

"I don't know what you're talking about," Magdalena muttered, but then she realized what the priest meant. With her hood and long hair she really looked a bit like Jesus in the mural paintings in the Schongau church as He rode into Jerusalem on His donkey.

The only things missing are the waving palm branches and the cheering crowd, she thought.

She dismounted and entered the cemetery, her legs trembling slightly as the priest remained on the stage, kneeling and praying.

"Eh, I can give you some solace, Excellency," she said. "I am not the Saviour but only Magdalena Fronwieser from Schongau, the wife of the bathhouse keeper. I'm looking urgently for my husband. Do you perhaps know where I can find him?"

The priest looked up, perplexed, and now Magdalena could see he was as pale as a shroud and trembling all over. Something seemed to be making him very anxious, and she could feel the anxiety coming over her now, as well.

What happened here?

"Not . . . the Saviour?" he stammered. He got to his feet and shook his head, as if awakening from a bad dream.

"My husband, the bathhouse keeper and medicus," she began slowly and gently, as if speaking to a child. "Where is he?" When she received no answer she continued. "Then do you know where the Schongau secretary is? Or my father, the Schongau executioner?"

The priest let out a shrill laugh, and Magdalena was starting to think he was not all right in the head.

"Ha! An executioner is someone we could put to good use here," he said with a giggle. "So many dead, so many culprits. I suspected it from the beginning, but I was silent. This is my sin, my great sin."

Nervously Magdalena looked around the deserted cemetery. Little drifts of snow covered the graves, and the wind whistled through the open church portal. A strange feeling came over her.

"Where are all the people?" she asked. "There are no lights in the houses."

The priest pointed to the west towards the outline of the mighty Kofel that had caught her eye earlier. "The mountain has called them," he mumbled. "They do evil things there, and I couldn't stop them. As God is my witness I tried to change their minds, but they . . .

they wouldn't listen. Only a few have remained here. The play could
have united us, but now that it has been called off . . ."

Completely wrapped up in his thoughts, the priest babbled on,
but he'd already turned away and was pacing like an animal in a cage,
shaking his head over and over. Magdalena realized she could expect
no help from him.

"Eh, thank you, Excellency," she said politely. "I must go on. As
I said, it's urgent."

She hurried out through the cemetery gate, mounted Franziskus,
and gave him a slap on the backside. "Sorry, old fellow, but it seems
we have to make another trip," she whispered in his ear. "Later you'll
get the biggest ring of salt in all the Priest's Corner, I promise."

Unexpectedly, Franziskus at once started moving, as if he'd
understood Magdalena.

As the babbling of the priest behind her faded into the distance,
she rode through the dark, abandoned lanes of Oberammergau,
squinting in order to see through the blinding snow. The Kofel was
on the other side of the Ammer, and if there was any truth in the
priest's frenzied prattle, many of the inhabitants of Oberammergau
were up there, perhaps even Simon and her father. At least one of
them should be able to tell her what had happened and where Johann
Lechner was. She'd have to go back over the bridge again, across the
pasture, and head for this strange mountain. Sooner or later she'd
have to come upon some people. This valley was so strange.

Magdalena turned right on to the main road that led through
the deserted village, but suddenly Franziskus froze, as if he'd seen a
ghost. In front of them, three riders entered the village, all dressed
in black. It made them seem even weirder that their horses were also
as black as night. Leading them was a single man on a dapple-grey
horse with his hood pulled far down over his face.

The Four Horsemen of the Apocalypse, Magdalena thought at once.
Am I dreaming?

The riders approached with infinite slowness, and Franziskus's flanks trembled, possibly because of the cold, but perhaps, too, because the donkey sensed, as did Magdalena, that something unspeakably evil had taken possession of this valley.

Twenty miles away, Barbara crouched down in her hideaway as the wind shook the shutters.

Ever since the previous afternoon she'd been huddled down in a storeroom hewn out of the rock in Martha Stechlin's cellar. It was so cold that even three thick woollen blankets weren't enough to keep her warm. Along the walls of the tiny recess were jars of pickled gherkins and sauerkraut, withered apples from the previous autumn, and other odds and ends. Sausages and hams hung from the shoulder-high ceiling. The strong odour of smoked meat, so tempting at first, made Barbara feel now as if she were choking. At the moment, she couldn't imagine she'd ever again have any appetite for sausage and sauerkraut, until then among her favourite foods.

Several times she'd pleaded with Martha Stechlin to let her out, but each time the midwife declined. Guards had come to search Martha's house twice, as they knew she and the escaped hangman's daughter were good friends, but they hadn't found Barbara, possibly because the entrance hatch to the storeroom was hidden beneath a shabby, mouldy, stinking sheepskin. Nevertheless, Martha didn't want to take any chances.

The wind moaned, and from somewhere far off Barbara heard something groaning and cracking. Barbara assumed it was a shingle that had come loose. A violent storm seemed to be raging outside. She couldn't help thinking of her sister, Magdalena, who was presumably somewhere in the Ammer Valley, where a May storm like this could easily usher in a wintery blast. Was that perhaps the reason Magdalena still had not returned with Johann Lechner?

Shivering, she wrapped the blankets the old midwife had given her more tightly around herself and brooded. Basically, she was still a prisoner. Would she have to spend her entire life in a hole like this? It all depended on whether Jakob Schreevogl could prove that the Schongau burgomaster was guilty of some wrongdoing. Only then would the dignitaries perhaps realize that Barbara's execution was intended to silence her. But for now it didn't look like that was going to happen. Ever since the day before, Paul had been watching the old cemetery in hopes that Melchior Ransmayer and Burgomaster Buchner would show up there again. But perhaps they suspected they might be under surveillance, and they did not appear. Secretly, Jakob Schreevogl had arranged for an inspection of the sacks at the building site, but had found nothing. Buchner would dissolve the town council at their meeting that night, and they still had no evidence against him.

Above her, the front door of the house flew open with a crash, and she shuddered. Had the guards come back again? Had someone disclosed where she was hiding? She could hear steps moving across the floor, then the hatch opened. She held her breath.

They are coming to get me! This time there is no way out.

But it was the almost toothless face of Martha Stechlin that appeared in the opening above her.

"I have some news," the old woman whispered. "Ransmayer is back at the cemetery – Paul just saw him there, along with a fellow in a tall, bell-shaped hat. It appears they're unloading something from a wagon there."

"The Tyrolean!" Barbara gasped. "So they're meeting again. You've got to tell Jakob Schreevogl right away."

"I'm afraid I can't – the council meeting has already begun."

"The council meeting?" Barbara blanched. "Does that mean it's already evening?" Down in the cellar she had lost all track of time. If the meeting had already begun, it was almost too late.

"Listen, Martha," Barbara whispered after a brief pause. "You must go to the Ballenhaus and try to speak with Jakob Schreevogl under some pretext. He's got to learn about what's happening there."

"You want *me* to go and speak with the second burgomaster during a council meeting where all the fine gentlemen are present in velvet and silk?" Martha laughed bitterly. "You forget I'm just a simple midwife. They'll never let me speak with the master Schreevogl."

"But you have to figure out how, and in the meantime I'll go to the cemetery and try to learn what's going on there."

"And I'm coming, too." Paul appeared alongside Martha, grinning. He'd evidently been standing there listening the entire time. "And I have my slingshot with me," he boasted. "With this we can make things really tough for that stupid doctor."

"You won't do any such thing," Barbara replied. "That's much too dangerous, and you're going to stay here."

Paul pouted. "But you said yourself I should keep my slingshot handy."

"I meant if I was in danger, or if you were, then perhaps . . ."

"But we are in danger!" Paul stamped the ground furiously. "I have to protect you, because Father and Grandfather aren't here. I'm the man here now. If you don't let me, I'll scream."

"For God's sake," Martha Stechlin groaned. "Don't do that."

"All right then, come along," Barbara said, trying to calm him down, "if that's what you really want to do, but don't shoot until I say so. Promise?"

Paul grinned mischievously, pulling the leather sling out of his trouser pocket and swinging it around so it whizzed through the air. "I promise. But in return I get some candied plums, just like the fat noblemen in the tavern down by city hall."

"When this is all over, you'll get so many candied plums they'll be coming out your ears," Barbara replied. With both arms, she boosted herself out of the trapdoor. "Now let's go, before Ransmayer slips through our fingers."

Wedged in between two guards, Simon stood atop the Döttenbichl staring at the many Oberammergauers gathered below around the hill. Some faces were contorted with hate, but most of the spectators seemed just curious or even indifferent. Simon knew these gazes from the occasional executions in Schongau. They were just waiting for the spectacle to begin, and happy they weren't standing up there on the scaffold themselves.

Alongside him stood Franz Würmseer, dagger in hand. He approached menacingly, as the guards forced Simon down on to the snow-covered, muddy ground.

"The verdict is unanimous," Würmseer proclaimed as he cast his eyes over the silent crowd. "The stranger must die."

"You mustn't do this!" cried Simon, struggling in vain to escape the clutches of his guards. "You know me . . . all of you. It's me," he pleaded, "the medicus from Schongau." He turned and looked down at the woodcutter Alois Mayer standing in the first row alongside some of the other actors in the Passion play. "I came to help you. How many of you have I visited in your homes as the medicus?"

Mayer was about to answer, but a young, tough-looking fellow dressed as a wagon driver cut him off. "Hold your tongue, Schongauer. We don't want any foreigners poking their noses around here. What comes next is all your fault."

"Faistenmantel hired him!" screamed an old woman to whom Simon had given a herbal ointment just two days ago for her gout. "He told me himself. They're probably working together to sell our village to the foreigners."

"What nonsense," Simon insisted. "I'm here because—"

"Truly spoken." It was the voice of Johannes Rieger, interrupting Simon's desperate plea. The judge strode forwards through the crowd and climbed slowly up the hill. "Don't you see what's going on here? First they sent just the Schongau medicus, then the Schongau secretary with his executioner. Who will they send next? For a long time, the people down on the Lech have had an eye on our beautiful town, and if we don't watch out, they'll seize power here, too. Just like this man here." Rieger pointed his walking stick at the groaning Konrad Faistenmantel, who was gradually regaining consciousness. The council chairman was bound to the cross by ropes on his hands and feet; his bald head had swollen bright red from hanging upside down, and blood continued to drip from it into the snow. "First he took your money, and now he wants to sell what remains of you to the Schongauers," Rieger continued. "I have proof that Faistenmantel wanted to meet with the Schongau Town Council. The papers with his signature were already prepared."

"That's a brazen lie," Simon shouted. "Don't believe a word he says."

He still could hardly believe that even the Ammergau judge was one of the conspirators – the whole valley seemed to be part of a dreadful conspiracy. Evidently they had long ago lost patience with the many foreigners. The children's bones that Simon had found suggested that Franz Würmseer and his accomplices had killed the labourers' children to sow fear among the immigrants and convince them to leave the valley on their own. The Faistenmantel family and some others who were on the Oberammergau Town Council had figured out what was going on and had to die for it. That's what must have happened.

Simon couldn't imagine that all of Oberammergau had known about the grisly sacrifices. Perhaps at first it had just been a small group, and the others had appeared at the meeting that night merely out of curiosity or hatred of Konrad Faistenmantel.

But through their terrible suspicions, Johannes Rieger and Franz Würmseer had accomplished just what they intended – to whip the Oberammergauers up into a mob. Anyone doubting Faistenmantel's guilt was now finally won over.

"Death to all traitors to our village!" someone shouted, and others joined in the chorus. "Death to all immigrants! We don't need you!"

Johannes Rieger had now reached the top of the slope with the cross. He stood next to Franz Würmseer in a defiant pose. "We cannot be sold," the judge said in a loud voice, "not to the Schongauers, and not to anyone else. This valley is free, and ever since the time of King Ludwig of Bavaria we have had inalienable rights. Anyone seeking to take them from us must die."

The earlier mumbling swelled up now to a thunderous cascade of shouts, roars, and the banging together of hoes and shovels as the Oberammergauers expressed their agreement.

"Death to the foreigners, death to the traitors!"

"Don't believe a word of what your judge says," Simon shouted desperately. "Children have been killed here. If you don't do anything to stop this now, you will be murderers yourselves."

But Simon's voice was drowned out in the roar of the crowd, and the guards pushed him back on to the ground, holding him by both arms in a vicelike grip as Franz Würmseer slowly brought the dagger up to his throat.

All the fanaticism had disappeared from Würmseer's eyes. He appeared cool and cautious now, and Simon thought he understood what the wagon driver had been trying to do all along. With the sacrificial ritual he was forging an inseparable bond between himself and the citizens of the town. After tonight, they would all be murderers. The act would bring the village together and no one would then be able to stop this shameful activity.

Snowflakes fell into Simon's eyes, and he had to blink. Strangely, at this moment he no longer felt any fear. Even the shouts of the villagers sounded muted, as if he were separated from them by a thick wall. All his thoughts at that moment were with Magdalena and his two sons, who would now grow up without a father. Endless grief came over him.

So this is the way it feels when you die . . . He squinted and waited for the painful, deadly blow. But it didn't come.

Instead, he heard a voice he knew only too well.

"Take your filthy paws off my husband, or my father will put you all on the wheel one by one and yank your guts out. By God, I swear he will!"

The guards loosened their grip a bit, and Simon was able to turn his head around. From out of the darkness, three riders clothed all in black charged at full speed up the hill. In front rode a man on a dapple-grey horse, and a donkey trotted alongside them.

And on the donkey rode a woman in a black robe who looked very, very angry.

17

Simon closed his eyes, then opened them again. But he still saw the same thing. *Am I dreaming? Am I perhaps already dead?* The strange riders and Magdalena had now reached the top of the hill, and at the same time almost two dozen soldiers, about half of them armed with muskets, emerged from the forest. They aimed at the spectators, who ran off in all directions, wailing and screaming. Stunned, Franz Würmseer and Johannes Rieger stood up above alongside the cross. Clearly, they couldn't comprehend what they were seeing.

"Nobody move!" commanded the disguised man on the dapple-grey horse. His hood hung down over his face, so that Simon couldn't recognize him in the dark. But he knew the voice.

"My men have orders to shoot anyone who tries to flee," he said in a commanding voice. "Those who remain will not be harmed. You have my word as the personally appointed secretary of the elector."

"Johann Lechner!" Simon scrambled to his feet, shocked. The two guards who'd been holding Simon tightly until a few seconds ago had already run off. He staggered as he looked down at the secretary, who reined in his horse at the foot of the Döttenbichl and removed his hood.

He held a pistol in his right hand, and his expression was imperious and determined. With his other hand he pointed up the hill.

"Cut the fat man down from the cross, and bring me the judge and this Würmseer fellow," he ordered some of the soldiers around him. "They are the main culprits; don't let them escape."

Franz Würmseer let out a loud cry of anger, ducked, and ran down the back of the hill, away from the crowd. A shot rang out, but the wagon driver just kept running into the forest and had soon disappeared in the darkness. Johannes Rieger, however, remained standing there calmly, holding his hands up, smiling, confident of his ultimate victory. His old arrogance had returned.

"It's good you came, esteemed colleague," he called out to Lechner. "I was trying to bring this crowd to their senses, but it appears they've got a bit out of control."

"He's lying," Simon shouted. "He's the leader of this conspiracy."

"Nonsense," Rieger replied coolly. "In any case I answer only to the abbot of Ettal."

"Whom I have already informed of your machinations," Lechner said. "A letter to our reigning prince, the elector, will be sent tomorrow." He nodded grimly. "But don't worry, you will receive a fair trial, if only to show Munich that a new hand is needed to rule in this valley."

Two soldiers seized the astonished judge, who offered no resistance as he was bound and led away. In the meantime, Magdalena had got down from her donkey and run up the hill. Breathing heavily, she embraced her confused husband and gave him a kiss.

"I actually intended to roast you slowly over a hot fire because you just decided all of a sudden to stay in Oberammergau," she said with visible relief. "Damn, if I didn't love you so much—" she said, shaking him. Suddenly she stopped short, and Simon saw she was pale and trembling all over.

"What . . . what are you doing here in Oberammergau?" he asked, confused. "You're clearly ill. You should be in bed at home and not in some godforsaken place like this."

"The same goes for you," Magdalena panted, feverish and trembling. "Are you . . . scolding me now for having saved you? Don't say another word, or I'll tie you to the cross myself."

Simon raised his hand, trying to calm her down. "I just want to know what's going on here, that's all."

"That is something I can explain to you, Herr Bathhouse Medicus." It was Johann Lechner on his dapple-grey horse, trotting up the hill. In the meantime, some men had untied Konrad Faistenmantel from the cross. The council chairman had a badly bleeding head wound, but otherwise seemed relatively uninjured. Lechner looked down on him from atop his horse with visible disgust.

"It appears we arrived just in time," the secretary said. "This crazy mob would actually have crucified their own fat council chairman." He snorted. "In fact, I could imagine something like that happening in Schongau now." Only then did he turn to Simon with a stern gaze. "I gave you and the executioner clear instructions to return home. And now look where I find you. Can't you do as you're told? I suppose I can find that stubborn Kuisl character somewhere around here . . ."

"Oh, no, I came by myself." Simon brushed the snow and mud from his shirt and trousers and hoped Lechner wouldn't probe any further. He looked down to where the crowd had been driven together by the guards; they were now crying and praying as they stood on the meadow in the moonlight. It was hard to imagine that just moments ago these same people had wanted to kill him. "I learned about this meeting and wanted to check it out all by myself," Simon continued. "That was stupid of me, and I should have let you know – but evidently you knew about it anyway."

"What did you think I knew about?" asked Lechner, still sitting atop his horse. Suddenly he looked at Simon with piercing eyes.

"Well, that Konrad Faistenmantel was about to report Würmseer and his henchmen on account of these grisly sacrifices, and was thus marked for death."

"Grisly sacrifices? That is certainly . . . interesting." Lechner raised an eyebrow. "Now please tell me more about it."

Simon quickly told him about the children's bones he'd discovered there a few days ago and his presumption that certain workers' children had been killed here in order to drive the foreigners out of the valley.

"I suspect that young Dominik Faistenmantel and Urban Gabler were about to talk and had to be eliminated," he concluded. "And Sebastian Sailer was plagued by a bad conscience and killed himself for his part in the crime."

"Because of these . . . sacrifices?" Lechner asked.

Simon nodded. He looked around the Döttenbichl, which was now almost completely enveloped in darkness. "The bones lie in some of the crevices in the rock. If you want to have a look . . ." He began to search, but Lechner called him back.

"Stop this nonsense. If there are children's bones lying around here, we'll find them tomorrow and give them a decent burial. What's more important now is to catch Würmseer. He's one of the masterminds behind this plot."

"Don't forget the judge," Simon persisted. "I'm convinced he knew about it from the very start, though he claims he's not involved."

The secretary dismissed the thought. "I have long suspected that Johannes Rieger had his finger in this, though I had no proof. It took this meeting to provide the evidence against him and Würmseer." He smiled. "I owe you a debt of gratitude, Master Fronwieser. Your evidence that Franz Würmseer had left behind secret messages put me and the black riders on the right track."

"Secret messages . . . Black riders . . . ?" Simon was now completely baffled. "I don't understand." But then he remembered the black riders who had come with Lechner and Magdalena. Once he had seen a black rider like that on the Döttenbichl. He looked out into the darkness, but the riders had disappeared. What did these ghostly apparitions have to do with Johann Lechner?

"The black riders are out looking for Franz Würmseer, who evidently has fled into the mountains," Lechner said. "For a long time they have been on the trail of him and the others."

"Because of the sacrifices?" Simon asked.

Lechner smiled. "No, not because of the sacrifices, but for something altogether different." He winked at Simon. "Both you and the hangman are clever, but not quite as clever as you sometimes think, Herr Fronwieser. Your observations were correct, but they led you to the wrong conclusion." He pointed at Magdalena, who looked exhausted and had taken a seat on a mossy boulder. "In contrast to your wife, who's exceptionally smart for a woman. I owe a lot to her, and I only hope her warning didn't come too late."

When Simon looked at her questioningly, she just shrugged her shoulders and smiled. She was pale and trembling, but seemed strangely relaxed, as if a great weight had been lifted from her shoulders. "I, too, didn't realize until the very end," she said. "But everything came together, and it all centres on a single matter that has already cost so many lives."

"And that would be?" Simon asked.

Magdalena began her story.

Under the cover of darkness, Barbara and Paul crept through the roads of Schongau towards the old cemetery next to the church. The wind howled, tearing at their clothes, while a cold rain lashed their faces. In weather like this it was unlikely they'd meet anyone here.

Barbara had learned from earlier late-night excursions that the night watchman always followed the same route and schedule as he made his way through town. She had bided her time at a corner close to the Cow Gate until he'd passed by with his lantern and halberd, and then she'd followed him. Nevertheless, she turned around cautiously from time to time. It was quite possible the guards were still out looking for her, though they probably assumed she had fled the town.

The moon had slipped behind the clouds, leaving the streets as dark as at the bottom of the sea. Barbara had brought along a large kitchen knife from Martha Stechlin's home, and she clutched it tightly. It gave her a feeling of security, even though she didn't really believe it would be of much use to her in a fight against two strong men. She feared a confrontation with them but hoped fervently that Paul's observations were correct and that Ransmayer and this strange Tyrolean were still at the old cemetery. There had been only one stroke of the church bell since Paul had brought his message, but the men might now be long gone, and then she would once again have nothing to go on.

And Buchner will finally get what he wants, she thought – *absolute power in Schongau. Perhaps even now the dissolution of the town council is being discussed in the meeting, and then even Jakob Schreevogl won't be able to change anything . . .*

The watchman announced the ninth hour in a loud voice, and the church bells resounded through the night. They had arrived at the low wall surrounding the cemetery, behind which the weathered gravestones and the shed for the building site became visible. At present, construction work on the steeple and chancel was proceeding very slowly even though new mortar, plaster, and bricks were being delivered every day. Barbara had often wondered what Burgomaster Buchner, who was supervising the construction, meant to build with all the materials.

The Tower of Babel?

Paul tugged at her dress and pointed towards two figures vaguely visible, standing in front of the shed. Barbara breathed a sigh of relief. Apparently they had not come too late after all.

The two men were engaged in an animated conversation, but the howling of the storm made it almost impossible to hear what they were saying. Barbara signalled to Paul, and they crept along the cemetery wall until they reached the crooked gate that was swinging back and forth and banging in the wind. They slipped through and ran hunched over from one gravestone to the next towards the shed. The temporary wooden structure seemed strangely out of place amid the rotten crosses and crooked gravestones. Alongside the shed was a pile of nearly a hundred sacks, evidently delivered that day and not yet brought inside. They were covered temporarily with a canvas sheet, which formed a small hill that provided Barbara and Paul a place to hide behind to spy on the two men. Carefully, Barbara climbed up on to the sacks and motioned to Paul to stay down below and wait.

From up above, she had an excellent view of the two men. Ransmayer was wearing his fine velvet jacket and a full-bottomed wig that he had to grip tightly with one hand because of the stormy gusts.

"We'll have to stop deliveries for the time being," the Tyrolean said in his harsh-sounding dialect. "It's getting too dangerous. Your secretary and his hangman are snooping around everywhere in the Ammer Valley, and now the black riders . . . It's too risky."

Barbara held her breath. Had the man been talking about her father? Before she could give it any more thought, the conversation continued.

"The old man won't be at all happy to hear that," Ransmayer grumbled. "Especially now that we'll soon have the possibility of storing much more and shipping it down the Lech. If everything goes well in the council meeting today, we can start using the entire storage facility in the Ballenhaus."

"But what you have here at the cemetery will be enough for weeks," the Tyrolean exclaimed, pointing to the sacks behind him. Barbara ducked down, terrified, but the man hadn't noticed her. "Who are you going to send this all to?"

Ransmayer chuckled. "You have no idea all the people we have on our list – we have buyers from Augsburg to Vienna. Because of the Turkish wars, all the customs duties have risen again, and the stuff is almost worth its weight in gold."

Barbara frowned. She had no idea what the men were talking about, but the Tyrolean had pointed at the sacks, so evidently they contained something very valuable. She had assumed the sacks contained building materials such as plaster and mortar. Carefully she pressed on a sack. Under the canvas it felt like there was something soft as flour. What could it be that was almost worth its weight in gold?

"We'll stop deliveries for a while, just the same. The last one to arrive here was dangerous enough," the Tyrolean replied. "Of course, more for the others than for us," he added with a hoarse laugh. "I'm going back to Tyrol to speak with my client there, and I'll get back in touch."

"Be careful," Ransmayer hissed, though he was hard to understand because of the storm. "If everything goes according to plan, the burgomaster will take control of the city today and then other trade routes will open up for us."

"There will be nothing in that for me if I'm hanging on the gallows," the Tyrolean said. Another gust of wind whipped through the trees and at the last moment the Tyrolean grabbed his hat before it could blow away.

It became harder and harder for Barbara to control her curiosity. Her assumptions were right. Burgomaster Buchner and Melchior Ransmayer were actually involved in some conspiracy, and it all had to do with whatever it was that she was lying on at that very moment. She had to find out what it was. She carefully removed the kitchen knife from where she'd hidden it in her boot and made a small incision in the canvas. Powder came out, but the cut was wider than she had planned and it trickled down over the sacks to the ground near where the two men were standing.

"We can find another contact," Ransmayer was saying. "You're not the only one in Tyrol who wants to do business with us."

Barbara suppressed a cry as the powder was carried by the wind and settled like dust on Ransmayer's full-bottomed wig. Still, the doctor didn't seem to notice.

"Believe me, it's just too dangerous," the Tyrolean persisted. "The German kaiser has given this matter his highest priority. The number of black riders on the entire stretch of this road has been doubled."

Ransmayer made a small step to the side, and the powder ran down into his collar. Barbara placed her hand over her mouth, and the powder on her fingers stuck to her lips. She stopped short.

What the devil . . .

The powder was grainy and had a salty taste. The clouds covering the moon parted for a moment and for the first time she could see the colour of this strange substance.

It was white.

White and salty, she thought. *Not plaster but simple . . .*

"Curses! What is this?" Ransmayer reached inside his collar, where the powder was still trickling down from his wig. He looked up, and his astonished gaze turned at once to a hateful grimace on seeing Barbara's head between the sacks.

"Cursed hangman's brat," he snarled. "This time I'll kill you myself!"

"Hangman's brat, you say?" Now the Tyrolean looked up, as well. At first he looked a bit confused, but then in one fluid motion he drew out a long, rusty sword hanging on his belt. "Damn! How many members of your family do I have to kill to get some peace and quiet?" With drawn sword, he ran around the pile of sacks in order to attack his victim from behind.

At that moment there was a loud shout and Paul stormed out from the rear of the pile. He swung his slingshot like a spiked mace, shocking the Tyrolean, who stepped back a pace. Pure bloodlust shone in Paul's eyes.

"If you even touch a hair on my aunt's head, I'll shoot you right between the eyes," he growled. "And you'll be as dead as a dormouse."

"Oho! Another little devil," the Tyrolean laughed, getting control of himself again. "You brood of hangmen are worse than the rabbits. If you wring one by the neck, two more come popping up out of the burrow."

Without hesitation, he swung his sword.

Barbara screamed as the storm continued to rage, the sacks she was standing on started sliding, and she fell towards Melchior Ransmayer, who tumbled into a growing pile of white powder.

"Salt?"

Simon stared at his wife. "All these dreadful murders were committed here just because of salt?"

Trembling, and dressed in a mud-spattered jacket, he stood alongside Magdalena up on the Döttenbichl next to the cross. She'd begun explaining it all to him, but he interrupted her after just a few sentences. What she was saying was just too bizarre. He also didn't know what Magdalena was doing here in Oberammergau.

"Don't underestimate salt," said Johann Lechner, who had got down from his horse. "Many bloody wars have been fought because of this apparently insignificant mineral, and mighty cities have been established or destroyed. Even our beautiful city of Munich is basically built on salt." Smiling, Lechner approached Simon and Magdalena with two soldiers at his side; they held torches, lighting up the gloomy hill behind them. "You know the old story," he said, turning to Simon. "If Henry the Lion hadn't set fire to the bridge belonging to the bishop of Freising, diverting the salt road through Munich, our capital today would probably still be an insignificant backwater town like Oberammergau – so you see how important this white powder can be."

"But we don't have any salt here," Simon interjected.

"Not here, but in Tyrol," Lechner responded. He took one of the torches and pointed it to the west, where high, dark rock walls stood out in the night. "And it's easy to reach through the neighbouring Graswang Valley. Our venerable elector has suspected for a long time that large quantities of salt are smuggled into Bavaria via that route, and from there to the entire Reich; because of that the country loses tens of thousands of guilders every year in taxes. The government has sent out men to patrol the entire route, but until now they have had no success."

"The black riders," Simon said, shocked. "So they're not mysterious, mythical figures at all – they really exist."

Lechner nodded. "They're well-trained men who inconspicuously keep an eye on the trade routes and, if necessary, strike without mercy. But even they were not able to get their hands on the smugglers, perhaps because the smugglers have developed a rather clever system of routes and secret signs – inconspicuous circles, stones, and twigs that provide information about unguarded routes and possible meeting places."

By now it had stopped snowing, and the moon shone brightly in the night sky, but Simon noticed none of that. He listened spellbound to Lechner's words. Suddenly there was a logical explanation for the strange things that had been happening the last few days. He had believed in the ritual sacrifices, the virulent hatred of foreigners, the bloody rites – but it was all much simpler, rational, and mundane.

The black riders and the strange stone circles, he mused. *There's nothing mysterious about them, they're just as real as the mountains, the valley, and the river. There are no riddles nor legends . . .*

The secretary winked at Simon. "Your father-in-law was so kind as to point out these circles to me yesterday. He told me you discovered a stone circle just like it and some other things on the Döttenbichl, and from then on it was clear to me there would soon be another meeting of the smugglers there. I was surprised, however, to find half of Oberammergau and even the Ettal judge there. Fortunately, I had enough men with me. Just today the elector himself sent me two dozen soldiers."

"Does that mean the Oberammergauers had been planning this smuggling operation for a long time?" Simon asked in surprise. He still couldn't believe there were dozens, perhaps even hundreds, of criminals involved.

Probably the whole village knew about it. How were we duped so easily?

"Well, at least the majority of them knew about it," Lechner said. "Especially the wagon drivers, led by Franz Würmseer. In our investigation we heard over and over again about a so-called Master. That was no doubt Würmseer, the leader of the gang. I think he's been involved in this for several years, ever since the trade route started going downhill." He shrugged. "It was just an assumption that the Ettal judge was involved in the matter, but the operation simply was so smooth it had to have protection from above. And that's the reason the government in Munich ordered me—"

"Just a moment," Simon interrupted. "Can you slow down a bit? Do you mean you didn't come to Oberammergau on account of this dreadful crucifixion, but only to break up this gang of smugglers?"

Lechner grinned slyly. "Let's say that the crucifixion was just the icing on the cake. The murder gave me an excuse to have a look, with permission from Munich, and I'm happy that you and your father-in-law went snooping around in the valley, too. To tell the truth, I even hoped you would. That provided the cover we needed to capture Würmseer and his henchmen."

Simon groaned. "So we were nothing more than a distraction."

"Oh, I wouldn't say that," said Lechner dismissively. "You two actually gave me the decisive clues." His gaze darkened as he looked down at the moonlit meadow, where the Oberammergauers were being led home by some of the soldiers. "It's still not clear to me, however, what the two murders and the suicide have to do with it and, above all, this crucifixion, but I'm determined to find out."

Simon hesitated. Something about Lechner's explanations seemed too smooth. It all fitted together a bit too easily. Perhaps he just didn't want to admit to himself that his assumptions were wrong. He picked up a torch, walked around the top of the hill with it, and after a while he'd found what he was looking for. Bending down, he picked up a white rib bone with light-coloured shreds of cloth, as if from a shirt, clinging to it. All were covered with a greenish slime.

"Bones of children," Simon said, holding the rib bone out for Lechner to see. "There are more of them here. How does that fit into your theory?"

The secretary shrugged. "They're just old bones. Perhaps in ancient times people were actually sacrificed here, but those are old superstitions that have nothing to do with our case."

"I don't set store in superstition any more than you do," Simon replied coolly. "I don't believe in magic, but in scientific facts." He carefully examined the tiny rib, then placed it respectfully on the ground. "The last time I wasn't so sure, but this time I'll swear that this bone hasn't been here for more than two or at most three years. And it comes from a child. Würmseer was always stirring up hatred against the foreigners and their children. Isn't it possible he—"

"Didn't you hear him?" asked Magdalena. "There were no sacrifices. We really don't have any time now for your crazy ideas. This smuggling ring is huge. It begins in Tyrol and goes far beyond Oberammergau. The smugglers are well organized and control the entire trade route, probably as far as Augsburg." She was visibly shaken. "I learned that myself in Soyen when I happened to fall into the hands of the smugglers. That's where the salt is reloaded into wine barrels so it can be sent along unnoticed. Afterwards, I briefly tasted the content of the barrels, and they were as salty as blood." She shook her head. "I didn't realize it all until I was on the way to Oberammergau."

"Which brings me to an important point," Simon said. "What in the world are you doing here? I mean, I understand you're angry at me because I stayed in Oberammergau. But I swear that was not because I was trying to learn more about these murders." He hesitated. "Well, let's say it was partly the reason, but basically I just wanted to earn a bit more money for our family, and Konrad Faistenmantel gave me an offer that—"

He stopped short, seeing Magdalena smiling and shaking her head wearily. "Oh, Simon, that's not so important any more," she said. "The only important thing now is Barbara. I'm afraid this accursed smuggling activity is threatening the life of my sister."

"Not just the life of your sister, but the whole town of Schongau," Lechner interjected. "Your wife brought me this letter from Master Schreevogl, and if what it says is true, then God help us." He quickly jumped on to his horse and gave a sign to the watchmen. "And now, let's go! We can discuss everything else on our way back to Oberammergau."

He kicked the horse in the side so hard that it neighed, jumped up, and galloped down the hill.

Barbara landed softly as Melchior Ransmayer let out a muffled cry. His perfume was so heavy and sweet that for a moment it nearly took her breath away. All around them, sacks were falling, bursting, and spilling their contents on to the ground. Instinctively, Barbara pressed the doctor's face into a pile of salt that the recent rains had transformed into a caustic mush. He bellowed with pain, as the salt apparently got into his eyes. For a moment he lay under the pile of sacks, unable to move, but cursing even louder.

"Ach . . . ach . . ." he gagged, spitting out clumps of salt. "Help!"

"I don't know if you really want to call the guards," Barbara gasped, pushing him back to the ground again. "They would no doubt quickly find out what's in the sacks, and that wouldn't be good either for you or for Burgomaster Buchner, would it?"

Ransmayer cringed, confirming Barbara's suspicions. Once she realized the sacks contained salt, not plaster, she quickly put two and two together. Buchner was the construction manager for the church, but work wasn't proceeding, as the construction site had always been just a pretext. Actually it was a hub for shipments of salt, used to evade customs on its way to the docks on the Lech. Now Barbara understood why Buchner and Ransmayer were trying to get her out of the way. They must have been afraid she would figure it out, having overheard their conversation in the church tower days ago. Ransmayer's function was no doubt that of a middleman, while Buchner was responsible for political matters. It was likely that most of the Schongau wagon drivers were involved in the plot. Whom could one trust in this town?

"You . . . you little bitch!" Ransmayer writhed around beneath the sacks like a slippery fish out of water, but he could already raise his head a bit and it wouldn't take long before he'd be able to free himself. "I'll wring your neck with my own hands – I'll break your neck like a chicken's!"

Frantically, Barbara looked around the construction site. Where were Paul and the Tyrolean? Her knife must have slipped out of her hand when she fell; it had to be somewhere around here. But it was too dark to see much more than the huge pile of salt on the ground, which was slowly turning into a mushy heap. Suddenly there was a loud cry of pain nearby. Barbara cautiously looked behind her and saw the Tyrolean holding his forehead and cursing. She breathed a big sigh of relief. Evidently Paul was still alive and had hit his opponent with his slingshot, but she couldn't see her nephew anywhere.

"Run, Paul, run!" she shouted into the wind. She could only hope that Paul was sensible enough not to take up arms against an experienced fighter with a sword. Just a moment later she heard an angry shout, and something small and furious jumped down from the tottering pile of sacks right on top of Melchior Ransmayer. It was Paul, attacking Ransmayer like a deranged kobold with his little woodcarving knife. Barbara ducked to one side to avoid being hit by accident. She knew her nephew. When Paul was overcome by one of his fits, there wasn't anyone or anything that could stop him. Like a legendary berserker, he flailed out at everything that crossed his path.

Sometimes he really scares me, she thought.

Ransmayer screamed like a stuck pig. His fear and the pain gave him extra strength, and he was able to pull the furious youth off him and hold him at arm's length, but not before the six-year-old had ripped off Ransmayer's wig and was holding it triumphantly in his hand like a rabbit pelt. In his other hand he clutched the woodcarving knife, from which blood dripped down into the mushy white salt.

"Ignaz, where are you?" Ransmayer shrieked. "Ignaz! The boy is killing me!"

Barbara noticed in fact that blood was dripping from the right shoulder of Ransmayer's velvet vest, and there was a long cut across his left cheek. Paul wriggled out of Ransmayer's grip now and went on the attack again, shouting furiously.

Barbara struggled to her feet and finally found her own knife half-buried in the salt not far away. She picked it up and looked around cautiously for the Tyrolean, but he seemed to have vanished in the darkness. Her heart was pounding. What should she do? She could no doubt polish off the injured, whining Ransmayer but not the trained swordsman. Barbara blinked her eyes.

Where, in God's name, is the Tyrolean?

"Paul!" she shouted at her raging nephew, trying to sound calm and sensible. "Listen, we have to get out of here. We'll get help, and then—"

A vague shadow rushed past her. The Tyrolean emerged from behind a sack of salt and grabbed little Paul like a puppy by the scruff of the neck. He shook him, and Paul's knife fell clattering on to the ground. The Tyrolean pulled out his own jagged sword-blade and put it to Paul's throat.

"Just one more careless move and this boy will lose his head," he growled at Barbara. "Now get up slowly and drop the knife."

Barbara looked into his eyes and knew he was serious.

Carefully she put the knife down and stood up, raising her hands.

"Don't be afraid, Paul," she said gently. "Everything will be all right if we do what the men say, you'll see."

Paul's eyes flashed, but apparently he recognized the seriousness of the situation and remained still. The Tyrolean grinned.

"I've got to admit he's quite a rascal," he said. "He'll be a good warrior someday if his hot temper doesn't get him killed." He laughed and turned to Melchior Ransmayer, who was holding up his hand to the heavily bleeding cut on his face. "The kid almost killed you. Ha! A little kid like that against a grown man. You can count yourself lucky if I don't go around telling everybody about that."

"My grandfather will cut you to pieces and hang your guts on the gallows," Paul snarled. "You'll see."

"Your grandfather is an old drunk," replied Ransmayer, who had got to his feet and calmed down a bit, putting his hand to his cheek, which was still bleeding. "If Master Hans doesn't chop his head off soon, he'll wind up choking on his own vomit in the street."

"I'll kill him! I'll kill him!" Paul shouted, lunging for Ransmayer again, but the Tyrolean grabbed him by the hair and yanked him back.

"Calm down, kid," he said. "Actually I was going to cut you down right here, but I like you. Let's see if I can't find some use for someone like you in Hall in Tyrol." He pointed at Barbara, and then at Ransmayer. "Quick, tie the girl up. We've got to find out what she knows and if she talked to anyone about us. The shipment leaves for

Augsburg tomorrow, and until then we must be sure nothing goes wrong."

Ransmayer nodded darkly, then took one of the ropes used to tie up the sacks and bound Barbara's hands behind her back. Briefly she considered resisting, but the point of the sword was just an inch away from Paul's throat. The Tyrolean had said perhaps he could use Paul, but that certainly wouldn't prevent him from killing the boy if she struggled to get away.

Melchior Ransmayer tied the knots so tightly that she let out a muted cry of pain. Then once again he checked the wound on his face. "This will never heal," he moaned. "It will leave a terrible scar."

"You're the doctor," said the Tyrolean, grinning, "so sew up the wound yourself. Or are you really just a bad doctor, as everyone says around here, huh?"

"How dare you . . ." Ransmayer seemed about to explode, but then he took a deep breath before continuing in a quiet voice: "You're right. We have to find out what this girl knows, but we can't do that here — there will be too much noise, and that would be dangerous. Let's go to my office, where nobody can hear us."

Suddenly, Ransmayer smirked and his eyes began sparkling with excitement. "This pretty wench and I were rudely interrupted during our last tête-à-tête." He giggled. "Well, this time we'll have all night."

The few houses in Oberammergau where lights were still burning showed Magdalena, Simon, and Johann Lechner the way back to the village. Magdalena was shivering despite the warm coat that Lechner had put around her shoulders.

The Schongau secretary had provided the Fronwiesers with two horses, so they arrived in the village before the others. Along the way, Magdalena finally told Simon what had brought her to Oberammergau and the difficulties she'd suffered on her trip. She was trembling all over now and had a bad cough, but at least the fever didn't seem any worse. What worried her most was her pregnancy, but she'd probably have to wait a few months to see if any harm had come to her unborn child.

"This Tyrolean who almost managed to drown me in the Ammer is probably the same person Barbara saw in Schongau with Melchior Ransmayer," she said to Simon, as they followed along behind the secretary. The donkey, Franziskus, trotted along happily beside them. He had got his helping of oats and was now peaceful as a lamb. Magdalena had decided nevertheless not to ride him any more.

"Master Schreevogl has long suspected that Ransmayer and Burgomaster Buchner are involved in some scheme," she continued. "Now we know that Schongau is at the centre of a large smuggling ring. In Soyen they are using wine barrels, but I suspect they have other ways to conceal their activities – boxes, sacks, concealed compartments for all I know. They probably keep changing the containers so as not to attract attention." She shrugged. "I'm sure the wagon drivers both in Oberammergau and in Schongau have a finger in this, as well as the two master wagon drivers, the raftmaster down at the Schongau landing, but also the little fish like poor Lukas, who was thrown into the Ammer by the Tyrolean." Magdalena sighed as they turned off the main road and entered town. "The poor fellow probably drowned, and all he wanted was to make a little money for his family, and had no idea what he was getting into."

"And do you think Barbara figured out what was going on between Buchner and Ransmayer, and for that reason they wanted to silence her?" Simon asked.

Magdalena nodded. "He didn't make someone plant fake evidence – the supposed mandrake root – in our house because he wanted revenge as a jilted suitor. Everything was planned coldly by Ransmayer and Buchner. It was, naturally, a big plus for Buchner and his people when the guards found the magic books. We have to get back to Schongau as soon as possible and—" Magdalena doubled over, clutching the reins tightly. Her stomach cramped up painfully like it was an anxious little animal.

Lord, don't let me lose the child. Not again.

"You're not going anywhere," Simon replied, placing his hand anxiously on her shoulder and trying to steady her. "You are sick. What you need now is a comfortable seat by the fire, a hot cup of camomile tea, and a bed."

Magdalena smiled wearily. "Except for the camomile tea, I'll agree."

"I must side with your husband," said Lechner. "Your work is done, Frau Fronwieser. Take a rest – you've earned it. That's the least I can do for you. Take care of yourself, and of Peter, who will surely be happy to see his mother tomorrow morning."

"But—" Magdalena objected.

"What has to be done in Schongau will be done," Lechner interrupted coolly. "By me, not by you, and that's my final word. I shall ride home with the soldiers and arrest Buchner, and I promise you that your sister will be set free." He shook his head. "Even though I'd like to throw her into the stocks for a day for the stupid things she's done. Those magic books should have been burned long ago."

"Well, then . . . all right," Magdalena replied hesitantly. She was actually happy that Lechner had made the decision for her. She felt so weak, and so incredibly tired. Until now the desire to reach Oberammergau in time to save Barbara had kept her going, but the turmoil on the Döttenbichl, the grisly sight of the crucified Faistenmantel, and above all the concern for her husband's life had taken their toll. Now that Lechner had received Schreevogl's letter, she broke down. All she wanted to do was to sleep.

When they finally arrived back in Oberammergau, lights were burning in every house. Soldiers were in the streets and they had confiscated a large wagon, in which sat Judge Johannes Rieger, his hands tied, along with other residents of Oberammergau, some wagon drivers, and the woodcutter Alois Mayer. Simon had told Magdalena that Mayer in particular had tried to frighten him with stories of little Venetian men and black riders, probably to keep him from poking around too much.

He could never have imagined that they would only awaken Simon's curiosity, she thought wearily. *An old family affliction!*

The Ammergau judge glared at Johann Lechner but didn't speak. Evidently he'd come to terms with his fate, for the time being.

"These are the ones we suspect of being members of the smuggling ring," the secretary declared. "We'll take them to the dungeon in Schongau for further questioning, and I hope very much their leader, Franz Würmseer, will soon join them there." He winked at Magdalena. "You see, your father has plenty to keep him busy. Where is he, anyway?"

"That's what I'd like to know," Magdalena mumbled. Simon had told her that her father had been gone since that afternoon to look for a suspect in the forest. But now it was the middle of the night. It was still raining lightly, and the wind whistled through the alleys. What in the world had her father been doing out there all this time?

"In God's name, stop!"

A carriage rumbled with great speed down the main road and stopped in front of the tavern. On the coachbox sat Abbot Benedikt Eckart, looking very angry. His cross was on a chain around his neck, blowing back and forth in the wind. He got to his feet, wavering, and shook his fist at Lechner.

"What you're doing here far exceeds your authority," he shouted, his voice crackling with emotion. "What's the reason for all these arrests? This is my district."

"Though it seems you have lost that authority," Lechner rejoined coolly. "Your Excellency, I suspect your judge, along with a number of residents of the village, of running a huge salt-smuggling operation.

This is a serious crime being investigated directly by the supreme ruler, the elector, and is not within the purview of ecclesiastical law. The evidence is so compelling that I must take Johannes Rieger and some other suspects back to Schongau with me."

"But . . . but . . ." stammered the outraged abbot.

"If you wish to complain, you are welcome to do that in Munich," replied Lechner, "but I think you'll soon be receiving a letter from the capital, in any case." He smiled. "Rumour has it that Munich is not completely satisfied with your judgement and plans a new administration for the district. It would be an honour for Schongau to offer our assistance."

The abbot fell back feebly on to his seat in the coach, clutched his wooden cross, and spoke a quiet prayer. Suddenly he appeared very old. Lechner paid no further attention to him but got down from his horse and motioned for Simon and Magdalena to enter the inn with him. Downstairs in the warm tavern were some soldiers just preparing to leave.

"Follow me," Lechner ordered, and led Simon and Magdalena up the stairs.

They ascended to the first floor and continued down a corridor to a door in the back. Lechner opened it and bowed slightly. "The ambassador's suite," he said, pointing inside. "This is where I always stay, but now it's at your disposal. I hope you have a speedy recovery."

"But this is—" Magdalena gasped.

"The least I can do for you," Lechner said.

The room before them was completely panelled in oak and magnificently enriched with carvings. In one corner a fire was roaring in a green-tiled stove, spreading its comfort and warmth. A chandelier hung from the ceiling with at least two dozen fragrantly scented white candles burning in it, and in the middle of the room stood a huge four-poster bed with furs and quilts spread out on it and a baldachin overhead like a canopy of the heavens.

"I know this is not the most elegant of places, but in these backwater towns one has to take what's available," Lechner said with a shrug. He pointed to a table with a carafe of wine as well as bread, cheese, and ham on it. "The same goes for the food. I hope you find it more or less acceptable."

"Oh . . . uh . . . yes, it is," Magdalena replied. "Completely acceptable." The room was so warm that she took off the wet coat. Then she sank into the bed and at once was overcome with exhaustion. Simon collapsed in a chair. In his filthy clothes he looked very much out of place in the regally appointed room. Strangely, that didn't seem to disturb him at this moment, as he sat there, lost in his thoughts.

"I'll leave you and your husband to yourselves now," Lechner said. "If you need anything, just let the innkeeper know. He's been told to fulfil your every need. Stay as long as you wish, and, uh . . ." He looked over at Simon with some disgust. "In case your husband should need a few fresh clothes, you'll find some things in the chest over in the corner, though perhaps not the right size. We'll meet again in Schongau."

Without another word, Johann Lechner left the room. For a while, the voices of the soldiers could be heard downstairs, then the whinnying of horses outside, and finally the rumbling of a number of wagons slowly fading in the distance. Soon thereafter, silence fell over the room, interrupted only by the crackling of the logs in the stove.

Magdalena closed her eyes and almost instantly fell asleep.

When she woke up, Simon was still sitting on the same chair at the table. The plate and cup seemed unused, and he was staring up at the flickering chandelier.

Magdalena rubbed her eyes and yawned. "How long did I sleep?" she asked, sitting up in the bed.

"Not long – perhaps one or two hours." Simon shrugged. "I don't know exactly." He looked out the window into the darkness. "All is quiet in the village, almost as if nothing had happened."

Magdalena was still weak, but the warmth in the room felt good. Her strength seemed to be returning even though she hadn't slept nearly enough yet. She looked lovingly at Simon. Was this the right time to tell him about her pregnancy? "Simon, there's something—" she started to say.

"I've been thinking," he interrupted. "About the salt smuggling and all the strange things that have happened here. There's something that's still not quite right. The bones of the children . . ."

She sighed. The good news would have to wait a bit.

"Can't you and my father just admit for once that you were wrong?" she asked wearily. "Where is he, anyway? You said before he was looking for a suspect. Where? In the mountains?" She'd never really been concerned about his safety as he was always so strong and clever. Perhaps he'd simply taken shelter somewhere from the storm. Nevertheless she felt a bit unsettled.

"I don't know where he is," Simon replied. "The last time I saw him he was looking for Xaver."

"Who is Xaver?" Magdalena asked.

"A fellow who probably knew about this gang of smugglers for a long time and, unlike the other villagers, didn't want anything to do with it." Simon told her about the young red-headed woodcarver whose family had been bankrupted by Konrad Faistenmantel, then he told her about the carvings of the Pharisees, the murder of Urban Gabler, and Sebastian Sailer's suicide in the Sacred Blood Chapel in Unterammergau. Magdalena listened in disbelief. Once again, Simon and her father had in a few days' time managed to get involved in multiple murders. It almost seemed as if they were attracted to crime.

Or that crime is attracted to them, she thought.

"I assume Xaver Eyrl wanted to take vengeance on the villagers," Simon said finally. "He opposed the smuggling, so he came back and distributed these Pharisee figurines to remind people of their greed and hypocrisy. It's possible he killed Gabler, too, but I don't really think so. I think that Gabler, a devout Christian, had a guilty conscience and was going to expose their operation, so one of the other smugglers had him killed. Perhaps Sebastian Sailer . . ."

"Who then hanged himself because of his shame and guilt." Magdalena nodded. "That certainly could be so, and these deaths weren't presaged in the Acts of the Apostles but were simply a chain of adverse circumstances. But how about Dominik Faistenmantel, the man who was crucified? You said that Xaver and he were friends – so he probably wasn't Dominik's killer. But who was? The smugglers?"

"That's exactly what I've been thinking about." Simon sighed. "I don't know how he fits into the picture. It's possible that both he and his father knew about the activity and wanted to expose the perpetrators. But why the elaborate staging with the cross? At that time it would have been far simpler just to strike him dead and blame the murder on a random criminal. In addition, Dominik was the son of the council chairman, a man who at least approved of the machinations of the smugglers. The murderer must have expected to incur the wrath of Faistenmantel's powerful family. It just doesn't make any sense."

"It would be best to ask Konrad Faistenmantel himself," Magdalena responded wearily.

"He's in bed, unconscious." Again, Simon shrugged. "The blow he got on the back of his head nearly killed him, and in addition he was hanging upside down on the cross. He can count himself lucky if he even partly recovers someday, but he certainly can't be questioned in the near future."

"Wouldn't it be good if my father were here now," said Magdalena, yawning. All the talking and concentration had made her tired again, and once more she lay down in the bed. "Surely he could help us," she mumbled.

Simon stood up, walked from the table over to the bed, and put his hand on her forehead. "The fever has subsided a bit," he said, "but you're still very sick. Sleep is the best medicine for you now. You'll see."

He grinned. "Your father will show up tomorrow at the latest. He's a damned tough old bird, as you know. Tomorrow we'll go over to visit Peter and then leave for Schongau."

"I wish I could go to him right now," she murmured.

"It's too late. He's surely fast asleep; we'll go to see him early tomorrow morning, all right?"

"You . . . you don't feel like solving any more riddles, then?" asked Magdalena as her eyes fell shut.

"No more riddles, I promise," he replied with a grin, "at least not until tomorrow morning."

"That's good. Oh, one other thing, Simon." She yawned. "I really think you should change your clothes. You stink."

With these words, she turned over on to her side, and the last thing she remembered before she drifted off to sleep once again was seeing Simon staring up at the ceiling, lost in thought. For the first time ever, he seemed completely indifferent to his appearance.

18

In THE DARKNESS, JAKOB KUISL STOMPED ALONG the narrow, slippery path up the mountain. His overcoat, leather collar, and linen shirt underneath were already soaking wet from the rain and his own sweat.

For nearly an hour the hangman had been following the light on the other side of the high meadow that he'd seen from down in the valley. The light continued moving ahead of him, up the mountain, around sharp turns, and up steep, slippery paths. Once or twice Jakob lost sight of it, but then it appeared again like a will-o'-the-wisp, luring him farther and farther into this inhospitable region.

For some time, Jakob had had his doubts that the person carrying the lantern or torch up the mountain could actually be Xaver Eyrl. Perhaps it was a poacher, a smuggler, or some other sinister individual, but that didn't dissuade the hangman from pursuing his suspicions. He was driven by an insatiable curiosity, a longing, as if the mountain itself had summoned him. He simply had to know who that was up there.

Whenever Jakob thought he was getting close, the light would suddenly appear in another place higher up the mountain. Whoever it was seemed to know shortcuts on the narrow paths that the hangman couldn't see in the darkness. Or was he following several men? A few times he thought he saw a number of shadowy figures walking along behind the light.

At least the snow had stopped, but it was still bitter cold. His fingers felt like wet and half-frozen twigs; rain and wind tore at his clothing. Peals of thunder rumbled over the Kofel and suddenly a flash of lightning briefly cast the slope above him in a dazzling light.

And then he saw it.

For a fraction of a second he could make out a line of men. The one at the front of the procession was holding a lantern and the ones behind carried hoes and shovels. All were wearing coats with pointed hoods. And they were very small.

Like dwarfs.

The little men from Venice.

The hangman had heard the stories of the little people not only from the Oberammergauers. His mother had often told him of them when he was perhaps four or five years old.

If you misbehave, the little men from Venice will come and get you. They'll take you to their mines in the mountains, where you'll hack and shovel and dig, and you'll never see the light of the sun again . . .

In Jakob's childhood imagination, the Venetians had worn hoods exactly like the figures he'd just seen walking along the rock face. Back then, he'd imagined their eyes gleaming with greed just like the cold gemstones they were searching for. There was even a song they'd sung as children about the Venetians, or the bogeymen, as they were also called. Jakob searched his memory, then started humming the long-forgotten melody.

The bi-ba-bogeyman, the bogeyman is back . . . He picks up little boys and girls and throws them in his sack.

Sometimes the song even mentioned a scythe. But Jakob had always known this was nonsense. In the old stories, the Venetians, the bogeymen, had always brought disaster.

They were the grim reapers, the messengers of impending death. *He brings along his scythe of death . . .*

Jakob remembered seeing a little man like these just a few days earlier, over in the Laine Valley. Simon had seen him too. What did it mean? Now he suspected the Venetians were looking for him. For a long time, the hangman had felt a longing to simply lie down, to sleep, to never wake up again. How often had he looked death straight in the eye – crying eyes, eyes pleading for mercy, hateful eyes cursing him and the authorities? So much suffering, so much death . . . He had been on this earth a very long time, almost sixty years; most men died much earlier.

Was he watching the approach of his own death up there? Had the Venetians beckoned to him?

The urge to know, to find out who or what was up there pressing on towards the summit, became stronger and stronger. Jakob ran, stumbling over the wet rocks. His eyes had already become sufficiently accustomed to the dark. The path was dangerous. There were slippery patches of snow and ice, twisted roots, and dangerous crevices in the rock. A few times he started to jump only to pull back at the last second on seeing the yawning abyss below. And each time that happened, he thought he heard evil laughter.

The bogeyman is back . . .

He turned another corner and was shocked to see that the light had disappeared. Cursing softly, he looked around and then climbed up on to the trunk of a tree that had been hit by lightning ages ago and peered out into the darkness. And there it was again, only a stone's throw away. It was no longer moving but quivering in place. When Jakob looked more closely, he could make out a slight pendular movement, almost as if the light was trying to send him a coded message.

"What in God's name . . . ?"

Jakob climbed a steep slope just below some dark rock formations. Another lightning flash lit up the night and he perceived a strangely shaped rocky spire resembling an admonishing finger; beneath it were rocks of all sizes, like huge dice cast there by the hand of a giant. The clouds had parted, and in the light of the moon he could make out an area strewn with rubble and fallen trees. Nearby there was a rhythmic sound – *clunk, clunk, clunk* – as if something metallic was pounding the rock again and again.

He brings along his scythe of death . . .

Jakob was about to turn around towards the sound when he noticed a sort of shelter on the steep, rocky slope. Rudely constructed, it consisted only of four short posts hammered into the rocky soil with a piece of linen or cloth stretched over them as a provisional roof. On the side exposed to the weather, stones were piled up, perhaps to protect against the strong gusts of wind.

A lantern hung on one of the posts, swaying in the wind, its metal handle squeaking, while the flame behind its sooty glass smoked and seemed about to go out.

The will-o'-the-wisp, Jakob thought. *I found it. I've reached my goal.*

As he ran towards it he heard a dry cough come from the shelter and again he heard the rhythmic *clunk, clunk, clunk* from the rock face; they combined with the squeaking of the lantern to form an eerie, discordant chorus. Carefully, the hangman reached for the larch-wood club dangling from his belt.

What in God's name is going on here?

He got to the shelter and peered over the pile of rock forming a wall. Behind it he saw what looked like a dirty bundle but on closer examination turned out to be a child wrapped in soiled furs and blankets. It was a girl about eight years old. She had a bad cough and her face was bony and gaunt; she looked like a dying little bird. Her dirty skin made the whites of her eyes stand out all the more as she stared anxiously at Jakob.

"Who . . . who are you?" she murmured feverishly. "Death?"

"I'm . . ." he started to say, but then he saw that the girl's eyes had closed again.

"He mustn't see you," she murmured.

The hangman frowned. "Who? Who mustn't see me?"

"No one must see us."

Jakob put his hand over the wall and brushed the girl's stringy blonde hair out of her face. Now he noticed that she also had a bandage on her forehead that was blackened by dried blood. She was evidently badly injured. "Child, what are you saying?" he asked in a soft voice, trying not to frighten her. "What's going on here?"

Instead of an answer, the girl pointed a trembling finger towards the place the metallic ringing was coming from – another high boulder, rising up dark and massive before them like a clenched fist.

Clunk, clunk, clunk . . .

Gently he pulled the blanket back over the injured child.

"I'll be right back," he grumbled. "Whoever did this to you is going to pay for it."

Then he stood up to his full height and took the lantern. Clenching his cudgel tightly, he proceeded towards the large rock; in the flickering light of the lantern he could see a dark hole in it.

The girl had taken him for the bringer of death. Now he really would be.

With a pounding heart, Barbara stared at Melchior Ransmayer as he ran his skinny fingers from her nose, down to her lips, and finally to her breasts. She was lying, bound hand and foot, on a sofa with pale red velvet upholstery. The doctor's face was less than a foot above hers, so she could smell his heavy perfume, but also his sweat, the odour of cooked onions, and the cheap brandy Ransmayer had been drinking. She was terrified and wanted to scream, but a dirty rag was stuffed into her mouth, choking her. From a corner of the room she could hear Paul, who was also bound and gagged.

"You're afraid, aren't you?" Ransmayer whispered in her ear. "But don't worry, if you do exactly what I say, you won't be hurt. But first you have to show the old doctor that you like him."

He giggled, and the Tyrolean seated alongside him snorted. "Stop this nonsense and just get to the point," he ordered. "The girl must tell us what she knows, and after that you can do whatever you want with her."

About half an hour before, Ransmayer and the Tyrolean dragged their two prisoners through the dark streets of Schongau. From far off they heard the calls of the night watchman, but the knife held at Barbara's throat had prevented her from crying out for help. Once inside Ransmayer's house, the men dragged them down a cellar stairway into a mouldy, smelly room lit only by torches that evidently served as a sort of laboratory.

Out of the corner of her eye, Barbara saw dozens of shelves full of vials and jars with nauseating contents. In one jar was a tiny human foetus with a monstrous head as large as the rest of its body, and in another a severed hand with nerves and blood vessels still trailing from it floated in a clear liquid. From another, an eye stared blindly at Barbara as she writhed back and forth helplessly on the sofa. The doctor, dried blood on his cheek, looked down on her as he moved his fingers towards the buttons of her dress.

"You like this, don't you?" he said, salivating as he undid the first button.

"Damn it! Stop that now. It won't get us anywhere." The Tyrolean seized the shackled boy and held him up like a piece of meat, then he turned to Barbara. "If you don't want me to hurt the kid, you're going to talk now, do you understand?"

When Barbara nodded her agreement, the Tyrolean set Paul down on the ground roughly. Then he came over and untied her gag. "Now don't do anything foolish," he said menacingly. "Nobody will hear you down here, anyway, so screaming would just be a waste of time." He leaned over and whispered in her ear. "But I'll see to it that this old lecher keeps his hands off you, so behave."

Barbara coughed and struggled to breathe as the gag was finally removed. "I . . . I swear that only Paul and I know about the meeting at the cemetery," she gasped. "Paul stole a ring of keys from one of the guards yesterday and tossed them to me through the window of the dungeon. I ran away, and since then we've been hiding out at the construction site next to the church. And we saw you before, too." That was such a barefaced lie that Barbara even amazed herself. The two men appeared uncertain, but presumably they couldn't imagine any other way she might have escaped from the dungeon.

The Tyrolean tilted his head to one side and chewed on his lip, then he bent way down until they were almost face to face. "I don't know whether to believe you, girl. You say the little devil here stole the key ring from the guard? Hmm. I wouldn't put anything past him, but this . . ."

"It's the truth," Barbara insisted.

"Let me have my way with her for a while, and then we'll learn the truth," Ransmayer hissed. "Believe me, you can't trust the Kuisl family even as far as I can spit. They're all liars," he said, undoing the next button on Barbara's dress. But the Tyrolean held him back.

"And what do you think you've learned?" he asked her in an almost friendly tone.

"Just . . . just that you're smuggling salt," she quickly replied. "Probably over the mountains from Tyrol, and in large amounts. Apparently Burgomaster Buchner also had a hand in it. He's the construction supervisor for the church where you deliver salt in bags labelled as mortar. The shed on the building site is where you store the salt for shipment, and the wagon drivers take it from there down to the raft landing on the river for shipment."

The Tyrolean smiled. "Smart girl, and pretty, too. I'd like to have somebody like you at home in my bed." He raised his hands apologetically. "But I'm afraid that's not possible, since there's something else about you that doesn't please me at all. You can't keep your mouth shut." He turned to Melchior Ransmayer and nodded. "I think she's said everything now."

Barbara wanted to scream, but the Tyrolean stuffed the gag down her throat again so all that came out was a muffled rattle. "She's all yours, Doctor, but when you're done we'll have to do away with your pretty toy. After all, you can't leave her locked up down here forever." He bent down to Barbara and stroked her hair.

"Hey, but there's also good news. I like the little rascal." The Tyrolean pointed back at Paul, who was still struggling with his fetters. "What's his name? Paul? Nice name. I'll take him back to Tyrol with me, and someday he'll be a good soldier." The Tyrolean laughed. "Or a murderer and cutthroat – it amounts to the same thing. Just look at me."

He grabbed the whimpering boy, took him under his arm, and carried him up the stairs like a bundle of rags.

The cellar door slammed shut, and now Melchior Ransmayer started unbuttoning Barbara's dress slowly, one button after the other.

"Now we'll make up for everything we missed in the last few days," the doctor whispered. "Believe me, Barbara, you will enjoy it, if only because it's the last time."

Clunk, clunk, clunk . . .

Jakob could still hear the rhythmic pounding that seemed to come directly out of the heart of the mountain. He stooped down and peered into the dark, waist-high hole in the rock face. With his broad shoulders he rubbed against the sides, so that a few small stones came loose and fell to the ground. He stopped short in the expectation that someone had heard him, but the pounding continued.

Clunk, clunk, clunk . . .

After turning around one last time to look at the shelter with the injured girl inside, now shrouded in darkness, he knelt down and crawled into the hole. He held the lamp up in front of him in order to see at least a few steps ahead. The passageway was supported at irregular intervals with beams that appeared rotted and cracked. Ice-cold water trickled down from the ceiling and under Jakob's collar. After a few yards he came upon a broken wooden tub and a rusty pickaxe, both of which looked like they'd been there for centuries. Shortly after that there was a fork in the passageway, and the rhythmic pounding clearly came from the right side, so he crept on towards the sound.

Fortunately, the ceiling here was a bit higher, so Jakob could stand for a few moments before leaning over and continuing. The supporting beams were now older and in poorer shape, however. They projected crookedly out of the rock and in some places were splintered and appeared to be held together by just a few remaining fibres. Once again Jakob bumped his shoulder on the wall and pebbles trickled down, but the sound didn't stop this time either.

Clunk, clunk, clunk . . .

And again the hangman came to a fork. The narrower passage on the right had collapsed and a large pile of rubble blocked the entrance. In the light of his lantern the hangman saw something white in the pile. He reached for it and dropped it immediately in disgust. It was an arm bone with shreds of mouldy clothing still adhering to it. Alongside it was an ancient leather shoe and the remains of a leather hat so fragile it disintegrated the moment he touched it. After further rummaging in the pile he came upon a rusty pick with a broken handle.

An old mine, he thought, *but it appears it's been abandoned for ages. Then where is the knocking coming from? Perhaps a ghost?*

He turned to the left and the sound got louder. Now he thought he could hear banging elsewhere deep within the mountain. Was it perhaps just an echo of the first sound? The entire mountain seemed full of noise, the beating of a great stone heart.

Clunk, clunk, clunk . . . Clunk, clunk, clunk . . . Clunk, clunk, clunk . . .

There was a bend in the passageway again, and Jakob stopped abruptly. Just in front of him, a few steps away, something was crouched on the rock floor, illuminated by the light of a lantern hanging on the wall. For a moment he was so astonished he didn't know what to do.

It was a little creature, not much larger than a child, wearing a leather hood pointed at the top and a leather smock. Its back was turned to Jakob and it was pounding the wall of the passage with a pick. Next to it stood a wooden tub filled with stones that glistened and sparkled eerily in the light of the lantern.

One of the little Venetian men, Jakob realized. *Is this possible, or am I dreaming?*

Cautiously he approached and stretched his hand out towards the creature, as if fearing it might vanish into thin air at the slightest touch. The creature had evidently not heard him and continued pounding the rock. When his hand had almost touched it, it seemed to suddenly sense his presence, stopped working, and turned around.

And Jakob looked into the face of a child.

A weary, pale child that stared at him in horror, as if he were a ghost. The child dropped the pick and let out a loud scream.

"Sh!" Jakob said, putting his finger to his lips. He had recovered from his initial shock. The child in front of him was no little Venetian man, but a human made of flesh and blood, a boy around ten years old with strands of red hair protruding from the front of his leather cap.

Children are working here, not dwarfs. Who does something like this to children?

"Calm down, I'm here to—" Jakob started to say, but the boy screamed again and stepped back, pressing his back against the wall and holding his hands in front of him for protection. The hangman suddenly realized how he must look to the children – a huge fellow dressed in a black, wet overcoat with a lantern in one hand and a club in the other, a strange giant the likes of which the boy had never seen before.

"Don't be afraid," said Jakob, trying to calm him down. Slowly he put the club down on the ground and approached the boy with his hands raised. "I'm not going to hurt you—"

Suddenly a voice rang out from farther inside the mountain. "What's going on here?" Moments later a large, muscular man appeared, holding a switch in his hand. His face was covered by as many pockmarks as blowflies on a slice of cake. Poxhannes.

"Damn it, Jossi!" he shouted at the boy. "Didn't I tell you if you made trouble again, I'd—"

He stopped suddenly on seeing Jakob in the passageway, and for a moment he seemed at a loss for words.

"Who are you, and what are you doing here?" he finally growled.

The hangman stood up as tall as he could in the low passageway. "I could ask you the same," he said, regretting that he had put his club aside. The fellow in front of him looked young and strong, and by his swagger it was clear he was ready for a fight. But it was also clear he wasn't very bright. He seemed to be racking his brains, trying to figure out what to do next. His pockmarked face brightened, then turned dark again.

"Ah, now I know," he said. "You're the hangman that the Schongau secretary brought along. I've heard you're poking around everywhere. How in hell did you find us?"

"What are the children doing here?" Jakob asked ominously, without answering the man's question. "They're working for you, aren't they? You make them slave away here in this mine looking for treasure. How many are there? Tell me, how many?"

"None of your damn business," the man growled, raising his switch.

"That girl outside," Jakob continued in a cold voice, "she had an accident here in the mine, didn't she? And you're going to let her die so nobody finds out about it." Jakob hesitated for a moment, but his thoughts were racing. He'd gone out to look for Xaver Eyrl, but instead he'd found all this. Something told him he was close to finally learning the grisly secret of this valley.

"And she isn't the only one," he finally continued. "Tell me, how many children have been killed in this death trap by falling rock? How many have been buried alive? And tell me about the two corpses on the Döttenbichl . . ."

"Shut up!" the man shouted. "Shut your god-damned mouth!"

"You buried them there," said Jakob, nodding. The man's reaction had confirmed that his assumptions were correct. "You discarded them there like a dead goat, but wild animals pulled them out again and my son-in-law found them."

The boy cowering against the wall of the passage between the two men spoke up. "Their . . . their names were Markus and Marie. It was three summers ago. I remember Marie well, even if I was still very small. I was afraid of the dark mine, and she always tried to console me . . ."

"Be quiet, Jossi," the man snapped. "The two of us will talk later. Now go over to the shaft on the north side and call the others to come. We'll meet in the large cave when I've finished with the old man here." He looked disparagingly at Jakob. The hangman was a head taller, but Hannes was younger and very strong.

"It was a mistake for you to come into the mine," the man said with a grin, pulling a hidden pistol out from underneath his belt. "I'll just let your corpse rot here, as I should have with the two children back then. But I was afraid the other children would be frightened, or they would remove the bodies. So I buried them on the Döttenbichl."

"What happened to Dominik Faistenmantel?" Jakob asked, his mind racing, considering what to do, but not taking his eyes off the pistol. "Did you kill him because he got wind of it? And the others? How many villagers were in on the plot? I found a wooden chip in the pocket of Sebastian Sailer after he hanged himself. It was broken off at the bottom. You drew them by lots, didn't you?" Jakob Kuisl came a step closer to his adversary. "He drew the shortest chip and therefore had to kill Gabler because he was going to talk. Am I right?"

The muscular fellow stared at Jakob in disbelief, then broke out in a laugh. "You have no idea," he scoffed. "For a moment, I thought you knew, hangman, but you have no clue."

Suddenly the patter of little feet could be heard in the passageway directly behind Jakob. The expression on his opponent's face showed this was not part of his plan.

"Good Lord, get out, all of you!" he shouted. "This is between the two of us. I'll see you all later outside. Now get out, you little brats."

"Jossi, what's going on?" asked a high, anxious voice behind Jakob, apparently that of a little girl. "Who are you talking to, Hannes?"

"Out, out, out!" he screamed. "Or I'll beat you to death like a pack of rabid mongrels."

Jakob knew that it was a mistake. Still, he turned his head to see who it was. The voice was so tender, so thin . . .

About a dozen children cowered fearfully in the low-ceilinged passage. The smallest was no older than five, about as old as Jakob's youngest grandson. They were all pale, with sunken cheeks, and their shoulder bones protruded from under shirts that were much too thin. Hunger, weariness, and fear showed in their wide eyes. The children looked like small, starving birds that had fallen from their nest. Unbridled anger rose up in Jakob Kuisl.

"You damned son of a bitch, I—"

As he was turning back to the man, he was hit by a powerful blow to the back of his head. Jakob saw lights flashing in the darkness, and he fell into an abyss. For a moment he thought he heard the malicious giggles of evil dwarfs.

Then the darkness enveloped him.

Melchior Ransmayer stood with his flies open in a corner of the laboratory and poured himself a glass of wine from a carafe. He was breathing hard, staring ecstatically at Barbara, who was still lying on the sofa. He'd untied her legs, but kept her hands tied over her head and to the back of the chair. Her dress was pulled up.

Ransmayer raised his glass to her. "Would you like a sip?" he asked with a wink. "It lifts your spirits."

Barbara stared silently at her tormenter. He'd pushed the gag back in her mouth so she couldn't answer, in any case. Her tears had dried up long ago, and all that remained were anger and contempt. In the final minutes she'd withdrawn completely into herself, where Ransmayer could not reach her. That was all that kept her going – the doctor could possess her body, but not her soul. When he attacked her she was already far away in the forest on a green meadow sprinkled with patches of red poppies. Only from far off could she hear the snorting and panting. She was now as cold as ice, infused with just a single emotion.

Hatred.

"Admit it, you liked it," Ransmayer said, taking another sip of wine. There were tiny red drops on his fleshy lips, and Barbara imagined it was blood.

"You women are all the same, after all," he boasted. "You need a firm hand. The fresher you are, the more you thirst for domination, isn't that right?" He put his hand to his forehead in mock astonishment. "Oh, excuse me, I forgot that you still have the gag in your mouth. I'll make you an offer – I'll take off the gag if you promise not to scream. Promise? It will be easier for us both that way."

Barbara didn't reply, but apparently he took her silence as agreement and removed the dirty wad of cloth from her mouth. Then he sat down alongside her on the sofa and patted her knee.

"It's really a shame we're so far apart," Ransmayer said as he sipped at his glass of wine, lost in thought. "I really like you, you know. Really. There's something so . . . wild about you, something you rarely find in women. Most of them are very plain. If you'd accepted my offer a few days ago – you remember, back in the street – perhaps everything would have been different. But then you went and eavesdropped on us in the church." He shook his head. "Bad, bad girl."

"Doctor?" It was Barbara's first word in a long time. Ransmayer pricked up his ears.

"Yes, my child?"

"I'll tell you a secret." She raised her head and looked directly at him. "I actually enjoyed it."

Ransmayer smiled. "You see, I knew it."

"Yes, I enjoyed it. Because with every single one of your pathetic snorts and contortions, I imagined how you're going to writhe around on the wheel when my father breaks your bones, from bottom to top, slowly, one bone after the other."

Melchior Ransmayer froze for a moment, then broke out in a scornful laugh. "You still don't understand, girl. We are the new authorities in town. If your father, the old drunk, ever comes back to Schongau, Master Hans will string him up like a vagabond for his disobedience. The hangman on the scaffold, what a show. That execution will be our first official act, and the people will love us for doing it."

"It's *you* they're going to execute," Barbara snarled. "My sister is on her way to Oberammergau with a letter for Johann Lechner, and it won't be long before the secretary returns." She glared triumphantly at Ransmayer. She should have actually kept this information to herself, but now in the face of imminent death, nothing mattered any more. "Then your whole stinking conspiracy will go up in a cloud of smoke," she snarled. "No matter what you do with me, your game is up."

"Frau Fronwieser with a letter . . . ?" At first he seemed so surprised that words failed him, but then he reacted quite differently than Barbara had expected.

He laughed – long and in a shrill voice, like an old woman.

It took a while for Ransmayer to settle down again. "That's . . . that's really priceless," he finally said, wiping tears from the corners of his eyes. "Of course, that letter is of no importance now, since at this very moment the Schongau Town Council is being dissolved and Matthäus Buchner is assuming all power. But I also happen to know that the letter you're speaking of never got to Oberammergau."

"Never . . . got there?" Barbara tried to control herself. Surely the doctor was bluffing. "How could you know that?"

Ransmayer sneered, and his face twisted into an evil grimace. "Well, I have another bit of news for you, Barbara. I wanted to save it for last, and I think now is the right time." He leaned way over and whispered in her ear.

"This letter never reached Oberammergau because your sister never got there. The Tyrolean told me already. He drowned your sister in the Ammer like a mangy cat." He put his hand to his mouth and giggled. "My condolences, girl. I was told your sister died with a long last scream before being swallowed by the waves."

Barbara felt as if a dark cloud had passed over her, threatening to engulf her.

Magdalena . . . Drowned like a mangy cat . . .

Now she remembered what the Tyrolean had said before in the old cemetery, and her whole body began to shake.

How many members of your family do I have to kill to get some peace and quiet?

She swallowed hard, and her voice was no more now than a low rasping sound. "My . . . sister . . . She is . . . ?"

Melchior Ransmayer grinned and nodded, evidently gloating over her horror. "Ignaz, that fine Tyrolean lad, drowned her two days ago in the Ammer near Soyen. Their paths crossed, no doubt, as he was delivering some salt, so she had to die." Again he laughed in a loud, shrill voice. "What irony. The only woman who could have helped Schongau was a dishonourable hangman's daughter, and now she's lying at the bottom of the river."

Barbara was about to scream, but Ransmayer stuffed the gag in her mouth again. "Calm down," he cooed. "Soon you'll join your sister, but before that the two of us are going to have a little more fun."

He was fumbling with his flies when suddenly a furious tumult could be heard upstairs. He paused and listened. "Damn, what was that?" he snarled.

He stood up abruptly and ran over to the cellar door. Hurried steps could be heard overhead, and finally the sound of doors slamming. The shouting continued, getting louder and louder, and a moment later the door to the cellar was flung open.

There stood the Tyrolean, gasping and holding his hand to his right cheek. Blood seeped out between his fingers.

"That god-damned bastard," he shouted. "I should have killed the brat right away."

"What happened?" Ransmayer asked, visibly unsettled.

"That little brat somehow managed to escape from his shackles. I told him his mother was dead and he went completely crazy. He kicked and struggled like a rabid dog. I have no idea how he got away."

Ransmayer's jaw dropped. "You let him get away?"

"Damn it, he bit off one of my ears! Look for yourself." The Tyrolean took his hand off his bloody cheek. Only shreds of flesh hung down from where his ear used to be. "That boy is an animal. I've never seen anything like it."

"You let him get away?" Ransmayer repeated, his voice getting shriller and shriller. "Do you have any idea what that means?"

The Tyrolean waved dismissively. "Don't worry. The council meeting is in full swing, Buchner is now in charge here in the city, and this boy is nothing but a dishonourable brat that nobody will believe. So what do we have—"

He stopped short on hearing a banging and splintering upstairs as someone evidently kicked in the front door, then the stomping of many boots coming down the cellar stairs.

"What the hell . . . ?" the Tyrolean started to say.

With her last ounce of strength, Barbara spat the filthy rag out of her mouth and started screaming as she never had before, pouring out in one cry all her grief at her sister's death and her hatred of the doctor. She didn't stop until a handful of heavily armoured soldiers stormed into the cellar, with Jakob Schreevogl close behind, breathing heavily. Alongside him was Paul, his face still spattered with the Tyrolean's blood, his eyes full of anger directed at his two tormentors.

"Your game is up, Doctor Ransmayer," Schreevogl shouted. "Schongau is ours again." Fondly he patted Paul on the head. The boy's eyes flashed like glowing coals.

"The boy came running towards us on the road," Schreevogl declared. "And it appears we've got here at just the right time. If Martha Stechlin hadn't told us about the smugglers' storage location, Buchner would already have taken over. But given the new information, the council decided differently. It is my assignment to arrest and interrogate you. What I see here will not gain you favour, to put it mildly." He beckoned for the guards to come, as he stared in disgust at Ransmayer's open flies. "Doctor Ransmayer, you are under arrest on suspicion of smuggling, high treason, and other revolting crimes that will, I hope, assure you a long, painful death. May God have mercy on your soul."

As the guards seized Ransmayer and the Tyrolean, Schreevogl came over to Barbara and gently released her fetters. He spoke to her quietly, as one would a little child.

"Everything will be all right, Barbara, the horror is over."

19

Jakob Kuisl could make out a sound – a steady *tick, tick, tick*, like that of a giant clock – coming from somewhere in the surrounding darkness. At the same time something was pounding rhythmically against his forehead.

The little Venetian men, he thought. *They're hacking at me with their picks. They're looking for diamonds and jewels inside my head.*

A piercing pain shot through him, as if the dwarfs had finally split his head in two. It ached like it did after a long night of heavy drinking. Brief memories flashed through him, then the dreams began to fade, and slowly he drifted back to reality.

The mine . . . the children . . . the man with the pockmarked face, the whip, and the pistol . . .

Once again, he felt something tapping against his forehead and he struggled to open his eyes, only to close them at once again with a cry of surprise, as a drop of water landed directly in one of them. Then he blinked to get the water out, sat up, and looked around carefully.

At first everything was just as black as it had been before, in his nightmare, but with time his eyes grew accustomed to the darkness and he could make out some vague outlines. Evidently he was somewhere deep in the mountain, in a sort of niche or small cave. He was lying on icy, wet rock, and cold water was dripping down on him from stalactites hanging from the low ceiling. His ears still rang from the blow he'd got from the pockmarked man, and he struggled to open his right eye, which was crusted with blood. At least he was alive, *but why?*

He shook his shaggy mane like a wet mongrel, setting off another painful spasm in his head, but he was finally able to think again, more or less. He had come across this old mine in the mountains where children had been put to work. Evidently this man had forced them to dig for ore and was trying to keep the matter secret – and it was for this reason he had left the injured girl outside in the rain, snow, and cold in that wretched shelter rather than returning her to the village. The pockmarked man had as much as admitted that at least two children had died in these unsafe tunnels. It was quite possible there had been others. Jakob was a witness, and so he had to be eliminated. The only reason he was still alive was no doubt that the dirty swine first wanted to learn who else knew about the mine.

Cautiously, the hangman began to explore his dark surroundings. The niche he was in was so low he was forced to stoop over. It seemed to be no more than a few paces wide, and he couldn't see a passageway. He moved to the left, then to the right, groping in vain for an exit, and after examining the walls in front of him and behind him and finding nothing but broken rocks, he realized the hopelessness of his situation.

He'd been buried alive, under tons of rock.

The pockmarked man had no interest in questioning him, he just wanted him to rot down here and probably thought the hangman was already dead. To make sure, the man had piled a few large boulders in front of the exit or perhaps even caused the passage to collapse.

Jakob began moving the rocks aside but soon weariness came over him, and he felt faint. He had to stop and lean against the side of the cave. His head wound was no doubt worse than he had first thought. Besides, he assumed his opponent had used a crowbar to move the heavy boulders in front of the entrance. Jakob had nothing but his hands, and as large and powerful as they were, they were no match for a crowbar.

Grimly, he pulled away a large rock, loosening some pebbles above and finally some larger rocks, blocking the entrance even more.

"Damn, damn, damn!"

Kuisl's curses resounded so loudly in the dark, damp space that more stones trickled down from the ceiling. There was a crunching sound not far away, and he stopped in shock, but soon started again lifting rocks one after the other. He couldn't give up, ever, for the sake of the children, even if he felt more and more like this Grecian fellow he'd read about once. Whenever he removed a stone, two more came down in its place. There was a loud rumbling as these rocks crashed into one another.

After a while, the hangman was gasping for air. He took a break, leaning on the cold rock wall and staring into the darkness. He almost laughed out loud – after all these months of neglecting himself, boozing, and getting howling drunk, God had sent him the earthquake a few days ago as a warning, but now once again God was scorning him. Jakob grunted angrily.

God just doesn't like hangmen.

He was finished.

Yet he'd almost solved the riddle – the many riddles in the valley. Someone was forcing the children into something like slave labour. Evidently it was all about gold, silver, or some other treasure in the mountain. Still, it was unclear what the murders of the actors had to do with the mystery. The man with the pockmarked face apparently feared that Jakob was on to him, that he knew something about the murders, but then he suddenly acted very self-confidently once he saw that Jakob didn't know the whole story. What was it that Jakob still didn't understand?

It has to have something to do with the children . . .

He was overcome with exhaustion and sat down on the cold stone floor of the cave, staring blindly into the darkness. Suddenly it all seemed so pointless to him. He'd been struck down by some young punk who hadn't even fought in the war. If he met his death down here, he really deserved it.

Old worthless mongrels were put out of their misery before they became a burden. Hadn't he thought he'd seen a Venetian, after all? A messenger of impending death?

Actually, he'd hoped for a better end than to die of hunger down in a damp, dark grave. Walling up a man alive was a favourite punishment, reserved mostly for the higher functionaries to avoid the disgrace of a public execution. Many years ago, Jakob's father had walled up a man convicted of counterfeiting, in the dungeon in Schongau. For days his desperate knocking on the wall could be heard, and since then the place was considered accursed.

Jakob assumed it would take weeks for him to die of hunger in this damp hellhole.

If he didn't lose his mind first.

Suddenly he thought again of the children in the mine, and their hungry, sad gazes. Those little urchins were buried alive down here, too, and they needed him. He'd have to free himself to prevent any more from dying.

A new will to live flared up inside him. He straightened up and began lifting the stones, one by one, as his thoughts raced. The mine looked like it had been abandoned ages ago, but apparently someone had started to dig there again – with success. He remembered the bucket next to the red-haired boy; there was something glittering inside it.

Even now he thought he saw a slight glitter on the wall opposite him.

He was stunned.

Am I going crazy?

The hangman was familiar with mica, that basically worthless mineral that glimmered alluringly in the dark. Mushrooms sometimes glowed mysteriously as well, but this light was stronger: light was actually reflecting off the wall.

"What the hell . . . ?"

Jakob stood up and moved towards the flickering light when suddenly he heard whispering behind the rock.

"He isn't here, Maxl," someone whispered. "Poxhannes probably already buried him. Let's go back before he notices we're not working."

"He wanted to help us, didn't he?" someone else whined. "He seemed like a very strong man – Hannes thought he was the hangman from Schongau, Peter's grandfather."

"Hey, you out there!" Jakob shouted. He hurried towards the light coming through the crack between the rocks, which turned out to be a lantern. Evidently, without being aware of it, he had cleared a space several inches wide to the passage on the other side. A slight draft was blowing through the hole. When he looked through he could make out some vague figures in the tunnel only a yard or so away. "I'm not dead, I'm here!"

The voices fell silent, and after a while someone asked cautiously, "Are . . . are you the Schongau hangman or a ghost?"

"By God, I'm the hangman. But if you wait much longer I will be a ghost, and I swear by my immortal soul I'll come after you little rascals and haunt you from now until Judgement Day!"

"It's really him, Jossi!" gasped a voice out in the passageway. "He's alive, and we have to help him."

"But maybe he really is a ghost . . ."

"Now you listen here, you two little wise guys," shouted Jakob, whose patience was running out. "Stop your silly chitchat. Is there some sort of crossbeam or bar out there? If so, hurry up and push it through the hole before I get angry – and I swear, that's something you don't want to see."

He heard a cracking and crunching, and then a splintered old support beam was shoved through the hole. He grabbed it and, using the beam as a lever, succeeded in pushing some of the large stones aside. His renewed hope, and also the fresh air flowing in through the hole, infused him with new strength, and soon the hole was large enough to crawl through.

On the other side, two boys about ten years old stared at him anxiously. One of them, the red-headed youth whom Jakob thought before was a little Venetian man, was holding a lantern. This time, however, he looked quite human in his ragged shirt and muddy trousers.

Human, and very vulnerable.

The hangman crawled over a few rocks and now stood directly before the two boys, who seemed to shrink in the presence of his imposing figure.

"And now, finally, tell me what's going on here," Jakob growled.

The two boys began to speak, first hesitantly, then without inhibition, like a gushing waterfall.

Outside the window of the Schwabenwirt tavern in Oberammergau, a barn owl called plaintively, like a crying child.

Simon startled and looked over at the shutters, shaking in the wind. He was still sitting by the table in the ambassador's suite in his filthy clothes that stank of cow dung, still too lost in thought to touch either the food or the wine. How he longed for a cup of coffee to keep him awake and help him think, but he doubted the innkeeper would have any of the exotic beans. Even the influence of Johann Lechner couldn't do anything to change that.

From time to time he looked up at the ceiling and at the chandelier holding the white candles that slowly burned down as the night steadily advanced. Wax ran down the iron holders, dripping on to the floor from time to time in front of the tile stove, forming little puddles that soon hardened.

He heard Magdalena's regular breathing coming from the bed and lovingly looked over at her. She was fast asleep. Her chest rose and fell beneath the thick covers and her face was rosy and not as pale as it had been a few hours ago. Evidently, her fever really had subsided.

He couldn't help thinking of Peter, who he hoped was sleeping just as peacefully over at Georg Kaiser's house. A warm feeling of affection came over him as he looked again at Magdalena. Basically, they had happy lives. The Kuisls were perhaps a dishonourable family, but at least they were a close-knit family that loved, quarrelled, and cared for one another. They always had enough to eat, a roof over their heads, and good reason to hope that their future would be better than their past.

Unlike some of the children here in this village, he thought darkly.

He shuddered, remembering the children's bones he'd held in his hands just a few hours ago atop the Döttenbichl. They'd been so small, so fragile. Had those children ever known the love of a father or mother? When they had bad dreams, were they comforted, rocked, or sung to sleep? Had there been more to eat than just unsweetened porridge and a hard crust of bread every day?

Well, at least they seemed to have friends. Martin was one, the boy who was now languishing with a black, festering stump of a leg in a cabin near the Laber with his sick mother and little sisters. Simon swore to himself he'd pay another visit to Martin before finally going home to Schongau. Basically, the case was closed, the murders were almost all solved, and the smugglers had been arrested. The two children had probably had an accident and wild animals had dragged their corpses to the Döttenbichl. Now it was important to help Barbara, who was clearly in serious trouble back home, but that was Lechner's job, not his, and his work here was done.

Or was it?

He couldn't stop thinking of the children's corpses – he remembered their names. Martin's mother had told him that day up on the Alpine meadow.

Markus and Marie.

And all of a sudden these names set off a bell deep inside him followed by a whirlwind of thoughts descending on him, crushing him in his chair. It was as if he'd been sitting here all these long hours just waiting for this whirlwind.

Markus and Marie . . . Markus and Marie . . . Markus and Marie . . .

Details of recent events came flooding back to him, and he grew more and more restless.

Finally, he jumped up and paced back and forth like a caged animal while Magdalena snored softly and shifted around in her sleep. From far off he heard the bells striking midnight, and he paused briefly to count the strokes.

Midnight. The hour of the mountain spirits, kobolds and dwarfs . . . I, too, once almost believed in them.

Then he stopped short. He couldn't remember ever hearing a church bell ring this late at night. Evidently the priest was still awake. On this night that had brought so much misfortune to the village, the venerable Tobias Herele was reminding the Oberammergauers of their guilt. Simon walked over to the shutter, opened it softly, and looked over at the church, whose steeple stood out in grey before the black backdrop of the mountains. The light was still on downstairs in the rectory.

And suddenly Simon knew what he had to do.

He looked over at Magdalena and hesitated. It certainly wouldn't help her recovery if he woke her now. On the other hand, she'd never forgive him if he took off on his mission without telling her.

Not if what he feared had actually happened.

He finally went over to her and gave her a quick kiss on the cheek. Unexpectedly, she opened her eyes at once.

"What is it?" she asked sleepily.

"There's something we have to check," Simon said. "Something very important. I hope it will finally bring us clarity."

Stooped over, Jakob Kuisl raced with Jossi and Maxl through the low passageways in the mine towards the exit. Occasionally he bumped his head against a low-hanging rock, which didn't exactly help his headache, but he persisted and ran on, driven by irrepressible fury. The two boys had told him only briefly what was going on down there, but it was enough to enrage him like a wild bull. It appeared the children were being used as cheap labour, as slaves whose lives weren't worth a heller. They all came from workers' families, and they all had to work in the mine at night and on their days off, looking for gold and silver. Jakob still hadn't figured out who in Oberammergau knew about it. He couldn't imagine it was just this stupid pockmarked fellow who evidently worked as a teacher's assistant in the village school.

"Poxhannes is furious," red-headed Jossi exclaimed, panting, as the three of them ran on. "He thinks one of us ratted about the mine. He drove all the others back down into the large cave and is beating them black and blue to make them tell who it was. We're the only ones who escaped."

"Now he surely thinks we're the traitors," Maxl said. "He'll kill us just as he did Markus. The poor kid didn't properly support a passageway, and it caved in. Marie was killed by the falling rock." He shuddered. "Poxhannes beat Markus with a club until he couldn't move any more, then he buried him, along with Marie."

"On the Döttenbichl, I know," Jakob said. "But there will be no more of that. This scoundrel won't beat kids any more, as sure as I am the Schongau hangman."

They were just turning a corner when Jossi suddenly stopped. They could hear a child crying somewhere, and again and again a loud, threatening voice.

"We're very close now," Jossi whispered, pointing the lantern towards the left, where a hole the size of a barrel was visible in the rock wall. "There's a cave back there that's probably even older than the mine itself. We found the bones of huge bears in it, and strange drawings of animals on the walls that look like they were made by a child."

"How long has this been going on?" Jakob asked. "How long has he been tormenting you?"

Maxl shrugged. "Many years. Jossi and I have been working in the mine since we were six, and before that there were others. He needs small children who can fit through the low passages."

"Just like dwarfs." Jakob nodded. It seemed that at least here, in the Ammergau Valley, there was some truth to the legends. "And do you find gold and silver?"

The wailing continued in the great cave below, and Jossi laughed bitterly. "If only that were so. But there's nothing here, just bits of mica, fool's gold, and sometimes alum. As far as I know, no one has ever found anything of real value here, but still he doesn't give up. It's like an obsession."

The hangman remembered having seen something sparkling in Jossi's bucket earlier, and had thought they were precious stones. But it was just mica sparkling seductively in the light of the lantern. There were no dwarfs, and there was also no treasure.

"But why does he make you keep digging here, when there's nothing to find?" Jakob asked. "That doesn't make any sense."

"As I said, he's obsessed," Jossi whispered. "Sometimes he sends us down to the Laber to dig in another mine, or to the old bear cave above Pulvermoos. But there's nothing there either. For about two years we've been working mostly at this mine in the Kofel. He sends us at the strangest times into the mountains – we never know when it will be our turn. Sometimes we work for a week without rest, like now, and we have to work at night, as well."

Jakob nodded. He remembered the little creature he and Simon had seen shortly before the avalanche in the Laine Valley. It must have been one of the children. With the leather miner's hoods, they could have passed for Venetians.

"You stay here," he whispered to the two boys.

He crept silently into the hole in front of them, which he was just able to fit through. The crying and the shouted commands as well as the whistling of the stick and the slapping sound as it hit bare flesh again and again became louder as he advanced. Jakob scooted a few steps forwards. He peered through an opening into a large cave with a ceiling high enough for adults to stand up in. Some rocks were piled up in front of the hole, partially blocking his view.

Just as in the rest of the mine, the rock ceiling was propped up with crumbling wooden beams and rough-hewn pillars made from oak trees. Burning torches were driven into cracks in the rock floor and they cast eerie shadows on walls where someone had sketched bears, stags, and hunters in shades of red and black. The drawings were faded and no doubt very old.

More than a dozen children were gathered in the cave, and one of them, a small boy, was leaning over a large rock and screaming while Poxhannes beat his bare backside with a stick.

"Give me the names of all the people you told about the mine," Hannes shouted. "The Ettal abbot? The Schongau secretary? If that hangman knows about it, then so does the secretary, doesn't he?

Who talked? Jossi and Maxl? Speak up before I rip the skin off your friend's arse."

"We don't know anything," a little girl cried, holding her hand in front of her face. "I swear we don't! Please stop beating Benedikt. You'll . . . you'll kill him!"

"First you brats are going to talk. Hurry up, I'm waiting." And again the teacher's assistant flogged away mercilessly at the boy. "I'm going to keep beating him until the culprit confesses. So what's your answer?"

Jakob had seen enough. He crept back into the passage and turned to the boys, who were waiting anxiously for him.

"Now listen here," he began in a whisper. "I have to know where the fellow keeps his pistol. A little while ago he had it with him, but he's not wearing it on his waist now, so far as I can see in this accursed darkness. So where is it?"

Maxl frowned. "Hannes takes it around with him and likes to show off. Once, as a joke, he held it to the head of one of the kids and pulled the trigger, but it wasn't loaded. But where it is now—"

"The chest," Jossi interrupted excitedly. "His chest is back there in a niche in the cave. That's where he keeps his lamp oil, the torches, and some other things that have to be kept dry. I'll bet he keeps his pistol there."

"Then I'll tell you what we're going to do," Jakob growled. "You go in there and distract him, and I'll follow just out of sight. If I can get to the chest before he does, then he's through."

"And if not?" Maxl asked anxiously.

The hangman shrugged. "I know pistols like his from the war, a single-barrelled Dutch wheel-lock gun, large calibre, but with just one round. The fellow better pray to all the saints that he doesn't miss, or I'll rip his arse off, so—"

Another loud scream rang out, and the boys froze. Evidently, Hannes had just hit the boy very hard.

"There's one thing I don't understand," Jakob said. "Why didn't you ask anyone in town for help in putting an end to this?"

"Because he threatened us," Jossi replied despairingly. "He keeps saying he'll see to it that our families are driven out of the valley. Just like many years ago, we workers would be chained to wagons and taken down to the Loisach. He said that if we even said a word, our families would be destroyed."

Jakob grunted with disgust. "That guy in the cave looks as dumb as an ox. Why are you afraid of him? A teacher's assistant? He doesn't have any power in the village."

Jossi looked at him, wide-eyed in terror. "But . . . but I don't mean Hannes," he said quietly.

Again there was a scream as the rod hit naked flesh.

And then, finally, Jakob Kuisl understood.

Peter couldn't sleep.

He lay in his bed up in the schoolmaster's attic, staring at the ceiling. The massive oaken beams looked like huge snakes hanging over him and threatening to fall down and devour him at any moment. A few times he drifted off and had bizarre dreams. In one he was in a narrow, damp cave somewhere in a mountain, and the walls had closed in on him until finally they crushed him like a bug. His days in Oberammergau had been too upsetting, especially today. He kept thinking of the conversation between Franz Würmseer and that gloomy man, the knacker, that he, Jossi, and Maxl had overheard earlier that day. There had been a secret meeting on the Döttenbichl, just as he'd told his father there would be, and it must be over now, because there had suddenly been a lot of noise out in the village late at night. He had peeked out through the shutters and seen many people outside, as well as soldiers in armour on horseback. A wagon had come clattering down the road and he got a quick glimpse of the Ammergau judge and a few other Oberammergau citizens with dark looks on their faces. What was going on out there? And how was his father? Was he all right?

But then Georg Kaiser came into his room, shooed him away from the window, and brought him back to bed. The schoolmaster had been very friendly but didn't want to tell him what had happened. Kaiser had told him only that tomorrow everything would be clear.

But for now he should go back to sleep.

After Peter had rolled back and forth in bed for another hour, he got up. In the room beneath his he heard sounds. Evidently Georg Kaiser was also awake. Surely the old man would understand if a boy had trouble sleeping on such a night. Kaiser was a warm-hearted, open-minded man, and Peter had become very fond of him. The schoolmaster had given Peter the feeling that he was something special. He valued Peter's drawings, his knowledge of Latin, his intelligence, and always enjoyed kidding around with him even though he was often very tired, sick, or strangely lost in his thoughts.

Barefoot and in his nightshirt, Peter groped his way across the cold wood floor, carefully opened the door, and tiptoed down the stairs. The door to the main room was ajar and a narrow ray of light fell out into the hallway. Peter went to the door and peered inside. He didn't want to disturb the old teacher unduly. If he was too busy, Peter would perhaps go to the library. Surely the schoolmaster would allow him to sit and read there for a while.

Kaiser was sitting at his desk, wrapped in his worn woollen jacket and frowning as he leaned over a pile of sheets and documents, stopping from time to time to scribble something into a file. Peter assumed the schoolmaster was still busy working on the play – but didn't they say the Passion play had been called off?

Unsure of what to do, Peter stood in the hallway watching the emaciated, bent-over man, who started shaking now with a coughing fit. Peter felt sorry for him. Clearly, Georg Kaiser was very ill and ought to be in bed and not working on that play. Perhaps Father could look in on him in the morning and give him some medicine, for example that delicious syrup that tasted like honey that he himself was given once in a while.

As if Kaiser had sensed his presence, he suddenly raised his head and looked towards the crack in the door. At first he seemed annoyed at Peter's visit, but then he smiled wearily.

"Come right in, lad," he said. "It seems like neither of us can sleep tonight. Everything has been a bit too much recently."

Hesitantly, Peter entered the stuffy but warm room. Kaiser motioned for him to come over and offered him a seat. "Would you like me to throw some wood on the fire over in the other room so you can sit there for a while and draw? It will soon start getting light, in any case, and your father will be coming then to see you."

Relieved, Peter nodded. He was about to leave when he happened to notice all the scribbled pages on the table. They looked very old, some were ripped, and others had little sketches on them that Peter couldn't quite make out – perhaps drawings of a stage, or something like that. Other pages were covered with symbols whose meaning Peter didn't know, depicting a sun, a moon, or an upside-down triangle.

"Is that the play everyone is talking about?" he asked curiously.

Kaiser looked at him hesitantly, then smiled. "It's an old version of the play," he finally replied. "Very old. I'm studying it, changing some passages, and taking out others." He sighed. "As you probably know, the play is very long, perhaps too long."

"But it's not going to be performed any more," Peter responded.

Kaiser snorted. "Not this year, but in four years. I wanted to finish the work." He raised his finger and looked at Peter amiably but sternly. "Something you should take to heart – always finish what you are working on."

Silence reigned for a while, then Peter pointed at the documents. "It's written in Latin."

The schoolmaster smiled. "You are right, lad, and in addition, in dreadful handwriting, rather difficult to decipher."

Peter studied the scribbled letters, which were sometimes so small and written so closely together that his eyes blurred. Sometimes the scribe used a rust-coloured ink that had been smudged in places and almost looked like dried blood. Still, Peter was able to read some of the words.

Aurum . . . argentum . . . divitiae magnae . . .

"It's talking about gold and silver," Peter said in amazement, as he ran his finger over the lines. "And great riches."

Kaiser was stunned, and took the parchment sheet away from him. "It seems you have better eyes than I do," he replied, blinking. "I haven't been able to read those lines. Let me have a look."

The schoolmaster put on his pince-nez and held the document very close to his face. "Aha!" he said finally, laughing softly. "It's about the passage in the Bible where Jesus drives the merchants and money changers from the temple. That's actually not part of the Passion, but a good story anyway. God knows who wrote that in the text."

"And this here?" Peter interrupted, pointing at another parchment full of crooked Latin letters, as if the scribe had been in a great hurry. "'When you come to the place where lightning struck down the oak, turn left until you come to a deep hole'," he translated slowly but fluently.

Peter looked at Kaiser in surprise. "Is that in the Bible, too?"

Suddenly, Kaiser's expression darkened, his eyes narrowed to slits, and between the eyelids the pupils gleamed like water in a deep, dark well.

"Your Latin is quite . . . astonishing for a seven-year-old," he said hesitantly, "but I really think it's time for you to go to bed."

At that moment, Peter noticed a sentence on another document that seemed strangely familiar. It took him a while to realize it was nothing he'd ever read, but he'd heard it. He remembered it well, probably because the words sounded so strange to him – the very words Jossi had spoken at the Malenstein when Peter was allowed to enter the children's secret hideout for the first time.

When the eagle utters its cry with both heads, stay on the narrow path in the shadow of the mountain . . .

A two-headed eagle had been scratched into the rock at the Malenstein, and after Peter had pointed it out, Jossi talked about the little men from Venice.

"The Venetians," Peter gasped. "Do they really exist, and is there something about them in these documents?" He frowned as always when he was thinking hard. "And why do my friends know what's in these papers?"

Georg Kaiser stood up abruptly, locked the door, and turned around to Peter.

"Because they are *my* little Venetians, Peter," he replied in a gentle tone of voice. "My dwarfs." He sighed deeply. "Your Latin is really much too good, Peter, and I'm afraid we two now have a little secret. Unfortunately, I don't know if I can trust you."

The schoolmaster walked over to Peter and bent down. Suddenly, he seemed very grey and wrinkled, like an ancient evil spirit that had come down from the Kofel to steal children. To take Peter along to a dark, dank place deep inside the mountain.

"Tell me, Peter," he whispered into the boy's ear, "can I trust you? Would you also like to become one of my busy little dwarfs?"

Deep within the mine, Jakob stared at the boys in disbelief, while nearby the sounds of the beating continued.

"The Oberammergau schoolmaster stands behind all this?" he finally asked in astonishment. "That little cripple who has been praising my grandson to the skies?"

The boys nodded anxiously. "Kaiser has two souls," Jossi said softly, as if fearing that even here in the depths of the mountain, the schoolmaster could hear them. "Good – and evil. Sometimes it seems like he's fallen into the clutches of an evil spirit. It's not that Kaiser doesn't like us. He doesn't even charge the poor children for our schooling. But sometimes the light is burning all night in his study, and we know he's brooding again over his old treasure maps and books. Then he can turn very angry and mean."

"Poxhannes is the one who comes into the mines with us," Maxl added in a whisper, "but we always have to report back to Georg Kaiser. When we come back and tell him we have found nothing, he becomes furious, calls us worthless riffraff, and threatens to expel our families from the valley. As the schoolmaster and writer of the Passion play, he has a lot of influence in the council."

"Does he know there's a badly injured girl up here?" Jakob asked.

Jossi nodded. "We told him, but he's probably afraid word would get around in the village about what we're really doing here. The other villagers think we're just working for Hannes chopping wood, picking up stones, or helping in the school's vegetable garden; nobody knows what we're really doing." He put on a gloomy face. "Most residents of Oberammergau don't even care, though some of our parents suspect something but they don't ask questions. I rarely see my father, in any case, and my mother has her hands full with my five younger brothers and sisters. She's just happy I am out of her way and have free tuition in school."

"So except for this Poxhannes and Georg Kaiser, no one in town has any idea what you're doing up here?" Jakob asked.

Maxl nodded. "No one, even though . . ." He hesitated. "Dominik Faistenmantel made some strange remarks once. He had his suspicions, but now he is crucified and dead."

"And I'm gradually beginning to suspect who's behind it," Jakob mumbled. "How could I have been so stupid? Dominik never really fitted in with the others."

"What do you mean by that?" Jossi asked, puzzled, but Jakob just put on an angry face and waved him off.

"That's of no importance. The only thing that matters now is that I have to get you all out of here, but first I've got to dispose of Poxhannes." He pointed to the opening in the wall. "You two go in there and lure him away from the chest. Don't worry – I'll be close behind you."

The boys visibly struggled with their fear, but they pulled themselves together and crept through the hole into the cave. A moment later, Jakob could hear his opponent's shout of triumph.

"Ha! I knew you two brats would come back when you heard the others whining," he crowed. "So, do you admit your guilt? Did you lead that fellow here? If you tell me the truth, maybe I'll show some mercy and simply beat the daylights out of you instead of letting you rot to death down here with the hangman." The loud *snap* of his stick sounded like a gunshot. "Speak up!"

Jakob Kuisl didn't waste any time. He squeezed through the hole, groaning, and saw Poxhannes approach the two boys threateningly. He watched in alarm as Hannes put down the stick and started waving around a large sledgehammer, grinning as the children screamed in horror.

"I told you to speak up, you little maggots!" Hannes screamed. "Well?" He brought the hammer crashing down on a rock, which burst into little pieces.

Jakob moved closer until he could see the chest tucked away in a niche at the back of the cave. The opening he'd just crawled out of was exactly halfway between Hannes and the chest. In his mind he calculated how many steps away it was.

Ten . . . fifteen . . . twenty . . . If he acted now, he could do it.

"Open your god-damned mouths!" Hannes screamed, swinging the hammer.

With both arms Jakob heaved himself out of the hole.

Now!

He tumbled to the ground like a wet sack, but quickly scrambled to his feet and ran towards the chest, which was held closed by leather straps but – thank God – had no lock. The other children gaped at him wide-eyed, as if they'd seen a ghost, and some screamed in shock, but Jakob didn't waste a second, running on, stooped over, towards the chest.

"You . . . you filthy traitors!" Hannes screamed as he now caught sight of the hangman as well. "Is this my reward for feeding you all these years? You've reported me? Now just wait . . ."

Brandishing the sledgehammer, he stormed towards Jakob, who opened the chest. There amid the damp canvases, filthy leather aprons, and torches lay the pistol. He grabbed it, turned around, aimed . . . and saw how Hannes suddenly stopped, and broke out in a wide, malicious grin. He was standing next to one of the oak pillars supporting the roof of the mine, and slowly raised the hammer.

"Very well, hangman," he said in a deep, threatening tone. "You have the pistol, but I have my nice little hammer. If you shoot, I have enough time to strike the column, and what do you think will happen then, hmm? We'll all go to hell together, you, me, and all the dear children. Tell me, is that what you want?"

Jakob hesitated and glanced up at the ceiling, which was brittle and crumbling, just as it was in other parts of the mine. It was entirely possible that there was nothing holding it up except the columns. He couldn't risk it.

Quietly he placed the weapon down on the ground, looked at Hannes, and waited for what would come next.

"Kick it over to me," Hannes ordered. "And hurry up."

Jakob nudged the pistol with his foot so that it slid across the floor to Hannes, who tossed the hammer into a corner. With a malicious grin he reached for the pistol and aimed it at the hangman.

"It will be an exquisite pleasure for me to take the life of a hangman," he snarled. "Go to the devil."

He squeezed the trigger.

There was a click, nothing else.

For a moment, Jakob stood there like a rock. When he first saw the weapon in the chest, he immediately suspected it might have got wet lying among all the damp canvases. But that was not a sure thing. Now he was too tired to be relieved. Screaming, he rushed at his enemy, who still held the pistol in his hand, befuddled. Only at the last moment did he drop it, spin around, and run as fast as he could towards the exit. Cursing, Jakob followed.

Jakob, you're getting old. Formerly, the fellow wouldn't have got away that easily.

At the end of the cave was a low passage, only a few steps long, leading outside. The exit was so far away from the other corridor that Jakob hadn't discovered it in the darkness. But now dawn was breaking, and in the first light of day Jakob saw Hannes run towards the makeshift shelter, grab Joseffa, the injured girl, by the collar, and shake her like a captured rabbit. The terrified girl let out a loud cry of pain.

"Stay right where you are, big fellow. One more step and I'll wring her neck," Hannes warned. "By God, I'll do it."

"Leave God out of this. I hate to mention you and God in the same breath." Jakob stopped and raised his hands. "Just calm down," he finally grumbled. "Let the girl go, and you can leave."

"Ha! So you can catch up with me later and throw me off the mountain?" Hannes laughed, but it sounded more like a howl of desperation. "Oh, no you won't. You're going back to the cave now, and I never want to see your ugly snout around here again, do you understand?"

Jakob nodded, and started backing off, step by step, towards the entrance to the mine. He crawled inside and was again engulfed in darkness.

"He'll surely kill her," cried Maxl, who had been waiting for him near the entrance. "He's so angry, and now that he can't kill you, he'll certainly take his anger out on poor Joseffa."

"Nobody here is going to take out their anger on anyone," Jakob said, trying to sound as calm and confident as possible. "The only one who's going to get hurt is your Poxhannes," he continued, lowering his voice. "And I'm going to smash his face until it's even uglier than it already is. Listen to me now – run down to the valley and back to your parents; I'll worry about Joseffa. Everything's going to be fine, and Hannes will never torment you again."

Jakob Kuisl couldn't help thinking of his two grandchildren, who were as old as many of these children. Even though they were the grandsons of a hangman, they had a family that cared about them and would do everything they could to protect them. These children, on the other hand, had no one to protect them. They needed him.

Jakob waited a while, then he crept back cautiously to the entrance. Outside there was nothing to see or hear except for a few birds that were starting to wake up. At least he could make out his surroundings in the first light of the morning.

He was on a steep slope strewn with massive boulders. Not far above him were jagged peaks, one in the form of a huge raised finger, and off to one side was the summit of the Kofel. The path he'd taken several hours ago was a mere stone's throw below him. It seemed to lead to the Kofel, though the trail soon disappeared around a corner.

Where is he?

Suddenly he heard a child's cry. It came from the right, where the Kofel was enshrouded in the morning fog.

He looked suspiciously up the steep slope towards the summit, which, from this point on, seemed forbidding and completely unclimbable. Still, the shout had come from exactly that direction.

The hangman tried to shake off at least the worst of the pain in his pounding head, then he slid down to the path below by the seat of his pants, scrambled to his feet, and ran off towards the Kofel.

Frozen with fear, Peter sat on his chair as Georg Kaiser patted his head almost tenderly. The schoolmaster's lips had curled into a lopsided grin that looked as if it had been pasted on. The friendly old man, the good friend of his father, had suddenly turned into something completely strange.

Peter still didn't know why Kaiser had become so angry or what the strange words meant that both the schoolmaster and Jossi knew. It had to have something to do with the old documents on the table, and it must be unrelated to the Passion play. To Peter they seemed to be enigmatic descriptions of how to find a buried treasure. By now he had also been able to figure out the meaning of the other Latin passages.

Where you see this sign, you will find many gold nuggets, said one entry alongside a drawing that looked like a bishop with his mitre and staff. There was another symbol that looked like a double rectangle next to the scribbled words: *The downward path leads to concealed secrets.*

Peter was choked with fear as Kaiser's fingers crawled like spiders through his hair and finally grabbed him by the scruff of the neck.

"I asked if I can trust you, Peter," the schoolmaster said in a soft but firm voice, "and you haven't answered yet. So what do you say? Can I trust you?"

Peter nodded hesitantly, and immediately the grip loosened. Then Kaiser sat down alongside him and smiled wearily. It was so strange – now he once again seemed like a kindly old grandfather.

"That's good, Peter," Kaiser said. "Very good, because I don't want to have to hurt you. I'd much rather tell you a story, the same one I told your father, though I left out the last part. Would you like to hear it, Peter?"

Again, Peter nodded silently. Georg Kaiser took a deep breath, and then he began his tale.

"Once, a long time ago, little people came to our beautiful Bavaria from the far side of the Alps. They were looking for ore and minerals used in making blue glass and bright and shining mirrors. But they also prospected for gems, gold, and silver. They were called the little Venetian men, bogeymen, or simply dwarfs. They weren't the kind of dwarfs you find in fairy tales, but simply short little men, hard-working miners. They had certain abilities that no others in the world did. They could actually smell the gold buried underground, as if it were truffles."

Kaiser chuckled gleefully, like a small child, before continuing in a gentle voice. "Whenever they found something valuable, the Venetians marked the way to their treasure with secret symbols so they might find it again – the sun, moons, rectangles, monks . . . Here in the valley there are also such signs pointing the way to a treasure, a great treasure, Peter. Ever since childhood I've dreamt of finding it."

"The Malenstein!" Peter gasped. "I've seen signs like that there – Jossi told me about them, the eagle that utters its cry with both heads . . ."

Kaiser recoiled, as if struck by a heavy blow. "That's . . . that's something he shouldn't have done, that bad boy. I'll have to punish him for that." He shuddered, then continued. "Yes, there are signs like that on the Malenstein, but also in many other places here in the valley, and a huge treasure awaits the person who can interpret them. It is said there's so much gold and silver in the mountains around the Ammer Valley that thirty mules would not be able to carry the burden. The signs say it. But they are often concealed and hard to read. Many people around here have tried to find the secret treasure. There are old mines all around the Weißenstein, and in other places where people have dug for these precious minerals. But no one has ever been able to find them." Kaiser gave a conspiratorial wink. "Because no one has the knowledge I do. But I still don't know where to dig."

Peter trembled and pointed at all the documents on his desk. "Do you mean . . . this knowledge?" Now Peter thought he understood why the schoolmaster had spent so many long nights brooding over the papers. What interested him so much was not the text of the Passion play, but something quite different.

Kaiser nodded. Reverently, he ran his fingers over the yellowing, tattered documents. "What you see here are the remnants of ancient Walen books – that's what they call the books with the secret drawings the Venetians left behind. I found them many years ago in the cellar of the church in Oberammergau when I was a young cantor looking around for sheet music and hymn-books. Since then I can't get the Walen books out of my mind." The schoolmaster's voice suddenly rose in a crescendo and his eyes bulged. "They're like a curse! It seems like every sentence in them conceals a new secret. For as long as I can remember, I've been in search of these secrets, and I know I shall someday find the Venetians' treasure. I'm almost there." The man lowered his voice and spoke in an almost pleading tone. "But for that I need my little dwarfs to go into the mines for me. I myself am too old and sick to do it. But you children can."

"You send Jossi, Maxl, and the others into these mines to search for your treasure?" Peter asked hesitantly. Slowly he began to realize what his friends had been keeping from him, why they always looked so pale and tired, and why they'd had to go away with Hannes the day before. "And how about Joseffa?" he asked. "Is she . . . ?"

"Why are you worried about Joseffa?" Kaiser suddenly screamed. "That stupid brat wasn't paying attention. The mines are dangerous, after all. I can't allow her parents to gossip about what happened, not now, when we have almost reached our goal. So she'll stay up in the mountains a bit longer. Didn't I always teach these boys and girls in my school free of charge?" he pleaded. "Wasn't I always good to them, and can't I expect at least a little humility and patience in return?" He patted Peter on the arm. "But rest assured that Joseffa is being well cared for – Hannes assured me of that. And in a few days, when we have our treasure safely in hand, she can return to her family. This time, we have found the right mine. All the signs point to it, and surely I'll soon hear that my little dwarfs have finally found the treasure."

Restlessly, Kaiser looked over at the shutters, where the light of dawn was slowly appearing between the slats. "Any moment now, Hannes should be back," he said with a nervous twitch. "I wonder where he is. I hope nothing has got in the way again. Spies are everywhere . . . and they want to steal my treasure. Your father and grandfather also ask too many questions."

Suddenly, a terrible thought flashed through Peter's mind. "These gruesome murders recently," he whispered, "do you have anything to do with them? Did the man on the cross, and the others, know about the mines, too?"

Kaiser tilted his head to one side and scrutinized the boy from head to toe. "Smart lad, aren't you? But don't worry about that. I'm—" Suddenly he was shaken so violently by a coughing fit that his saliva splattered on to the parchment documents. To Peter's horror, the saliva was blood-red.

Georg Kaiser clung to the top of the table, and it was a while before he'd recovered. "Do you understand now, boy, why I finally have to uncover the secret of the Venetians?" he gasped. "I'm . . . I'm dying. But first I'm going to find that accursed treasure, I swear. It's been haunting me all my life. I simply have to get my hands on it." He rose to his feet and paced the floor, constantly turning to look towards the door. "Just where is Hannes?" he mumbled. "Tonight they were searching far back on the right side of the mine, and all signs say this is the right place. I finally decoded all the signs correctly, and all I needed were these final clues. The treasure is there – it must be."

Some cows mooed out in the barn, a rooster crowed somewhere in the distance, but otherwise silence reigned. Georg Kaiser sat down again and took Peter's cold, trembling hands. The boy felt like death itself had reached out to him.

"You're a bright lad, Peter," Kaiser said, "just like your father. I always liked him, and I like you, too, but damn! I just don't know if I can trust you." Suddenly tears welled up in his eyes. "I almost have it, do you understand? If you betray me now, all these greedy Oberammergauers will run off into the mountains and take what belongs to me, what I've been seeking for such a long time. I could threaten the other children – I told them I'd expel them along with their families from the valley if they ever revealed my secret, that I'd turn Würmseer and the other council members against them, but I can't threaten you, Peter. I can only take you at your word." Kaiser looked the boy straight in the eye, their faces almost touching, and Peter thought he could smell his disease, a bitter smell like that of burned milk. "Tell me, Peter," he whispered, "can I trust you?"

Peter nodded silently as the schoolmaster stared at him with empty black eyes, little drops of blood still clinging to his lips. For a while, silence prevailed.

"Give me your word of honour, Peter," Kaiser begged, "that you won't tell anyone, not even your father. Promise."

Peter still didn't know why the old man suddenly appeared so terrifying. It was like in a dream, Kaiser seemed bewitched. Peter was so frightened he couldn't speak a single word, his lips were sealed, and he simply stared at the schoolmaster, who began shaking his head sadly.

"You leave me no choice, Peter," Kaiser whined. "I have to make sure you keep silent – at least for the next few days, then it will all be over."

He nodded emphatically before continuing. "The old bear cave is the best choice. There are a few small rooms in the back where no one will hear you. Of course, we'll have to tie you up, but I'll tell Hannes to bring you something to eat every day, and I'll have a candle put in there for you, as well. It probably won't last longer than a week, and then . . . Hey!"

Peter had jumped up and was about to run for his life. He couldn't help thinking of the nightmare he'd had that night, and the idea of being locked for days in a dark cave almost drove him crazy. He tried to reach the door, but Kaiser grabbed him and pressed him down on to the floor with his long, gout-swollen fingers. Peter flailed about like a wild beast driven into a corner. He tried to crawl forwards towards the door, but Georg Kaiser was unyielding.

"Don't . . . make . . . such a fuss!" he panted. "Think of the treasure. We all have to make sacrifices."

Peter tried to scream, but Kaiser held his hand over the boy's mouth. Despite his frail health the old man managed with his other hand to slip his belt out through the loops of his housecoat and quickly started tying Peter up.

"I swear I didn't want to," he mumbled as if in a trance, "but nothing else can go wrong tonight. Not so close to the end."

As the first rays of sunlight crept over the mountains, Jakob ran, panting for breath, along the slippery path to the Kofel, where the cry had come from. Poxhannes had to be somewhere up there with the little girl. No doubt he planned on hiding among the rocks as the hangman ran past.

Jakob's head still throbbed from the blow he'd received, and his heart was pounding, but he ran as fast as his legs would carry him. When he'd heard the child's cry for help, he realized that God had given him a second chance. For the last two years, the hangman had been drowning all his grief over the death of his beloved wife, as well as the anger at his son, Georg, leaving them, in wine, beer, and liquor. He had nearly drowned in self-pity. It had taken that earthquake here in the Ammer River valley to shake him out of his lethargy.

He had actually left the evening before in search of the woodcarver Xaver Eyrl, but then he had come across these sad, lost children up here, and one of them was now facing death. Jakob had to agree with young Maxl, who said Poxhannes would probably take out his anger on the little girl. The cry earlier was like a plaintive cry from heaven to lead him back on to the straight and narrow path. All his life he had tortured and killed people, and now he was being called on to save a life.

An eye for an eye, a tooth for a tooth, he thought grimly.

Despite the tension, he felt strangely light and free as he continued running towards the summit. On the left, the slope fell off precipitously, but now it was light enough for him to see the path. Occasionally he ran past flat stones piled up to make little towers called cairns to mark the way. A cold wind was blowing and diaphanous clouds whirled all around him, gradually dispersing.

After a while, the path ended suddenly at a flat area just below the summit. Jakob looked around and discovered nearby a path leading back down into the valley. A second, barely visible path led upwards, between massive boulders. He went a few yards up the trail, then frowned. Was it possible for Hannes to climb up here with the little girl? It seemed more likely he would have chosen the path that went down.

He was about to take the trail down when he noticed a scrap of green cloth hanging on the branch of a dwarf pine. He reached out for it and rolled it between his gnarled fingers. The girl, Joseffa, had been wearing a forest-green skirt, though it was badly soiled. No doubt Hannes had been dragging her along behind him and the skirt had got caught on the tree – so they really were somewhere up on the summit.

Jakob groaned. He had never told anyone, but if there was one thing he hated even more than open water under a boat, it was deep chasms. Every time he looked down into an abyss he was overcome with vertigo, and his legs began to tremble like those of a hysterical old woman. He almost hated Poxhannes more for making him climb this high peak than for hitting him on the back of the head.

Panting hard, he struggled up the path. The fog was parting now, revealing a sheer cliff falling at least five hundred feet with a large field of debris at the bottom. The hangman's eyes were riveted straight ahead. The path led past the rock wall, rising gently at times, and at other times more steeply, but always upwards. In places it looked as if someone ages ago had cut steps in the rock, but they were possibly also of natural origin.

Jakob's shirt was drenched with fog and sweat, as if he'd jumped into a deep, cold lake, and the air was turning cooler. He took a few final, cautious steps before reaching the summit – or at least what he thought was the summit. The fog up here was so thick he could hardly see his hand in front of his face. The wind tugged at his hair and beard, but except for the sound of the wind and the squawking of a few Alpine crows, there was nothing but silence. Had he missed something?

After some hesitation, the hangman decided to act.

"Joseffa!" he shouted into the fog. "Are you here somewhere?"

A muffled cry came from somewhere nearby.

"Joseffa!" he shouted again, but this time there was no reply.

Jakob cursed under his breath and sat down, exhausted, on a rock. In the dense fog, Hannes and his hostage could be almost anywhere. Perhaps he'd just thrown her over the cliff as unnecessary ballast.

He was about to call a third time when God sent him another miracle. Or perhaps it was just the wind that sometimes took strange turns so high in the mountains. It suddenly changed direction and blew the mist away like the tuft of a dandelion, and instantly the summit was bathed in the warm red light of the morning sun.

Hannes and the child were standing only about fifty feet away.

Together with Magdalena, Simon hurried through the dusky lanes of Oberammergau towards the schoolmaster's house. He doubted that Georg Kaiser would already be awake at this early hour. But what he'd learned in the church made him run faster instinctively. Priest Tobias Herele was anxious almost to the point of going mad. It had taken some time to get the necessary information from him, but in the end, the priest helped them, no doubt because of his guilty conscience at being silent for so long. Simon ground his teeth and ran even faster. There were some things he'd have to clear up with his old friend, things that couldn't wait.

Especially since his son Peter was in Kaiser's care.

Simon was not so much worried about Peter's welfare, but what he'd learned had troubled him. Magdalena, too, running along beside him with her robes blowing in the wind, was anxious. She was still suffering slightly from the fever and the exhaustion of the last few days, but she insisted on accompanying him to Kaiser's house.

"I still can't believe it," Simon panted. "I've known Georg for so long. Perhaps there's a reasonable explanation for all this."

"No matter what the explanation is, my son won't stay one minute longer in that house," she replied, completely out of breath from running. "At least not until we know more about all this." She stumbled and nearly fell in the wet, muddy street, but Simon caught her at the last moment.

"Don't you just want to stay in the tavern and wait for me until—" he started to say. She looked at him angrily, and abruptly he fell silent. He sighed. When his wife had set her mind to something, nothing would change it, not even illness. Magdalena had in any case been irritable and nervous recently, and even before her near drowning in the Ammer she'd been pale and had to sit down often.

She couldn't be very ill, could she? Simon wondered with growing anxiety. *Perhaps I should give her a thorough examination.* But then he saw Magdalena's determined expression and decided to put it off for the time being.

The cattle were lowing in the barn, a few shutters started opening, and soon the Oberammergauers would rise and begin their day's work as if nothing had happened the night before. Through the windows of some houses, Simon and Magdalena could see kindling being lit, or a fire already blazing in the stove, but the schoolmaster's house was still dark. On closer examination, Simon could see light slipping through the cracks of the shutters in a room downstairs; he signalled to Magdalena.

"It looks as if the old man is still sitting there brooding over the Passion play," he whispered. "It was no doubt a hard blow for him when the play was cancelled."

"Or he's up to something else," Magdalena answered softly.

Simon was about to hurry to the door and knock, but Magdalena took him by the sleeve and held him back.

"First I want to know what's really going on in there. What we learned in the church worries me." She tiptoed up to the shutter and peeked through the crack. Suddenly she let out a muted cry, and a moment later ran towards the entrance and threw herself against the door. It flew open and Magdalena raced down the hall towards the main room.

"Magdalena!" Simon called after her. "What in God's name . . ." Without finishing his sentence he stormed in after her. Whatever it was she'd seen, it must have been something horrible. A gnawing suspicion came over him that something might have happened to Peter. He ran after his wife down the hall and into the main room.

What he saw there made his blood freeze.

His old friend Georg Kaiser was kneeling alongside the table, which was piled high with old parchment documents, and at his feet lay Peter, with his hands and feet tied. Kaiser had stuffed scraps of paper in the boy's mouth, and his face had already turned blue.

"Peter, Peter!" Magdalena screamed as she rushed at Kaiser and started pummelling him with her fists. "Let him go, you monster! Let him go at once."

But the schoolmaster was as if in a trance, stuffing more and more paper into the boy's mouth.

"I must . . . do this," he mumbled. "He must not betray me, not when we're so close to the end. The treasure . . . my treasure!"

"Simon, do something!" Magdalena shouted.

Simon threw himself on to Georg Kaiser, who fell against the table with all the documents, causing it to tip over with a loud crash, and only then did Kaiser turn away from his victim, as sheets of paper flew in all directions.

"I . . . didn't mean to harm him," he gasped. "But why did he have to resist me? Why can't he realize how important this is? Stupid boy . . ."

Panting and coughing, Peter lay among the yellowed, partially torn sheets of paper, struggling for breath. Magdalena bent down to pick the scraps of paper out of his mouth, then she untied the ropes and took her son in her arms.

"Everything is all right now," she whispered. "Your mother and father are here with you now, my love. All is well."

"He didn't promise!" Kaiser wailed as he lay among the pieces of the smashed table, coughing in fits. Then he struggled to his feet, and walked around picking up the tattered documents with trembling hands. "What shall I do now? He will tell all the greedy Oberammergauers about my treasure. I . . . I just wanted to put him away for a few days in the old bear cave. He would have been fine, just like all the other girls and boys. I wanted nothing but the best for them."

"Good Lord, what are you saying, Georg?" Simon asked, wiping the cold sweat from his brow. Secretly he suspected that he already knew what his friend meant.

I was right, and the priest was speaking the truth.

"The Walen books," Kaiser said as he continued picking up the documents from the floor. "I must save them. They are the only ones left and they must not be lost."

Abruptly Simon took his old friend by the shoulders, turned him around, and slapped him in the face. Kaiser shook, but his gaze became a little clearer. Suddenly he began to cry and collapsed into Simon's arms. "I am so sorry," he whimpered. "I don't know what came over me. It's that treasure . . . It's driving me crazy!"

"I think it did that a long time ago," said Simon. He took the documents from Kaiser's hands and led him carefully to the bench in front of the stove, where the old man settled down listlessly. He was coughing hard, and now for the first time Simon saw the spots of blood on his jacket.

Consumption, he thought. *I should have noticed it earlier. It's already got to his lungs and he hasn't much longer to live.*

Consumption was one of the worst plagues in human history, and it had spread more and more in recent years. Victims literally wasted away as bit by bit they spat out pieces of their lungs. Only God could help them. Kaiser's sunken cheeks, his rattling cough, and above all the bloody saliva indicated he'd been suffering for a long time and was probably beyond help. Simon could only hope that Peter hadn't been infected by the old man.

Magdalena, in the meantime, had sat down with Peter as far away from Kaiser as possible. She rocked her son on her lap and cast angry glances at Kaiser. "Monster," she hissed. "My father, the hangman, will put you on the wheel for this, starting at the bottom and working his way up – the most painful way."

Kaiser laughed dryly and convulsed into a new fit of coughing. "The hangman won't have to torture me and kill me," he finally gasped. "My sickness will do that all by itself. All I wanted was to find the treasure I've been looking for all my life."

"We went to see Tobias Herele, Georg," said Simon as he inspected some of the documents more closely. "He told us that you send workers' children to the mines to help you, but nobody actually knows what you're having them do there, not even Herele, though he said it had been going on for a long time. He's right, isn't he? You force them to work for you."

Kaiser nodded, seeming almost relieved it was all over now. "They . . . are my little dwarfs," he replied with a weary smile. "The word *force* sounds a bit harsh. I was always good to them."

"Really?" Simon's voice was now ice cold as he looked at his old friend with disgust. "Magdalena and I went through the church registers for the last few years that contain all the records of births and deaths, and do you know what stands out? There are so many children from poor families who died under very strange circumstances. Often the records mention accidents during work in the forest or from avalanches. Some of the children were simply listed as missing and never found again – Markus and Marie, for example. They were just eight years old when they died. You buried them up on the Döttenbichl, didn't you?"

"It wasn't me, it . . . it was Hannes," Kaiser said as he clapped his hand to his forehead. "He told me they'd died in the mine from falling rocks. They were unfortunate accidents, I swear."

"The priest confirmed that all these dead children came from your school and worked for you," Simon said coolly. "What a remarkable coincidence. The children who died or disappeared were working for my old friend, and in the eight years since your return to Oberammergau there were almost a dozen of them."

Simon pointed angrily at Kaiser, who was staring down at the floor. "And that's how I found out it was you. I kept asking myself what didn't seem right in the story of Markus and Marie, and then in the Schwabenwirt tavern it came to me. You said you didn't know the two children, and that they'd disappeared far before your time. But Markus and Marie disappeared just three years ago, and you've been here much longer than that. You knew them well, Georg, better than most of the other children. The priest said you took special care of them. I asked myself why my old friend was lying to me."

"They were all accidents," Kaiser wailed, burying his face in his hands. "Accidents! I cried my eyes out over poor little Marie, and Markus, too." He nodded energetically. "The mountains are dangerous, especially the Kofel, that old demon. And in return I took the dear little ones into my school free of charge."

"How kind," Magdalena replied wryly. "What a trade-off – school lessons in exchange for the chance to slave and die. And now you almost got my son."

"I just wanted to silence him for a while," Kaiser shrieked. "Peter is bright. He has read the Walen books and figured out what my dear, hard-working dwarfs are doing, but he didn't promise me he'd keep his mouth closed."

"The books are about treasure," Peter said hesitantly, sitting in his mother's lap. His breathing was still laboured, but at least his face wasn't as blue as it had been just a few minutes ago. He was trembling all over. "Jossi and the others are probably up in the mountains now," he whispered. "I saw them leaving with Poxhannes last night."

Simon picked up a few of the papers on the floor and glanced at them. Slowly it came to him what they said. "The Venetians," he finally mumbled, "I remember. You told me about them, Georg, back in the graveyard. Do you really believe there is some kind of treasure here in the valley?"

"Ha! Not just *some* treasure, but the greatest treasure of all time." He suddenly laughed again, as if nothing had happened. "Believe me, Simon. When I was a little boy still living here in the village, my mother used to tell me about the little men from Venice and their treasures. I have never forgotten, and when I'd finished my studies in Ingolstadt and returned to Oberammergau, I found these old texts in the cellar of the church. It was a stroke of destiny." He pointed to the yellowing sheets of parchment on the floor. "They come from the Walen books. God knows how they ever got there – perhaps some treasure-seeker donated them to the church. And ever since then, they've been haunting me, Simon. I've lost my wife, I am dying now myself, and my whole life was not much more than the stuffy, grey life of a schoolmaster. The Walen books and the treasure are the only two things still left to me."

"And do you really believe these bizarre lines will lead you to the treasure?" Simon asked suspiciously. He read a passage at random: "With a hand like this, gold can be found . . . Take the black dog along and let him guide you." He shrugged. "It all sounds very mysterious, doesn't it?"

"Exactly." Kaiser laughed. "They are symbols and riddles, Simon. Don't you understand? Only I can read them, and I am about to lift the veil of secrecy. For years I've been digging in the old mines and caves around here in search of this treasure."

"Not you, the children," Magdalena said bitterly. "You've forced them to work for you, and accepted their deaths as the cost."

"But . . . but I love them just the same," Kaiser persisted. "The children mean everything to me, my hard-working little dwarfs. I didn't kill any of them."

"Perhaps not directly, but slowly and insidiously you sucked out their life and let them die, which is almost worse," Simon replied. He walked over to Kaiser and bent down to him. "Furthermore, you are responsible for the death of Dominik Faistenmantel," he said softly. "You are a cold-blooded murderer, Georg. You just don't want to admit it."

Kaiser recoiled as if he'd just taken a heavy blow. "So . . . you know," he said, trying to avoid Simon's eyes. Suddenly he seemed very small and weasel-like, and Simon was overcome with disgust at his old friend.

He nodded. "And I knew from the start that something was not right here, Georg, even back when you brought me out to see the stage in the graveyard. But I couldn't say what it was. But today, as I was thinking of Markus and Marie, even more things came to me that just didn't make sense. For example, the pulley."

Kaiser looked at him, astonished. "The pulley?"

"Well, the first time I stepped out on to the stage in the graveyard, I said no one person could lift that cross by himself. You concurred, even though as director you knew, of course, that there was a pulley for the cross. You wanted to divert attention from yourself." Simon shook his head. "I even saw the pulley then, as well as later during the rehearsals. It was lying atop a pile of ropes on the stage, right next to the wheelbarrow. That, too, betrayed you."

A mischievous smile passed over Kaiser's face. "So you noticed? Together with Hannes I took the unconscious Dominik in the wheelbarrow from my house to the graveyard, and in the excitement I just left it there." He frowned. "Unfortunately, I had to let Hannes in on it, as I could never have done it myself. Ever since, that greedy fellow has been demanding a larger share of the treasure. He can go to hell, along with all those greedy Oberammergauers."

"Later, I saw the wheelbarrow in your garden," said Simon. "If I had looked for wheel tracks that first night, I'm sure I would have found them leading from your garden to the graveyard." He laughed bitterly. "But who would suspect a good friend, one who is also weak and sick and therefore would never be considered as the culprit? Nevertheless you played it safe and planted that incriminating page of text on poor Hans Göbl."

Simon leaned down and glared at Kaiser. "I assume that Göbl took those pages along with the bundle of papers when he left your house on the night of our arrival. Am I right? At the inquest you made sure this page and the argument between the two were mentioned." Simon turned away in disgust. "You planned this cold-blooded murder, Georg, in such a way as to deflect all suspicion from yourself. You used me, and I almost fell into your trap."

"He found out," Kaiser cried. "Dominik Faistenmantel came to my library that evening to discuss his role as Jesus. I left him there alone for a few moments and he discovered the Walen books on a shelf. He wanted to know about them and kept asking questions." The schoolmaster lowered his voice so much that it almost sounded like the growling of a dog. "He wanted part of the treasure in order to start a new life far from Oberammergau. We started to fight, and I hit him with the poker – it all went so fast, I lost control . . ." He hesitated. "Just . . . just as I did a moment ago when I attacked your son . . ." He shook his head, unable to continue. He cast a pleading glance at Magdalena, who was rocking Peter in her arms, avoiding any eye contact with the old schoolmaster.

"You and Hannes took the unconscious Dominik out to the graveyard in the wheelbarrow," Simon continued. "You suspected he was not yet dead and couldn't bear the thought that he knew your secret, so you unclothed him, tied him to the cross, and hoisted it up with the pulley. Am I right?"

"By God, you are!" Kaiser laughed bitterly. "I thought it was an appropriate end for Jesus in the Passion play. I took his clothes and threw them in the stove here. Shortly before dawn I returned to the graveyard, as I realized I had taken things too far. Dominik had to die. So I climbed up to him on the ladder just to make sure he was already dead. I removed his gag to make it all even more mysterious." He smiled as if he'd pulled off a practical joke. "I knew of course that there had been arguments about his role in the play and thought it was a splendid idea to let these quarrelsome Oberammergauers bash one another's heads in over it."

"No one suspected you, the kindly old schoolmaster who also lost his star in the play when Dominik died. The murder was well staged, worthy of a theatre director, and a perfect diversion. Even I was fooled." Simon shivered. "It must have been a painful death up there on the cross, just like the death of our Saviour, but this time with no resurrection."

"Dominik threatened me," Kaiser snarled. "He was going to extort money from me and tell everyone if I didn't share the treasure with him. I had to act."

"And so you simply killed him," Magdalena said. "Georg Kaiser, you are a murderer and a monster, and my father will soon deal with you."

For a long time, no one said anything. It seemed that for the first time Kaiser understood the havoc he'd wreaked over all these years. He lowered his head and sobbed, coughing from time to time.

"For a long time my father-in-law and I have wondered what the connection was between all these murders," Simon said finally, shaking his head in disbelief. "The answer is there is no connection at all. The murder of Dominik Faistenmantel had nothing to do with the other crimes. Urban Gabler was killed by Sebastian Sailer because he was going to expose the salt smuggling. Sailer must have followed him out on to the moor. Then Sailer killed himself out of despair, because now he was a murderer." Simon laughed dryly. "A simple murder motivated by greed, and a tragic suicide, but along with Dominik's crucifixion and the earthquake in the valley, enough to set off wild speculation about strange supernatural events. But all the legends and tales were almost enough to drive me crazy, too. Usually the truth is so trite by comparison."

Kaiser raised his head. Suddenly he seemed strangely relieved, his expression relaxed, but then he started coughing again.

"It's really such a shame," he gasped, looking at Peter, who was still sitting anxiously in his mother's lap, and beckoned for him to come over. "You ... you don't need to be afraid of me any more, boy. The demon that possessed me has disappeared. If you will do me one last favour ..."

"No!" Magdalena shouted. "My boy won't do you any more favours, and we won't stay one more minute in this evil house."

"My ... My cough syrup," Kaiser cried. "It helps the worst of the pain. It's over there on the mantel. The ... little glass vial, would you get it for me, Peter?"

Peter looked at his parents questioningly, but Simon shrugged. "Just give it to him, son. I'll examine him later and give him something stronger. Opium, perhaps – we'll have to see."

Peter walked over to the mantel and returned with the small blue bottle.

"You're a good lad, Peter," Kaiser said with a smile, taking the bottle from the boy and emptying it in one gulp.

"Ah, that's better," he mumbled as he wiped his lips. He set the vial down carefully on the tile stove. "Much better."

"You realize I'll have to report your crimes, Georg," said Simon, picking up the earlier conversation, "despite our long friendship. You've committed a gruesome murder and you've sent innocent children into dangerous mines where some were worked to death for your dreams."

Kaiser nodded. "I know I've sinned. The treasure blinded me. And yes, I'll suffer the consequences of my crime." He smiled. "But not before a worldly court."

"What do you mean by that?" Simon asked in surprise.

Kaiser got up from the bench, stretched, and wrapped his arms around his torso, as if he suddenly felt very cold. "Well, when it became clear to me I was dying of consumption, I decided to make up my own mind on when this suffering would end. All I wanted to do was to find the treasure." He stooped down and picked up some of the crumpled papers still strewn across the floor, carefully smoothed them out, and studied them. "My consolation is that only I can solve these riddles. It took years, but no one after me will be able to do that, no one will ever retrieve the treasure."

Simon jumped to his feet. "My God, did you . . . ?" As Kaiser's gaze drifted to the little vial on the stovetop, Simon was suddenly gripped with horror. He'd been so engrossed in his thoughts that he'd missed this most obvious thing.

Georg Kaiser tipped forwards like a sack of flour.

Gagging, his face ashen, he fell headfirst into his yellowing documents.

In the light of the morning sun, the hangman and Hannes stood face to face, as if frozen in time. Hannes had wrapped a leather cord around little Joseffa's neck and was holding her tight with it, like a dog. Wide-eyed, the girl stared at Jakob, who slowly began to move forwards.

"Not one more step, hangman!" Hannes shouted as he backed away towards the cliff. "Or Joseffa will fly like a little angel through the clouds."

"Is that all you know how to do, boy?" Jakob growled, while trying to sound as calm as possible. "Torture and kill little children? Why don't you come and fight someone your own size?"

"You're the expert on that, hangman – torturing and killing," he shouted back, with a grin. "Besides, you're too old for me to fight. It wouldn't be any fun. I'd just feel sorry for you."

"I'm enough of a man to handle a pimply weakling like you." Jakob took a step forwards, but at once Hannes tugged at the leather leash. Joseffa let out a muffled cry and fell on her knees just a step away from the precipice.

"Believe me, I'm not kidding," Hannes screeched. "I'll toss her over if you don't immediately turn around and go back down."

The hangman raised his hands. "Calm down," he grumbled, "there's no need for this. I'm leaving." Joseffa stared at Jakob with pleading eyes as he calmly turned around and disappeared between the boulders. As soon as he was out of sight, he stopped and looked around hectically. As the fog dispersed he noticed a tiny path on the right, probably used by mountain goats. It led down slightly beneath the summit and curved back to the top of the cliff. He hesitated briefly, then took the muddy path strewn with goat faeces leading back just a hand's width from the edge of the abyss. Was there another route to the summit? If he managed to approach Hannes from behind without being noticed, perhaps he could attack him before he could do anything to the child. Cursing under his breath and with knees trembling, the hangman groped his way forwards.

The bastard deserves to die just for making me do this.

The path led past an old abandoned shelter along the edge of the cliff. Once again, Jakob remembered why he hated the mountains. They seemed to him like living, evil creatures bent on throwing him off their giant backs. Jakob tried hard not to look down. He stared straight ahead, where the path turned and finally ended on a ledge about fifteen feet below the summit. At this point the cliff fell off steeply, finally ending in a field of boulders far below. A few mountain jackdaws flew up, screeching excitedly, and a bit farther away an eagle circled lazily.

Jakob waited a moment to see if the jackdaws had perhaps warned Hannes, but on hearing nothing, he quietly said a prayer and began to climb the wall, groaning. There were rock overhangs where he could get a grip, but some of them were loose, crumbling under his fingers while he frantically looked for another hold. The short ascent was extremely tiring and dangerous.

He avoided looking down but could clearly sense the abyss below trying to pull him in. In addition, the wind blew upwards like a poisonous breath directly from hell. Bit by bit, and as silently as possible, he worked his way upwards. He was choked with fear such as he'd never known before, and streams of sweat poured down his back.

Just don't look down.

A few times he almost slipped, but each time he managed to find another handhold. He paused to listen and could hear the muted cry of a child not far away.

"Hold your tongue, girl, there's no point now," Hannes growled. Jakob was shocked, realizing that his opponent had to be very nearby somewhere just above him.

"Ha! You see? Your great saviour is a coward," Poxhannes continued. "He just ran off," he chortled. "And now what am I going to do with you, hmm? You're just a burden. If I throw you over, I'll be doing everyone a favour. You'll never get better anyway, and your

parents would just have to feed you until you died. Come on, now,
let's get it over with."

There was a stifled gurgling sound, then Jakob heard something
being dragged across the ground. Jakob's heart beat faster. Clearly,
Hannes was about to throw the child over the cliff. With trembling
hands, Jakob pulled himself up the last few inches and now he could
see Hannes just a few steps away, dragging Joseffa by the leather
strap.

They were coming right towards him.

Fortunately, Hannes had his back to the cliff and didn't notice
Jakob's face, covered in sweat. Joseffa let out a tiny cry of relief.

"No, no!" Jakob whispered, but it was too late. Hannes turned
around and saw him. With a grin, he dropped the leather strap, took
a few steps towards Jakob, and swung back his leg, preparing to kick
the hangman straight in the face.

"Ha! Now you'll both fly through the clouds directly to hell,"
he cried triumphantly. "Give my greetings to the devil when you—"

The words stuck in his throat as Jakob suddenly grabbed his
leg with his left hand and pulled. Hannes shouted with surprise,
while at the same moment the hangman let go with his right hand,
a spontaneous action he almost immediately regretted. He fell, still
holding tightly to Hannes's foot, and the two tumbled to the narrow
ledge below the summit. Jakob groaned as he felt his shirt rip and
sharp stones tear into the flesh on his back. The precipice was just a
few inches away.

It took his opponent just an instant to recover from his shock. He
scrambled to his feet, tottering slightly, then attacked Jakob, who in
the meanwhile had also got to his feet. Above them, Joseffa's shocked
face appeared.

"Run, girl!" Jakob called up to her. "Run back to the valley,
quickly. I don't need you here now."

It had taken just a fraction of a second for the hangman to look up, but Hannes used that moment to attack. The schoolmaster's assistant was almost as tall as Jakob and strong as a bull. Moreover, he wasn't wounded and seemed accustomed to the high altitude. Jakob had trouble warding off the punches he threw and kept backing off closer and closer to the edge. Once again he could feel the wind pulling him by the legs, and he began to tremble. He blocked his opponent's blows with his forearm, then finally went on the attack himself. His punches were off the mark, however, and the constant awareness of the yawning abyss alongside distracted him. A broad grin passed over Hannes's face as he noticed Jakob's uncertainty.

"Soon you will learn to fly, hangman," he hissed. "Give up, old man, you're as good as dead, you just don't know it yet."

Jakob remembered all the men he'd ever fought. His whole life had been one long fight. He'd often battled far stronger and more experienced fighters than this pockmarked fellow who was half his age, but he felt exhausted nonetheless. His fear of the abyss robbed him of his strength, but it was more than just that.

There's no end to it . . . never . . .

Once again, Hannes's blows rained down on him, and he was now at the very edge of the abyss. One more step and he'd plunge into the depths.

The exhaustion and despair in Jakob's eyes seemed to give Hannes more strength, and with a triumphant cry he jumped at his opponent.

Then Jakob did something unexpected.

He didn't fight, he didn't strike back, he just let himself fall backwards into the abyss. *For Joseffa . . .*

A piercing scream sounded in his ears as Hannes raced past him into the void. For a moment he watched as Hannes flailed his arms, then Jakob landed hard on another ledge below, which for a moment knocked him unconscious. When he came to, he instinctively looked for something to hold on to, reaching out to grasp the branch of a mountain pine growing out of a crevice in the rock. The branch started to bend, stones trickled down, but then the little tree held, at least for the moment.

Swinging gently back and forth like a pendulum, he clung to the thin branch over the abyss. Hannes was nowhere to be seen.

Jakob continued to sweat, and his fingers began to lose their grip on the damp wood. This was a real, living nightmare. He had never before felt fear like this, which paralyzed him and made his muscles cramp. To the right, about an arm's length away, a crooked rock chimney led to a part of the cliff that was not as steep. Jakob blinked as dust clouded his eyes. If he made it over to the rock chimney, perhaps he had a chance, but to do that he'd have to jump – and to do that in his present condition seemed to be about as improbable as dancing over the clouds. His fear of the void below crept through every fibre of his body.

Moreover, he was getting increasingly tired and beginning to doubt himself. Was all this effort even worth it? Wasn't it better just to close his eyes and simply give up, to let himself fall? A tiny, high-pitched voice suddenly spoke to him, whispering in his ear.

Why struggle, Jakob? The children are safe. Who needs an old drunken hangman? Why all the effort?

He turned around to the place where the sound was coming from and for a moment thought he saw a little man dressed in black with a pointed hat and evil eyes staring out at him from the rocky outcrop behind the pine tree.

The Venetian, he thought. *The bogeyman. Now he has come to get me after all. Mother, God rest her soul, was right.*

Again he heard a voice, this time silky, almost singing.

Let it go, Jakob. It's over, you've had a long life. Sooner or later the end comes for everyone. Who needs you any more?

"Who . . . needs . . . me . . ." Kuisl gasped.

His head started to spin.

He wanted to let himself go and fall into this huge, soft bed that had opened up below him, when suddenly he thought of his grandson Peter.

Just a single image flashed through his mind. He remembered how Peter had come running towards him a few days ago in the Oberammergau graveyard with outstretched arms and nothing in his eyes but joy at this unexpected meeting with his beloved grandfather. The image vanished, and was replaced by a new one. He could see little Paul, that hot-headed, boisterous child who sometimes made him think of himself when he was young, and how together they'd built waterwheels down at the river and carved wooden swords. He thought of his children, Magdalena, Georg, and Barbara, his family, with whom he was often so ferocious but whom he loved more than anything in the world. And suddenly he was quite sure.

"They need . . . me . . ." he groaned. "They need . . . me . . ."

The hangman was not yet ready to go.

Jakob began to swing his huge body back and forth. The pine loosened a bit more, but it didn't give way. Finally, he'd swung far enough to jump to the rock chimney. He climbed on to it and crawled down until he'd finally reached the top of the slope. There were a number of mountain pines growing down here that he could hang on to. He slid down, reaching out for branches and rocky projections. Now everything happened as if in a dream. Later he would remember that he'd finally reached the debris at the bottom. He crawled through the scree, slipping again, falling, and setting off little avalanches that nearly buried him. But he kept getting back up, kept groping his way towards the bottom, where the first tall trees grew – beeches with green leaves providing shade. "They . . . need . . . me."

He finally sank down under the trees, found some melted snow in a depression, and bathed his grimy, scabby, bleeding hands in the cold water, then he lay down to sleep.

The last thing he remembered was the vague form of a little man with a pointed hat who shouted with disappointment and finally disappeared somewhere between the boulders.

"Salt, we need salt!" cried Simon frantically.

Georg Kaiser lay in the middle of the room among all his documents. The schoolmaster quivered all over, and his arms and legs twitched uncontrollably. Magdalena jumped up and ran out into the hallway, where there was a small kitchen in a niche. She knew why Simon needed salt so urgently. Georg Kaiser had obviously poisoned himself – there had been something other than cough syrup in the vial. If they infused him with lots of salt water, he would perhaps vomit before the poison could take its full effect. Magdalena looked around excitedly for the little pouch of salt usually found next to the fireplace and hurried back into the room. She couldn't help thinking what a miracle this white powder really was, something men in this valley had died for.

Salt can kill, yet without salt, there is no life. It really rules the world . . .

Whether it would help Georg Kaiser at this point was doubtful. The schoolmaster thrashed around like a fish on dry land, and the poison had probably penetrated too far into his body. Magdalena's suspicions were confirmed when she returned and saw Simon's discouraged expression. Her husband had cradled the head of his old friend in his lap and shook his head sadly. Kaiser mumbled a few final, incomprehensible words.

"The . . . the Walen books," he gasped. "Care for them, Simon. You are the only one I want to have the treasure, not . . . not these greedy Oberammergauers with their accursed Passion play. I . . . I could never stand the play . . . It was much too long . . ."

"You must spare yourself, Georg," Simon said softly. "Perhaps the poison is too weak . . ."

Kaiser coughed, and it took a while for Magdalena to realize he was laughing. "Believe me, this poison is not too weak," the schoolmaster said in a rasping voice. "I made it myself from wolfsbane, a beautiful blue flower that blossoms here in the mountains in summertime . . ."

Magdalena looked at Peter, who was staring in horror at the twitching man, and took her son in her arms. When she heard it was wolfsbane, she knew at once that there was no cure. Wolfsbane, or devil's root, was the deadliest plant she kept as a bathhouse operator. It was said the blue blossoms came from the saliva of the Grecian hound of hell, Cerberus, and that sometimes even touching it led to death. A vial like the one Kaiser had prepared could not fail to have its intended effect.

The schoolmaster now became weaker and weaker. "So . . . so cold," he mumbled. "Can't feel anything any more . . ." One last time his head shot up and his fingers dug into the papers all around him. "The Walen books . . . my treasures . . . Simon, see to it that . . ." He collapsed and his eyes glazed over.

A strange silence spread through the room, almost as if time stood still for a moment, but then the birds started chirping again outside and the first rays of the morning sun passed through the slats in the shutters. Life went on in the village.

"It's over," Simon said sadly, closing Kaiser's eyes. He gently placed the head of his old friend on the ground and released the documents from his claw-like fingers. "Even if he was a murderer, he once meant much to me." Simon sighed. "He was like the father I always yearned for."

"Yet in the end, he was a monster," Magdalena added harshly. "I actually liked your deceased father. Maybe he was peculiar, but he was not possessed by the devil." She shook her head. "Well, at least not when he was sober."

"It was these Walen books that cast a spell over him," said Simon, pointing at the crumpled papers surrounding Kaiser's head like a halo. "The thought is appealing," he conceded. "Hundreds of secrets all pointing to a huge treasure. A treasure hunt . . ."

He began to gather up the papers and started reading with a thoughtful expression on his face. "Listen to this," he said after a while, turning to Magdalena. "'Here, where a chasm opens up like the mouth of a fish, you will acquire great wisdom'." He frowned. "Hmm. That could be a fountain or also a puddle in a mountain brook. Do you remember seeing, up in the Ammer Valley . . . Hey! What are you doing?"

Magdalena had ripped the pages out of his hand and started picking up the other documents from the floor.

"You're right," Simon said excitedly. "First we have to sort them and put them all in order so we can read them, and perhaps they'll make more sense then. Georg Kaiser would surely be proud if we . . . Stop! Are you crazy?"

Magdalena walked over to the tile stove with the stack of papers in her hands. She opened the little door for stoking the fire and was about to toss them inside.

"What are you doing?" Simon shouted angrily, pushing her aside. "Have you lost your mind? These pages could lead us to a treasure. Don't you understand what that would mean for us? We could say goodbye to this life as dishonourable people. We could move to another town and begin new lives. Georg Kaiser had almost figured it out, and perhaps we just have to look a bit more. You're crazy if you throw these documents into the fire now."

"You're the crazy one!" Magdalena slipped away from him and began feeding the papers one by one into the fire.

"What . . . what are you doing?" he shrieked, his head turning red as a beetroot. "How dare you destroy something my old friend bequeathed to me? Stop right now, or I'll do something I'll regret." He raised his hand and was about to strike Magdalena.

"Stop, Father," shouted Peter, running towards him. "What are you doing?" He wrapped his skinny little arms around his father and clung to him for dear life.

Simon stopped, confused, with his hand still raised as Magdalena stared at him with a mixture of ridicule and horror.

"Don't you see what these Walen books are doing to you?" she said finally, shaking her head. "They really are cursed." She pointed at Georg Kaiser's corpse on the floor. "There's your dead friend, he just breathed his last, and you are crying bloody murder and want to beat your wife just because of a few accursed sheets of bizarre scribblings. Is it really worth it, Simon?"

Slowly Simon lowered his arm. "No . . . it's not. It's really not worth it. I'm sorry, Magdalena. It's as if I was—"

"Possessed, I know." Magdalena smiled. "But I excuse you because you are my husband and I love you." She motioned to Peter to come over. "And now, both of you, help me destroy once and for all this devilish claptrap."

The three stood in front of the stove and continued throwing the papers in the fire. Once Simon stopped and held one of the documents between his fingers, lost in thought. "And you really think . . ." he started to say. But the stern look on Magdalena's face silenced him at once.

Simon cast that sheet into the flames as well. Holding one another by the hand, father, mother, and son watched as the pages were gradually consumed by the flames.

At the Malenstein, keep an eye out for . . .

And then this riddle as well disappeared in the smoke and fire forever.

When Jakob opened his eyes, he thought at first that the cruel bogeyman had returned to get him. Attentive eyes stared at him from beneath a leather hood, and little fingers ran over his crushed limbs.

"He's alive," whispered a gentle voice.

"But how is that possible? He fell off the steep cliff, I saw it myself!"

"He must have a powerful guardian angel, or perhaps it's that death is afraid of the hangman."

That voice was, in contrast to the two others, deep and masculine. Jakob blinked. The morning sun blinded him, and he still felt like he was dreaming. Dwarfs knelt all around him, washing his face and tugging on his clothes.

"Filthy Venetian riffraff," he grumbled. "I don't have any jewels, I . . ." But then his vision cleared, and he saw they weren't dwarfs standing around him at all but children, many children, certainly more than a dozen. Among them was little Joseffa, leaning on Jossi for support, and Maxl, along with the other boys and girls from the cave.

"Didn't I tell you to go back to your parents?" he growled weakly. "Troublemaking kids, don't even listen to the hangman . . ."

"You should be happy these children didn't go back down into the valley but kept looking for you," came a deep voice that seemed strangely familiar, "or you'd soon be food for the ravens. You badly need medical help."

Jakob slowly turned his aching head – and froze.

"Damn! Xaver Eyrl," he gasped, "I've been looking for you everywhere."

The young woodcarver grinned. He'd folded his huge arms and was looking at the hangman lying in front of him in the meadow. Eyrl's red hair shone like fire in the sun. "Well, it seems I've found you, and not the other way around," he said. "It's lucky for you I'd just gone to the old mine looking for a place to hide, and the children told me you were lying up here in the meadow." He winked at Jakob.

"I thought I'd come up and have a look at my hangman. Our last meeting wasn't especially cordial, you know."

"You knew about the mine?" Jakob asked, puzzled.

Eyrl shrugged. "Of course I know about the mine on the Kofel, and so do many old residents of Oberammergau, but I had no idea the schoolmaster and Hannes were searching for gold and silver there. The children told me everything."

"Hannes . . . ?" Kuisl asked, exhausted.

"We found him dead at the bottom of the cliff, nothing but a smashed puppet, his eyes wide open in terror. I don't know what the last thing he saw was, but it was certainly nothing pleasant."

"Ah . . . the black bogeyman," Jakob mumbled. "That's what he saw."

Xaver Eyrl looked at Jakob in surprise. "What did you say?" But the hangman just shook his head, which made it ache again.

"Oh, forget it, but it's good you're here so I don't have to keep looking for your rotting corpse any more. So listen here . . ." Jacob tried in vain to get up. "Xaver Eyrl, I'm arresting you under suspicion of . . ." He groaned and fell backwards again. Small pebbles trickled down into his open wounds and he started to pass out.

"Hmm. To tell you the truth I don't think you're in any condition to arrest anyone," Eyrl responded, "not even a rabbit. Otherwise I would never have considered coming to the sickbed of my hangman and torturer." He grinned, showing a row of white teeth. "But in any case, you are on the wrong track. It wasn't me. At least, I didn't kill anyone. I'm not guilty of anything except poaching." He leaned far over to whisper something in the hangman's ear. "I'll tell you a little secret. I just saw the charcoal burner, the one who has been secretly bringing me bread and cheese the last few days. He was down in the valley and told me excitedly about all the things that happened since yesterday. The accursed smuggling ring has been broken and Judge

Rieger has been arrested and taken to Schongau. Finally justice will prevail and you won't need to search for me any more. My job is done."

"Smugglers' ring?" Again Jakob tried to sit up, but he collapsed again. "Damn!" he cursed, "I . . . I thought there was more to this than just a few ghost stories, but . . ." He tried to concentrate, which just made his headache worse. His whole body ached as if every single bone were broken.

"You really need to rest," said little Jossi, standing alongside Xaver Eyrl. "You're badly injured."

"Has it got to the point where a child must tell me what I can and cannot do?" he asked, but he lay still because the pain was too great.

Quickly, the children stripped off his torn shirt and washed his upper body and face with ice-cold meltwater. The hangman groaned but let them do as they wished.

"How about not asking any questions for a few moments, but just listening?" Eyrl suggested. "I'll tell you what happened, and you'll let the children wash your wounds."

Jakob nodded silently and Xaver Eyrl began. First he told about the smuggling ring led by Judge Johannes Rieger and the deputy burgomaster Würmseer, then the hidden signs, and the black riders. Half the village was involved in smuggling, he said. Then he told Jakob briefly about what had happened the night before on the Döttenbichl.

"The Schongau secretary is now in charge here in the valley," he said finally. "And as the executioner, you'll no doubt soon meet Rieger again in your home town. The only one to get away was Franz Würmseer, but the black riders will catch up with him." Eyrl nodded his satisfaction. "I've got my revenge."

"Does that mean you knew about this smuggling all along?" asked Jakob as the children dabbed his wounds with freshly picked shepherd's purse.

"All of Oberammergau knew about it, but no one said anything; they kept silent while they were paid off." Eyrl's face suddenly turned red with anger. "Only my father and I resisted. Father said it was unchristian — we couldn't earn money carving figurines of our Saviour and at the same time line our pockets with ill-gotten gains. When Father threatened to report the matter to the abbot, the citizens of Oberammergau ruined us financially. My father left the valley and died in misery. I swore vengeance."

"So you returned and distributed those Pharisee figurines," Kuisl said.

"I wanted to remind the smugglers of how evil they were and force them to face up to it. The old bathhouse keeper, Landes, along with Gabler, Würmseer, and Sailer — almost the entire town council — were involved in the operation. Even old Faistenmantel knew about it, though he didn't get involved, probably because he knew there would be trouble sooner or later. Nevertheless, I wanted him to have a Pharisee, too. Konrad Faistenmantel could think only of himself, unlike his son Dominik, who was a lovable dreamer." Eyrl seemed to relax. "The two of us played together a lot when we were kids."

"But why were you silent when I questioned you?" asked the hangman. "You could have confessed it all to the abbot."

"You forget that Judge Johannes Rieger was also present there, and he was one of the masterminds of the smuggling operation. If I'd even said a word, he would have denounced me as a liar and made sure someone would kill me even sooner. That's the reason he calmed down when you said there was more to my break-in at Konrad Faistenmantel's house." He smiled. "But then came the earthquake and my chance to escape. Sometimes the earthquake seems like a gift from God."

"You're not the only one to feel that way," Jakob said.

By now, the children had cared for his wounds, at least for the time being, but Jakob still was not able to stand up by himself. Evidently his left leg was broken. Eyrl looked at him, trying to figure out what to do.

"You'll never get back to the valley like that," he finally said, shaking his head. "And the children can't carry you." He sighed. "So I'll have to do it."

Jakob coughed, and realized he'd lost two teeth in his fall. "You mean you will carry your own hangman?"

"I can't believe you'll charge me. For doing what? Distributing little figurines and poaching deer now and then?" Xaver Eyrl laughed. "Actually, I meant to wait a few days before showing my face in town again, but under these circumstances . . ." He scratched his head, then motioned to the hangman. "So come on, hangman, jump up on my back."

"You forget I'm very big," Jakob objected.

"And I'm very strong. We can stop and rest now and then."

Jakob shook his head doubtfully, but then he let the children get him to his feet. They helped him stagger over for a few steps, like an old dancing bear, until he got to Eyrl. The woodcarver grabbed his arms, wrapped them over his shoulders, and pulled him up.

Xaver tottered a bit, but then he started walking forwards. Like two demonic creatures merged into a single monster, the hangman and his former victim marched down from the Kofel into the sunlit valley.

Surrounded by a cluster of laughing children.

EPILOGUE

ON A SUNNY MORNING IN JUNE UNDER A CLEAR blue sky, the largest and most spectacular execution in recent decades took place in Schongau.

From as far away as Landsberg, Augsburg, and beyond, people streamed into town to witness the execution of the former burgomaster of Schongau, Matthäus Buchner, along with his accomplices. The crowd was so great that the spectators had to search for good places to stand in the adjacent fields. Lodging in Schongau was so tight that farmers rented out their barns, and the pedlars, musicians, actors, and hawkers of sacred images did a brisk business.

Despite his treasonous activity and involvement in the salt-smuggling operation, Buchner, as a patrician, had the right to a speedy beheading. People said later that he stood up straight and without much fuss for the final blow, but that was no doubt because Jakob Kuisl carried out the execution with just one powerful stroke of the sword. The blow came so fast and clean that for a moment Buchner's head remained atop his torso before finally tipping over slowly, to the accompaniment of loud murmurs in the crowd. Just as deftly, the executioner beheaded the former Ammergau judge, Johannes Rieger, who received his just punishment as the ringleader of the band of Oberammergau smugglers.

Afterwards, Jakob turned and stared grimly and defiantly into the crowd as if expecting an apology from everyone who until recently had cursed him as an incompetent drunk.

"It's hard to believe that despite his age he managed to deliver such powerful blows with the sword," mumbled Wilhelm Hardenberg, an old patrician and councillor. "Especially since rumour has it that he fell in the mountains near Oberammergau and broke his leg. Two weeks ago he looked pretty bad, and now he's just limping a bit with the splint."

His colleague on the council, the pharmacist Magnus Johannson, agreed. "He still is certainly the best hangman in all of Bavaria, even if there are some people who didn't see it that way until recently and wanted to call on Master Hans from Weilheim to be their hangman." Johannson cast a sarcastic sidelong glance at Hardenberg, then he shook his head. "This Master Hans is a strange fellow, not only because of his white hair. Compared to him, our hangman is a true paragon of joyful living, even though . . ." – he hesitated – "they say he doesn't drink a drop any more." He laughed. "You'll see . . . In his old age our hangman will become a crotchety old Calvinist."

"God forbid!" Hardenberg shook his head indignantly and crossed himself. "Well, in any case, we should thank God that this dreadful conspiracy has finally been brought to an end."

The two patricians nodded in silent agreement, leaving unmentioned the fact that they, like most of the other councilmen, had been loyal followers of Buchner until just a short while ago. Secretary Johann Lechner had decided to prosecute only Buchner, and he required the other members of the town council to renew their oath of office to the city before releasing them. In this way, Lechner could be certain to have especially loyal patricians in the future.

Ignaz the Tyrolean and Melchior Ransmayer, who as accomplices of Buchner followed him to the scaffold, were less fortunate. In the presence of some officials from Munich they were tortured for three days by Jakob until they finally told everything about their salt-smuggling scheme, and since they were neither nobles nor patricians they could not expect an even half-painless beheading, but at least the secretary waived torture on the wheel, which would have been appropriate in this case. The two were hanged by Jakob Kuisl as common thieves, though the Tyrolean made a much more dignified impression than the doctor.

On the way to the execution site in the knacker's cart, Melchior Ransmayer howled the entire way, begging for forgiveness and calling to his former influential patients, who lowered their gazes as the cart passed by. On the ladder up to the gallows he fidgeted and wriggled so much that Jakob had to tie him with ropes like a bundle of rags. People laughed on seeing that Ransmayer, without his full-bottomed wig, was almost bald, and in his death struggle his eyes popped out like the eyes of a fish.

While Jakob tugged on the Tyrolean's feet to break his neck and shorten his suffering, he let the doctor dance around at the end of the rope until his feet finally stopped quivering. The spectators in the front row seemed to notice something like a triumphant flash in the hangman's eyes, though how could you say that for sure about someone wearing a hood?

By early afternoon, the executions were finally over. The crowd dispersed and went to the noisy taverns. For the torturing, beheadings, and two hangings, Jakob received twenty gleaming new guilders and an entire roasted sheep, which was eaten with great gusto that evening in the hangman's house, along with copious amounts of beer and wine.

"And you really don't want anything to drink?" Magdalena asked her father in surprise as he chewed contently on his leg of mutton. "People say you—"

"People say all kinds of nonsense when they've got time on their hands," he answered. He grinned and patted his well-rounded belly. "A man must drink, too, and the water in the Tanners' Quarter isn't fit for much more than tanning hides. I'll stick with small beer – it doesn't taste quite as bad as the water, and I can still stand up after three mugs of it. Perhaps others should do that, as well."

The hangman cast a suspicious glance at his younger daughter, Barbara, who at that moment was toasting one of the knacker's journeymen and already seemed a little tipsy. Magdalena breathed a sigh of relief when she noticed Barbara's smile. Her younger sister still sometimes woke up at night bathed in sweat when the memories of that terrible night with Melchior Ransmayer returned. She had aged just in the last month, but she had also become more mature, and her visits with the young men became less frequent.

"You should be happy that Barbara is enjoying life again," Magdalena said, turning to her father. "What she experienced over the last few weeks was dreadful, and I hope she can someday forget the horrible things Ransmayer did to her."

There was a loud cracking sound as Jakob broke the leg of mutton straight through with his powerful hands. "I should have put the bastard on the rack," he growled, grim-faced. His fall in the Ammergau mountains had left him with not just a broken leg and a wide gap between two teeth, but some bad scarring. One of the large scars was on his forehead, giving him an even more fearsome appearance.

"I'm glad, though, that Lechner didn't order that cruel punishment," Magdalena replied. "It's just not appropriate any more in these modern times. Lechner showed mercy with the other Oberammergau smugglers and ordered a few blows with a stick and some time in the stocks. He knows he still needs his people." She squeezed her father's hand. "And believe me, Ransmayer will rot in hell a long time for what he did."

"Hell exists already here on earth," said Jakob, angrily pounding the table. "Damn, if Paul hadn't been able to slip away, who knows . . ." His voice trailed off. Evidently the consequences were too dreadful to consider.

Magdalena turned around to look at the other guests. And at the opposite end of the table sat the midwife Martha Stechlin, engaged in an animated conversation with Jakob Schreevogl. The patrician wasn't going to miss this opportunity to pay a visit to the dishonourable hangman's family after the executions, even though it would surely earn him some disapproval from his colleagues.

Martha Stechlin had actually been able to get Schreevogl and a few of the younger council members to leave that contentious meeting weeks ago, and the piles of salt they discovered in the old graveyard had provided the decisive evidence. After that, things proceeded quickly. Schreevogl had demanded a search of Ransmayer's house, and on their way to the house Paul had come running towards them. The subsequent hearings had left Burgomaster Buchner with no other choice than to admit everything, allowing him to escape the same torture on the rack he himself had ordered for Barbara just a few days earlier.

"Stop right now and die like a proper chicken!"

Shouting and waving his wooden sword, Paul chased after a rooster that ran under a table in the main room and disappeared, clucking loudly. He, too, had recovered remarkably well from the events of the last few weeks, though sometimes his callousness seemed a bit frightening to Magdalena. She herself had survived the fall into the Ammer as well as the fever that followed. There was no bleeding, and Martha Stechlin assured her there had been no injury to the child she was carrying. In the last few weeks she'd developed a healthy appetite and had worn wider skirts. She smiled. It was really astonishing that Simon still hadn't noticed, but he was completely absorbed in his work with the many patients who'd been anxiously awaiting his return from Oberammergau.

Paul's older brother, Peter, was completely absorbed in a volume of anatomical sketches from Georg Kaiser's library. Among the possessions of the deceased schoolmaster they had found a will in which he bequeathed all his books to Simon, including the valuable illustrations of human anatomy by Andreas Vesalius. The many fine books helped Simon significantly in coming to grips with the betrayal and horrible death of his old friend.

Magdalena couldn't help remembering Jörg Abriel's magic books, which were now well preserved in the city archives. *Out of Barbara's reach*, she thought with relief. These books, like the Walen books, seemed to have a strong magical attraction and could put a curse on anyone who wasn't careful. Anxiously, Magdalena glanced at Peter, absorbed in the pages of anatomical drawings.

Perhaps all books have something magical about them, she thought. *Just letters on a page that turn into images, scenes, and conversations in our minds.*

"Did you hear the latest from Oberammergau?" Simon asked loudly, breaking Magdalena's train of thought.

He wiped his greasy mouth and began his account. "The messenger who brought me the books told me that the mine on the Kofel has been closed and the bodies of the two children given a decent burial in the cemetery." He smiled. "And now that Lechner has been put in charge of the Ammergau district as well, the workers should be better off. Little Joseffa and poor Martin from the meadow above the Laber have recovered, as has Konrad Faistenmantel. After what the Oberammergauers did to him, he intends to move to Nürnberg. I'm sure the greedy old man will get even richer selling the carved figurines there."

"But what about the Passion play?" Magdalena asked.

"Well, the Oberammergauers intend to perform it again in four years, in accordance with tradition, and this time they'll earn their money honestly. It will be their grandest production yet." Simon laughed. "These stubborn mountain folk really seem to believe that someday people will come to their dumpy little town from all over the world. You've got to credit the Oberammergauers with one thing, at least – they have as much drive as they do imagination."

"Did they ever find that accursed Würmseer?" Jakob wanted to know as he picked little pieces of meat from between his teeth.

Simon shook his head. "Only his coat, near the Falcon's Cliff. He must have taken it off in order to make faster progress through the mountains. In the days since the late-winter weather, warm weather finally set in again up in the mountains and there were a number of avalanches. Many Oberammergauers think Würmseer lies buried beneath one of them. In a few years, though, the Kofel will spit him up again."

"The Kofel is always seeking new victims," Jakob mumbled under his breath.

"What did you say?" asked Magdalena. But at that moment there was a whinnying of horses outside in the street, and soon thereafter the squeaking sound of coach wheels. Magdalena listened in surprise. "I know only one person who could come and visit us in a coach," she said with a frown. "But he hardly ever sets foot in our Tanners' Quarter."

There was a knock, then without waiting for a reply, a soldier with a gleaming cuirass entered. It was one of the new young recruits placed under Lechner's command by Munich authorities because he was now responsible for the Ammergau district as well.

"His Excellency the secretary wishes to speak to the hangman and his family!" the soldier announced, clicking his heels together. "At once."

"Well, if this is the new era you were talking about before, I'd rather be back in the old one," Jakob said, turning to his eldest daughter. Nevertheless, he got up and went outside. Magdalena and Simon followed him.

Outside, Johann Lechner sat upright in his coach. He made no move to get out, but held his silk handkerchief in front of his mouth and fanned himself.

"The stench here in this quarter," he said in a muffled voice through the handkerchief. "Perhaps we should do something about that – a ditch underground for the sewage, perhaps, but there I go, dreaming again." He sighed, put the handkerchief back in his pocket, and turned to the Kuisls.

"I won't disturb your gathering for long, but there are a few things I wanted to discuss with you as soon as possible. First of all, my compliments on the executions." The secretary nodded his appreciation. "It seems you still are very accomplished in your work and I'd thus like to ask for a small favour. What do you think of the idea of not burying the four corpses, but preserving them in brine and hanging them from the frame of the scaffold? They should last at least a year that way and leave a lasting impression on anyone thinking of undermining the salt monopoly of our esteemed Bavarian elector."

Jakob nodded hesitantly. "That's a bit unusual, but it could be done. It will cost a few guilders extra." He scratched his huge nose. "But surely you have not come to our stinking section of town just to tell me that."

Johann Lechner smiled. "Of course not. There are two other reasons requiring my presence here. The first concerns the investigations of your daughter Barbara . . ."

Magdalena was shocked. She thought that after all the horrible events, Barbara would now be found innocent, though of course there was still the accusation that she'd possessed books of magic.

"I have had another look at these . . . uh . . . magic books belonging to your ancestor," Lechner said, turning to Magdalena, "and I share your opinion that they are not instructions for witchcraft but simply records of interrogations. Therefore, they should have long ago been consigned to the town archives, but in view of the statute of limitations with regard to these cases, we can temper justice with mercy. As far as the second matter is concerned, I must be more severe . . ."

Magdalena's lips tightened. What could that be? What offence had they committed without even realizing it?

Johann Lechner looked disapprovingly at the hangman's crooked house and again fanned himself with his handkerchief. "A house like this is certainly not worthy of a doctor, and I insist that at least you and your husband move up into town. Your father can stay down here in the Tanners' Quarter, if he wishes."

Magdalena looked at the secretary, perplexed, and for a while Simon didn't know what to make of it, either.

"Not . . . worthy of a doctor?" he stuttered. "What doctor? I'm afraid I don't quite understand."

"Well, after the death of Melchior Ransmayer, once again we do not have a doctor in Schongau." Lechner rubbed his temples, as if the caustic stench down here was giving him a headache. "I have read in the town statutes that the council may appoint a bathhouse medicus as the town doctor, if necessary, and I find this is now the case. Schongau needs a doctor, and why shouldn't that be you? People in town say you don't make such a bad impression."

"Do you mean . . ." Simon stuttered, still unable to fathom what he was hearing.

"Are you stupid or just deaf?" Jakob growled. "Lechner is appointing you town doctor even though I still think you're a total quack."

"Oh, Father!" Magdalena said with a laugh. "Just be quiet so the Herr Secretary doesn't change his mind."

Johann Lechner looked at Simon, waiting for an answer. "So, what is it? Do you want to be our new town physician and take over the heritage of your deceased father?"

"I . . . I do!" Simon stood up straight like a soldier, overwhelmed by the news. "And I will be a good doctor in this town, with the grace of God, with new methods, that are so—"

Lechner waved him off. "Spare me your explanations. A simple *yes* would have sufficed. As of tomorrow you can take over the office and house of your accursed predecessor. We'll talk later about the lease." Carefully, the secretary folded his silk handkerchief and put it back in the pocket of his waistcoat. "It will be adjusted according to your new income, which will of course be somewhat higher than that of a bathhouse keeper. Doctor Ransmayer had many well-to-do patients, as you know, myself included. And now farewell."

He waved to the coachman, who cracked his whip, and the coach rumbled away, soon disappearing behind the houses of the Tanners' Quarter, leaving the Kuisls standing in the muddy street – Jakob, Magdalena, and Simon, who still couldn't fathom his incredible good fortune.

"I am Schongau's new town physician," he said. "If only my father were here to see this. A doctor of medicine."

"Now don't puff yourself up like that," Jakob snapped at his son-in-law. "What will you do that you didn't do before? You'll cure people, but with glib, high-sounding Latin words."

With his not-yet-completely-healed leg Jakob hobbled back to the hangman's house, where his grandsons eagerly awaited him. It was apparent that there had been a fight again. Paul's wooden sword was broken, Peter's precious book of drawings bore a few dark juice stains, and both boys were bawling at the top of their lungs. Their grandfather, the hangman, grabbed them both by the scruff of the neck and took them down to the Lech to build a little millwheel out of oak bark.

Longingly, Simon looked on as his sons left. "Those two can sometimes make your life miserable, especially Paul." He sighed. "But it's almost impossible now to imagine life without them."

"That's what you call family," Magdalena replied with a smile. She winked at him, rubbing her bulging belly, which until now had been well concealed under flowing skirts. "Now that we're talking about it . . . it's good we'll soon be moving into a larger house."

"Do you mean . . . ?"

Magdalena pursed her lips facetiously. "Apparently the new Schongau city physician, this distinguished doctor of medicine, has failed to recognize all the signs of his own wife's pregnancy." She started counting them on her fingers. "A rounding in certain places, nausea, tiredness, dizziness, hunger . . ."

"I thought you were sick," Simon protested.

"Well, the good doctor clearly still has things to learn from a simple midwife and bathhouse keeper." She laughed and took him in her arms. "Now let's go inside again and drink to the new Schongau doctor – and the new life in my body. I have a clear feeling that fate has great plans for this little girl."

Simon frowned and carefully stroked the slight curvature of her abdomen. "It will be a girl? How do you know?"

"As I said, you still have a few things to learn from me." She gently pulled away from him and returned to the main room, where the sound of cheerful people well provided with food and beer could be heard. "Even if I am just a dishonourable hangman's daughter," she said with a smile and a feeling of profound happiness. She was back home.

AFTERWORD

(WARNING TO CURIOUS READERS! AS ALWAYS, READ
THIS PART ONLY AFTER FINISHING THE BOOK! OR AS
THEY WOULD SAY IN GOOD OBERAMMERGAU GERMAN:
KONNSTNEDLESNPRATZNWEGSAUPREISSDAMISCHER — FREELY
TRANSLATED: CAN'TYOUKEEPYOURPAWSOFFYOUSTUPIDIDIOT?)

AFTER READING THIS NOVEL, THERE MAY BE
some who think of the Oberammergauers as stubborn, quick-
tempered, and hostile to everything strange and new – in short, what
Munich people call "petty, angry mountain people". That is, of course,
nonsense. The Oberammergauers are a most delightful people –
creative, sensitive, worldly, democratic, friendly, open to any discussion,
and only at times a bit, well, let's say *reserved*.

The result is that inquiries from curious, know-all, upstart writers
from Munich are sometimes put off indefinitely. Telephone calls aren't
answered, the right people are hard to find. This region is so divinely
beautiful that people there simply don't take the time to deal with such
mundane matters, but eventually, one can get together with them, on a
long hike through the mountains or to the top of the Kofel. Those who
take the time to get to know Oberammergauers will learn that they . . .
but you know this already.

I had planned to write a Hangman's Daughter novel about the
Ammer Valley for a long time. The region is one of my favourite hiking
areas. Even as a small child, like many other kids from Munich, I hiked
up the Laber, climbed the rocky Ettal Mandl with the horrified shouts

of my mother ringing in my ears, hiked tearfully and under protest over the three summits of the Hörndl, went cross-country skiing through the Graswangtal, and after that splashed about in the Oberammergau swimming pool (my reward for all the strenuous trips through the mountains that even four-year-old Bavarians have to take).

Still, as with every novel, it took a key moment to release my imagination, and in this case it was before a concert with my soul band, Jamasunited, in Oberammergau. I arrived a few hours early. The sun shone from the bluish-white Bavarian sky, and I felt bored, and so I started hiking the same paths I'd known as a child. Down below, in the green, flowering meadows, was the famous Passion Theatre, and behind it the towering Ammergau Alps – and at that moment I knew that the setting for my next Hangman's Daughter novel would have to be here. After all, the history of this place is the perfect backdrop for a historical novel.

In the year 1633, the Plague came to the Alpine foothills, claiming more than eighty victims just in little Oberammergau, and the people there swore they would put on a Passion play every ten years if they were spared after that. They have kept that vow up to the present, though twice the play had to be cancelled. The author of the oldest text of the Passion play, by the way, was the Oberammergau schoolmaster Georg Kaiser. I have taken many other proper names from the old chronicles – the Faistenmantels, Eyrls, Göbls, and so forth. Any further details about these historical figures are of course purely fictional. I'm sure Georg Kaiser, like all the inhabitants of Oberammergau, was a respectable man. And the Schongau secretary Johann Lechner never sought to seize control of the beautiful Ammergau. The judicial administration was situated in Ettal and Murnau.

Nowadays, the Passion play is an enormous spectacle, attracting hundreds of thousands of guests every year from all over the world, and incidentally filling the town's coffers with millions (although only once every ten years). More than two thousand Oberammergauers take part in the play, among them four hundred and fifty children. The male actors, according to the traditional "hair and beard decree", must not cut their hair or beards for more than a year. The whole village functions in a state of emergency: those not appearing on the stage sing, make costumes, or construct the sets.

During the early decades, however, the Passion play must have been similar to the way it is depicted in my novel – a minor event, not widely known, that took place in the cemetery, where the gravestones were turned over to allow room for the participants.

Many other scenes in my novel have a factual basis. The mysterious little men from Venice (the *Walen*, derived from *Welsch*, the earlier word for *Roman* or *foreigner*) are not my invention. They really existed, though they weren't dwarfs but ore and mineral prospectors from Italy who came to the Alps mostly in the fourteenth and fifteenth centuries. Often they dug for alum and cobalt, two materials necessary in the production of the extremely valuable blue glass. Local people usually thought of foreigners as gold diggers, and because of their unfamiliar language, strange pointed hats, and usually small size, legends about them circulated all over Europe. In their so-called Walen books and use of strange signs, the little Venetians were thought to be pointing the way to hidden treasure. Many of our fairy tales and legends about dwarfs originate with them.

Strange signs and symbols, and even a small mine in the area around Oberammergau, and that mysterious ancient sacrificial site on the Döttenbichl are said to originate with the little Venetian men.

For much of the background information for this novel, I am indebted to the excellent chronicle of Father Joseph Alois Daisenberger, who lived in Oberammergau in the nineteenth century. Daisenberger describes, among other things, mining ventures in the Ammer Valley, which were, however, already suspended by the sixteenth century. It is likely that prospectors at that time were searching for silver and gold. Some minor earthquakes are also mentioned in that chronicle, two of them in the eighteenth century. There was a major earthquake in 1670 in the not-far-distant town of Hall in Tyrol, just a few months after the events in the novel. Most of the town towers were destroyed in that quake, and additional quakes followed. At that time, the people must have viewed such a quake as a punishment from God, and it's easy to see how the hysteria surrounding the event could have further intensified the panic.

It's quite likely that salt was smuggled via the Graswang Valley and Oberammergau in the direction of Schongau. Since the Bavarian dukes and later the electors had a monopoly on the salt trade, they dictated the prices and demanded outrageous tariffs, making the smuggling of salt by the wagon drivers an extremely attractive source of extra income, presumably in the Ammer Valley as well. The so-called black riders also really existed, and even today smugglers communicate with secret signs.

If the Oberammergau region in my novel seems too cold and dark for the month of May, remember this was the time of the so-called Little Ice Age. On average, Germany was two to four degrees colder than it is now. Winters were cold and long, summers were rainy, and many of the things we think of as idyllic now were just hard work for the people at that time. Nature was viewed mostly as the enemy – for example the gently flowing Laine, which can turn into a raging torrent in the springtime even nowadays and bring floods to the valley. In addition, no person in his or her right mind would ever think of climbing a mountain just for fun or hiking through the valley in the summer's heat unless it was absolutely necessary.

Times change . . .

A historical novel also doesn't exist in a political vacuum. This book was written at a time of controlled right-wing demonstrations everywhere in Germany, and later the conflict over the increasing number of refugees arriving before our very doors here in Europe. I've seen some dreadful comments on Facebook by people who have been indoctrinated by right-wing hate groups. From time to time I've tried to respond, and sometimes I've become so angry it was difficult to continue writing.

During my research for this novel, one of my lasting impressions was of a seventeenth-century report in the Daisenberger chronicle. At that time, the abbot of Ettal denounced what he called the *overpopulation* of the valley. The homes of the poorest residents were demolished, their stoves smashed, and those who wouldn't leave on their own were put in chains by thugs, tossed on to carts, and driven down to the Loisach, where rafts were waiting to take the outcasts. True to the motto "The valley is full", some people today want to deal in the same way with the so-called immigrant rabble.

The upshot was that after the Thirty Years' War there was serious underpopulation in the valley, workers were in short supply, and messages were sent to the expellees asking them to please come back. Not a single one did.

And thus the land turned into a barren wilderness.

It is important to emphasize that outbreaks of xenophobia like those described in this novel were and are still possible everywhere, not just in the Ammer Valley. History repeats itself, and it appears that we rarely learn the lessons of the past. Perhaps interest in my novel will provide not just excitement and entertainment but an opportunity to rethink some of this.

ABOUT THE AUTHOR

OLIVER PÖTZSCH, born in 1970, has worked for years as a scriptwriter for Bavarian television. He is a descendant of one of Bavaria's leading dynasties of executioners. Pötzsch lives in Munich with his family.

ABOUT THE TRANSLATOR

LEE CHADEAYNE, translator, is a former classical musician and college professor. He was one of the charter members of the American Literary Translators Association and is editor in chief of the *ALTA Newsletter*.